SAXON: *The Book of Dreams*

TIM SEVERIN, explorer, film-maker and lecturer,
has made many expeditions, from crossing the Atlantic in
a medieval leather boat to going out in search of Moby Dick
and Robinson Crusoe. He has written books about all of them.
He has won the Thomas Cook Travel Book Award; the Book of
the Sea Award, a Christopher Prize, and the literary medal of the
Academie de la Marine. He made his historical fiction debut with
the hugely successful Viking series. *The Book of Dreams* is
the first in the new Saxon series.

* * *

'As always, Severin excels in his palpable sense of history
and adventure, rich period detail, thrilling battle sequences and
fascinating, larger-than-life characters who strut their hour upon
his epic stage . . . a gripping start to what promises to be
another all-action historical series'
Lancashire Eve~~ning Post~~

TIM SEVERIN

SÆXON

VOLUME ONE

The Book of Dreams

PAN BOOKS

First published 2012 by Macmillan

First published in paperback 2013 by Pan Books
an imprint of Pan Macmillan, a division of Macmillan Publishers Limited
Pan Macmillan, 20 New Wharf Road, London N1 9RR
Basingstoke and Oxford
Associated companies throughout the world
www.panmacmillan.com

ISBN 978-1-4472-1214-0

1 3 5 7 9 8 6 4 2

A CIP catalogue record for this book is available from the British Library.

Map artwork by Stephen Raw
Typeset by Set Systems Ltd, Saffron Walden, Essex
Printed and bound by CPI Group (UK) Ltd, Croydon CR0 4YY

The Book of Dreams

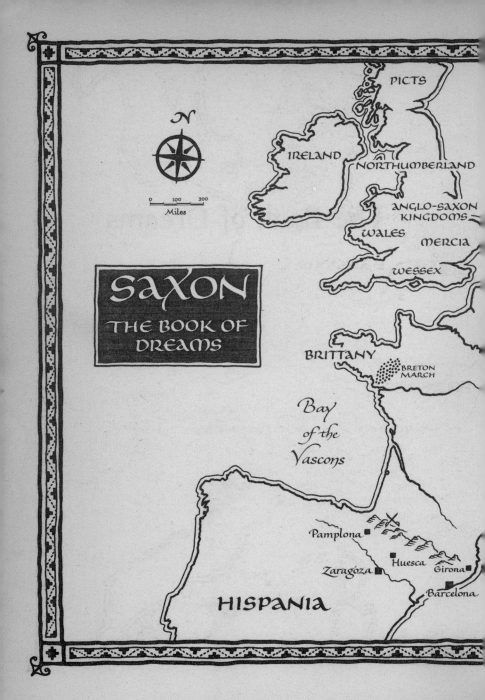

N

0   100   200
Miles

PICTS

IRELAND

NORTHUMBERLAND

ANGLO-SAXON
KINGDOMS

WALES

MERCIA

WESSEX

SAXON
THE BOOK OF
DREAMS

BRITTANY

BRETON
MARCH

Bay
of the
Vascons

Pamplona

Huesca

Zaragoza   Girona

Barcelona

HISPANIA

Prologue

AACHEN, FRANKIA, 780 AD

Sorely wounded, Roland felt his death coming upon him.
He made his way to where a great block of marble stood.
Raising Durendal, he struck the stone with all his strength.
The sparks flew and the rock was scored, but Durendal did not break.
Three times he struck the rock.
Still the blade did not shatter.
Lamenting, Roland laid himself face down on the grass,
his sword and the oliphant beneath him,
and prepared to give up his soul to God.

I put down my pen and wait for the ink to dry. I am pleased to see that my letters are neat and evenly spaced. I learned the new script under the critical eyes of the men who persuaded the king that it should be made standard throughout his realm. I sit straighter on my stool to ease the nagging cramp in my spine and try to ignore the low incoherent muttering to my right. An Irish priest, ruddy cheeked and bald, has an irritating habit of talking to himself at his desk. It is mid-January in Aachen and the royal chancellery is full of draughts; every few minutes the priest wipes his streaming nose on the sleeve of his gown. He is making notes of what he has seen and heard at court, and has already confided to me that he is writing a biography of our lord and master.

'I shall call it *The Life of Carolus Rex*,' he said, his Latin tinged with the musical accent typical of his island.

A dull title for a colourful topic, I thought. But I restricted myself to enquiring why he embarked on this labour when the notaries of the imperial secretariat were being paid to compile the official record.

'My dear Sigwulf,' he replied, 'the wisdom of the ancients tells us that when great men die, the story of their deeds deserves more than burial in mouldering archives. Their lives must be celebrated in classical prose, enduring and invigorating.'

I wonder just how lively his prose will be when, between sniffles, he adds, 'With God's help, my book will be read and re-read for generations to come. It will not be some fanciful yarn recited by the fireside or sung to a simple tune that soon fades from memory.'

He is wrong, of course. Tales of the tongue can be more vivid than tales of the pen; they endure just as long, as I know from personal experience, and they are more widely remembered.

However, the priest's disdainful remark plants an idea in my mind: I will write a story about the brave, chivalrous and noble man who was my patron and my friend. He also saved my life. My tale will be my way of keeping his memory bright. At times he could be arrogant, vindictive, headstrong and greedy for wealth, yet all agree that his death is a tragic loss. Few, if any, know that I abandoned him in his final hour. That is why I begin this homage with the moment of his dying.

I still grieve for him.

Chapter One

'RUN! RUN FOR YOUR LIFE, you fool!' the man yelled. He was meant to be my bodyguard and had sworn to my father that he would protect me. He grabbed me by the arm and spun me round so I faced away from the disaster. Then he gave me a hefty shove between the shoulder blades so that I had to take a few steps just to keep my balance. A moment later, he took his own advice and barged past me, racing off with great leaps across the turf, tossing aside his shield and sword. I stood there stupidly, my head still ringing from the blow of some missile, probably a slingstone, which had struck my helmet. Behind me I heard the whoops and shouts of the Mercians. They had smashed our feeble line with their first charge. The majority of our men had come to the fight carrying their seaxes, though the way they gripped their weapons made it look as if they were about to trim and lay a hedge rather than use them as the lethal fighting blade that had given our Saxon people their name. The rest arrived equipped with clubs, staves and the hatchets they used for chopping firewood. A few brought bows and a handful of arrows more suitable for hunting small game. None of them thought to bring along spare bow strings. I had noticed one man armed only with a thresher's flail. My father should never have ordered them into battle.

Our plan had been to stop the Mercians at the hill crest. Two deep and shoulder to shoulder, we shouted our war cries and waved our pathetic weapons, more to keep up our spirits than in real defiance. It was a late spring day full of sunlight with the cloud shadows chasing across the downland. The breeze had the faint salty tang of the distant sea and fluttered our family banner – two black stags on a yellow field. My father managed to extract a few extra cheers from our men as he rode up and down in front of our battle line. But you had only to compare his scrawny horse with the sturdy charger of the Mercian commander waiting at the foot of the slope to know the difference in our resources. My Uncle Cyneric and my two brothers took their places in the front line. I, as the king's youngest son, was stationed a little distance to the rear. My duty was to direct our pitiful reserve, a score of elderly churls and the same number of household serfs.

Only the slope was in our favour. We reasoned that the Mercians would not attack up such a steep hillside. But they came on regardless – a terrifying mass of warriors stamping and hallooing, beating their leather-covered shields with their heavy iron swords. They were confident in the knowledge of a dozen victories over petty kingdoms like my father's. They out-numbered us, two to one.

Still dazed, I twisted round and looked over my shoulder. The Mercians were wading among our men, crushing any hint of resistance. A man toppled backward as the bronze boss of a Mercian shield smashed into his face. I saw swords and spear butts rising and falling as they cut down or spiked anyone who showed a glimmer of fight. I recognized a farmer who had visited our great hall only last week to pay his tithe. He was a slow-spoken gangling man who was half a head taller than those around him and wore a metal helmet like my own. God knows where he had found it, but it did him little good. A Mercian swordsman feinted at his face, then smoothly dropped his blade and hacked him across the legs. The farmer tumbled to the ground like a slashed nettle. Desperately I looked for any sign of my father. He was nowhere to be seen. Our flag was tangled around its staff and swaying back and forth. Seconds later it was dragged down and disappeared. A riderless horse, wild-eyed with terror, bolted past me. I recognized the beast as the one that my oldest brother had ridden. He too must have fallen. The triumphant howls of the Mercians were beginning to fade. They were running out of breath. Here and there our men were falling to their knees, hands clasped, pleading to be spared. That would limit the massacre; it made no sense to injure a prisoner who would soon be a slave.

One of the Mercians, a thick-set warrior in a leather jerkin sewn with metal plates, caught sight of me. I was standing by myself, numb with awful knowledge. His bearded face split into a covetous grin. He must have glimpsed at my neck the glint of the thin gold torc I had received the previous winter when I began my sixteenth year. He had no intention of sharing such loot with his comrades. Without a word, he began to run purposefully towards me. He had taken several strides before I gathered my wits and began to flee. I ran without hope. As a child I had never been able to run fast. My brothers had mocked me for being so sluggish, and they scarcely bothered to pursue me, knowing the chase would soon be over. Now it was the same. I heard the feet thudding on the turf behind me, the reverberation growing louder as the gap closed. Soon my breath was rasping in my throat, and my knees hurt. My loosely fastened helmet bounced on my head and slipped forward until all I could see was a yard or so ahead of me. I had dropped my sword but realized too late that my buckler was still strapped to my left forearm. I tried in vain to shake it free, but only succeeded in throwing myself off balance. I had gone no more than fifty yards when I became aware of the looming presence of the Mercian closing in. I heard his panting and sensed his air of easy triumph.

Then something solid crashed into me from behind, and I fell forward, face down into the sun-baked ground. I caught a whiff of sweat and greased leather mixed with the sweet smell of bruised grass as a heavy weight dropped on my shoulders. Someone was kneeling on my back. My helmet flew off and rolled clear. A hand was grasping my hair, pulling my head upward; for a ghastly moment I thought the Mercian was stretching my throat ready to cut it. Then his hand pushed forward sharply and my forehead slammed down on to the earth. Pain jolted through me. I tried to feebly squirm away, but the grip on my hair held fast, and the Mercian raised my head and battered it against the ground a second time. This time I did not resist. I welcomed the wave of blackness that engulfed me.

For more than a month I had known that this would happen.

*

I came to my senses, still lying face down. Someone had lashed my wrists together with a strip of rawhide. My face was now pressed against cracked and hardened mud. The slime on my cheek had the smell of chicken droppings. I stifled a groan and raised my head to look around. It was mid-afternoon, the sky had clouded over, and I was sprawled in the yard in front of my father's great hall, my own home. A large group of Mercians was clustered in front of the building, still dressed in their war gear. They were joking amongst themselves and taking turns to step forward and pick up an item from a pile of goods heaped on the ground. I recognized the helmet I had been wearing at the battle and, with a lurch in my stomach, my father's long ornate sword. To my right was the man supervising the division of the booty. He was seated on a tall carved wooden seat, which had once been my father's place of honour. The Mercians must have dragged the better furniture outside when they looted the hall. The man sitting in my father's place was middle-aged with a thick powerful body and heavy rounded shoulders. His hair was curled and greased and elaborately piled up on his head. Even without the crown that he wore for his image on the coins from his royal mint I had no difficulty in recognizing Offa, King of Mercia. I lowered my head back into the farmyard filth and lay still, gathering my thoughts. The sight of my father's sword confirmed that he must have perished on the battlefield. I doubted that my two brothers had survived. My gold torc was gone, of course. I could feel the bruise around my throat where my captor had wrenched it away; doubtless it was now hidden in his clothing. I toyed with the idea of denouncing him but decided it would serve no purpose. To the victor, the spoils. Last autumn, Offa had sent a message to my father, demanding to be acknowledged as his overlord and a payment of tribute. When the demand had been rebuffed, Offa had used the excuse to invade. Our battered little kingdom would first be raped, then either become a tributary of Mercia or absorbed directly into Offa's domain, which already included much of England.

I had already dreamed it in vivid detail: an antlered stag was grazing peacefully on a lush meadow when a huge dangerous-looking bull, led by a vixen, emerged from the dark forest in the distance. With the vixen scuttling a few paces ahead, the bull advanced. Too late, the stag raised its head and confronted the intruder with its antlers. The bull charged and gored its victim to death while the vixen screamed her encouragement. I had woken, drenched with cold sweat, realizing the screams were my own.

Rough hands were hauling me to my feet. Someone – I presumed he was the Mercian warrior who had captured me – took me by the elbow and marched me over towards King Offa. The pile of booty was gone. Now it was time to dispose of the prisoners of war.

A group of well-dressed men stood behind the royal seat: the royal councillors. To my shock and utter disgust my uncle Cyneric was among them. He must have surrendered very early in the fight and been spared. The look he gave me, a mixture of shame and arrogance, told me all I needed to know – he was now King Offa's man.

'This is the only surviving son, my lord,' said my escort.

Offa looked me up and down with hard, grey eyes. He saw a raw-boned young man of ordinary height, dishevelled and filthy, dressed in a tunic and leggings, strands of lank yellow hair flopping over his dung-streaked face.

'What is your name?' Offa asked. His voice was gravelly, and he spoke with the thick vowels of his own dialect.

'Sigwulf, my lord.'

The royal mouth twisted into a sardonic smile.

'Victorious Wolf. Not very appropriate.'

My turncoat uncle stepped forward from the councillors.

'He is the youngest son. There was another . . .'

A raised hand cut his sentence short. Cyneric was already being treated like the vassal he had become.

'So what are we to do with you?' Offa asked me.

I stared down at the ground and said nothing. We both knew that the sensible step was to put me to death, ensuring the direct bloodline of the kingship died with me. I wondered if my uncle had been dealing in secret with the Mercians before the invasion. His wife was one of Offa's distant cousins. The marriage was meant to be a bond-weaver, one of those alliances that cement friendships between neighbouring kingdoms. In this case it had been the reverse. Perhaps the screaming vixen had been her.

'Stand closer, lad. And let me see your face,' growled Offa.

I shuffled forward and raised my head, flicking aside my long hair. At that precise moment the sun broke through a gap in the clouds and lit up the farmyard. The light fell full on my face as

I found myself staring directly into the grim countenance of the man who was bold and ambitious enough to style himself Rex Anglorum, King of the English.

He flinched, just briefly, and then made a small movement as if to cross himself before he stayed his hand.

I was born with dark-blue eyes. This is quite normal among my people, and usually the colour of a baby's eyes changes to a lighter shade of blue when they are a few months old. Sometimes their eyes turn to grey, and very occasionally to brown. But something different happened to me. The colour of my right eye did alter, gradually becoming a greenish hazel, while the left eye faded to the normal pale blue. By contrast my twin brother – of whom I shall write later – underwent the opposite. His left eye changed colour, and his right eye remained the same. To many in our community these were certain signs of the Devil, all the more so because in the pain and difficulty of giving birth to twins, our mother died.

Whatever fate King Offa had in mind for me changed in the instant that he saw my mismatched eyes.

I sensed the hesitation in the king's manner as he tried to devise a way of eliminating me without doing me an injury. He was thinking that harming anyone who bore the Devil's mark would invite trouble from the Wicked One.

He turned to question my uncle.

'What do we know about this youth?'

'His father's pet, my lord,' answered my uncle. I could hear his bitter dislike of me in his voice. 'Too precious to be sent away for fostering like his older brothers. Taught how to read and write instead of how to hunt and make war.'

'Not dangerous then?' Offa raised an eyebrow.

'I wouldn't say that,' my uncle replied hastily. 'He is slippery, not to be trusted.' He produced a sycophant's smile, nastily deferential. 'Maybe Your Majesty should have him tonsured and shut up in a monastery.'

Incarcerating an unwanted person in a monastery was an effective way of putting them out of sight and mind.

A more thoughtful expression appeared on Offa's face.

'What are his manners like?' he asked, as though he was enquiring about the training and discipline of a house dog he was considering buying.

'He should know his place among his betters,' my uncle admitted grudgingly. 'He was brought up in the great hall.'

'Languages?' This time the royal question was addressed directly to me.

My tongue felt thick and dry in my mouth.

'Only Latin,' I mumbled.

There was a long pause as Offa regarded me seriously.

'Clean him up and find him some decent clothes,' he announced finally. 'Mercia has a better use for him.'

'And what has the king decided?' The question came from one of the royal councillors, a greybeard with the air of someone long in the royal service. His obsequious tone indicated that his query was a customary one, designed to allow Offa to show off his wisdom.

'He'll go to live with the Franks. Their king has been asking for someone to be sent from Mercia as an earnest of our good relations. If he's as educated and personable as is claimed, he'll make a good impression. Well scrubbed, he could even be quite good-looking. That should keep the Franks off our backs.'

Offa was cleverer than I had given him credit for. It was the custom for rulers to send family members to live in other courts. Officially they went as guests and as a gesture of trust and friendship between kingdoms, but in reality they were kept as hostages. They lived in their new homes until they died or were recalled. Should war break out, they were killed out of hand. As the only surviving scion of a noble family, I could be passed off as a suitable pledge of Mercia's good neighbourliness as long as my Frankish hosts did not enquire too closely. If they did discover I was not as important as had been made out, they would put an end to me and that would suit Offa just as well.

The king turned towards me again.

'You will not come back,' he said flatly. He did not need to say that if I did return, I would forfeit my life.

I kept my expression neutral but, strange to say, his judgement caused a sudden thrill of excitement to run through me. I was to be an exile without hope of return, a wanderer. Offa had not demanded my allegiance, and therefore I no longer had a lord. To many in our close-knit society, this would have been a terrible sentence. There is a special term for such an outcast. I would be *winelas guma*, a 'friendless man', living without protection, prey to all who would harm or exploit him. Yet for as long as I could remember, I had wanted to travel to foreign lands and see how others lived. Here was my chance. Perhaps I would even find a place where I would feel less of an outsider and my mismatched eyes would not arouse such unease.

The court of the Frankish king was as promising a destination as I could have wished for. Even our rustic villeins had heard of Carolus. For more than a decade he had ruled Europe from the dark forests beyond the Rhine to the sunlit plains of Lombardy and west to the ocean. It was such an enormous area that there were rumours that one day he would be crowned the emperor of Europe, the first true emperor since the days of Rome. His court must surely attract all manner of exotic and unusual folk. Perhaps I would blend in with them despite my unusual appearance.

'You have three days for the funeral rites,' Offa grunted. With a twinge of conscience I realized that I had been thinking only of myself. My father and two brothers had been proud of their warrior heritage. They would want that I gave them a fitting burial rather than lament their passing.

'A request,' I said.

Offa's chin came up as he glared at me. A scruffy and defeated youth whose life he had just spared was not expected to make requests.

'What is it?' His tone was truculent. For a moment I thought he was going to change his mind about my exile and order my execution instead.

'That my personal slave goes with me,' I said.

Once again Offa glanced towards my uncle.

'Is this slave of any value?'

'Hardly, my lord,' answered Cyneric. He did not bother to keep the sneer from his face. 'He's a defective cripple. An outlander who can barely string two words together.'

'He looked after me throughout my childhood,' I interrupted. 'I am in his debt.'

'And you in mine,' said Offa coldly. 'Take your worn-out slave with you, but he has cost you a day's grace. The day after tomorrow you will be escorted to the coast and put on the first ship sailing for Frankia.'

Chapter Two

OSRIC, MY BODY SLAVE, had been to sea before, that I knew. My father had bought him from a travelling dealer who must have heard that the woman looking after my brother and me was refusing to touch us after she noticed something strange about our eyes. The other household servants had been equally frightened.

'Make a good babysitter, he would. He's quiet and gentle and, with that gammy pin, not likely to run away,' the slaver had said as he showed off a battered-looking, scrawny man, perhaps thirty years old with skin the colour of a fallen autumn leaf. The unfortunate man had evidently been in a very bad accident, for his head was permanently canted over on a slant and his left leg broken and set so badly that it was crooked.

'Where does he come from?' my father had asked.

The dealer had shrugged.

'I got him down in the west country, part exchange for a couple of brawny lasses fit for mine work. Locals found him washed up on the rocks, like a half-dead mackerel. Probably off a tin ship that wrecked.'

My father had looked doubtful.

'Worth owning someone as hardy as that,' the slave dealer had wheedled. 'Any other man would have died. Besides, he doesn't understand any speech so he won't be taking up any wild ideas and gossip.'

My father had allowed himself to be persuaded. He'd paid a

few coins and named his new slave Osric as a joke; his namesake was a rival kinglet in neighbouring Wessex, a man famously vain of his good looks.

Over the years Osric became an essential, silent member of our household. He spoke so rarely that many visitors thought he was a mute. Growing up in his care, however, I knew that he learned our language in secret. When alone with his two charges, he would talk with us, though only a few words at a time. As I grew older I came to the conclusion that he preferred to stay withdrawn, locked away in his battered body.

'Are you afraid of the sea after what it did to you?' I asked Osric as we had our first glimpse of the distant blue line on the horizon. We were travelling on foot, since Offa had seen no reason to provide us with horses, only a couple of Mercian armed guards plodding along behind us, out of earshot.

Osric gave a slight shake of his head. We had left the burgh at daybreak two days earlier. There my father and two brothers lay side by side under a single, fresh barrow grave. I had buried them hastily with the few paltry goods that had survived the Mercian sack – a handful of damaged and long-discarded weapons, some cheap ornaments, a few pottery jugs and bowls and the bones of the pigs slaughtered for the funeral feast. These would have to suffice for their banquet in the afterlife. The only item of real value in the grave was my father's best hunting hound. A courser with a glossy dark-red coat and a nervous temperament, the creature had panicked and run off during the battle and had escaped becoming part of the Mercian plunder. We were digging the burial pit when the hound reappeared, slinking on its belly across the raw earth, whining as it sought its master. I coaxed the dog closer, looped a cord around its neck and strangled it. Then I carefully laid the body at my father's feet. He had loved the hunt.

Now he would at least be accompanied in the afterlife by his favourite hound.

Only a handful of our people had attended the funeral rites. They were too scared of incurring my uncle's displeasure. He was their new master, and their daily drudgery would continue as before. Slave or freeman, it was better not to anger him. Their taxes would be heavier now that King Offa would demand his share.

With Osric limping beside me, I came down the worn track that led to the cove where the trading ships called. A tubby, high-sided vessel lay on the damp sand of the shoreline, tipped awkwardly on one side. At first I thought something was wrong and the vessel had run aground, but then I noticed the rim of seaweed further up the beach and realized that the water's edge must advance and recede. I had never seen the tide before.

The captain of the vessel had set up his tent at the spot where the track came down to the strand. A heavy-set man, his pot belly held in by a thick leather strap, he had a notched stick and a knife in his hand for counting off the bundles of fleeces and hides his crew were busy sorting through. He turned and scowled at us as we approached.

'What do you want?' he snapped. His gaze went past me and took in our two Mercian guards. Clearly he recognized them as King Offa's retainers. It was in his interest not to offend the most powerful ruler along the coast but he resented being interrupted.

'Passage for myself and my slave,' I said, keeping my chin down. It was an old trick I had learned. It meant my long fringe of hair flopped forward and concealed one eye.

'Where to?' The response was blunt.

'Any port on the mainland. I am on my way to the Frankish capital.' I tried to make it seem as though the two Mercians were my honour escort, not my guards.

'I don't take passengers.' He hooked a thumb in his belt and looked me up and down. He was calculating what fare he could extract from me. The clothes that Offa had provided were far from luxurious. My only baggage was a leather satchel, supplemented by the pack that Osric carried. Altogether I cut a seedy figure.

'I am travelling at King Offa's request. Here is his authority,' I said grandly, pulling out a parchment from my satchel. It was nothing more than the brief letter written by Offa's scribe, introducing me to the court of the Frankish king. I gambled that a captain who needed a tally stick would not be able to read. 'We can pay for our passage,' I added sweetly. Offa's reeve had grudgingly provided a few silver coins for travelling expenses, scarcely enough to cover our costs.

The captain took a half-step forward, trying to snatch a glimpse inside my satchel to see if it contained anything of value. I closed the flap quickly.

'All right. Four pence for each of you,' he said after a pause.

'Four pence for the both of us,' I countered.

The captain's eyes flicked back towards our two guards. They were leaning on their spears, looking bored. One was picking his nose.

'Payment in advance.'

I counted out the coins — Offa's currency, of course — and dropped them into the out-thrust palm. The captain belched as he slipped them into the purse that he then tucked inside the front of the tunic. 'We leave on the next high water.' He nodded in the direction of Osric standing silently a few paces to one side. 'Your slave can help load cargo.'

I bridled at his tone.

'He will do no such thing,' I snapped.

The captain treated me to a look of such insolence that I was about to drop my hand to the dagger in my belt. Then I remembered that Offa had not trusted me with a sword or knife in case I tried to attack my guards and escape.

The captain shrugged and deliberately turned his back on me, before bellowing at his sailors to hurry up with the work.

It was dusk by the time the cog – as I later learned was the name for such a vessel – was loaded. I could see her beginning to lift and rock on the incoming tide. The captain was ignoring us so Osric and I waded out thigh deep and hauled ourselves aboard. Behind us the two guards, their task accomplished, began making their way back up the path. Doubtless they would report to Offa and my uncle that they had seen us safely on our way.

There was a good deal of grunting as the sailors came aboard and hauled on a heavy, wet rope hanging over the vessel's side. It must have been tied to an anchor set some distance off the beach. The cog bumped several times on the sand, and then began to back her way out into deeper water. The moment she was properly afloat, there was a different flurry of activity. The men ran here and there, unfastening, hauling and re-fastening ropes, untying the sail, hoisting it, fitting a long wooden handle into the shaft of a massive paddle that hung down into the water. I presumed it was the device which guided the ship. The captain shouted and swore, directing his men to their tasks with strange commands whose meanings were a mystery to me. I understood about one word in five. I looked on, trying to grasp what was happening, and every few moments I was shouldered out of the way by an impatient sailor.

Eventually the big, single sail flapped and banged, then filled with a great groaning of the mast and a twanging of ropes. All of a sudden the deck tilted beneath my feet and I had to sit down on the planking before I fell over. Out to sea the sky was darkening, and the wind seemed stronger than it had been on land. There was nothing to be seen ahead of the ship except an expanse of grey-blue water flecked with an occasional wave. I was feeling queasy already. I wedged myself in a corner and fought down my rising panic. A wave slapped against the side of the ship which gave a shudder, and a few flecks of spray fell on my face. I licked my lips and tasted the saltiness.

I closed my eyes and an image swam up into my mind. I could not push it away. It was my brother's face, greyish white, the sodden hair clinging to the scalp. It was how he had looked when I found him. Both hands grasped tendrils of the weed he must have seized as he tried to claw his way to the surface. Around one ankle looped a single thick, slimy snake: the massive lily root that had wrapped around his foot and held him down as he gulped desperately for air.

It was only a small pond. In summer, clouds of gnats and midges danced above its surface like swirls of smoke. In winter, it froze over, and the cowmen smashed the ice so that their beasts could drink. The pond was as much a part of our lives as the sheep pens and the cattle byres, and we had known it since early childhood. As toddlers we had made mud pies on its rim, and in later years tested our aim by throwing stones at floating twigs. The still water was so black that it was impossible to judge the depth. Nothing and no one warned of its dangers.

We were six years old and that afternoon we were climbing in an ancient alder tree. It was early autumn and the deep green leaves were still thick on the branches. They concealed just how far the alder overhung the pond. Normally Osric would have been in attendance but was suffering one of his recurrent fevers and had stayed in the slave quarters. My brother and I were alone when the branch beneath him broke. He gave a cry of surprise and crashed down through the foliage. I heard the heavy splash as he struck the water. I swarmed back to the ground as fast as I could, skinning my hands and knees on the tree bark. The moment my feet touched the ground I ran to the edge of the pond. The inky black water was swirling and eddying, but there was no sign of him. Dismayed, I stepped into the water. Immediately my feet sank deep into the sucking slime, and in another two paces I was up to my waist. I lost my footing and fell backwards, the water closing over my head. Neither my brother nor I could swim and I panicked. I scrambled back to safety and crawled out on the bank on all fours. Then I ran home, seeking help.

There was only one person in our inland burgh that could swim – Osric – and he was handicapped by his deformity. It was he who dived down again and again until we recovered my brother's body. We dragged it out and lay on the bank. The water trickled from his clothing and he was utterly limp. His head flopped over to one side. A pinkish froth oozed out from his mouth and nostrils. He looked small and helpless. I was numb with shock and pain. It was as if half my existence had been torn away, and I turned aside unable to watch. On the ground nearby lay the broken alder branch that had caused the accident. The raw splintered end was changing in colour from a creamy white to reddish-orange. According to our village elders, it was Nature's warning that the alder tree harbours evil in its veins.

*

I must have passed out with sea-sickness. The next thing I knew was someone kicking hard on my outstretched foot to rouse me. It was shortly after dawn on a dreary overcast morning and I was still seated on the deck. I could not remember ever feeling so ill. My limbs would not move, and there was a nasty sour taste in my mouth. I must have vomited in my wretchedness. I looked up at the captain of the cog who stood over me, gloating.

'Too rough for you, pretty boy? That was nothing more than a little chop,' he said, smirking. 'Get up!' He kicked me again, even harder.

The ugly menace on his face made me reach feebly for a handhold. Shakily I pulled myself to my feet. My knees were weak and I swayed, unable to keep my balance. An abrupt heave in my gut caused me to turn and grab the edge of the ship. I thrust my head out over the sea, closed my eyes and retched violently. I felt as though I wanted to die.

The captain hauled me back by the collar. 'Tie him up,' I heard him say. 'We'll see what he's got in that satchel. Later we can find what price he'll fetch. Some dried-up old spinster might like to have him close to hand.'

I turned to face my tormentor, hoping perhaps that the sight of my ill-matched eyes might deter him. But the brute noticed nothing. The daylight was too murky to make colours stand out clearly.

'Get me a length of codline,' he shouted to one of his crew standing a few feet away. As the man hurried off, I saw a hand rise up behind the captain's head as if from nowhere. An instant later an arm clamped around the captain's neck and jerked his head backward. There was a quick glint of something sharp and pointed, the hand struck forward, and all of a sudden the captain was frozen in place, his eyes bulging in shock. Whatever was held in that hand was now against his throat, just below his right ear. A bright red squirt and then a trickle of blood dripped down on the soiled fabric of the captain's tunic.

Osric's dark face appeared over the captain's shoulder. No one had paid him any attention until now. He must have scuttled across from wherever he had spent the night. Now he was clamped like a deadly spider on the captain's broad back.

The sailor sent to fetch the codline took a half-step towards the pinioned captain as if to go to his help. His movement produced a scream of pain, and a gurgled command for the sailor to stay back. The flow of blood onto the captain's collar increased a fraction.

I had no idea where Osric had obtained his weapon. It must have been a tiny dagger or a sharpened spike. Perhaps he always carried it on his person. The sailors had not bothered to search a crippled slave. Certainly they hadn't expected him to spring to the defence of his master.

'Knife,' Osric said to me. Shakily I reached out and took the captain's knife from his belt.

The captain gave another squeal of anguish as Osric dug the point of his weapon a little deeper.

The crew of the cog gathered in a threatening group, barely a couple of yards away. They had recovered from the shock of seeing their captain taken prisoner and were watching us closely, calculating how to rescue him. I counted five men and one further sailor at the wooden bar that steered the ship. One of the men closest to us made a furtive gesture. He was signalling something to the steersman, who in turn jerked the wooden bar abruptly. The big sail above my head flapped thunderously and the slope of the deck beneath my feet suddenly altered. I clutched for support. But whatever it was that the sailors had planned, Osric knew what they were doing. He kept his fierce grip on the captain and shouted some sort of command. He emphasized the order by twisting the point of the blade in the captain's neck. His victim let out another yelp of pain, and his back arched in anguish. The steersman hurriedly pushed the wooden bar back to its previous position, and the angle of the deck returned to what it had been before.

'Pull in the little boat,' said Osric to me. He nodded towards the back of the ship. I looked in that direction and saw that the cog was towing a small open boat behind her. I had been too seasick to notice such matters before.

Unsteadily I made my way to the rope tied to the boat and began to haul it in. It was surprisingly difficult, but the effort made me feel a lot better. When the boat was close under the side of the cog I fastened the rope tight and stood waiting.

'Move!' ordered Osric, jabbing again with his blade. He obliged the captain to sidle sideways around the edge of the ship until the two of them had joined me.

'Cut that big rope!' Osric said to me, nodding towards a rope as thick as my wrist tied at the base of the mast. I had seen the sailors use it to haul up the sail at the start of our voyage.

I still had the captain's large knife in my hand. The cog's crew had murder in their eyes as they watched me begin to saw through the heavy rope. It took several minutes. When the last strands gave way, I had the good sense to jump backwards. The big sail came slicing downward and collapsed in a great heap on the deck.

I ran back to rejoin Osric and the captain.

'Now take away the helm,' Osric told me. I had no idea what he was talking about until I followed his glance and realized he meant the big wooden handle controlling the ship's direction.

I walked across the deck towards the steersman and when he hesitated to step aside I raised the blade of the captain's knife menacingly; I was beginning to enjoy myself. He retreated, and I found I was able to pull the wooden bar free. Osric did not need to tell me what to do next. I threw it overboard.

In a couple of strides I was back with Osric and the captain, whose tunic front was now stained with blood. The cog was no longer moving through the water but was wallowing awkwardly, heaving up and down, turning this way and that, pushed by the wind.

'You first,' said Osric to me. I scooped up my satchel and

Osric's pack and dropped them into the little boat. I swung myself over the side of the ship, hung for a moment, then let go. I landed awkwardly in the little boat, falling in an ungainly heap. I recovered myself as Osric joined me, dropping nimbly down from the cog. Without a word he took the captain's knife from my hand and slashed through the rope that fastened us to the larger vessel. Instantly the gap between us widened as the wind blew our boat away.

I looked to Osric for guidance. He was busily untying a pair of oars that had been lashed in the boat. Only then did it occur to me how Osric's broken leg and twisted head had made very little difference to his agility aboard the cog. For a man with his handicap, being on a ship was altogether different from being on land.

Something plunged into the sea nearby, throwing up a little spout of water. I looked up. Someone on the crippled cog had found a bow and arrows, and in his rage was shooting at us. But we made an almost impossible target, and very soon we were out of range. The last I saw of her, the cog was drifting helplessly away into the distance, the small figures of her crew gathered on deck trying to raise sail.

I took the oars from Osric and he showed me how to slide them through two rope loops to hold them in place as I settled on the bench and made ready to row.

'Which way?' I asked.

He pointed. I could see only the waves around us. Then the rowing boat rose on the crest of a large wave, and far in the distance I saw a low grey line. It had to be the coast of Frankia.

I turned to my task and took a pull at the water. One oar dug into the sea, the other waved in the air. I nearly fell off my bench. Rowing a boat at sea was not going to be easy.

Osric had found a wooden implement that looked like a grain

shovel with a short handle. He began using it to scoop loose water from the bottom of the boat and back into the sea. He paused for a moment and reached inside his shirt. He pulled out a purse that I recognized had belonged to the captain of the cog, and passed it across to me. As I took it, I opened my mouth, about to thank him for saving our lives, when I saw that my words were not needed. Osric was doing something which I had not seen since the day my brother drowned, a death for which he had blamed himself.

Osric was smiling.

Chapter Three

WE CAME ASHORE ON a beach of round, smooth grey stones. Two urchins stood up to their knees in the shallows and watched me clumsily row the last few yards. The boys had been gathering shellfish and cautiously retreated as I climbed out of the little boat. The land swayed slightly as I walked towards the boys with a smile fixed on my face.

'Can you take us to your homes?' I asked.

They looked at me blankly. Without a word, they turned and ran, the stones clattering under their bare feet as they disappeared over the dunes at the back of the beach.

Osric and I picked our baggage out of the boat and began to trudge after them. With an afterthought, I stopped.

'Let me have that pack for a moment,' I said. He took off the pack and I searched among the garments that I had managed to save from my home: shirts and underclothes; a pair of spare shoes and a rolled-up cloak; an extra tunic and sandals for Osric; an embroidered belt; leggings. There was nothing else. I used the captain's dagger to trim a strip of cloth off an old shirt and wrapped it around my head, covering one eye. At home everyone had known about the colour of my eyes, but now I was among strangers and it would be best to leave it to others to suppose that the bandage concealed an empty socket.

Osric looked on and said nothing. He closed the pack and swung it on his back, and together we resumed our journey. We crested the slope and, a short distance away, hurrying towards us across an expanse of boggy ground thick with reeds was one of the two lads we had seen on the beach. He was accompanied by a man dressed in the long brown robe of a priest.

They halted in front of us, barring our way. The priest was an old man, so bony and shrunken with age that his threadbare gown hung loose upon him. His face was deeply lined and only a few wisps of grey hair surrounded his tonsure. He regarded us with a mixture of curiosity and mild suspicion. He had lost most of his teeth so he mumbled as he spoke. It hardly mattered. I did not understand what he was saying, only that he was asking a question, and his tone was not hostile.

'We would welcome your help,' I said in Latin.

He looked at me in surprise, as I did not have the appearance of someone with an education.

'The lad tells me that you came out of a small boat,' he said, switching to the same language.

'We're travelling to the court of the Frankish king,' I replied.

Again he looked surprised.

'I supposed you are shipwrecked mariners or perhaps pilgrims. We sometimes see pilgrims from across the water, on their way to Rome.'

'We had to abandon ship,' I lied.

I was met with a puzzled look.

'There has been no storm.'

'A fire on board,' I invented hastily. 'The cook was careless. The other passengers and crew got away in another boat. If you could set us on our way, I would be grateful.'

The old priest hesitated, looking uncertain.

'Carolus, our king, could be in any of a dozen places. He has no fixed residence.'

It was my turn to be taken aback. I had imagined the great

ruler of the Franks to be living in a splendid palace in a settled capital, not wandering from place to place like a nomad. Life would be more difficult if Osric and I had to go searching his vast kingdom to catch up with him.

'But most likely he is at Aachen in this season,' said the priest. 'He is engaged in building works there, an extraordinary project I understand.'

'Then perhaps you could tell me the best way there, and how far we must travel,' I said.

'What about your boat? Will you be leaving it behind?'

I guessed that the priest considered a small boat to be an item of considerable value.

'I will be glad if you accept the boat as a thankgift. I have no further use for it,' I said magnanimously.

The priest glanced at Osric standing crookedly a pace behind me.

'You will need the permission of my abbot if you and your companion are to go any further.'

He spoke a few words to the boy. Doubtless he was telling him to go to the beach and secure the boat before it drifted off for the lad scampered away over the dunes.

'Come with me!' he said, 'There's a village nearby where you can rest. Tomorrow we will go on to the monastery and meet the abbot.'

We squelched along the footpath which wound through the reed beds. The priest led the way, splashing through the puddles. The ragged hem of his gown was dark and sodden. We skirted several large ponds, their dark brown water still and silent. I shivered at the memory of my brother's death.

'My name is Lothar,' he said over his shoulder. 'You were fortunate that I was in the area when you arrived, or no one would have understood you – they speak their own local dialect. The village belongs to my monastery and is a very poor place. The families live by fishing and by collecting whatever is cast up along the shoreline.'

From his tone of voice I gathered that he was still not fully convinced that Osric and I were genuine castaways.

'I didn't see any fishing harbour,' I said.

'The coast here is too exposed to heavy winter storms. The villagers keep their boats in a river mouth nearby, and in bad weather they net the inland ponds.' He could no longer restrain his curiosity. 'Where did you learn to speak Latin so well?'

'My father arranged for a priest to teach me.' I did not say that the priest had been on the run. Bertwald was being pursued by the Church for theft and had arrived with his mistress in tow, a wild-looking slattern with a dramatic bush of wiry, auburn hair. My father, who believed in the Old Ways, took pleasure in giving shelter to a renegade from a religion for which he had no use. Bertwald had stayed with us for nearly ten years, with little to do except breed children and instruct me, his only pupil. Together he and Osric had been the two great influences of my growing up and I was only just beginning to appreciate how good a teacher Bertwald had been. Besides Latin, he had taught me how to read and write and even some grammar and logic. When he was drunk he would boast about the importance of the foundation to which he had once belonged. He'd claimed it had its own school and a library with fifty books. But in the end his loose talk undid him. One of our local Christians betrayed him to his former bishop and he had left as hastily as he had arrived.

We reached the fishing village, a huddle of small huts thatched with reeds. There were nets everywhere. They were heaped outside doors, draped over roofs, stretched between posts to dry, and strung out at a convenient height so they could be repaired. Every able-bodied man who was actively employed was mending nets. Unsurprisingly, the place reeked of fish.

Our supper was stale bread and shellfish stew, and we passed the night in one of the huts, asleep on mattresses of discarded nets. When we rose in the morning, we too had a distinctly fishy smell.

'We'll bathe when we reach the monastery,' Lothar assured me. It was not yet full daylight, and a dozen villagers joined us. In the half-darkness each man was bent forward under the weight of a large wickerwork pannier strapped to his back. I thought I heard a faint creaking as if their burdens were alive.

The dawn came, dull and grey and with not a breath of wind as we walked inland. The ground rose gently, the landscape changing from wet marsh to dry uncultivated heath. Flocks of small birds rose from the low bushes on either side of the path, and a large hare lolloped away before stopping and turning to look back at our little column as we tramped along. It was a wild and desolate place and we saw no sign of human habitation. After three hours we stopped briefly for a meal of chewy strips of dried fish washed down with lukewarm water from leather bottles. There was no conversation. The accompanying villagers were a taciturn lot. They sat on the ground, not removing the panniers from their backs. Eventually, soon after midday, we came to an area of open woodland and finally saw some buildings. Our guide quickened his pace. 'We should arrive in time for nones,' he said.

I had been expecting his abbey to be something substantial and impressive, yet the place could have been mistaken for a large farm sheltered by an outer wall.

We plodded in through the gate and found ourselves in a large unpaved courtyard surrounded by stables, cattle byres and storage sheds. The abbey itself formed one side of the yard and was no bigger than my father's great hall. A priest on his way in through the abbey's entrance door turned and called out greetings. Lothar waved to him but our silent companions who had tramped up from the coast ignored him. They went directly to a large stone trough set to one side of the yard. One by one, they halted in front of the trough, bent forward at the waist, and a colleague unfastened the lid of the pannier. Out from the basket poured a writhing brown and black mass. It cascaded over the porter's head and landed wetly into the trough and slithered and thrashed. An image flashed into my mind of the lily root that had drowned my brother and my stomach heaved. The villagers had been carrying a delivery of live eels, most of them as long as my outstretched arms. They knotted and wriggled, vainly trying to climb up the sides of the trough and escape.

Relieved of their burdens, the porters were already making their way back towards the gate. They wanted to be back in their homes by nightfall.

'How often do they bring eels up here?' I asked the priest.

'Every second month. They net them in the ponds and keep them until it is time to pay their tithe.' He looked pleased with himself. 'One of God's wonders. Fish of the sea and fish of the rivers come and go with the seasons, but eels are always there. A constant crop.'

A strikingly dressed figure emerged from the doorway of the main abbey building and darted across the courtyard to inspect the roiling mass of eels. A short, balding, rotund man, he wore a pink tunic of fine wool with dark-blue leggings and orange cross garters. His fashionable shoes had long, pointed upturned toes and were bright yellow. There was an expensive looking chain around his neck.

'There's Abbot Walo. You can explain yourselves to him,' said Lothar.

I noted a jewelled Christian cross suspended from the neck chain.

'You have done well, Lothar,' said his abbot, rubbing his hands together briskly. The crucifix bobbed up and down on his paunch. 'There is enough here to meet our obligation.'

Abbot Walo reminded me of an active plump bird with bright plumage, an impression strengthened by the beady-eyed look he gave me.

'And who are you?' he demanded.

'He came ashore near the village and says he is on his way to the king's court,' explained Lothar.

'My name is Sigwulf,' I broke in. 'I am travelling to the Frankish court at the request of King Offa of Mercia.' I had no need to mention Osric. Clearly he was my attendant, however worse for wear.

'Any proof of this?' demanded the abbot.

I produced the letter that Offa's scribe had provided me. The abbot's flamboyant taste in clothes was misleading. There was evidently a sharp mind behind the colourful exterior. He quickly scanned the document and handed the parchment back.

'King Offa's mark is known to me.' He stepped back a half a pace though not before I caught a whiff of his perfume. 'Lothar will see you to our guesthouse after a visit to the lavatorium.'

Before I could apologize for my own smell, he added, 'If you're not in a hurry to get to Aachen, you can accompany my eels. They leave in the morning.' With that, he turned on his heel and strode off.

'A remarkable man,' said Lothar, watching his superior leave.

'How long has he been your abbot?' I asked. Walo did not strike me as very devout.

'Less than three years. He was sent here to improve the revenues.'

'His previous abbey must have been sorry to lose him,' I said tactfully.

'Oh no, he was directly created abbot by the king. Previously he was assistant to the royal chamberlain. Very efficient.'

I tried to recall whether Walo had a tonsure. Probably not. I sensed that Lothar was getting fidgety and remembered that he was keen to attend afternoon prayers.

'I don't want to delay you any further,' I said. 'My servant and I can look after ourselves now.'

Lothar brightened, evidently relieved to be rid of us.

'I'll show you to the lavatorium before I go to chapel.'

He led me and Osric into a small outbuilding attached to the main abbey. Bertwald had described how his grand abbey had a washroom with running water delivered through lead pipes and running down a stone trough. Here, though, were just four large wooden tubs of water standing on a stone flagged floor with a hole cut in the outside wall as a drain. Lothar splashed water on his face and hands, and then hurried off to his devotions. I washed more thoroughly, Osric handing me fresh clothes. As soon as Lothar was out of sight, I gestured to Osric that he could also use a tub. I knew that my slave was meticulous in his personal cleanliness.

Afterwards, as I waited for Lothar to reappear, I wandered about the courtyard, peering into various outhouses and sheds. I had never before been in an abbey or even in a Christian church, and, in truth, I had no religion, but Bertwald had talked enough about the Christian life for me to pretend that I was a believer.

I discovered the well, a bakery and a smithy, and also the laundry room where I left Osric to wash our dirty clothes. Everything seemed to be very well-run and orderly, a testament to the efficiency of Abbot Walo. With divine service in progress, there was no one about, and I finished up in the stables, enjoying the peaceful sounds of the animals as they snuffled and munched and moved about on their straw bedding. Unusually, two oxen were stalled beside the half dozen horses. At home my father's tenants had kept plough oxen: working animals which were well treated in return for good service. By contrast these two beasts were more like pampered pets. Their tawny coats had been brushed until they gleamed, coloured thread wound around their horns, and their hooves had been oiled and polished to a shine. I gathered up a handful of hay and went to offer it to them.

'Keep your hands off!' warned an angry voice. I was so startled that I jumped. A squat, powerfully built man had appeared in the doorway behind me. He set down the wooden water bucket he was carrying and scowled as he stepped past me and took the hay from my grasp.

'I meant no harm.' I said.

'No one touches those beasts, except me,' said the stranger. A gross reddish-purple birthmark disfigured the left side of his face, extending from his hairline down to his neck where it disappeared under his collar. In his heavy wooden clogs, homespun breeches and smock he looked like a farm worker rather than a priest, and his Latin was heavily accented and clumsy.

'I was trying to find the guesthouse. Perhaps you can direct me?' I said.

'How should I know? I sleep next to my cattle,' he answered rudely.

I left the stable and found Lothar outside, looking for me.

'I see you've met Arnulf,' he said.

The surly stableman was standing in the doorway of the stable, hands on hips, making it plain that I was not to come back and bother his precious oxen.

'Perhaps someone should remind him that an abbey is a place of welcome,' I grumbled. I was still smarting from the rebuff.

'Arnulf's not with the abbey. That's his wagon there.' He pointed towards a vehicle standing in one corner of the yard. It had the usual four large, solid, wooden wheels and a single shaft.

Someone had fixed an enormous coffin-shaped wooden box on the flat bed where the load was normally stowed.

'For our eels,' explained Lothar. 'Arnulf has been hired to carry them to Aachen. That's what Abbot Walo meant when he offered you a way of getting there.'

*

I had difficulty getting to sleep that night. Every time I closed my eyes I was tormented by unpleasant images of eels knotting and unknotting, and I was fearful of the nightmare that awaited me. Curiously, when I did eventually fall asleep I dreamed instead of an enormous horse made of metal that gleamed and sparkled. It came towards me at a ponderous walk. On its back was a bearded rider, also made of metal. He was dressed in a short cloak and a military-looking tunic. The beast came closer and closer until it loomed over me. I could feel the warm breath from each nostril so large that a bird could have nested there. The giant rider's legs were bare and his feet, encased in heavy boots, hung level with my face. I sank to my knees, fearful that I would be crushed. At the last moment the horse stopped and stood still, one enormous hoof raised over me. I looked up, shivering with fear. The rider was staring down. His face was unknown to me. He raised an arm in a gesture which I did not understand and drops of blood seeped from his eyes.

I awoke to find that I had overslept. Sunlight was pouring in through the guesthouse window and with it the sound of splashing water and a strange thumping sound. I rose hurriedly and went to the door and looked out on the courtyard. A gang of workers, slaves by the look of them, was standing in line and passing bucket after bucket of water drawn from the well. The last man in the chain was up on the wagon next to the wooden chest. Another slave stood next to him. Each time a full bucket arrived, he lifted up a heavy wooden lid for a moment, the water was tipped in, and the lid was slammed shut. It was this that made the thumping noise. I guessed that the eels had already been transferred into their new home.

Osric was beside the tail of the wagon. He had spent the night in the servants' dormitory and our pack lay on the ground beside the wagon. Arnulf had already harnessed his two oxen to the shaft, and the two beasts were standing motionless, drools of saliva hanging from their jaws. I called to Osric that I would join him in a moment, and was rewarded with a black look from Arnulf as though I was about to cause a delay. The wagoner carried a long light wand in his hand.

The water carriers finished their labour. The man dealing with the lid banged it closed one last time, hammered in a wedge, then jumped down to the ground. I watched as Arnulf took up his position, facing his two huge beasts. He made a low clucking sound with his tongue, and the two oxen stepped forward with surprisingly short dainty paces. Behind them the massive vehicle rolled forward on its thick wooden wheels as though it was weightless. Arnulf walked backwards, facing his animals. He reached out with his long wand and very gently touched it to the outside ear of the right-hand animal. Without changing gait the two oxen shifted the balance between them so that the wagon turned away from his touch and headed directly for the abbey gate. Behind them a thin, dark trail was drawn across the earth of the courtyard as water dripped from the eel tank.

I wasted several minutes going in search of Lothar. I wanted to thank him and to say goodbye but there was no sign of him, nor of Abbot Walo. Slinging my satchel over my shoulder, I ran out through the gate to catch up with Osric. The wagon had gone barely fifty yards. It occurred to me that I had no idea how far it was to Aachen, or how long we would take to get there at a stately walking pace.

Chapter Four

As it turned out, that leisurely journey was a delight. Summer came earlier on the mainland than at home, and the air was warm yet not hot enough to trouble Arnulf's oxen. An occasional shower kept down the dust along the road without turning it to mud. We walked for up to six hours a day, stopping from time to time to rest the beasts and give them forage and water. At night we camped by the roadside or stayed in the guesthouses of monasteries, of which there were a remarkable number. We were on monastery business so room was always found for us, and we were given food and fodder to take on the next day's travel. The scenery was very like what I had known at home. The rolling hills were covered with oak and beech forest, and the farmers had cleared the bottom lands for crops of barley, rye and wheat. They lived in small hamlets, surrounded with vegetable plots and orchards, and it was clear that they were prospering. Their houses, built of wood, straw and clay were substantial, and it could take us twenty minutes to walk past the full length of a single field.

It took some time to win Arnulf over. He always went on foot in front of his two beasts, his guide wand over his shoulder like a fishing rod. In the beginning Osric and I ambled along at the tail of the wagon, out of sight and too tactful even to hang our baggage off the vehicle. Arnulf treated us as if we did not exist. At each halt, if he talked, it was only to his animals. He tended

to them, petted them, walked around the wagon, carefully checking the wheels and axles and the load. It was not until we came
to the first river ford that Osric and I were able to gain his
grudging acceptance. Arnulf stopped the wagon in mid-stream to
allow the oxen to stand in the water and cool their hooves. I
nodded to Osric and took down the bucket which dangled from
the tail of the wagon. Moments later the two of us were busily
topping up the eel tank with river water. Arnulf did not thank
us, but at least he waited until we had finished our work before
he clucked his tongue again and the oxen began to move. Later in
the afternoon he cut two leafy branches and gestured that we were
to walk beside the oxen. We were to use the whisks to keep off
the flies and midges that appeared as the sun began to sink.

Each mile increased my sense of well-being. I was in no hurry
to reach Aachen and, for the first time in my life, I felt I had some
control over my destiny. I was gaining in confidence and the only
precaution I took was to replace the makeshift bandage which
covered one eye. Passing through a small market town, I found
a saddler to make me a proper patch of soft leather with thongs
to attach it firmly in place. When I came to pay, there was a
difficulty. He refused Offa's silver coin, saying it was not legal
tender. He directed me to a Jewish moneychanger who offered,
for a twenty per cent commission, to take in all my Mercian
silver and give me King Carolus's money in its place. Without a
moment's hesitation I tipped out the contents of my purse. While
the Jew weighed and scratched each coin to test for purity, it
occurred to me that this was the last time I was likely to see King
Offa's image. At least I hoped as much.

Our journey also altered Osric. Exercise and the long days
spent in the sunshine began to improve his health and posture.
He held his head a little straighter, and by slow degrees his limp
became less obvious as his crooked leg strengthened. He became

much more relaxed and out-going. Previously he would have restricted himself to a few words at a time. Now it became possible to exchange a few sentences with him, though he would rarely start the conversation.

'Would you rather have stayed on and served my uncle Cyneric?' I asked him. It was the third day after leaving Abbot Walo's monastery and the two of us were seated on the grassy verge of the highway. Arnulf had called a halt in the noonday heat and was fussing over his oxen in the shade of a gigantic chestnut tree.

Osric rubbed a hand along his twisted leg to massage the spot where the bone was crooked. 'There was nothing to keep me there.'

'King Offa may yet arrange to have me done away with. What would you do then?'

'That will be for fate to decide,' he said with a shrug. 'Right now I'm looking forward to reaching Aachen and seeing if what I've heard about King Carolus is true.'

'What have you been told?'

'He has strange habits. He doesn't keep normal hours, takes naps in the afternoon, wanders about his palace unescorted and wearing normal everyday clothes, nothing to mark him out as being the king, sometimes even summons his council meetings in the dead of night.'

'It sounds as though you've been talking to his servants.'

'Abbot Walo was several years as an official in the palace administration. When he was appointed to the monastery, he brought his butler and cook with him. They enjoy talking about their time in royal service.'

'Is that just gossip or did they meet Carolus in person?'

'The butler claims he met the king once, in a corridor very late at night. Carolus stopped him and asked him a lot of questions about the palace staff, who did what, and where they were from. He apparently likes to know everything that is going on. His staff is in awe of him.'

I thought about Osric's reply. My father had been respected at a distance by his people. King Offa's subjects feared their overlord. King Carolus sounded like no monarch I had ever heard about.

'About the royal family? What are they like?'

'Carolus has an illegitimate son who, it is widely believed, will inherit the throne.'

Again that sounded unusual. Kings normally did not recognize bastard children.

'Doesn't he have anyone closer to him?'

'He's a lusty monarch, and has had several concubines and sired several children, most of them girls.'

There was something about the way Osric made the last remark that made me look at him questioningly.

He allowed himself the sliver of a smile.

'I was told he likes to keep the girls very close. But that's just gossip.'

With that enigmatic remark, Osric rose to his feet. Arnulf had started his oxen on their steady plodding advance along the highway, heading west.

*

We met other wayfarers along the road – beggars, itinerant craftsmen, pedlars trudging from hamlet to hamlet, their packs crammed with everything small and portable from knives to needles. Dirge-like songs in the distance warned of the approach of bands of pilgrims on their way to a shrine. On market days there were farm carts laden with produce, children running alongside, live chickens dangling upside down, pigs trussed and squealing in the back. Everyone overtook us if they were travelling in the same direction except for those on crutches or with toddlers in hand. Horsemen swore at us. They shouted at us to clear the road. Arnulf ignored them, and they were forced to find a way around us. As they drew level, his angry scowl and the ugly blotch on his face was enough to deter them from complaining further.

Only once did Arnulf turn his wagon aside for other road users. A small party of mounted men came towards us, ordinary looking except that they had a small escort of soldiers. Arnulf promptly veered his wagon to one side, and they rode on past, stony-faced. Then a hundred yards down the road, one of them turned his horse and came back to us. He was a young man, a clerk perhaps. He reined in and asked Arnulf a series of questions – how long he had been on the road, where he was from, where he was going and how much he had paid at the last three toll points. His answers seemed to satisfy the young man who had given a curt nod and trotted off to rejoin his companions.

'Who was that?' I asked. I had never seen Arnulf so respectful.

'King's commissioners,' he said. 'Sent out with royal orders and the power to demand explanations. They poke and pry, making sure that the kingdom is running smoothly.'

'Why do they have an armed guard?'

'For show. No one would dare interfere with them.'

'Are we near Aachen then?'

'This forest is the king's hunting preserve.'

It was a lonely, gloomy place, mile after mile of dense woodland. Evening was coming on and as the light faded I had an uneasy feeling that someone was tracking us from within the forest margin. But whenever I looked, I saw nothing. I mentioned my worries to Arnulf but he only grunted. Eventually we found a clearing where we could halt for the night. It was not worth lighting a fire, so we ate a meal of cold ham and bread provided by the last monastery kitchen, and lay down to sleep under the wagon. The two oxen, obedient as well-trained dogs, ate their forage and then sank down on their knees to rest.

Sometime later a faint scratching sound woke me. I raised myself on one elbow and peered out. A bright moon in a cloudless sky gave enough light to cast shadows. Everything seemed normal. I could make out the bulky outlines of the two oxen, and I heard the faint sound of chewing cud followed by the deep rumble of an animal gut. Beyond the beasts was the black margin of the forest, and somewhere deep in the forest an owl hooted. I sank down and lay quietly, wondering if I had been woken by the sound of a rat or fox investigating our provisions. Abruptly there came a stifled yelp. Two dark figures dropped on the ground beside the wagon and silently ran off into the dark woods. I scrambled to my feet. Looking up at the eel tank, I saw the lid was ajar. My shout woke Arnulf and Osric, and they joined me in time to see the first serpent shape slither out of the tank.

Arnulf let out an oath.

'Get the lid back on before we lose the lot!'

I reached out to haul myself up on the wagon. In the darkness my hand landed on something wet and slime-covered. It twisted away like a slippery muscular rope. I fought to overcome my revulsion. Putting my foot on the axle hub to use it as a step, I was knocked off-balance by the weight of a large eel which flung itself down the side of the wagon and struck me in the chest. It disappeared into the darkness, snaking rapidly across the ground. I gritted my teeth and swung myself up until I was standing next to the tank. I pressed down hard on the lid, trying to force it shut. It would not close: an eel was trapped halfway. It thrashed in panic, flailing against my arm and gripped itself around my wrist. Then Arnulf was beside me. He had the wooden mallet he used for securing the axle pins. He hit out, striking the escaping eel which twisted clear and was gone. I felt the lid drop into place and dull tremors as more eels attempted to force their way out. Arnulf had located the wedge that the thieves had removed and hammered it fiercely back in place.

'Bastard thieves must have given themselves a bad fright,' he said as he finished. He gave me an odd look. I realized that my eye patch had slipped in the excitement. He could see that both my eyes appeared normal. Fortunately it was too dark to make out any colours.

'I never knew that eels could move so fast,' I mumbled, turning my head aside.

He spat over the side of the wagon.

'They go mad when they know that rain is coming.'

It seemed an odd thing to say on such a fine clear night, but the next morning a grey-black line of thunder clouds was massing on the western horizon as Arnulf harnessed the oxen. The clouds spread rapidly, blotting out the sun, and the light dimmed though it was not yet noon. All around us the forest waited in baleful silence until we heard a moaning sound in the far distance. A savage wind came tearing through the trees. The leading gusts ripped off leaves and sent them swirling through the air in a mad dance. A lone raven flashed past, helpless in the gale and was whirled out of sight. Soon the upper branches of the trees were bending and twisting as the main weight of the storm raced across them. There was a random cracking and snapping as twigs, then thick branches, broke free and came spinning to the ground. A long-dead and enormous oak, gnarled and its heart already rotten, leaned sideways until the roots gave way. Then it came crashing down with a thump that shook the ground, half blocking the roadway and prising a massive clump of brown earth, the size of a small cottage. Within the wind's howl was a drumming noise, and finally the rain arrived. Heavy rain drops rattled on the ground; puddles appeared in an instant and joined together.

Rivulets of yellow-brown water raced down the slope and turned into churning streams.

Arnulf's oxen were halted by the ferocity of the storm. They stood patiently, their tawny hides soaked to a dullish brown, their hooves gradually sinking into the mud. Osric and I crouched in the shelter of the cart, the water rising around our feet. Arnulf pulled up the hood of his cloak and hunched in the lee of his beasts. For perhaps an hour the storm beat down on us, and then eased to a steady, soaking rain. We began to move. The oxen sloshed through the mud, and the wheels of the cart left deep grooves that instantly brimmed with rainwater. I imagined I could hear the eels thrashing and roiling excitedly in their tank.

Heads down, we plodded on, scarcely noticing that we were finally leaving the forest. The rain continued all that day and the next night, a miserable time spent under the wagon once again. At dawn on the second day it was still raining heavily as we took to the road once more. There were no other travellers, and when I finally looked up and took an interest in our surroundings, I saw that we were approaching the outskirts of a large, sprawling township.

Arnulf pointed. A mile ahead of us the ground sloped upward. There, surrounded by a web of scaffold, were by far the largest buildings I have ever seen. Still under construction, they already dominated the town.

'Big Carl's newest palace,' Arnulf said, wiping the rain from his face. His wet birthmark glistened like sliced beetroot.

He led the way deeper into the town. The citizens were all indoors, shutters closed against the sheeting rain. Stray mongrels and pigs scavenged in the miry side lanes and flooded ditches. The closer we came to the new palace the more substantial were the houses. I assumed they belonged to wealthy merchants and members of the royal entourage. Occasionally a servant or a slave on some errand darted between the houses, dodging the spouts of water gushing from the roofs and gutters. Drenched, we slogged on until we had entered on the royal precinct. It was a vast building site. Materials lay everywhere: heaps of timber; piles of cut stone; stack upon stack of bricks. Here at last was some activity. Under long, low shelters and out of the rain carpenters were shaping huge beams with saw and adze. Men heated and hammered metal in a dozen smithies, stonemasons carved and split, and smoke oozed from an odd-shaped building which, to judge by the great heap of clay beside it, was a brick kiln. We passed a makeshift roof under which a team of men was walking round and round a circular pit, pushing on a heavy beam. Glancing into the pit I saw that paddles attached to the beam were mixing a sludge of what looked like grey-brown porridge and realized they were mixing vast quantities of mortar.

As we trudged past them, the function of several different, half-finished structures became apparent. A massive rectangular building had the same proportions as my father's mead hall. I guessed it would become some sort of grand meeting chamber. Beyond it a large octagonal building was taking shape and was well advanced. The arched framing of its roof was in place and formed the skeleton of a great dome I guessed was destined to be a royal church. I also made out the foundations and lower walls for what would be a long arcade. It was not just the size and scale of the structures that amazed me: I had never seen bricks used in this way. At home we built our walls with wood and clay and capped them with thatched or tile roofs that had to be replaced regularly. Here the monumental walls were being put together with thousands upon thousands of sturdy rust-coloured bricks with an occasional course of cut stone. Any observer would know that the buildings were intended to endure forever.

Arnulf guided his two oxen through the churned-up mud

towards a cluster of older buildings. Shortly before reaching them, he halted his beasts.

'This is where our roads part,' he said in his usual blunt manner. 'I report to the seneschal's office,' he paused briefly. 'And thank you for your help on the journey. I doubt we will meet again.'

He walked away to stand beside his oxen, clicked his tongue and the wagon creaked off through the mire. I was sorry to lose his company for he had proved to be an honest man, and had been patient in allowing Osric and myself to use him as our teacher so that we could learn to speak the Frankish tongue. Quite a few of its words were similar to my Saxon speech, and Osric and I had practised together so that we already had a good working knowledge and were improving daily. My last glimpse of Arnulf was the tip of his wand waving above the eel tank, more like a fishing rod than ever.

Osric and I were left standing alone in the rain, and I took the chance to switch my eye patch from one eye to the other. I had discovered that if I left the same eye covered for too long, I had difficulty in seeing with it afterwards.

The nearest shelter was the porch of the part-finished octagonal building I had noted earlier. I ran across and removed my sodden cloak, trying to avoid dripping water on a couple of priests already loitering there.

'Could you tell me where I might find the office of the court chamberlain?' I asked.

The taller of the priests, a gaunt man in his fifties with a freckled complexion and a high forehead, gave me a sharp look.

'Where are you from, young man?' he asked in a precise, deliberate voice that matched his scholarly appearance.

I explained how King Offa had despatched me to the Frankish court.

'I thought I recognized the accent, though your Latin is more than adequate. I see you've brought your weather with you.' The priest drew his gown more tightly around him and peered up at the leaden sky. 'It looks as if this rain's set in for the rest of the day.'

'I'm hoping to report my arrival to the chamberlain's office,' I reminded him.

He grimaced.

'You'll find the government at a standstill. The rain has kept everyone away, and the floods. The fords are impassable and the current in the river runs too strongly for the ferries.'

I wondered whether I should turn round and try to catch up with Arnulf. He should have reached the royal kitchens by now, and at least there would be hot food there.

Osric limped across to join us. He looked woebegone, splatters of yellow mud on his tunic. He seemed to have shrivelled.

'You've done well to get this far,' observed the priest, eyeing us, 'one with difficulty seeing, the other walking.' He seemed to make up his mind about something. 'If you will follow me . . .'

He set out across the sea of mud towards a substantial two-storey house, one of a handful of newly completed buildings. It stood alongside the great half-finished meeting hall, and two sentries armed with heavy eight-foot long spears guarded the entrance. They seemed to know our guide for they saluted him, banging the hafts of their spears on the ground which sent a spray of rain dripping from the rims of their iron helmets. He led us inside, and then up a staircase. The place had the atmosphere of a private residence rather than any office. Two more guards were stationed each side of a large double door where he knocked. A voice called to us to enter and we stepped into a spacious, plainly furnished room. In the centre was a broad table on which stood a clay model of the palace as it would look when completed. Near-by were a number of low stools and a tall upright wooden chair which reminded me of my father's high seat in the mead hall. On the walls were a few rather faded hangings depicting hunting scenes. The only colourful item in the room was a large cross, exquisitely carved and gilded and placed at one end of the room on a low plinth.

At the window with his back to us stood a tall, thick-set man gazing moodily at the rain. He had an arm around the shoulders of a young woman.

'What is it, Alcuin?' the man asked, turning to inspect us. He stood well over six feet and everything about him was on a similar, rather daunting scale. A big round head sat on a thick neck. He had a prominent nose, large grey eyes, and, though he held himself straight, his stomach protruded slightly. I judged him to be about fifty years old, for the hair at his temples was turning white. His most striking feature was his moustache. Long and luxuriant and blonde, it hung down a good six inches each side of his mouth and was carefully groomed. The two hairy strands provided an unexpectedly close match to the two long, blonde braids of the much younger woman at his side. Glancing between them, I concluded that they were father and daughter, not lovers as I had first suspected.

'Two travellers who I thought might interest you,' said our guide.

The big man gazed down at me. He was soberly dressed in everyday Frankish indoor costume of a long, dark-brown belted tunic over grey woollen trousers. His wool socks had leather soles in place of shoes, and were held up by strips of cloth wrapped around his legs. He wore no jewellery, though the young woman had a showy necklace of polished amber pieces, each the size of a pigeon's egg. She had her father's sturdy build which, thanks to her belt with its gold filigree, gave her a voluptuous figure, wide-hipped and full-breasted.

'What is your name?' the big man asked me. His voice was surprisingly high-pitched for such a big man.

'Sigwulf,' I replied, 'and this is my slave, Osric.'

'They are just arrived, sent by Offa, the king of the English,' explained the priest.

Intelligent grey eyes searched my face.

'I see you had good weather during your travels. You have a deep tan.'

'Until three days ago we enjoyed nothing but sunshine.'

'And the sunlight hurts your eyes?'

'An imperfection from birth I prefer to keep covered,' I answered cautiously.

'A strange imperfection. It seems to shift from one eye to the other.'

I didn't know what he was talking about. I fumbled for an answer.

'The skin around your left eye is lighter where the sun has not touched. Yet you are wearing the patch on the other eye,' he explained without a trace of irony.

I felt myself flush with embarrassment and glanced across at the priest, Alcuin. He was standing with his hands concealed in his sleeves, looking imperturbable.

'It would be a courtesy if you removed your eye patch,' Alcuin suggested.

Reluctantly I reached up and removed the leather cover to my right eye. I remembered how Offa had recoiled.

This time it was very different.

The big man in front of me stared at me closely for several moments.

'Interesting,' he said finally. 'We are told that Alexander of Macedon had just the same condition. His eyes were of different colours. It was a mark of his uniqueness.' Ignoring Osric, he turned to the priest. 'We welcome this young man. Find him a place with the paladins and see that he gets fresh clothing.'

It was clear that we had been dismissed, and the priest bowed. Tactfully, I did the same, and the three of us left the room. As the door closed behind us, I remembered Offa's letter still in my satchel.

'I forgot to give the chamberlain the letter that King Offa prepared for King Carolus,' I said to the priest.

The priest raised an eyebrow.

'That wasn't the chamberlain. That was Carolus himself, properly known as King of the Franks and Lombards and Patrician of the Romans.'

I was mortified that I had failed to recognize the most powerful ruler in the west.

'But he was dressed so plainly . . .' I stammered.

'He loathes wearing costly or fashionable clothing,' said the priest. 'Almost as much as he detests being idle. It drives him to distraction. Most of his councillors are using this rain as an excuse to take the day off so he has little to do. I thought he would find your presence a brief diversion.'

I reached into my satchel for the now water-stained parchment.

'Then shouldn't I leave this letter with his secretariat.'

'I'll deal with it,' said the priest taking it from me. 'Incidentally, I come from Northumberland myself. I'm one of the king's advisers.'

'Thank you for all your assistance. I hope I will have the chance of meeting you again,' I said.

Alcuin smiled thinly.

'You will. Another of my duties is to drum some learning into the heads of royal "guests" like yourself. King Carolus cannot abide idleness in others, any more than in himself.'

I readjusted my eye patch over my left eye.

'I hope the king will not object if I continue to wear this.'

The priest shrugged.

'As you wish.'

He escorted us back to the entrance hall and spoke to one of the guards.

'Have one of your men show this young lord to the quarters for royal guests, and then take his slave to the stores to fetch suitable clothing for him.'

A gust of wind drove the rain horizontally into our faces as we emerged into the open. Osric and I followed the soldier as he ran for the lee of the unfinished meeting hall, then led us around a corner of the building. My eye patch made me blind on my left side and, in trying to keep up with him, I blundered into a massive stone block standing waist high in my path. I was about to step around it when something made me look up. A chill ran down my spine. The stone block was the pedestal of a remarkable statue. It was a bronze horse, twice life size. Every detail was precise – the flaring nostrils, one hoof raised, the arched neck. On its back a rider wore the same short military tunic and heavy military boots I had dreamed of and he was making the same gesture with his arm. The only difference from my dream was the rider's face. This time he did not look down at me, but stared straight ahead, and it was rain which trickled down from his sightless eyes, not blood.

Chapter Five

FROM THE OUTSIDE, THE QUARTERS where the paladins or royal 'guests' were housed could have been mistaken for an army barracks. A long, low barn of a building, it was located at the far side of the palace precinct. The guardsman left me at the threshold and went off with Osric to the royal stores. Eager to get out of the rain, I eased open the heavy door and slipped inside. I was in a room that stretched the full length of the building. Watery-grey light filtered in through a row of small windows. Tables and benches filled the spaces between the double rows of posts holding up the timber roof. The walls were lined by sleeping booths. There were damp areas on the earth floor where the thatch had failed. A fire trench held cold cinders and ash. The place not only looked like a barracks but had the same smell and fug.

A dozen or more men were idling away their time on a rainy day. Most were about the same age or a few years older than me and I took particular note of one shaggy fellow, off by himself to one side. He was seated on a wooden stool and moodily whittling a piece of wood. A much older white-haired man was playing a board game against a dashing-looking opponent whose skin was almost as dark as Osric's. The others were seated at the central table, leather bottles, drinking horns, cups and bowls in front of them.

'Hello, Patch,' said one of them, noticing me hesitating in the doorway. He had curly chestnut hair and an open, smiling face. 'Come to join the palace companions?'

'As King Carolus wishes,' I replied, hoping my Frankish, learned from Arnulf, was not too rustic to be understood.

'And where are you from?'

'King Offa of the English sent me.'

'Isn't that where that curmudgeon Alcuin comes from?' asked his companion, a chubby, soft-looking individual with melancholy brown eyes.

'He's from further north,' I said.

'Stop blathering, Oton, it's your turn,' snapped a man I judged to be approaching middle age. His thick, black eyebrows over deep-set eyes made him look fierce and short-tempered, an impression enhanced by his impatient tone.

The man called Oton nodded towards an empty place at the table.

'Patch, take a seat. Pay no heed to Anseis here. He's a thick-skulled Burgundian, and they don't have much by way of manners.'

'Oton, you're keeping us waiting,' growled Anseis.

I sat down at the table. Oton closed his eyes for a moment's thought, then opened them and declaimed:

'I saw a beast whose stomach swelled behind him, fat and bloated.

A strong servant tended to him, and filled his stomach with what came from afar, then travelled through his eye.

He gives life to others but does not die. New strength revives in his stomach.

And he breathes again . . .'

Oton looked around the table.

'What did I see?' he asked, and I realized the company were amusing themselves by posing riddles. It had been the same in my father's mead hall after a banquet.

There was a long silence.

'Come on, you lot. It's easy enough,' urged Oton.

'A stomach swelling behind him,' murmured the cheerful

young man with the curly hair. He raised himself slightly off his bench and let out a long, deliberate fart. 'Is that a clue?'

'Berenger, you're disgusting,' said Oton.

'A bellows, that's what you saw,' said the dark-skinned man who had been playing the board game.

'Correct. Your turn, Engeler,' said Berenger.

Engeler took a moment to smooth down his long, glossy, black hair and adjust the cuffs of his expensive silk shirt. I guessed that he was someone whom women found attractive, and he knew it. He posed his riddle:

'*A queer thing hangs down beside a man's thigh, hidden by his clothes.*

It has a hole in its head, and is stiff and strong, and its firmness brings a reward.

When the man pulls up his clothing, he wants the head of that hanging thing to poke the hole that it fits and has often filled before.'

Berenger guffawed.

'Trust you to be thinking of sex,' he said.

'Not at all,' replied Engeler with mock seriousness. 'It's you who has a dirty mind. There's nothing lewd about my riddle.'

I knew the answer but held my tongue.

'The solution is "a key",' said Engeler with a grin. 'Now have a go at this next one, Berenger, and try to keep your thoughts pure.' He paused, and then began:

'*A certain something swells in its pouch, grows, and stands erect, lifting its covering.*

A proud bride lays hands on that boneless marvel, the king's daughter covered that swollen object with clothing . . .
What is it?'

Berenger sat silent.

Engeler had a sly twinkle in his eye.

'Anyone know?' He turned to me. 'How about you, Patch?'

'Dough,' I said quietly.

There was a moment's silence. I could almost hear the others wondering what to make of me.

'So Patch, now it's your turn,' said Oton.

I thought back to father's drinking sessions and dredged up one of his favourite puzzles, and said:

'Four strange creatures travel together, their tracks were very swart.
Each mark very black. The bird's support moves swiftly, through
*   the air, underwater.*
The diligent warrior works without stopping, directing the four
*   over the beaten gold.'*

I sat back on my bench and waited for the solution.

'A horse and wagon,' volunteered Engeler.

I shook my head.

'Something to do with a dragon flying through the air, diving underwater,' was Oton's suggestion.

Again I shook my head.

'Give us a clue,' said Berenger.

Unexpectedly, the shaggy-looking fellow spoke up. He put aside the piece of wood he was carving and said, 'You use words to describe things without saying what they are.' He spoke in a heavy, deliberate way.

'Sounds crazy to me, Ogier,' observed Berenger.

'At home our poets do it all the time,' Ogier said. 'They say the sea is the whale road; the sun is the sky candle.' He resumed his whittling of the piece of wood.

I didn't want to make the company feel foolish so I said, 'Ogier is right. In my riddle the "bird's support" is a feather, and the diligent warrior is a "man's arm".'

A voice behind me said, 'Then the four curious creatures

travelling together are a scribe's four fingers, and the feather is a
writing quill leaving an inky trail.'

I turned to see who had worked out the correct answer. Tall
and good looking, he had just emerged from one of the sleeping
cubicles and held himself with an easy grace. Fair skinned, he had
a straight nose and grey eyes and hair the colour of ripe wheat.
Also, there was something vaguely familiar about him. It took me
a moment to realize that he reminded me of King Carolus. It was
as if the newcomer was the king as a younger man. I tried to stand
up from my bench, ready to bow to him, but I was awkwardly
placed and came up against the table and fell back on my seat. My
clumsiness brought a smile to his face. He showed white, even teeth.

'Don't get up,' he said. 'My name is Hroudland.'

'I'm Sigwulf,' I replied, 'and you have the correct answer.'

Hroudland came and sat down across the table from me.

'A lucky guess,' he said. 'But I haven't worked out what you
meant by "beaten gold".'

'My riddle was an image of a man writing in ink with a quill
on parchment that has gold illumination,' I answered him.

'You should try that out on my uncle. He's keen on anything
that's got a religious slant,' Hroudland said.

'Your uncle?'

'My mother is one of King Carolus's sisters.'

I had just opened my mouth to respond when I was interrupted by Anseis asking, 'Is it true that the king is planning a
campaign against the Saracens in Hispania, Hroudland?'

'Not this year. The season's too late,' said Hroudland.

'In the south you can keep an army in the field almost until
Christmas,' observed Berenger.

'That's something you should discuss with Gerard,' said
Hroudland looking across at the white-haired older man.

The riddles were forgotten. The conversation veered off into a discussion of how long it would take to raise an army, the speed of its supply train, the correct proportion of archers to foot soldiers to cavalry, the correct tactics for fighting Saracens. As they talked and argued, I learned that the old man Gerard came from the south and that when King Carolus went to war, my fellow royal guests served as officers in his army.

The discussion was bringing back bitter memories of the only battle I had ever fought in, and I excused myself from the table. Osric had returned from the royal stores with an armful of clothes, and I found myself a vacant sleeping cubicle where he laid out my new wardrobe. When he withdrew, I lay down on the cot and closed my eyes. It had been a long day and I was tired. Almost instantly I was asleep.

My twin joined me or, rather, his fetch came to sit on the side of my cot. He looked as he always did when he visited me in my dreams – pensive and calm, not the ghastly corpse of his death. He had aged at the same pace as myself, and sometimes I wondered if I was looking in a mirror, rather than seeing someone who had been dead these past ten years.

For a long time he sat without speaking, occasionally looking around the little alcove. 'What do you make of them?' he eventually asked.

As always, I did not reply. There was no need. My brother always answered his own question.

'Learn what you can about them. Suspect the one you come to trust, and trust the one you suspect.'

Then he stood up and left.

*

I was awake before sunrise. For a few moments I lay snug in my cubicle, recollecting where I was. Then I rose and dressed quietly in the Frankish costume that Osric had delivered for me – linen undertrousers and shirt under a belted tunic, and woollen leggings held in place by criss-cross garters. Osric had located a pair of laced leather boots of the right size, and only the long cloak in the shape of a double square delayed me. It took some time in the darkness to work out that I should place it over my shoulders so that it hung in front and behind, with a slit on each side.

I walked softly across the room, careful not to wake my new companions, and let myself out. During the night the rain had stopped. The air smelled of dampness and mildew. Only the faintest glow showed where the sun would rise. I made my way cautiously through the shadows, trying to retrace my path to where I had seen the statue of the horse.

I had gone perhaps a hundred paces when I realized that I had lost my way. I decided it would be wiser to wait until the daylight was stronger and I could get my bearings. I stood in silence for some time, watching the buildings gradually take shape out of the darkness. It was a strange sensation to know that I was in the heart of the largest, most powerful kingdom in the western world and had already met its supreme ruler face to face. Yet I knew almost nothing about it. If I was to find my proper place within it, I would have to learn its manners and customs. The prospect excited me.

All of a sudden there came the most hideous scream. It was a cry of such anguish that the hair rose on the back of my neck. Instinctively I reached for my dagger, only to remember that I had left it behind. The source of that terrible scream was very close. Weaponless, I hesitated. Then the ghastly wail came again, even more desperate than before, and I knew I had to intervene. Someone was being attacked and needed urgent help. The screams had come from the far side of a builder's shed. I took a deep breath and dashed around the corner, my heart pounding, not knowing what I would find. I half-hoped that my sudden appearance might frighten the assailant off his victim, or if I yelled loudly enough to raise the alarm, someone would come to help.

I came skidding around the corner of the hut only to find no one there. There was a large heap of rough-sawn logs and an open muddy space. Pale smears of sawdust showed where the carpenters had been at work. I slithered to a halt, puzzled. The light had strengthened enough to cast faint shadows. Something moved in the gloom, low down beside the timber. I tried to make out what it was, half expecting to see a badly wounded victim lying in the mire. Again nothing. Then out from the shadow strutted a bird. It stood taller than a chicken, with large feet and a small, fine head on a gracefully curved neck. The body was almost the size of a goose and, though it did not waddle, the creature had a stilted, ungainly walk. The tail was very odd. The bird dragged behind it a drooping train of feathers out of all proportion to its size. I was still puzzling about this strange creature when it raised its head and uttered that same spine-chilling, ugly scream. Once again my heart raced, but by then I knew what was in front of me. Near my father's house had been the ruins of an old Roman villa, once the home of a rich merchant. On its mosaic floor had been depicted all manner of exotic creatures, lions, sea monsters, fish, ducks and . . . peacocks.

'Escaped from the king's zoo,' said a voice I recognized, and Alcuin materialized from the shadows, giving me yet another scare that morning. 'I'm sorry if I startled you. I take a stroll after lauds. It helps clear the mind.'

'That creature has a shocking call,' I commented.

'The voice of the devil, the gait of a thief, and the body of an angel,' replied Alcuin.

The bird heard our voices, turned towards us and slowly raised its tail into an enormous fan. Straining with effort, for a moment the creature looked as if it would topple forward on its beak. Despite the comic stance, I was impressed. The Roman mosaics had not come near capturing the magnificence of the live display.

'The hundred eyes of Argos,' I said.

Alcuin gave me a shrewd glance.

'Where did you learn that?'

'A tale my tutor told me at home. He loved the ancient stories,' I replied.

'A priest?'

I nodded.

'He would have done better to tell you that the patterns of the peacock's fan represent the all-seeing eye of God.'

I decided to tease.

'And the flesh of the dead peacock doesn't corrupt? So it mimics the eternal body of Christ.'

Alcuin showed a flash of irritation.

'Pure myth. If this bird is mauled by one of the king's hunting dogs, you will find that the body rots just like any other fowl.'

He began herding the peacock across the ground, as if he was a goose girl, and I helped him.

'What other animals does the king have in his collection?' I asked.

'Bears, a leopard or two, cranes, wolves, some monkeys, several types of snake – most of them survive only a year or two before they die.'

'How do they get here?'

'Some are brought by hunters who've heard of the royal menagerie. The more exotic animals are sent by foreign rulers, as gifts.'

I saw my opening.

'What about that metal horse, the big statue? Was that a gift?'

'That came from Italy, from Ravenna. It represents a Roman emperor, Theodosius. Carolus asked for it to be sent to him.'

'A strange request.'

'Not really. Theodosios was a Christian emperor in Rome. He spread the word of Christ with his conquests. Carolus sees him as an example.'

I said nothing, wondering whether my dream was of the Roman or the Frank.

The peacock stalked ahead of us, not hurrying. Now it stopped and uttered another of its raucous wails. In response a servant appeared at a run. He must have been one of the keepers of the royal menagerie because he had a small bag of grain in his hand. He sprinkled a trail of seeds on the ground and the peacock pecked at them until he was close enough to grab the bird.

Alcuin watched the captive being carried away.

'How are you settling into your new quarters with your new companions?' he asked.

'I'm still trying to put names to faces.'

'Their families are influential and from all over the kingdom and beyond.'

'The one called Hroudland claims to be the king's nephew.'

'That's correct but his mother remarried; he doesn't get on with his stepfather who is one of the king's chief ministers. Life is quieter if they are kept apart.'

'There's a big, shaggy fellow in our lodgings who doesn't say much. Just watches.'

'Son of the Danish king. He's a hostage for his father's good behaviour. But a steady man and reliable.' Alcuin stopped and faced me. 'Sigwulf, if you take my advice you will do the same. Look and listen and keep your own counsel. Among the so-called royal guests there are rivalries and hatreds swirling beneath the surface. Beware of them.' Somewhere in the distance a church bell sounded. 'That's the signal for a royal council. I'll see you this afternoon, in class.'

I watched him walk away. He had the confident stride of a man who knew his own mind. His warning had been remarkably like my brother's.

*

I got back to my new companions in time for a breakfast of meat broth thickened to a porridge with barley meal and washed down with beer. There was a cheerful atmosphere at the table.

'Any good on a horse, Patch?' asked Hroudland. He pushed aside his empty bowl and stood up. He was almost as tall as his uncle, though not as heavily built.

'Just the basics,' I said, thinking of the dozen horses we'd owned at home; they had been ordinary nags that we'd ridden when hunting and they'd served as pack animals to carry back the deer and wild pig we'd killed.

'Then you have much to learn,' said Hroudland, laying his hand on my shoulder in an unexpected gesture of friendship.

There was good-natured banter as all of us, including white-haired Gerard, filed outside where a cluster of servants was waiting. They were burdened down with an impressive assortment of weapons – helmets and body armour, swords and shields, javelins and heavy lances. Only Osric was empty handed. Followed by our attendants we set off along the muddy footpaths, and once again Hroudland picked me out to say a few words, but quietly this time.

'Expect a little foolery.' His glance indicated Engeler and Oton walking ahead of us.

'I hope I didn't give offence last night,' I said.

'Some people are touchy, or they resent a quicker wit than their own. You would do well to doubt the first beast that is offered to you.'

We reached the edge of a paddock. A herd of some thirty excited horses was milling around, whinnying and occasionally baring their teeth at one another, their hooves splattering mud. The animals were larger, stronger and more spirited than any I had seen at home. Most were stallions. Grooms darted here and there to catch particular animals, and even to my untrained eye, the horses that they led out were clearly the best ones in the herd. Meanwhile our attendants were busy helping their masters to put on padded surcoats and mailed jackets, baldricks, helmets and thick gloves. Finally they assisted them into the saddles of their selected horses and handed up the weapons.

I stood apart, watching warily.

'Patch needs a horse, too.' My armed companions had gathered in a group and were looking down at me. I could not make out who had spoken, but it sounded like Berenger. Two of the grooms ran back into the paddock and, after an interval, led out a spare horse, ready saddled and bridled. They held the animal, waiting for me to mount. I walked towards them, knowing that I had to go through with the performance. Any fool would have known that they were restraining an animal that was difficult, perhaps dangerous. The creature was very angry. Stiff-legged and tense, it was showing the whites of its eyes, with nostrils dilated, and lips drawn back to show yellow teeth. Each groom had one hand on the bridle, the other tightly grasping the horse's ear, twisting it downward to induce submission.

A third groom helped me up into the saddle, and even before I was settled in place, the beast was let loose. The grooms dove for safety, and immediately the horse beneath me bucked violently. I made no effort to stay in the saddle, but let myself be thrown clear, dropping one shoulder as I cartwheeled through the air so I landed unscathed into the soft mud. I had not expected the horse then to launch an attack. The animal spun round and, as I was trying to rise, lashed out at me with its rear hooves. Fortunately I was still on all fours, and I felt the hooves slash past my head. Next the horse bolted off for a short distance and turned, whinnying with rage, ready to rush at me. By that time I was running through the muck and climbing up the wooden fence of the paddock like a frightened squirrel.

My mounted companions had broad grins on their faces.

'You knew that was coming, didn't you?' Oton said. He sounded disappointed.

Walk, trot, canter, gallop, and stand – the rest of the morning was spent in a series of mounted exercises on a nearby training field. Again and again my companions divided into opposing teams, rode to the opposite ends of the field, then turned, levelled their lances, and came charging towards one another. At the last moment before collision, the team's leader gave a great yell, he and his companions suddenly pulled up their horses, spun round and galloped away, pretending to flee and draw on their opponents. Then, moments later, they would wheel about and face their rivals again, weapons ready. It was all about keeping formation, controlling the horses, riding knee to knee, coordinating their manoeuvres. The air was filled with excited shouts and commands, the snorting of the horses, and the thud of hooves. Then, in smaller groups, they rode at straw-filled dummies and either hurled their javelins, or if they were carrying lances thrust and stabbed before withdrawing to reform and attack again with swords and axes. Finally they divided into pairs and, this time with wooden blades, they chopped and hacked at one another's shields until exhausted.

I took no part in the war drill. Instead I observed, with Osric standing at my shoulder.

'He's more accustomed to a pony,' observed my slave. He was watching Ogier who rode his horse, leaning far back, his legs extended straight downward as if he was walking. Unlike the others, he rode without stirrups.

I was curious to know how my slave was so knowledgeable but at that moment Hroudland came thundering past us at a gallop, cocked his arm and hurled a javelin. It thumped into the target, dead centre. He let loose a great full-throated whoop of triumph.

'What about him?' I asked. I could see that the king's tall nephew was a first-class horseman. He guided his animal with the lightest pressure on the reins as if he and his mount were one.

'He's good, but impetuous,' Osric answered.

'Then who's the most competent among them?' I enquired.

'That one there,' he replied. He nodded towards a man to whom I had paid little attention the previous evening. Gerin was a taciturn, rather grim figure, a big loose-limbed man with close cropped hair and hard eyes. Now he carried a plain, red shield and I had noticed his tendency to hang back and watch his companions in their manoeuvres.

'He doesn't need to practise,' said Osric, 'he's a professional warrior.'

Hroudland rode up to us. His horse was very distinctive, a roan stallion with dark patches on its neck and rump.

'Time to get you cleaned up, Patch,' he said in a friendly voice. I was still grubby with mud from my tumble in the paddock. He jumped down from his horse and handed his war gear to an attendant and pointed towards a low red-roofed building in the distance. 'I'll introduce you to my uncle's main indulgence.'

Side by side, we walked towards the building, leaving our servants to catch up with us. The rain clouds had gone, and the earth steamed gently in the hot sunshine. Hroudland waved a hand, taking in the construction work going on around us.

'It'll be years before this place is completed to my uncle's satisfaction. Sometimes I feel as cooped up as one of the animals in his menagerie.'

'I met the king yesterday,' I said. 'There was a young woman with him. She looked so much like him that I guessed she was his daughter.'

'That could have been Theodrada or Hiltrude or Gerswinda. I've several female cousins. It's difficult to keep track.'

'She wore her hair in two long braids.'

He pulled a face.

'Most of them do. It's the fashion.'

'Are any of them married?'

He gave me a sideways glance of amusement.

'Thinking of a local bride already?'

'No. Just curious.'

Hroudland's face took on a more serious expression.

'The king's not keen on having sons-in-law.'

I was dull enough to ask, 'Why's that?'

'Possible rivals to the throne. He keeps the girls at home and close to him.'

'How do they feel about that?'

'As I do . . . overly confined. Mind you, they have their own ways of compensating.'

With that ambiguous remark, we had arrived at the colonnaded porch of the red-tiled building. There was a faint smell I could not identify. It reminded me vaguely of rotten eggs. I followed Hroudland across the porch, through a small entrance hall, and then into the centre of the building. The sight before me was so unexpected that I came to a sudden halt. There was no roof. The building was open to the air, designed to enclose a large expanse of grey-green, opaque water. All of a sudden I knew what the smell had reminded me of. It was the rotting stench of the bubbles which had risen from stagnant water when we pulled my brother's drowned corpse from the pond. The same smell had clung to his slimed clothes as we laid him out on the bank.

Hroudland was regarding me with concern.

'Are you alright, Patch? You look as if you're about to faint.'

I shook my head.

'I'll be fine,' I assured him.

'The thermae, the royal baths,' Hroudland announced, 'and the main reason why my uncle chose to build his palace here.' He crossed to the edge of the water and dipped his hand into what I now realized was a tiled pool. 'See for yourself, Patch. The water emerges from the ground already warm.'

I forced myself to crouch at the rim of the pool and touch the sinister surface of the water. It was warm, almost hot.

Hroudland began taking off his clothes.

'My uncle suffers from aches and pains in his joints. He spends hours in the water. It does him good. He's even been known to conduct a session of the Council, half-immersed.'

I straightened up and stepped back. My fear of water had returned as strongly as ever. The evil smell only increased my revulsion.

'Come on, Patch!' Hroudland chided me. 'It doesn't matter if you can't swim. The water's not deep.'

'I'm sorry. I can't,' I mumbled.

Hroudland was naked now except for his undershirt, open at the neck. He had the sculpted muscles and slim legs of an athlete. 'Nonsense. I'll see that you don't drown.' He made a playful lunge and grabbed me by the wrist as if to pull me closer into the pool.

Panicked, I wrenched away my arm and stumbled backward to escape. Not seeing where I was going, I reeled into Berenger,

Oton and the others just entering the bathhouse. Berenger gave me an odd look as I blundered my way past them, across the entrance hall and out into the open. Only then did I stop as I fought to catch my breath and ignore the tainted air.

Chapter Six

A COUPLE OF HOURS LATER Osric found me among the half-finished palace buildings where I was watching a master carpenter scarf together two oak beams for a roof timber. By then I had regained my composure.

'Count Hroudland told me to bring you to the royal stables. He'll help you select a suitable war horse,' he said.

'Count Hroudland?' I asked.

'His title. He's waiting for the king to assign him a region to govern.'

'You seem to be well informed.'

Osric glanced around, making sure that we were alone.

'One of the paladins' servants is curious about you. He asked whether you had ever been at King Offa's court.'

I felt a prickle of unease.

'What did you tell him?'

'I didn't answer him directly. He told me that he had once been to England with his master, Gerin.'

I thought it strange that Gerin had said nothing when I mentioned Offa's name the previous evening. But, on reflection, I remembered that Gerin had played no part in the conversation. He was not someone who seemed like he'd volunteer much information about himself. Still, I wondered what he had been doing at Offa's court.

'Osric, see if you can find out more. If Gerin is King Offa's agent, it will affect our future here in Aachen.'

'I'll do my best. I think the servant mainly wanted to boast about how widely he had travelled.'

As I looked into Osric's lean, dark face with its expression of watchful intelligence, it occurred to me how much our relationship had changed in the days since Offa had sent me into exile.

'Osric, I've never thanked you properly for dealing with those treacherous pirates on the cog,' I said.

'Those cut-throats would have sold me on,' he replied quietly. 'I would rather continue to serve a master I know.'

'That's not what I mean. I'd prefer not to treat you as before, as if nothing had happened.'

He gave a small, eloquent shrug.

'You have no choice. Here at court everyone expects there to be a great distance between master and slave. If it were otherwise, people would be suspicious.'

'Yet without your help I doubt I will survive the court's dangers,' I said.

His voice kept its level, rational tone.

'That is why we must keep a distance between us, at least for others to see. Servants and slaves always gossip among themselves, and I'll be more useful to you if I am accepted as no different from the rest, and keep my ears open.'

Reluctantly I had to agree with his reasoning.

'What do you think of Count Hroudland?' I asked.

'He has the qualities and failings of someone born to high privilege. He's self-confident and decisive, but that makes him high-handed and he is not easily deflected from what he wants.'

'Should I trust him?' I asked.

Osric paused while he considered his reply.

'I think so. He has a sense of honour.' Then he added, 'And he will not take kindly if we keep him waiting.'

*

Hroudland met us at the stables.

'I'm sorry about the prank this morning. There was nothing I could do to stop it,' he said briskly.

He led me along the double row of stalls until we came to a stocky bay gelding standing looking out at us and placidly chewing a wisp of hay.

'Here's the ideal animal for you, Patch. Eight years old, calm and steady, yet with enough spirit for the front rank of a charge.'

The horse stretched out its head, snuffling my scent and allowing me to stroke its velvety nose.

'I appreciate your advice. I just need to learn to ride properly,' I said guardedly, for I was puzzled why the count was showing such concern for me.

My face must have revealed my caution, for he said quietly, 'Also, about what happened at the baths this afternoon, I apologize if I alarmed you.'

'It's nothing I want to talk about,' I replied stiffly, feeling clumsy and ungracious even as I said it.

The count, clearly not a person who allowed a moment's awkwardness to deflect him, pressed on.

'Now you've got a war horse, you'll need weapons to go with it. I've arranged with the seneschal to collect whatever we require from the royal armoury. He's sending a clerk to meet us there, so let's go before he changes his mind.'

We set out across the palace grounds, striding at such a rapid pace that Osric with his lameness had difficulty in keeping up with us.

'The king is being very generous to me,' I said.

'Think nothing of it. He owns vast estates, and his tenants supply all that his household requires.'

I recalled the shipment of live eels hauled for hundreds of miles across country.

'Even swords and armour?'

'Especially swords and armour, and the soldiers to go with them,' said Hroudland firmly. 'When my uncle launches a campaign, everyone is obliged to contribute to his armed host, whether he's a count or abbot or a lowly freeman with just a cottage and two cows.'

'That must take a lot of organization.' I had been wondering how the Franks came to dominate less purposeful nations.

The count was dismissive.

'A swarm of inky clerks keep endless lists of everything from beds and mattresses to spare sets of harness and carts. The chief nobles are obliged to hold stockpiles of material whether it's barrels of wine or bundles of firewood.'

On the far side of the royal precinct we arrived before a substantial building of cut stone with barred windows that I would have mistaken for a prison. A small, unsmiling man with the guarded look of a store clerk was waiting outside in the evening sunshine, holding his wax tablet and a bunch of keys on a large ring. He had two attendants with him.

'Good afternoon, my lord,' he said to Hroudland. 'I understand you wish to take away a full set of weapons for a cavalryman.'

'Indeed, I do. I will select the items myself,' answered Hroudland curtly.

'The law requires me to remind you that any arms that are issued must remain within the kingdom. They cannot be loaned or sold abroad.'

'I know, I know,' said the count testily. 'The weapons are for my companion here. I can vouch for him.'

The clerk unlocked a stout wooden door and led us inside and I saw at once the orderly hand of the ledger-keepers. The armoury was arranged in sections. Nearest were the projectile weapons – javelins, bows, bundles of arrows. Beyond them stood stack after stack of spears, neatly sub-divided according to length and weight, as pikes for foot soldiers or lances for cavalry. Next came edged weapons – swords, axes and daggers. Finally there was the defensive equipment with rows of wooden shields and a small pile of helmets and some body armour.

Hroudland walked slowly along the array of weaponry. Quickly he found me a lance and a couple of javelins. He rejected an axe as unnecessary and picked out a plain shield with an iron boss which he said needed a new leather strap. The clerk made a note on his tablet and said it would be provided. Finding the right armoured jacket took longer. The metal plates sewn to the fabric made the garment very stiff and restricted the wearer's movement unless the fit was correct. The choice of helmets was very limited – the clerk made cautionary noises about how expensive they were – and Hroudland reluctantly agreed to take one under which I had to wear thick wool and leather skull cap. A pair of heavy gauntlets completed the outfit. By then the two attendants had their arms full of my war gear.

'Now for the most important item – his sword,' announced Hroudland.

We were escorted to the farthest corner of the armoury where a dozen swords were racked. Hroudland scanned the selection with a critical eye.

'Is that all you've got?' he demanded.

'Fine craftsmanship, every single one of them,' said the clerk primly.

Hroudland reached out and removed a sword from the rack.

'Antique!' he announced, hefting it in his hand.

He held it out to me.

'Look, Patch, the edges of the blade run parallel almost to the tip. That makes a sword heavy and awkward to use.'

The clerk bridled.

'A fine weapon nevertheless.'

'But no use to my friend here,' retorted the count, replacing the weapon. 'I've heard that you've got one of those new Ingelrii swords here.'

There was a distinct intake of breath by the store keeper.

'Not a genuine Ingelrii,' he said.

'Let me be the judge of that,' said the count.

Reluctantly, the clerk went to a large wooden chest, unlocked it, and lifted out a long item wrapped in cloth. I could smell oil.

'This is it,' he said, handing the object to Hroudland.

The count unwrapped the oiled cloth and revealed a sword, its blade the length of my arm. I was disappointed. From the clerk's behaviour I had expected something much more spectacular, perhaps a glittering blade and a handle encrusted with jewels. Instead I saw a workaday weapon with a plain iron handle. The only decoration was a small, insignificant crystal set into the triangular pommel.

Hrouldland swung the sword through the air, testing its balance. Then he examined the blade closely.

'You're right,' he said. 'This is not an Ingelrii blade. He would have signed it.'

The clerk gave a self-satisfied smile.

'As I told you. We received the sword as a tithe payment from one of the Burgundian monasteries. We have no idea who was the swordsmith.'

The count whipped the sword through the air, and then said, 'It's not an Ingelrii. But it's as good. We'll take it.'

'I do not have the authority to let it out of the armoury,' snapped the storekeeper.

Hroudland fixed him with a glare.

'Would you like me to raise the subject with my uncle?'

'No, no. That won't be necessary.' The man was clearly unhappy with the arrangement.

Hroudland put the sword hilt in my hand.

'Now, Patch, how does that feel?'

I swung the sword tentatively in a small arc. It was remarkably light and well balanced.

'Note the difference in the blade, Patch,' Hroudland said. 'It tapers all the way to the point. That makes the weapon an extension to your arm. Also the quality of the steel is exceptional.' He peered inside the sword chest. 'I see there is a scabbard and baldrick to go with it,' he said.

Knowing he was beaten, the clerk nodded to one of the attendants and the sword's fittings were added to our collection.

Hroudland was looking pleased with himself as we walked back down the length of the armoury.

'I should have driven a harder bargain with you, Patch. That sword is unique. You'll have to find a name for it.'

'A name?'

He laughed.

'Every really good sword has its own name. Mine is Durendal, "the enduring one". The king presented it to me personally, a great honour. He has its twin, Joyeuse.'

I rather doubted that I would ever be enough of a warrior to wield a famous sword, and was about to say that 'Joyful' was a strange name for a deadly weapon, when I was distracted by Osric calling out, 'Master, this would be useful.'

My slave had veered off towards a rack of bows and was

tugging something out from behind the display. It was another bow but not like all the others. Their staves were as tall as a man and either straight or slightly curved. He had spotted a bow at least a third shorter in length and its stave had a peculiar double curve. He held it up to show me.

Osric's interruption annoyed Hroudland.

'A bow is a foot soldier's weapon. Your master rides into battle on horseback,' he snapped.

Osric ignored him, and before Hroudland could say anything more, I said quickly to the storekeeper, 'Would it be possible to take that bow as well?'

The storekeeper looked between us, obviously enjoying the apparent disagreement between his visitors.

'Of course. Bows are cheap, and that one is worthless.'

'And a quiver with a raincover and couple of dozen arrows,' Osric insisted.

The clerk treated him to a sour glance and nodded. Osric began to search through bundles of arrows, picking out the ones he thought suitable.

The clerk added these final items to his list on the wax tablet, snapped the cover shut, and escorted us from the building, clearly eager to see us on our way.

As Hroudland and I left the armoury, Osric was arranging with the two attendants that my new equipment should be delivered to him for cleaning and safe keeping. Hroudland insisted that I keep the sword with me.

'Your slave and the bow are too misshapen to be of much use,' he observed unkindly as we headed back to our quarters.

I resented the malice in his remark.

'Osric may be a cripple, but I trust him to know what he is doing. He's saved my life once already.'

Hroudland gave an apologetic smile.

'Sorry, Patch. I didn't mean to offend you. If that bow keeps you safe from danger, then your slave is welcome to it.'

His remark left me wondering, once again, what danger he had in mind.

Chapter Seven

THE SUMMER PASSED, the great storm and flood forgotten as I settled into the daily routine of my companions. I discovered that the bay gelding knew more about cavalry manoeuvres than I did, and I scarcely had to touch the reins in the mock charges and retreats. Instead I could concentrate on handling lance, javelin and shield. But I still felt clumsy compared to my companions, though I did better in the single-handed contests with blunted weapons, improving until I could hold my own with the likes of Oton and Berenger, the weaker members of our company. However, I never matched experts like Gerin or Hroudland, even though the latter showed me how to favour my left-hand side where my eye patch always left me exposed.

During those sham fights it was never far from my mind that King Offa might decide one day that it was better if I was dead. It was not unknown for there to be a fatal accident on the practice field, and I found it strange to be swinging a blunt sword blade or feinting a jab with a lance at someone who might possibly become an agent for the Mercian king. Afterwards, relaxing in the royal guesthouse, I developed a habit of watching my companions and trying to gauge just how much I could rely on them, because I was very conscious that I was a latecomer to their fellowship.

Berenger, always cheerful and open, was very easy to get on with. His sense of humour appealed to me. I was often the first person to laugh at his jokes so that he would fling an arm around my shoulders and proclaim that I must be his long-lost brother. The older man Gerard of Roussillon was more difficult to get to know, yet behind his reserve lay a kind heart and a tolerance born of long experience. I spent many evenings talking quietly with him, learning more about the Frankish world, and he appreciated the deference I showed him. But it was with Hroudland that I soon fell into an easy friendship despite the difference in our backgrounds. The count was open-handed and impulsive. One day, at his own expense, he sent his tailor to measure and make me a new and fashionable wardrobe. On another occasion he suddenly insisted that I accompany him to a meeting with a high-ranking official, telling me that it was the best way for me to see how the court worked. During those evenings when the paladins stayed in their quarters, discussing or arguing among themselves, he would often turn to me and for my opinion as if I was his advisor and confidant. Eventually I found a quiet moment, away from the others, to ask him why he was so considerate to me.

'Patch, one day my uncle will give me a province to govern in his name,' he answered. 'When that day comes, I will need to be accompanied by men on whom I can depend for good council.'

'But you have other comrades who can give good advice. Berenger, for example; you've known him far longer than you've known me.'

Hroudland treated me to one of his aristocratic stares, part amused, part condescending.

'I recall the first evening when you arrived among the paladins and they were exchanging riddles. I remember noting that you were both quick-witted and level-headed. I value that combination.'

'I hope I won't disappoint you,' I replied, for the truth was that I was flattered that the count had singled me out to be his particular friend after such brief acquaintance, and I already knew that there was one way in which I could be of use to him. Hroudland was headstrong and outspoken. From time to time he offended men like Engeler. They resented his royal connections and were jealous that he was so handsome and gifted. In future I would take it upon myself to smooth over the quarrels that the count left in his wake.

*

Some days after Hroudland had taken me to the royal armoury to select weaponry, Osric arranged to meet me at a wooded area close to the king's animal park. It was a quiet place, away from prying eyes, and he arrived carrying a long, thin object concealed in sacking. I guessed it contained the curiously shaped bow he had found.

'I've managed to restore it to working condition,' he said, extracting it from its wrapping. The bow was a little over four feet long and, to my eye, its design seemed to be back to front. The hand grip in the centre of the bow was where it should be held, but the stave curved in the wrong direction, away from the archer.

Osric saw that I was bemused. He reached into the neck of his tunic and pulled out a length of cord. 'Count Hroudland wouldn't be happy if he knew that one of his better shirts provided this thread. I've made a bowstring from silk.'

He dropped one of the bowstring's end loops over the tip of the bow stave and settled it into a notch. Then he placed the end of the bow stave on his instep and pressed down strongly. The bow bent, reversing its curve so he was able to slip the other end of the bow string in place.

'A long soaking in warm oil has brought the limbs back to life,' he murmured, running a finger lovingly along the gleaming length of the weapon.

He handed it to me.

'Try it.'

I gripped the weapon firmly with my left hand and pulled back on the cord. I was able to bend the weapon into a gentle curve, no more. Osric gave me the single, iron tipped arrow that he had brought with him.

'See how far this goes.'

I prided myself on being a good archer. At home I had often used an ordinary long bow for hunting and I was more accurate with it than anyone else in our household. Now I nocked the arrow, drew the strange bow as far as I could, took aim at a nearby tree trunk, and released.

The arrow whipped away and thumped into the target, driving the tip solidly through the bark and into the wood.

'Why didn't you make one like this for me when I was a boy?' I asked Osric wonderingly. I had not expected the arrow to fly so true and with such force.

'Because I don't have the bowyer's skill,' he replied. 'Look more closely; it is made of five different parts: the belly, the two arms and those two end sections called the siyahs.'

I examined the weapon in my hand. I could see the complex construction and also how several different materials were tightly glued together.

'The wooden part looks something like our bows at home,' I remarked. 'Heartwood to the belly, sapwood to the back.'

Osric's slight smile contained a hint of pride.

'This bow is made of wood, horn and sinew. Each element was gathered at the right season, selected and prepared, carefully fitted. It will have taken at least two years to make.'

'How did it come to be gathering dust in the royal armoury?'

'War loot?' Osric said with a shrug, 'A neglected gift to King Carolus that no one knew how to use properly?'

I was intrigued.

'What sort of range does it have and still be accurate?'

'At seventy paces a competent bowman should put his arrows into a target three spans across,' he paused deliberately, 'at a gallop.'

I thought I had misheard. As Hroudland had said, only foot soldiers used bows.

'You mean from horseback?' I asked.

Osric noted my disbelief.

'I can teach you how to do it. Either on foot or on horseback.'

It took me no more than a moment to realize my opportunity. Here was my chance to excel in the paladins' warrior games. I would surprise and shock my companions.

'And against someone wearing armour?' I asked.

'With the right arrow head, seventy paces is also your killing range.'

That settled it. A thrown javelin might hit the target at twenty paces, but I would demonstrate how my arrows could empty a saddle at three times the distance.

'Then I want you to teach me,' I said to Osric.

'You will have to be patient.' He gave a mirthless smile. 'And for once you will find your eye patch is a help. You aim with the right eye only.'

So I became Osric's pupil. While my more energetic companions wrestled, lifted weights, competed in races on foot while wearing armour, or held swimming contests, I would slip away and practise my archery. Osric showed me the correct stance when I drew the bow, how to control my breathing, allow for the wind, time my release. He explained the exercises to strengthen the muscles in my back and arms, and insisted on hour after hour of target practice. I enjoyed it all, and Osric was no more than honest when he said that I was a natural archer. By the time the leaves began to turn, I was close to achieving the standard he expected – sending arrow after arrow into a target as broad as a man's torso, at seventy paces. I was still on foot, for he said that shooting from horseback would come later.

*

King Carolus required that once a week all the paladins received formal instruction in a topic of his choosing. Like reluctant school children we assembled in the entrance porch of the royal chancery. It was temporarily housed in an annex of the great unfinished church and through the open doorway we could glimpse the earnest-looking monks and scribes. Some were at their desks, heads down and hunched over documents. Others stood in little groups conferring, while a secretary with a stylus took notes on a wax tablet. Porters and messengers bustled past us with expressions that told us we were standing in the way of what really mattered in the kingdom.

One day it was Alcuin himself who emerged to tell us that our topic for the day was to be geography.

Beside me Berenger muttered, 'Thank the Lord! I feared it would be theology.'

Alcuin pretended not to have heard.

'I will detain you only a few minutes, but it will be long enough to demonstrate that geography has its uses in war as in peace,' he said coolly. He gave no hint that he already knew me, and he brought us into the chancery and led us directly to a broad trestle table covered with biscuit-coloured tiles of baked clay laid side by side like the squares on a games board.

I studied what was scratched on them – the names of towns, rivers, provinces. I was looking at a great map of the kingdom of the Franks and the neighbouring lands, a portable map ingeniously made so it could be dismantled and reassembled wherever it was needed.

'We use this for planning, both civil and military,' Alcuin was saying. He walked round the table to its far side. 'Here, for example, is Byzantium, the capital of the Eastern Emperor. Over there,' he waved his hand, 'is the northern sea.'

I recalled the model of the palace I had seen in the king's chambers. There had been no documents or written material in his room. It occurred to me that Carolus could neither read nor write, and that this map of tiles was as much for his benefit as for the clerks in the chancery.

Alcuin reached into a small wooden box and produced a number of figurines, miniatures of men, horses and oxen.

'What sort of child's toys are those?' interrupted Anseis rudely.

Alcuin remained unflustered.

'Do you play tafl?' he asked.

'Of course.'

'In that game you calculate which of your opponent's squares are vulnerable and which squares hold threats?'

'Naturally.'

'Then think of this map in the same way. It tells you who lies beyond your immediate neighbour, and with whom you should form alliances.'

Anseis snorted with disdain.

'I don't need that map to tell me what I already know.'

'But this device will also allow you to plan your campaigns and plot your strategy—' Alcuin paused for dramatic effect '—which is why our king and lord asked me to teach you some geography. He may want your advice about where he should next send his armies.'

Alcuin now had their complete attention; they were like a

pack of hounds that have heard the first, faint sound of the huntsman's horn.

'If you were to advise the king, what would you say should be his priority?' he asked.

'Finish off the heathen Saxons,' grunted Gerin. 'We've been fighting them for years. One last push should do it.'

Alcuin placed the clay figures of a man, a horse and an ox, facing outward on the tile labelled SAXONIA.

'So here we assign some infantry, cavalry and a supply train for the task. You will have to bear in mind that the king's host will be entering densely wooded country. It will be slow work for them.' He indicated some cross-hatching incised in the tiles. I guessed it represented forests.

'I disagree,' said Gerard. 'The Saracens are a greater threat than the Saxons. They've attacked us once and will do so again.'

I recalled that Gerard's home was in the far south bordering on the Mediterranean and had been ravaged by Arabs from Africa.

Alcuin placed several more figurines on the tile marked SEPTIMANIA.

Hroudland was stalking eagerly around the table, looking at the map from every angle.

'The best campaign is one that brings glory and also pays for itself. If we overrun the Avars, their treasure will fill our coffers for years to come.'

Alcuin arranged some miniatures, this time in the east, on CARINTHIA.

'What is your suggestion?' asked Alcuin. He was looking directly at me.

The little figures on the table were facing in opposite directions, widely scattered and vulnerable. My reply would sound cautious and dull compared to the opinions of my companions.

'I would begin by asking the king whether he really needs to extend his kingdom. It is already immense and it prospers.'

'And if he does decide to send out his army?' Alcuin asked softly.

'Then he must first secure his borders; make sure that no enemy invades while his troops are elsewhere.'

'Which is precisely what I and the other members of his council have been telling him,' said Alcuin. He began collecting up the figurines and returning them to the box.

My companions sensed that the lesson was over and began to head for the door. A clerk came over and requested Alcuin's presence at a nearby conference with some other priests. But I lingered beside the table, staring down at the map. It was more detailed than I had first noticed. Thin, meandering grooves were rivers; straight lines almost certainly the old Roman roads. Someone had drawn a comb through the wet clay before it was fired, leaving ridges and furrows to indicate the extent of mountain ranges. I allowed my imagination to wander across the modelled landscape as I devised a make-believe itinerary for myself. I sidled slowly around the table, selecting which of the towns and cities I would choose to visit. Their names were not always easy to make out. I bent over the table, concentrating so hard with my single eye that it made me light-headed and giddy. In places the tiles had dark blotches where the clay was poorly mixed, and the lettering was indistinct. The tile labelled SAXONIA, for instance, showed an irregular dark stain the colour of dried blood where Gerin had proposed mustering an invasion army. I shivered, not knowing if this was a portent. Then a glint from the far side of the map caught my attention. It was a pin prick of light, unmissable. Curious as to what caused it, I walked around the table and looked closer. A speck of shiny material had been exposed when the mapmaker scraped his comb through the clay to mark the range of mountains dividing the kingdom from the Franks from the lands of the Saracens. The speck glittered, both malevolent and enticing. Gently I touched my index finger to it and was shocked to feel a tiny pinch of pain. As I withdrew my hand, a single drop of my bright red blood dripped on the tile. This time I knew, without question, it was an omen.

*

In early September came my first royal banquet and my life changed yet again. The feast was to celebrate the completion of the cupola on top of the royal basilica. For weeks the masons had been attached like spiders by safety ropes around their waists as they nailed in place the last tiles, the sound of their hammering drifting down to us. The banquet was to be held in the as-yet-unfinished Council Hall, the massive rectangular building whose shape had reminded me of my father's mead hall, though on a far larger scale.

'Don't expect too much,' Hroudland said to me as we loitered with the other guests outside the entrance, waiting to be summoned inside. 'This place is little more than a shell, and the builders are standing by to stretch a canvas awning to keep us dry.'

I glanced up at the sky. It was midday and the air had the first edge of autumn's chill, but the few clouds did not threaten rain. I felt self-conscious in a short cloak of very expensive dark blue velvet trimmed with marten fur which Hroudland has loaned me for the occasion.

'Who's going to be there?' I asked.

'Carolus, of course, with Queen Hildegard, and young Pepin, whom everyone presumes is the heir to the throne, though it's not official. Plus whichever of his other children care to come along.'

'It sounds rather casual,' I said, feeling relieved.

'Carolus dislikes formal banquets. He much prefers taking his meals with just his family.'

'And what's your opinion of your cousin Pepin?'

'It's difficult to think of him as my cousin. Carolus never formally married his mother though she was his concubine for years.'

'I thought the king was deeply religious, a devout Christian who believed in marriage.'

Hroudland gave a cynical laugh.

'The king is a Christian in whatever way suits him. He uses the Church to his advantage.'

At that moment a trumpet flourish announced that the guests were to proceed into the building.

As we filed inside, Hroudland whispered, 'Stick close to me. Otherwise you might finish up sitting next to some ancient bore. There'll be plenty of those.'

The absence of a roof made the interior of the Council Hall feel even larger than it really was. The enormous brick walls with their double lines of windows towered around us, open to the sky, and I could see a flock of doves wheeling in the air high above us. Finally completed, the place would be able to hold at least three or four hundred people, but now only the area next to the main entrance was being utilized. Two long tables had been set up, facing one another with a large open space between them. A smaller table, raised on a low plinth, had been placed across the end of the open space. This table was covered with a white and silver cloth, and gleamed with a display of gold ewers, goblets and other costly vessels, among them a remarkable salver carved from solid crystal and rimmed with a broad gold band inlaid with enamels of every colour.

Hroudland steered me to the long table on our left. Here the dishes were of silver and gilt, and the drinking vessels were beakers and cups of blue-green glass, some of them cleverly shaped to resemble traditional drinking horns.

'This table is for the likes of us, the companions of the court,' the count said, pulling out a bench. We sat down next to one another as Gerard, Oton and the others took their places nearby, along with several other people I did not know.

Hroudland nodded towards the far table.

'Over there, you'll see the king's councillors and advisors.'

I followed his glance. Alcuin was with a group of priests. A couple of places away from him sat a middle-aged man in a yellow silk tunic. He had a clever, foxy face and a shock of iron-grey hair. As I watched, he happened to look in my direction and I had the impression that he was taking note of my presence at the table alongside Hroudland.

Again the trumpet sounded, and I nearly fell to the floor as the bench beneath me tipped when everyone jumped to their feet. I clutched at Hroudland and hauled myself upright in time to see the king enter through a doorway which I guessed must lead to his private residence. He was dressed in the same costume as I had seen him previously wear, with the addition of a long embroidered cloak of dark purple held with a gold buckle. He wore no crown or symbol of rank, but his great height and confident stride were more than enough to establish his commanding presence. Crossing to the raised table, he faced the assembled company, lifted one hand briefly to acknowledge his guests, and sat down. He looked bored. We remained standing. After a short interval a group entered through the same door and took their places on either side of the king. They were all women with just one man among them. He was in his late teens and I guessed he was Pepin, the king's heir presumptive. I had not expected him to be a hunchback. But my attention was drawn to the young woman who had been with Carolus when I was introduced. She was wearing the same heavy amber necklace, but this time her long blonde braids were coiled up on her head, and she wore a headband encrusted with small jewels. Beside her were three other young women, ranging in age from their teens to early twenties. There was no mistaking the strong family resemblance.

'Who's the girl with the amber necklace?' I muttered to Hroudland as we resumed our places.

'That's Bertha. If she's the girl who caught your fancy, you'll have your hands full. That's true, isn't it, Oton?'

Oton, who was seated opposite us, rolled his eyes in mock horror.

'She'd eat you alive, Patch.'

A relay of servants was passing along our table, serving food and drink. I sipped cautiously at what was poured into my cup. It was red wine, the best I had ever tasted.

'We never drank anything like that at home,' I commented approvingly.

'You've got Anseis to thank for that,' said Oton. 'His family's Burgundian estates are obliged to send fifty barrels a year to the king.'

I noticed Anseis scowl; he must have been thinking that the vintage was wasted on foreigners like myself.

Oton reached for a loaf of bread and broke off a chunk, then passed it to me.

'Here, Patch, have some of this. It's flavoured with caraway and poppy seeds. The trouble with banquets is that Carolus only likes boiled or roast meat, no fancy sauces.'

A large dish had been set down in the middle of the table, heaped with what appeared to be a heap of twisted, dark-brown sticks.

'Can you pass me a couple of those,' I asked Berenger, who

was seated on my other side. I had recognized smoked eel and wondered if it was a relic of my trip with Arnulf and his ox wagon.

'Can't wait for the hunting season to begin,' complained Berenger, regarding with distaste the boiled pork and dumplings that had been put on our plates. 'Venison and wild boar on a spit is something the cooks can't ruin.' He called across to Gerard, 'I've a riddle for you:

I am black on the outside, wrapped in a wrinkled skin,
Inside I contain a fiery marrow . . .
I season delicacies and the banquets of kings,
But you will find in me no quality of any worth . . .'

Gerard gave a rueful smile and said, 'No need to go on. You've made your point.'

He produced a small pouch from his sleeve and carefully extracted three or four black seeds which he passed across. Berenger laid them on the table and smashed them to powder with the handle of his dagger. He saw me watching him.

'Patch, you're good at solving riddles. What's the answer to mine?'

'I have no idea,' I said.

Berenger picked up a few of the broken grains on the tip of his knife and said, 'Put these on your tongue.'

I did so. The fiery taste made me grab my wine cup. I took a deep gulp to wash out my burning mouth.

'The answer is "pepper",' said Berenger, grinning.

As we ate, a group of musicians entered the hall and began to play. The noise of their fiddles, pipes and drums made conversation difficult so I covertly studied the guests at the councillors' table. Several important-looking men wore chains of office. I supposed they were the high officers of state, the seneschal, the count of the palace, the high chamberlain, and the keeper of the royal stables. This last individual, Hroudland had told me, commanded the royal guard. Alcuin and his fellow priests sat in a group, forming a sombre block of brown and drab among the other splendidly dressed dignitaries, whose costumes were bright with rich reds and blues, their necks and fingers heavy with gold jewellery. I presumed they were the dukes and counts whom the king appointed to rule the provinces. Among them the foxy-faced man whom I had noticed earlier was in earnest conversation with his neighbour, but something told me that he was very aware that I was watching him.

'Who's that in the yellow tunic, the one with the shock of grey hair?' I asked Hroudland when the musicians finally began to put away their instruments.

Hroudland glanced across the hall.

'That viper is my stepfather, Ganelon,' he said icily. 'He's a charlatan and opportunist.'

I would have liked to have found out the reason for his dislike but a hush fell on the assembly. A man carrying a stool in one hand and a small harp in the other had walked into the open space between the tables.

Berenger gave a low groan of dismay.

'This will be worse than theology,' he said.

The newcomer set the stool down, bowed to the king, and announced loudly, 'With your permission, my Lord, today I tell of the great warrior Troilus, son of King Priam, and how he met his death at the hands of the noble Achilles.'

Beside me, Hroudland said in a low voice, 'Another of my uncle's foibles. At meal times he loves to hear the tales of ancient heroes.'

The bard cleared his throat, placed one foot on the stool, set his harp upon his knee, and after plucking a few chords, launched into his tale. I watched the king's face as I tried to decide whether he was genuinely enjoying the performance. He sat expressionless, not eating, only toying with a piece of bread with a large, powerful hand on which a massive gold ring was set with a large ruby.

I already knew the Troilus story. It had been a favourite of my old teacher, Bertwald.

The bard droned on. He had a high-pitched, rather irritating voice, and an unfortunate tendency to lay the stress on the wrong words. I began to sympathize with Berenger's dismay, and wondered how long the performance would last. The wooden bench was uncomfortable.

The bard plodded through his narrative: Troilus was the most beautiful youth in Troy, a famous warrior, and an adept handler of horses. Daily he went beyond the city walls to exercise his chariot team on the plain before Troy. Afterwards he brought them to a sacred grove to water them at a spring. Knowing his routine, the Greeks set upon him. But he defeated them, wounding king Menalaus, and even put the renowned Myrmidons to flight. When word of this humiliation reached Achilles, the greatest champion of the Greeks, he vowed to exact revenge. He put on his armour and hid in ambush at the sacred grove.

The bard paused. He took a sip of water and fiddled with his harp, tightening a couple of strings. I knew he was doing it for dramatic effect.

Incautiously I muttered to Hroudland, 'He's not mentioned the main reason why Achilles had to kill the youth.'

Either the king's hearing was abnormally acute or I had taken too much of Anseis's wine and spoken louder than intended. A high-pitched royal voice barked, 'You! If you know the story so well, why don't you finish it?!'

I looked up, dismayed. Carolus was glaring at me with those large pale eyes, his mouth set in an angry line.

'Go on, young man,' he rasped. 'Show us you can do better.'

I felt the blood drain from my face. The king continued to

stare angrily at me. I was aware of the sudden silence, the entire company watching and waiting for my reaction. Engeler made a faint, clucking sound with his tongue. He was enjoying my humiliation.

Perhaps it was a further effect of the wine, but somehow I found the courage to get to my feet. Without looking at the king, I walked over to where the bard was standing, harp in hand, a look of disgust on his face.

With an ironic gesture he offered me the harp, but I waved it aside. I was no musician. Smirking, he retreated a few paces and stood with arms folded waiting for me to make a fool of myself.

I drew several deep breaths as Bertwald had taught me to do if I was to speak in public.

'My Lord,' I addressed the king. 'There was a prophecy known to all the Greeks. It said that if the beautiful youth Troilus lived to reach full manhood, Troy would never fall. For that reason — above all others — Achilles knew he had to slay the golden youth. So Achilles lay in wait at the sacred grove, and when Troilus came there with his servant, he burst from ambush.'

I saw the king relax. He sat back in his seat, and nodded.

'Go on,' he commanded.

By now the wine had certainly gone to my head. The audience seemed to soften and blur around me. I knew they were still there, waiting and listening. But I was in my own empty space and I could fill it with my words. I raised my voice.

'Achilles fell upon Troilus. He caught him by his long and lustrous hair, and dragged him off his horse. Then on the sacred soil he beheaded him. Then he cut off his parts and hung them beneath the armpits of the corpse so that Troilus's ghost would never come to haunt him.' I paused and licked my dry lips. The spirit of tipsy courage had taken complete control. 'Troilus's mutilated corpse was carried back into the city, and the Trojans raised a great wailing. They lamented the loss of their youthful prince, but above all they remembered him for his grace and for his surpassing beauty. He was the darling of the people, and none grieved him more than Polyxena, princess of the Trojans. She was the fairest of all her sisters, tall and beautiful. Her eyes were lovely, her long hair the colour of ripe wheat, and her body was well-proportioned. She melted men's hearts.'

I finished the final sentence and bowed to the king. As I lowered my head, I deliberately allowed my eyes to rest for a brief moment on Bertha. She was staring at me, her eyes wide.

The bard treated me to a look of pure loathing as I walked past him and returned to my seat. The hum of general conversation resumed. Hroudland thumped me on the back as I sat down beside him. My knees were shaking.

'Well done, Patch!' he chortled.

The servants had already begun ladling out the next course of the banquet. I picked up my spoon and took a mouthful. It was an evil-tasting pottage of chicken in a spinach and bean broth, heavily flavoured with garlic. Vaguely I heard the musicians start up again. I was too spent to say anything and I kept my head down, eating quietly.

All of a sudden, there was an agonizing spasm in my stomach as if a dagger had been jabbed into my gut. Bile surged up. My throat constricted and I felt I could not breathe. Next there came a great roaring in my head and a red curtain descended across my eyes. I felt myself falling forward, and everything went black.

Chapter Eight

SOMETHING HARD WAS forced between my teeth, and then a trickle of fluid ran down the back of my throat. I coughed and nearly choked. I did not have the strength to lift my eyelids. Worse, my heart was pounding in a frightening way, its beat irregular.

A faraway voice said calmly, 'You must swallow.' I knew the speaker but I was too confused to remember who it was. I swallowed.

Time must have passed, for when I regained the strength to open my eyes, it was to see Osric's familiar face. He was leaning over me, a narrow tube in his hand. He inserted it again into my mouth.

'Drink as much of this as you can,' he said.

Obediently I sucked on the liquid. It had no taste and left a sticky coating on the inside of my mouth. My stomach churned and my bowels had turned to water. I felt so weak that I could not move my limbs.

'Lie quietly,' said Osric.

I must have drifted off to sleep for when I came to my senses again, it was night. By the light of a single candle Osric sat beside me, and once again he made me drink the sticky liquid. I was lying on some sort of bed and had soiled myself. The bed linen stank. Feebly I tried to sit up, but he pushed me back down with his hand.

'Here, chew,' he said, and dropped into my mouth a lump of some substance which crumbled into powder as I bit into it. He held a cup of water to my lips and I swirled down the thin paste. It tasted of nothing. Again I drifted off into blackness.

*

When I awoke a second time, it was to find that I had been washed and dressed in a clean bed gown. Osric was gone, but Alcuin was sitting patiently on a stool, his face grave.

I looked about me. I was lying in a small, plainly furnished room. Daylight entered through a window in the whitewashed walls.

'Where am I?' I asked.

'The king's house, a room where the crown couriers rest between trips.'

'What happened?'

'You ate something which made you so violently sick that you were brought here, the nearest place.' The priest folded his hands in his lap. 'Perhaps it was a food which you were not accustomed to. There were times when it was thought you might die. Prayers were said for you.'

I detected a hesitation in his voice.

'Was anyone else taken ill?' I asked.

'The old man, Gerard of Roussillon, suffers the same symptoms, but they began some hours later. He managed to get back to his own bed. He breathes with difficulty and is getting weaker.'

I remembered Osric dosing me.

'My slave Osric must treat him with the same medicine he gave me. It seems to have been effective.'

'As could have been our prayers,' Alcuin reminded me quietly, but he agreed to my request and got to his feet. 'When you are strong enough, you will be able to return to your own quarters.'

No sooner had he left the room than a worried-looking Count Hroudland and Berenger appeared in the doorway. I managed to raise my head and greet them. Hroudland's face lit up with relief.

'Patch, it's good to see you awake,' said Hroudland. 'There were times when we thought you were finished.' He came across to my bed and laid a hand on my brow. 'The fever has broken, thank God.'

'Fallen on your feet again, Patch,' Berenger said, his usual jaunty self. 'Convalescing in the royal household.' He grinned. 'I always knew that banquet food was bad, but I had no idea quite how awful it could be.'

I smiled weakly. My stomach felt as though a horse had kicked me in the gut.

'Get well quickly, Patch,' Berenger continued. 'There's to be a grand hunt in two weeks' time, the first of the season. You wouldn't want to miss that.'

Hroudland was pacing up and down the room, looking agitated.

'Patch, do you have any idea what could have poisoned you?' he asked.

I shook my head. I could remember eating smoked eel, pig meat with dumplings, and then some of the chicken and vegetable pottage.

'Perhaps it was something I drank,' I said.

'All of us enjoyed Anseis's wine, yet only you and Gerard are sick.'

'What are you trying to tell me?'

Hroudland chose his words carefully.

'That someone may have harmed you deliberately.'

It took me a moment to grasp his meaning.

'Are you saying that someone tried to poison me? Why would they want to do that?' I was astonished.

He hesitated.

'You are known to be my close friend. It could have a warning aimed at me, or simply an act to hurt me.'

'I still don't understand.'

'The king has said that he will appoint me to the next important post that falls vacant. Others seek that post for themselves. They see me as an obstacle to their own ambitions.'

I thought back to Alcuin's opaque warning about dangers lurking in the court.

'That seems a very vague threat,' I said.

'Then there's Ganelon.'

It took me a moment to realize whom he was talking about.

'You mean your stepfather?'

'He loathes me. The feeling is mutual. He thinks I'm trying to turn my mother against him. He'll lose much of his wealth and power if she divorces him.'

I recalled how the man in the yellow jerkin had watched me during the banquet. But surely it was impossible that Ganelon would have been able to carry out a deliberate poisoning so quickly. Also I found it difficult to believe that that a family feud could be so bitter that it would extend to murder. I told myself that my illness was probably an accident and I would be more careful what I ate in future. First, though, I would check with Osric. He had known how to cure me, so he might know what had harmed me.

Berenger had started to tell a bawdy joke when the door opened and my fourth visitor of the day swept in, someone so completely unexpected that I goggled: it was Princess Bertha.

Berenger immediately broke off his tale and bowed.

'We were just leaving, your highness,' he said smoothly. At the same time he treated Hroudland to a meaningful glance. The two of them made for the door and, just as they were leaving, I was startled to see Berenger turn round and, behind the princess's back, wink.

I had still not got over my surprise when the princess said, 'I am so pleased to see that you are recovering.'

She was looking lovely in a pale-blue gown of some soft, clinging material gathered at the waist with a thin silver belt. Her long yellow plaits hung free as when I had first seen her, though now the amber necklace was missing.

'It is kind of you to come to see me,' I mumbled.

'You told the story of Troilus so beautifully. My father says you are a natural storyteller.'

The princess's voice was husky and musical, and she had the same direct manner of speaking as her father. She walked over and sat down beside my bed on the stool that Alcuin had used. A hint of rose perfume reached me. She smoothed the front of her gown over her bosom.

'His regular bard is furious.'

Briefly I wondered if he had been furious enough to warn me off with something poisonous in my food.

'Sigwulf is a nice name. It's a pity that everyone calls you Patch.'

I wondered how she came to know this detail, but already she was reaching to remove my eye bandage.

'That should be more comfortable.'

I felt vulnerable without the eye patch, almost naked. Then I remembered that she had been in the room when her father had commented on my different-coloured eyes.

Now she was looking at me with great interest, searching my face. She was so close I could see that her own eyes, which I had thought were blue, verged on grey like her father's. The lashes were as blonde as her hair, the eyelids faintly freckled. Her broad well-shaped brow, fair skin and straight nose made her very attractive in the way the Franks admired. I found myself trying to decide whether she had used berry juice to add colour to her lips.

She sat looking at me without speaking. I kept my head turned towards her, scarcely daring to breathe. I wanted the moment to last as long as possible so that I could absorb exactly how she looked and would be able to recall it in every detail. She radiated a gentle warmth and softness that was overwhelming. I was captivated and hesitant, afraid to say anything, fearful of making a mistake, yet hoping that somehow she would read my thoughts.

With a confident, graceful movement she reached out one hand and touched a finger to beside my right eye, then my left.

'You are a very remarkable person,' she said.

I could not ignore the physical contact. I reached up and took the outstretched hand, opened the fingers and kissed her palm. This time there was the scent of oil of almonds.

Without a word, she rose to her feet, crossed to the door and put in place the little wooden wedge that locked the latch. In another two paces she had returned to my bedside. She undid her silver belt and peeled back the shoulders of her gown and let it fall to the floor. All that remained was a loose undershift, and she slid out of it with the same fluid movement that brought her beneath the blanket beside me. She was facing me, and I wrapped my arms around her and felt the soft pressure of those magnificent naked breasts. Her arms gathered me in, and after a long hungry kiss, I felt her hands removing my bed gown.

*

Later, as we lay side by side, I felt utterly content. What had happened was the most natural thing in all the world, yet it far surpassed any pleasure that I had imagined.

'I have never felt like this before,' I murmured.

'I know,' she said. She gave a slow, lazy smile and placed her hand across my chest. 'It was the first time, properly.'

'Yes,' I admitted. 'The girls at home steered clear of me. They thought I was bewitched.'

'But not bewitching?' She crooked her fingers so the nails dug lightly into the flesh, and then drew her hand slowly downward. 'That was only a beginning.'

I thought I heard someone at the door and my heart jumped into my mouth. I seized her wrist to halt her hand.

'There's someone coming!' I blurted.

She sat up, quickly but without panic. A moment later she had left the bed and was stepping into her shift. She pulled on her gown and fastened the belt with neat, sure movements. I noticed that her hands were steady. Even her long braids were undisturbed.

She leaned over me and gave me a brief but genuine kiss. For a moment there was a glimpse of the swell of those breasts that only minutes earlier I had enjoyed.

'That was only the first time,' she whispered, and then she straightened up, boldly stepped to the door and released the latch.

There was a brief pause, and when nothing happened, she opened the door. The corridor outside was empty. I cursed myself for being so nervous, for cutting short our time together.

Without a backward glance she glided out into the corridor and was gone, leaving me craving her.

*

I stayed another four days and nights in the king's house, longer than necessary for my recovery. The reason, of course, was Bertha. I was besotted with her, and she came to my bed twice more. It turned me into an unusual patient, dreamy and distracted yet fretful, because when I was not longing for her return, I was worrying that our intimacy would be discovered. I could think of nothing else but the two of us. Eventually, when it was obvious that I was well enough to return to my normal quarters, Osric came with fresh clothes for me to wear. Only then did I remember to ask him what medicine he had given me.

'I'll show you next time we have archery practice,' he said. 'It's the juice from a certain plant that grows near the menagerie.'

'You knew it would cure my sickness?'

'I only guessed.'

'So you're not sure what poisoned me?'

'I can't be certain, not yet.'

I thought about the crushed pepper grains that Berenger had given me to taste, and asked Osric if they could have been the cause.

He shook his head.

'Only if there was some other substance mixed in.'

'Count Hroudland thinks someone put it in my food on purpose.'

Osric gave me a long, hard look.

'That's possible.'

'He believes it was done because I am known to be his close friend. Someone wanted to warn him, or hurt him.'

A veiled look came over Osric's eyes.

'The count has enemies but there could be other reasons.'

I tried to make a joke.

'Are you saying that from now on I should employ a food taster?'

He didn't smile.

'If the poison was what I think it was, it could have got into your food deliberately or by accident.'

'Well, one thing is sure: if old Gerard mixed something with those peppercorns, it was by accident. I'm told he was also very sick.'

'Unless he deliberately took a smaller dose to distract attention,' Osric replied.

*

But when I saw Gerard in his cubicle, I knew he could have had no part in my poisoning. He looked dreadful. The flesh had fallen away from his bones, and his face was a sickly orange-yellow. He lay in a cot, propped up on a bank of pillows. There were great dark rings around his eyes and they were sunken in their sockets and also had a yellowish tinge. He greeted me feebly.

'Patch, whatever it was that your slave gave me saved my life.'

I tried to sound cheerful, though I feared that the old man was not yet out of danger.

'I am as much in debt to Osric,' I said. 'I'm sure his treatment can restore your body fully.'

Gerard gave a ghost of a smile.

'I'm leaving it to the priests to save my soul. But whatever the outcome, I would want to show some gratitude.' He fumbled under his pillow and, with an effort, pulled out a square package wrapped in cloth. He pushed it across the blanket towards me. 'Maybe you will accept this, though it's never been much use to me . . . until now that is.'

I unwrapped the package and found that it contained a medium-sized book, which had been ill-used. The leather cover had once been handsome. There were still the tracings of fine toolwork, and a flake or two of gold leaf. There were several gouge marks as though someone had kicked the book like a football across rough ground.

Gerard sank back on his pillow.

'I've owned that book for years. Can't say I've done anything about it.'

'How did it come into your possession?' I asked.

'It was found in the baggage train of the Saracens after we drove them into the sea. That was a long time ago. When I was just a youth.'

I turned the book over. The back cover was torn away. The last pages were gone. The exposed parchment was water-stained as if it had been left lying in a puddle. I hesitated to open it for fear that it would fall to pieces in my hand.

Gerard lay limp, drawing breath before he could speak again.

'May I examine it?' I asked. Books were rare and precious, even in such bad condition. It was most unusual to find one in private hands.

'Of course.'

I opened the book at random and saw the line upon line of writing, beautifully executed and regular. To my chagrin, it meant nothing to me.

'It is written in the Saracen script,' Gerard said.

I suppressed my disappointment.

Gerard allowed himself a bleak laugh.

'My father offered it to one of the monasteries as a gift. But the priests turned it down. Said it was the work of idolaters and would pollute their library of holy books.'

I began leafing carefully through the pages. The water had soaked right through the book, and then dried, leaving the material fragile. But the writing itself was clear.

'I'd be fascinated to know what is written here. If only I knew someone who could translate it,' I said.

'Have you thought about your slave Osric?'

I looked up in surprise.

'It hasn't occurred to you that he has Saracen blood?' The old man seemed faintly amused that I hadn't thought of this for myself.

'I haven't seen many Saracens,' I admitted.

'I have, and I would say that your slave's homeland was either in Hispania or Africa.'

I thought over his suggestion. Osric was swarthy, but his complexion was no darker than several other people I had known when growing up.

'Even if he is a Saracen, I doubt he can read or write,' I said.

Gerard eased himself gently against his pillows.

'Ask him nevertheless. If he can read the book, maybe he'll find a recipe for another potion, one that will speed my recovery. Everyone knows that the Saracens are skilled healers.'

The old man was visibly tiring. I turned my attention back to the book in my hands. The soaking had stuck the first page to the inside of the cover, and I carefully peeled it apart. Here, at last, I could recognize some writing, though not what it meant. Bertwald had taught me the Greek alphabet before he fled the Church hounds, though I suspected he knew little of the language itself. On the first page was a single word in Greek script. I presumed it was the book's title or perhaps the name of its owner. Letter by letter I deciphered what was written and silently rehearsed how it might be spoken.

Gerard had fallen asleep. His breathing was laboured and shallow, his head rolled to one side. I thought about replacing the book under his pillow, but feared that would disturb him. Instead I wrapped it back in its cloth cover, tucked it under my arm and set out in search of Osric. If the book did contain medical information that would help the old man, I should locate a translator as quickly as possible.

*

I found my slave at the stables, questioning the head groom whether my bay gelding would run straight when the reins were left slack, or veer to one side. Before he had his answer, I called him outside and together we walked to a spot where we could not be overheard.

'Old Gerard believes you saved his life by giving him that medicine,' I said.

'He's not out of danger yet. There could be a relapse.'

Osric's eyes flicked towards the parcel I was carrying.

'He's given me a book that he thinks is a leech book and contains medical knowledge which might help his recovery.' I hesitated, fearing to cause offence. Few people would like being mistaken for a Saracen.

Osric regarded me impassively.

'I can't read it,' I stumbled on. 'Maybe you can?' I had committed myself now. I took the book from its cover and handed it to Osric.

Osric opened the book without a word, and glanced inside. Then he raised his head and looked straight at me.

'Gerard supposes that your homeland may be Hispania or Africa,' I said, feeling the colour rising to my cheeks.

Osric did not move a muscle.

I grew more embarrassed under his silent gaze.

'Whether he's right or wrong makes no difference to me. I'm just trying to help him.'

Eventually Osric let out a long, slow breath.

'It has been a long, long time since I held a book like this in my hands. I should be able to read what is written here, provided the content is uncomplicated.' He looked down at the volume and slowly turned the pages.

I waited for his assessment. The time dragged by.

Finally he said. 'Gerard is wrong. This is not a book of medicine.'

I was crestfallen. Worse, I regretted that I had intruded on Osric's life before he was enslaved. If he had wanted me to know about his origins, he would have told me long ago.

'What is it?' I asked.

'I don't know for sure. There are some words that I do not know.' He pointed. 'Here it says that a man who dreams he is flying means that he will gain great riches.' He turned over several more pages and selected another section. 'Here is something about clouds and wind.'

He closed the book and handed it back to me.

'If I had enough time perhaps I could make sense of it.'

I took the volume from him.

'Osric, whether you are Saracen, Christian or pagan matters not to me.'

'Where I come from, it would be said that is God's will,' he assured me with a wan smile.

I left Osric at the stables and went in search of Alcuin. He was standing before the porch of the chancery, deep in conversation with another priest whom I recognized as Odo, the king's chief architect. They must have been discussing the next stage in the construction work because they turned to face the chapel and pointed upward at the new roof and were exchanging comments. I waited until they had finished their conversation, then approached Alcuin and asked if he could help me with the meaning of a Greek word.

'What word is that?' asked Alcuin.

'Oneirokritikon' I said.

My pronunciation must have been astray, for he asked me to repeat slowly what I had said.

It took me three attempts before I got it right, then Alcuin smiled and said, 'Ah! I have it now. "Oneir" is a dream or vision. "Kriticon" comes from "kritikos", which means able to discern or judge. So your word means something like "the interpretation of dreams". Does that make sense?'

I felt a shiver of apprehension. I had never breathed a word to anyone, even Osric, about my disturbing dreams, or how my dead brother's fetch sometimes appeared to me. If this alien book was genuine, it would allow me to unravel what my visions signified.

Suddenly, I was not at all sure that I wanted to be able to peer into the future. I feared that I would become a helpless onlooker, condemned to watch events unfold, knowing the outcomes, however sinister, yet tortured with the knowledge that I was unable to alter them.

Chapter Nine

I HAD LITTLE OPPORTUNITY to brood on what I should do with the book. Two days later I was riding out of Aachen with a cluster of courtiers, setting out for the first royal hunt of the season. The company fairly buzzed with excitement. An untold number of verderers, trackers, dog handlers and huntsmen had spent weeks preparing for the great occasion. The weather was clear and crisp, with a lingering trace of early morning mist, and the tall figure of king was in the lead. He was mounted on a towering, big-boned stallion and setting a brisk pace.

After two hours in the saddle we were deep within the royal hunting preserve. I recognized the road; it was the same track that the eel wagon had travelled to reach the capital, and I wondered if we would get as far as the place where the brigands had attempted to rob us. I doubted if I would be able to identify the exact spot because everything looked so different from what I remembered of those rain-sodden days. Then the forest had seemed heavy and foreboding, pressing in on us. Now it had an awe-inspiring majesty. The centuries-old trees were enormous. Their upper branches thick as a man's waist were still green with the last of the summer foliage. But the leaf fall had begun so the ground below them was russet and brown stretching away between the huge moss-covered tree trunks as far as the eye could see, deep into the gloom of primal woodland. Our cavalcade was no more than a temporary disturbance in this immensity. We brought a bubble of cheerful noise and activity – the thudding of hooves, creaking leather, snatches of conversation, bursts of laughter, a sudden oath as someone swore at a clumsy horse that stumbled. Yet as soon as our company had passed, a vast and timeless silence would seep back, only broken by the brief, ancient noises of the forest.

I was thinking how insignificant was our intrusion into such surroundings when Oton rode up beside me. He reined in his horse so we were riding knee to knee. His chubby face was pink from the rattling motion of our trot.

'Patch, how are you and the delicious Bertha getting along?' he asked.

I was startled out of my reverie.

'I haven't seen her since I left the royal household,' I answered.

'Berenger tells me that she was at your bedside,' he said with a spark of mischief in his eyes.

'She came to see how I was getting on,' I retorted, trying to keep my voice dispassionate.

'Only as far as your bedside?'

I coloured.

'I have no idea what you mean.' I knew I sounded less than convincing.

'Bertha is not easily denied,' he said, laughing.

I gritted my teeth. The truth was that I would have much preferred to stay back in Aachen with the chance of meeting the princess again. But that had been impossible. All royal guests were required to attend the hunt. Only Gerard had been excused, on the grounds of ill-health.

'Oton, leave off teasing him. You're just jealous,' said Hroudland's voice, and the count rode up on my other side. His roan stallion stood several inches taller than my bay, and I found myself looking up at my friend.

'Jealous?' Oton sniggered. 'Not me. But perhaps you should tell him. Could save him from a broken heart.' He pulled his horse's head aside and dropped back out of earshot.

'What's he talking about?' I asked Hroudland.

'Bertha's reputation as a man-eater,' said the count curtly.

I gaped at him.

'But she's the king's daughter!'

'Precisely. She gets what she wants.'

A hollow feeling grew in the pit of my stomach. I had been cherishing what had occurred between me and Bertha, every moment of it. I was smitten with her.

Hroudland saw my distress.

'Patch, don't take it to heart. Bertha and her sisters treat the court as their private hunting preserve, rather like this forest around us.'

'But surely their father does not allow it,' I protested.

'Rather the reverse.' Hroudland was matter of fact. 'The king knows his daughters have a healthy appetite in that direction. They've inherited it from him. He prefers they indulge themselves casually, rather than marry and produce children who would complicate the succession.'

I was speechless.

Hroudland lowered his voice.

'A word of advice, Patch. The king looks the other way, but he does not want to be made a fool of. So be discreet. And remember that you are not the only one.'

I turned aside, unable to face my friend. I was appalled that my affair with Bertha was neither secret nor special. I wondered how many of my companions had been her lovers before me. At the same time I wanted desperately to believe that what had passed between the two of us was genuine. Buffeted by these conflicting thoughts, I had to admit that I knew very little about women, least of all what to make of Bertha's behaviour. I angrily kicked my horse into a canter.

*

At length our cavalcade turned off the road and made its way down a grassy track, which widened in a broad clearing. Here the advance party of our servants, including Osric, had set up tents and pavilions, dug fire pits and latrines. There was a park for the wagons, which had brought in supplies of food and wine, stacks of fodder and firewood, a line of temporary stalls for our horses, enormous barrels with water for drinking and washing. The place resembled a small village.

We dismounted and were assigned to our tents. I was put with Hroudland, Berenger and Ogier. I was glad I did not have to share with Oton, for the thought that he had lain with Bertha sickened me.

'The head huntsman will explain about tomorrow,' Hroudland said to me. 'Listen carefully because my uncle takes his hunting very seriously.' He had thrown off his riding cloak and cap, and stretched to ease his muscles. 'The king likes the first hunt of the season to be by lance, though God only knows why he chooses to risk his life in that way.'

'Have there been many accidents?' I asked.

Hroudland ran his fingers through his hair.

'Not yet, though it's only a matter of time.'

At that moment a brief note sounded on a hunting horn.

'That's our signal to assemble. Come on! We want to be where we can see what's arranged.'

Together we walked to where the company was gathering in a circle. Standing in the middle of a patch of bare earth was a small, grizzled-looking man dressed entirely in leather that had been dyed dark green. Around his neck hung the metal hunting horn that had summoned us. Hroudland pushed our way to the front and I looked across the circle to see the king himself, directly opposite. Some five or six places to his left was Ganelon, Hroudland's stepfather. As at the banquet Ganelon caught my eye, before looking away to where Hroudland stood.

The green-clad man held up his hand to quieten the chatter of the onlookers.

'That's Vulfard, the king's chief huntsman,' the count explained.

'Your Majesty and my lords, Greetings!' The huntsman spoke with the confidence of a man who knew every detail of his profession. 'Tomorrow we should have good sport – a hart of eighteen points.'

There was a collective intake of breath among the spectators.

'A once-in-a-lifetime beast!' Hroudland hissed in my ear.

I saw the king perk up. He straightened his back and shoulders, standing even taller.

'My men have been watching this animal for months, long before the rut began,' announced the huntsman. He stepped to one side of the circle, pulled a long hunting knife from his belt, and leaned down to mark a small cross in the dirt.

'This is where he is now . . . and here—' he moved across the circle to stand directly in front of me '—is where we plan to bring him.' The point of the knife made another cross in the earth. 'With His Majesty's permission, I propose to establish our line from here to here.' The knife described an arc extending out in each direction from the second mark. 'The final sector has been fenced with hurdles to bring in the quarry.' The blade scratched a V-shape leading to the second mark. 'Until the hart has started between the hurdles, strict discipline must be observed. Otherwise he turns back and we lose him.' The little man paused and looked up at the king.

Carolus nodded at him to continue.

'I have three dozen men to drive the beast. Their hounds will be on leash. They will move him by gradual stages. We already know the tracks he favours.'

Vulfard gazed around our faces. Raising his voice and speaking slowly, he said, 'This hart is uncommonly wary. He may surprise us and leave his normal paths. If he comes your way, you must turn him back, but carefully. On no account panic him. Once he is turned, you may sound your horn as a signal. Just once and softly, like this.' He raised his hunting horn to his lips and blew a short, gentle note. 'Then we will know how the beast moves.' He frowned at us. 'Allow other creatures to pass, be they boar, hind, or any stag of less than twelve points.'

Many in his audience were nodding their agreement, clearly excited.

'What about an urus?' someone called out.

There was laughter as the huntsman answered, 'You'll have no choice. You'll be flattened.'

The king himself now stepped into the circle and addressed us, his high-pitched voice carrying clearly.

'Fellow huntsmen, this hart is a noble quarry. Tomorrow, when he falls, the death notes will ring out loud and clear so that all living creatures will know of his passing.'

'What are death notes?' I muttered to Hroudland.

'The hunting call that signals the death of the quarry. Sometimes the king sounds the horn himself. It means the end of the day's hunt.'

The king left the assembly and began making his way towards the largest of the pavilions. It was a massive affair, larger than most cottages, striped in red and blue.

An assistant to the chief huntsman approached Hroudland and asked him to attend the dispositions. I accompanied him to where

Vulfard was assigning each person to a place in tomorrow's line. He recognized Hroudland immediately and put him close to the king. He looked at me doubtfully.

'Have you hunted hart before?' he asked. His tone was polite but cautious.

'At home we hunted deer for meat,' I answered.

'By force or by stable?'

I looked confused, so he explained: 'Was it with a bow and on horseback, following hounds? Or waiting for a driven beast?'

'On horseback, with hounds.' I was exaggerating. I had seldom gone hunting, leaving the chase to my more sporting brothers.

Vulfard chewed his lip.

'Do you know the basic calls?' he demanded.

I hesitated, and then guessed.

'A single note if the quarry is passing to your left. Two quick blasts if he goes the other way.'

The huntsman shook his head.

'Wrong.'

'Perhaps he can stand beside me in the line,' suggested Hroudland.

Vulfard shook his head.

'No, my lord. Only the most experienced hunters will be near the centre. A novice could ruin the day for everyone.'

'I'm sure you can find a spot somewhere for him,' Hroudland coaxed.

Vulfard acceded grudgingly.

'He can stand there.'

He jabbed his knife point in the dirt. I saw he had put me at the extreme left-hand end of the line, farthest from the centre and the least likely place to see the great stag. Vulfard fixed me with a stern look.

'Just remember, stay quiet and do not disturb the drive. I'll send my son with you to help out. You'll need to be up early.' He turned away and began to interrogate the next man.

'I fear tomorrow is going to be very tedious for you,' said Hroudland as we strolled back to our tent.

'Well, at least I've been placed out of harm's way,' I said lightly.

'I've tried to persuade the king to change his routine but he insists that his first kill of the season is by lance alone, and the quarry has not been run until exhausted.'

'I would have thought that facing a boar would be much more dangerous than a stag.'

The count frowned at me.

'That shows how little you know about hunting. Tomorrow, if all goes to plan, a great hart will be guided to where the king waits with a lance in his hand.'

'And then?'

'There's an old saying that if you are injured by a boar, call for a healer. If hurt by a stag, call for a priest.'

'Why does the king expose himself to such a risk?'

Hroudland shrugged.

'To demonstrate that he still has courage and skill with weapons. It has become a ritual.' He made a sweeping gesture with his arm, taking in the entire forest around us. 'More than a hundred men, packs of hounds, weeks of preparation. Let us hope that all goes well tomorrow, and the king makes his kill. Otherwise he will be in a bad humour for months.'

'And what if this monstrous stag avoids the drive and escapes the hunt?'

Hroudland laughed and slapped me on the shoulder.

'Then, Patch, it will be up to you. If you see the stag escaping, you are allowed to shoot it with an arrow.'

'Why the laughter when someone asked about an urus? What is it?'

'A wild cow, but bigger than the biggest ox. Horns twice as long. Only a few left in the forest, if any. If you see one coming at you, just climb the nearest tree.'

*

A tickling sensation on my ear woke me next morning. I opened my eyes to find a faint pre-dawn glow seeping into the tent. The previous evening, knowing the night would be cold, I had lain down under my cloak, fully dressed. I sat up and irritably brushed aside the long feather that had been used to rouse me. Someone was squatting beside me.

'Time to go,' said a stranger's voice.

There was something not quite right about the words, but it was too dark to recognize the dark shape that scuttled out of the tent ahead of me.

The morning chill ate into my bones as I pulled on my boots. Outside, the ground was wet with dew, and I could just about make out Osric's distinctive limp as he came across the camp ground. He was leading two horses. I paid a quick visit to the latrines and, seeing a glow in the kitchen tent, found that the cooks were already up and preparing breakfast for the hunters. I carried a loaf of good barley bread and a flask of hot ale across to where Osric was waiting for me, holding the reins of my bay gelding.

'Eat it while it's still warm,' I said to Osric, tearing off a chunk of bread and handing it to him. Slung across his back, he had my bow and its arrow quiver, the leather flap securely fastened against the damp. The stranger had his back to me as he tightened the saddle girths of a large, shaggy pony. When he turned, I saw he was a lad in his teens.

'Farthest to go, soonest to start,' he said in that same blurred manner of speaking. He was a big, strapping youth, though his arms and legs were too short for his body. Belatedly I noted the round face and almond shaped eyes, the lids half-closed.

I supposed him to be an ostler, employed to help at the hunting camp. Then I noticed the battered hunting horn dangling from a cord around his neck, also the greasy cap he was wearing. It sported a long feather, the one he used to wake me, and was dyed forest green. I guessed it was a cast-off from his father, Vulfard, and the young man was our escort for the day.

'What's your name?' I asked.

There was a heartbeat of a pause.

'Walo,' he blurted, bobbing his head awkwardly.

'Then, Walo, show what we must do,' I said encouragingly.

My words were met with another duck of the head, quick and enthusiastic this time. Without warning he stepped forward, took me by the leg and threw me up on to my horse. He was surprisingly strong. I had scarcely settled in the saddle when he had done the same for Osric so that he was astride the pony. Then, to Osric's astonishment, Walo vaulted up in front of him, gathered up the reins, and banged his heels into the pony's ribs. We crossed the camp site at a fast trot, Osric almost falling off when Walo swerved the pony to one side to lean over to pluck up a lance he had left stuck in the ground. Moments later we plunged into the forest.

We rode in near-silence, the spongy ground absorbing the sound of hooves, the air heavy with the musty smell of rotting leaves and damp soil. Even in the dim light Walo was absolutely confident of our path though I failed to discern any sign of a track. The trees, mostly huge oaks, were widely spaced and allowed us to travel unimpeded but they offered no clues of our progress or direction. Once, when I turned in the saddle, I could not make out from where we had come. In every direction the forest was the same – full of shadows, brooding, limitless. There were a few signs of life. A late hunting owl flew up from behind us, gliding low over our heads, and then swooping away without a sound, a pale blur that vanished into the trees. A little while later, a dog fox loped across our path, nose close to the ground as it followed a scent. The creature was so intent on its prey that it failed to notice us until we were almost on top of it. It stopped, one paw raised, and turned its head to inspect us. It stood there motionless and unafraid as we rode past. I could make out the slanting yellow eyes, alert with interest.

The land ran level for the most part though occasionally we had to ride down into a small gully, splash across a rivulet of dark-stained water, and then up the far bank. After the best part of an hour, Walo reined in. We had arrived at a gap in the woodland, an open space dotted with clumps of birch and willow. Apparently this was the place allotted to me for the hunt. Pointing off to our right into a stand of beech trees, Walo explained that the line of hunters extended in that direction as far as the king's position in the centre of the line. If we were to see any game, it would come from ahead of us or to our right.

We dismounted and tied the horses to a tree stump hidden behind a willow thicket. Osric strung my bow and handed it to me. Walo jammed the butt end of the lance into the ground, squatted down on his heels and waited beside it. I wandered about, seeking the best spot to give me a clear view of any game that might come towards us, however unlikely that might be. I had just found a suitable location when I saw Osric bend down and pick something from the ground. I went across to see what he had found.

'Death cap,' he said. He held out a pale golden-yellow mushroom.

The mushroom looked harmless. I would not have hesitated to eat it.

'This is what poisoned me?' I guessed.

'The vomiting and dizziness were clues. But I wasn't sure if it grew locally.'

'Perhaps it got into my food by accident.'

'Perhaps,' he said, though he sounded unconvinced. He tossed away the deadly fungus and brushed all traces from his fingers. 'Yet it was the ideal poison. No one would notice a mushroom added to your plate.'

'What about Gerard? He too was sick.'

'Maybe someone wanted him out of the way as well.'

Behind us Walo uttered a low, clucking sound. I turned to see him gesturing that I should pay attention to the hunt. I walked back to my place, carrying my bow and took up a post facing into the line of beech trees.

For a long while nothing happened. The forest was silent. The only activity was from a flock of small dun-coloured birds. They were feeding in the willows to my left. They twittered and chirruped, hopped restlessly from branch to branch, then abruptly flew away, wings whirring. I thought I heard the distant sound of a twig snapping. A foraging jay chattered, and I caught a glimpse as it winged its way through the tops of the beeches.

To pass the time, I attempted to reconstruct what had happened during the banquet when I had been poisoned. I tried to picture the bowl of pottage as it was set in front of me, whether I had seen any slivers of mushroom mixed in my food, and who had served me. But inevitably my memory kept sliding away to the happier image of Bertha seated at the high table, and how beautiful she had been with her braids looped up and held in place with a headband. I recalled in vivid detail how she had looked at me when I completed my tale of Troilus and Polyxena.

A deep, rasping cough jerked me out of my day dream.

Directly in front of me, not thirty paces away, stood a colossal stag. The giant creature was staring at me belligerent and challenging. I had never seen such a towering animal. At the shoulder it was as tall as I was, and the rack of antlers rose another four feet above that. I was so close that I could see the nostrils opening and closing as the creature tasted my scent. The animal's head and thickly muscled neck was in proportion to its immense size. A broad, shaggy pelt of matted grey-brown hair covered the chest. I had no idea how it had emerged from the forest and appeared right in front of me.

I froze.

For a long moment the creature gazed directly at me. I felt small and puny. Then, slowly, the majestic spread of antlers, six or seven feet across, swung away as the hart turned its head and began to walk slowly past me. I had been judged as harmless.

I felt a nudge on my elbow. Osric had crept up behind me the moment the hart had turned away, and was prodding me with an arrow he had taken from the quiver. I looked down. It was a war arrow, the heavy iron head three inches broad and designed to pierce scale armour.

The hart was moving to my left, away from the line of waiting hunters. There was no hope of turning it back toward them. I took the arrow, nocked it to my bowstring, and glanced across at Walo. The lad was half-crouched, mesmerized, his mouth slack and his gaze fixed on the great deer. He turned to face me and saw the question in my face. He nodded.

I drew back the bowstring, felt the heavy shaft slide smoothly across my left hand, and in the same movement, released the arrow.

I had practised my archery so often that there was no need to take deliberate aim. Some instinct told me exactly where to place the shaft, and the heavy arrow slammed into the ribs, just behind the shoulder.

Until that moment I had never appreciated the force of the curved bow. My arrow struck at the perfect angle. It plunged deep into the body cavity and ripped through the vital organs. The huge beast ran less than fifty paces, and then with a hoarse grunt, buckled at the knees and sank to the ground.

Walo was on the stag in a flash. He darted behind the stricken animal, dodged the kicking hooves, and crawled under the sweep of the antlers. At risk to his life he drew his hunting knife across the throat. It took three deep cuts before twin bright red spouts showed he had succeeded in despatching the animal.

The great head dropped to the ground and lay there, twisted at an ugly angle by the massive antlers.

Walo got to his feet unsteadily, his face and jerkin splashed with blood. He gazed down at the great corpse, and a tremendous smile spread across his face. Then he broke into a gawky dance, capering up and down with delight.

'What do we do now?' I asked him. I could scarcely believe that it had all ended so quickly.

He stopped his jig and fumbled for the hunting horn dangling from the cord around his neck. Putting it to his lips, he blew three or four unsteady notes. The effort was beyond him, and he tried a second time. On the fourth attempt he succeeded in completing what I supposed was the death call.

There was no response from the silent forest.

We began to gut the huge animal. It was a mammoth task. By mid-morning we were not halfway through butchering the carcass, though we had succeeded in retrieving my lucky arrow, undamaged. It had slid between two ribs and pierced the heart. We sliced and cut, pausing to pass a whetstone between us and sharpen our knives and to listen for other hunters. We might as well have been alone in a wilderness. We worked until we were hungry, and Walo went to fetch bread and hard cheese from a saddlebag on the pony and a leather bottle of ale. I wandered off in search of water to clean my hands made sticky with blood. I took along the arrow to wash and smooth the blood-stiffened feathers.

Among the willows was a shallow puddle left by the summer rain. I knelt down and was washing the fletching when I heard the sound of a hunting horn. It was very far in the distance, several short calls followed by a longer note. I stood up to listen. The forest had fallen silent. Next came the alarm call of the jay, and then the sound of animals on the move, coming in my direction. As I watched, a group of half a dozen hinds moved across a gap in the thickets some fifty paces ahead of me. They were walking quietly, unhurried and unafraid. Cautiously I backed away, not wishing to frighten them. Varnulf had instructed that all lesser quarry must be allowed to pass freely. I reached the spot where I had left my bow when I happened to look toward the line of beech trees.

For a moment I thought I saw a ghost. A great stag was stepping out from the treeline. I shut my eyes tight and opened them again, thinking it was the fetch of the animal I had just slain. But this animal was slightly smaller, a lighter brown, and the rack of antlers was not as broad. Nevertheless I counted fourteen tines.

Instinctively I reached for my bow. My movement alerted the stag which turned its head to look in my direction. I stood stock still until the stag took a few more paces. Then slowly, very slowly, I set my lucky arrow to the string, and drew the bow. But the quarry was suspicious. Step by step it advanced, anxious to follow its group of hinds, yet wary of danger.

The stag was within killing range, yet I waited. My arms and shoulders aching with the strain, hoping for another mortal shot. Then Osric called to me to hurry to join him before all the food was gone. His shout caused the stag to wheel round and take a great leap towards the safety of the treeline. I loosed.

My arrow caught the beast in mid-air, striking well back along his body. I saw the hindquarters twist and droop as the injured beast landed. Then it gathered its strength and sped away among the beech trees, the crashing sounds of flight growing fainter and fainter in the distance.

'What was that?' demanded Osric, emerging from the brush-wood behind me, a cheese rind in his hand.

'Another hart, almost as big. I wounded it.'

'Badly?'

'I think so. It was running crookedly.'

'Quick, before you lose it. Walo and I can bring on the horses.' He ran back and fetched the lance that Walo had stuck in the ground and handed it to me. 'You'll need this to finish him off. In the woods it'll be more use than the bow. But take care.'

Alone, I set out in pursuit of the wounded quarry. I ran at first, a slow jog because the trail was easy to follow and I did not believe I had far to go. The hart had left a line of marks on the forest floor where its hooves had scuffed up the leaves. Here and there were sizable splashes of blood. In a few places I saw fresh scrapes on tree trunks where the wounded creature had blundered into the trees, and the antlers had knocked away the bark.

But gradually the trail grew indistinct, and I slowed to a walk. I was being drawn deep into the forest. The dense foliage filtered out the daylight and made it difficult to pick out the tell-tale signs. I worried that I might walk past the carcass of the beast if it had dropped dead. Worse, there was the risk of stumbling upon the wounded animal, as it was ready to attack. I recalled how my father had insisted that no trackers ever went after a wounded stag unless they were accompanied by dogs. So I looked about me carefully, peering into the dark shadows as much for ambush as for signs of blood or hoof prints. I kept a firm grip on the lance.

I had almost given up all hope of finding my quarry and was ready to turn back when I heard a sudden panicked thrashing not far ahead. I had come up upon the beast, and once again scared it into flight. I broke into a run, determined not to let it escape. But after a short distance the sounds suddenly stopped, and I was at a loss. I stole forward, taking each step quietly, straining my ears.

I came to the lip of a narrow, steep gulley. A dense tangle of ferns and brambles choked the little stream which ran through the bottom of it. I heard a bubbling, wheezing sound, looked down and saw the wounded stag. It was lying sprawled on the stream bed, deep pink froth coming from its jaws. My arrow must have pierced the lungs. A fresh scar in the earth bank showed where the creature had tried to leap across and failed. It had tumbled into the gully and, unable to rise, was very near death. Very cautiously I eased myself over the edge. The bank was too steep for me to stand upright so I sat back on the slope and allowed myself to slide down the bank. The sides of the gully were slick with wet leaves, and I dug in my heels to control the speed of my descent. When I reached the bottom of the gully, I circled round, keeping well clear of the antlers to where I could get a clear thrust with the lance. Not taking my eyes off the quarry, I sidled into position and drew back my weapon. I was about to stab down when something whipped past my head and there was a soft thump just beside me. I turned my head and was shocked to see the haft of an arrow sticking out of the earth bank to my right. It had buried half its length into the soil.

I yelped with anger and fright, just as a second arrow whizzed past, so close that I felt the wind of its passing. 'Watch out, you fool!' I screamed. I looked up at the bank above me to see a figure duck back out of sight. All thought of killing the stag had gone from my mind. I scrambled my way up the slope to confront the idiot hunter. But by the time I reached the crest there was no one there. Whoever had aimed the arrows had fled and there was no hope of catching him.

I waited to get my breath back and for the pounding of my heart to ease. If the archer had been a hunter, he would have stayed. My thoughts went back to the thief who had tried to rob the eel wagon. The forest was home to brigands and outlaws, but I could see little reason why one of them would want to kill me. This was not the time of hunger, and there was plenty of game in the forest so it could not be for the stag's carcass. Possibly I had stumbled on the outlaws' lair. If so, I was not aware of it.

Lying on the ground was a hunting horn. The cord had snapped. I picked it up, wondering if it was a clue to the archer's identity. But it was a commonplace instrument, made of wood with a mouthpiece carved from bone. Many foresters carried them. Thoughtfully, I knotted the broken cord and hung the horn around my neck. Then I slid back down into the gully to collect the two arrows that had so nearly killed me. Genuine hunters identified their own arrows with dabs of paint or coloured thread. It allowed them to reclaim spent arrows and settle conflicting claims about who had slain the quarry. Both the arrows I extracted from the soft earth carried broad iron tips, capable of killing man or beast. But neither had any distinguishing marks so there was nothing to be learned from them. Angrily I snapped them across my knee and tossed the pieces into the undergrowth. Such arrows were expensive, and at least the mysterious archer would be denied their use in future. At the same time I was increasingly uneasy that what had happened might not have been an accident.

There was no longer any need to despatch the stag. While I had been dealing with the mystery archer, the animal had died.

To make sure, I touched a fingertip to one of the huge, wide, unseeing eyes. There was no reaction and I turned away. The splintered stub of my own arrow protruded from the animal's side. It had been snapped when the animal fell. I left the arrow where it was. Osric and Walo could retrieve it later, and I would fit the broad head to another shaft. I wanted to keep my lucky arrow.

I clambered out of the gully and set off back the way I had come. I held on to the lance for defence but I had the feeling that there would be no more trouble that day. Instead, after an hour of walking, I knew that I had a different problem: I was completely lost. The forest track I had chosen to follow had petered out. All around me the trees looked the same. Suddenly I was thirsty and fiercely hungry. I had not eaten since before dawn and even then only a few mouthfuls of bread. The day's events had been exhausting, and it was now well into the afternoon. I was tired and did not relish the prospect of spending the night alone in the forest.

I had not seen any large game animals during my walk so I did not risk ruining the king's sport. I raised the hunting horn dangling against my chest and blew a soft double note, hoping Osric and Walo were somewhere quite close and would hear me. There was no reply. I tried again, louder. This time there was a response, a single short call. Relieved, I turned in that direction and began to walk.

Half an hour later I had not reached my companions and was again losing confidence. I feared that I was walking in a circle. Once more I sounded the hunting horn, and to my relief it was answered. I headed in that direction.

So it went on. Every five or ten minutes I blew a single note on the hunting horn, heard a reply and used it as my guide. I pressed forward, more quickly now, walking confidently. I was intent on catching up with Osric and Walo and returning with them to the main camp before dusk. I noticed how the forest around me was different. Previously there had been wide open spaces between the great trunks, now there was more undergrowth and brushwood. Occasionally my way was blocked and I was obliged to turn aside. When this happened for the third or fourth time, I looked more closely. I saw I had walked into a line of wicker hurdles, artfully covered with fresh branches.

I had blundered into the fence that Vulfard's men had erected to guide the game towards the king.

By now I was too exhausted and hungry to care. Besides, the day was so far advanced that the hunt should have been finished some time ago. I trudged forward, following the line of the fence, until I heard the sound of voices. Soon afterwards I emerged into a clearing and stopped dead. The king and his royal hunting party were standing together in a group, their backs to me. Attendants were serving food and drink from trays.

Hroudland was the first to notice me hesitating at the edge of the forest. He came forward, his face full of anxiety. To my surprise he did not ask where I had been. Instead he blurted, 'Patch, make yourself scarce. The king is furious.'

I was utterly taken aback.

'What have I done?'

'Played the noisy fool and ruined the hunt for everyone else.' My friend sounded resentful.

'Bring that oaf over here!' ordered an angry voice. It was the king and he had a face like thunder. Vulfard, in his green garb, lurked behind him, looking devastated.

My stomach growled with hunger as I walked forward. The group of courtiers nervously cleared a space around the infuriated king. Only Hroudland had the courage to step out and accompany me as I approached his uncle.

Carolus was fuming. He caught sight of the hunting horn dangling against my chest.

'Hroudland, take that away from him. I never want to hear its note again,' he stormed.

'Your Majesty, I beg forgiveness,' I stammered. 'I was lost and trying to find my way.'

'No wonder, you numskull. You couldn't find your arse with your own hands.' The king swung round and confronted Vulfard. 'You said you sent your son to keep an eye on this buffoon!'

'I did, my lord,' answered the huntsman. He was shrivelled up with embarrassment. 'The lad will get a whipping when he gets back.'

'Walo is not at fault,' I intervened.

'He knows well enough not to blow the death call in jest, and wreck the hunt,' snapped Vulfard.

'But the hart was dead,' I said.

There was the pause of a heartbeat, and then the king growled, 'What hart?'

'A large one, maybe eighteen points.'

I saw derisive looks appear on the faces of the royal party. Ganelon, Hroudland's stepfather, was smirking.

The king narrowed his eyes.

'You claim that you killed a hart of eighteen points?' He sounded incredulous.

'Yes, Your Majesty.'

He turned to Vulfard.

'Can this be true?'

The huntsman shifted uncomfortably.

'Possibly. We never saw the beast ourselves.'

'I know that!' the king snapped. 'Your dimwit son and this lout frightened off every creature for miles around, puffing away like low musicians at a fairground.' The king swung back to face me. 'When did you kill this wondrous beast?' His voice dripped with sarcasm.

'Shortly after we reached the place in the line assigned to us, Your Majesty.'

'And you are sure it has eighteen points?'

'The rack was larger than the other one.'

The royal eyebrows shot up.

'What other one?'

'Back there, it appeared a little while later,' I said weakly, indicating the forest behind me. 'It had only sixteen points.'

'Are you saying that today you killed two beasts, each fit to be royal quarry?'

'I intended no disrespect.'

The king studied me for a long moment, scowling. Then Vulfard coughed discreetly.

'I think he tells the truth, Your Majesty.' He indicated to one side. Walo and Osric were entering the clearing. They were on foot and leading the two horses loaded with great slabs of meat. Dangling from the saddle of my bay gelding was an immense rack of antlers.

The king turned back to face me. He scowled, and for a moment I thought he was going to strike me. Suddenly he threw back his head and burst out in a great roar of laughter.

'I hereby ban this young man from our forests and any future hunt of ours.'

I bowed my head obediently, and stared at the leaf mould on the ground. If I was forbidden from the forest, then I was unlikely ever to learn the identity of the mysterious archer who might have been an assassin.

Chapter Ten

NEXT DAY I WAS DISMISSED. I was ordered to Aachen while the king moved camp to a different area of the forest for another week of hunting. Hroudland later told me that his uncle's good humour was restored when he personally killed a pair of wisents, bull-like animals with great shaggy hides, which ran wild in the forest.

I would have been happier if the king had stayed away even longer. Discipline in the royal household was slack in the king's absence, and that made it less of a risk to continue my relationship with Bertha. Timing my visits carefully, usually well after dark and when the guards were drowsy, I was able to make my way discreetly to Bertha's room on the ground floor and spend several nights with her. She encouraged my attendance and I was so smitten by her that I was convinced her affection for me was genuine, whatever Oton and the others claimed about her appetite for men.

'We must think of an excuse for you to become a regular visitor,' Bertha murmured. Her father was expected back in the next few hours, and we were lying side by side in her bed, contented and warm in the darkness. Before first light I would creep away to my own quarters.

I yawned and stretched.

'I hate having to get up in the dark and cold when it is so delightful here.'

'You were talking in your sleep just now.'

'I must have been dreaming.'

'About me, I hope.' She leaned over and her tongue flicked around my ear. I shivered with delight.

'I can't remember.' I slid my arm under her shoulders and drew her towards me. She pressed herself against me and I gloried in her softness and warmth for a few more precious moments.

At length she drew back so I could get out of bed.

'You should try to remember your dreams. They could be important,' she said.

'I know,' I said neutrally. With a sudden upwelling of melancholy I recalled my dream of a bull attacking a peaceful stag, and how it had been a portent of my father's death and the destruction of his kingdom. I did not care to reveal just how important they were.

'My father believes in his dreams.'

I groped for my shirt where I had dropped it.

'Does he tell you about them?'

'Yes. Especially when they worry him.'

'What was the last dream he confided to you?'

'A man attacked by a pack of wolves. He could not see who the man was, but it was in a wild place, among rocks and trees. The man was blowing a horn, desperately signalling for help. It never came.'

I smiled into the darkness.

'Your father won't be worrying about that dream any longer. I made a fool of myself with a hunting horn recently. I'll tell you about it some time.'

'Were you attacked by wolves?' I was pleased to hear the note of genuine concern in her question.

'There were no wolves. I was lost.'

'Then that's not what the dream was about.'

I decided to tell her about the Oneirokritikon.

'There's a book that explains what dreams really mean.'

I heard her sit up in bed.

'Have you seen that book?' she asked.

'I have been given a copy, but it's written in Saracen.'

'You must get it translated!'

She sounded excited, and I already knew her well enough to guess that she had some scheme in mind.

'But I don't even know if there's any truth in it. It could all be rubbish, written for the credulous.'

'You'll never know until you've read it,' she said.

There was no response to that, so I stayed silent.

'My father tells his family about his dreams, no one else. He hopes we might be able to explain them to him.'

'Then perhaps I can write out a translation of the book for him.'

'My father doesn't know how to read.'

Now I saw what she had in mind.

'You mean I would become his interpreter of dreams.'

'Exactly! Through me.' There was triumph in her voice. 'And that way you will become a trusted member of the inner circle.'

*

Translating the Oneirokritikon was not as difficult as I had feared. Alcuin provided a desk in a quiet side room in the chancery and supplied writing materials. I took Osric's dictation as he unravelled the sentences.

'The author's name is Artimedorus,' said Osric as we began.

'He doesn't sound like a Saracen.' The goose feather was fresh, and I was having problems getting the ink to flow smoothly.

'He's a Greek. He states he will offer proof of the fulfilment of dreams and refute those sceptics who mock the art of divination.'

I wiped the tip of the quill clean with a fresh rag and loaded it again with ink.

Osric ran his eye along the next few lines.

'Artimedorus claims that for many years he has been collecting books of dream interpretation and consulting diviners of the marketplace, so now he provides a truthful guide on the subject.'

'Sounds promising.' I bent to my task.

'There are two categories of dreams,' Osric translated. 'Those which reflect the present, and those which foretell the future. The former need no explanation. Thus a sick man is likely to dream of doctors and his illness; a lover dreams of the person he holds dear. When they awake that was the end of the dream and it had no significance.'

My quill was still giving trouble. I discarded it and cut a replacement.

Osric waited until I had caught up with his dictation.

'Master, should I summarize the Greek's ideas?' he asked. 'I fear he is rather pedantic.'

'Pick out the practical advice,' I replied. Bertha would be expecting quick results on how to interpret dreams.

Osric leafed through the pages.

'The dreams of the second category can either be literal or allegorical.'

'Does he give examples?'

'For a literal dream, he cites the case of a man travelling aboard ship who dreamed he was in a shipwreck. The next day his vessel sank. Artimedorus claims to have spoken to the man himself. He goes on to say that such dreams come true so often that we should not be surprised.'

I had no need to ask Osric how a dream could be an allegory of the future. My dream of the aggressive ox led by a vixen attacking the stag had been an image of King Offa's invasion of my father's kingdom. There was a much more important question I had to ask. The answer might protect me against future dangers.

'Does Artimedorus say whether it is possible to induce a

prophetic dream – by swallowing extracts of powerful herbs before sleeping, for example?' I asked.

I had already told Osric about the unknown archer, and he guessed my thoughts.

'So you would have been prepared for what happened during the hunt?'

I nodded.

Osric spent a long time searching the pages of the Oneirokritikon. Finally he shook his head. 'He only warns that dreams that are the result of having eaten or drunk too much are not to be relied on.'

'Osric, do you ever dream?' I ventured to ask.

'Only nightmares I would sooner forget,' he replied quietly.

*

We worked on the translation for over a week before I received my next summons to the king's residence. Leaving Osric to puzzle over obscure Saracen phrases, I set out across the royal precinct. The weather had turned bitterly cold and a thick coating of frost covered the raw piles of building materials with glittering crystals. I felt sorry for the workmen balanced on the scaffolding of the half-finished audience hall, their hands wrapped in rags against the chill wind. They were still mixing mortar and setting courses of bricks. The construction work was behind schedule and the king was insisting on having the building in time for Christmas.

To my surprise the guards at the main entrance to the king's residence directed me to a side door. Here an under-chamberlain met me and escorted me to a small reception room, comfortably furnished with low stools and soft rugs and with a fire burning in the corner. To my delight, Bertha was waiting for me. The moment the door closed behind me, I started forward, about to embrace her. The warning look in her eyes stopped me.

'So this is the man of dreams,' said a slightly mocking voice. Standing off to one side was a woman who, I guessed at once, had to be one of Bertha's sisters. The two were very alike. They had the same fair hair, blue eyes and creamy, slightly freckled skin. But the stranger lacked Bertha's voluptuous curves and was not as tall. She seemed more mature, more worldly, and I presumed she was the older of the two. She was eyeing me with an expression of curiosity tempered with disbelief. I wondered if she was comparing me to her sister's previous lovers.

Bertha wasted no time in coming straight to the point.

'Sigwulf, this is Adelaide, my sister. Our father has had a dream that could be important.'

I could tell by the way that Bertha held her hands clasped in front of her, her face animated, that she was excited.

'He told us about it yesterday. We want you to interpret it for us.' She cast a conspiratorial glance towards her sister.

'I'm less than halfway through translating the dream book,' I apologized.

'I'm sure you can locate the part that matters.'

Her high-handed manner irritated me. Then I remembered that she was a king's daughter.

'I'll do what I can,' I said.

Adelaide moved across the room to stand beside her sister.

'Do you find this dream book believable?' she asked.

'I haven't had time to judge.'

'So now's the time to put it to the test,' Bertha interrupted eagerly.

'It's not as simple as that . . .' my voice trailed away. I wanted to please Bertha but I was beginning to wonder if I was wise to have spoken to her about the Oneirokritikon. I had a feeling that there was more to the sisters' questions than they were letting on.

I sensed that I was approaching something sensitive, a dangerous topic that I was not equipped to handle.

'What are these difficulties?' asked Adelaide. Her voice was low and musical but there was a probing edge.

I prevaricated.

'The interpretation of a dream depends on so many factors – the time of the dream, the status of the dreamer, his or her health, whether the dreamer has anxieties.'

Adelaide waved aside my excuses.

'You know my father's status – he's the king. He dreamed shortly before midnight. It's no secret that he's a light sleeper, and he awoke soon afterwards.'

It was clear that she was not someone who was easily diverted.

'Perhaps Your Highness could relate the contents of the dream,' I suggested.

'Our father dreamed he was travelling through a foreign country. He had no idea where it was. The people dressed strangely and they spoke in languages he did not understand. He was invisible to them so they ignored him even when he tried to engage them in conversation.' Unexpectedly Adelaide hesitated. She flushed slightly as if embarrassed.

'Go on, Addy,' said her sister. 'That patch Sigwulf is wearing is a fake.'

'What really troubles my father is that in his dream he had only one eye. The other had been lost,' said Adelaide.

I relaxed. Artimedorus had written about dreams of blindness or the loss of an eye in a chapter that Osric and I had already translated.

'There are two possible explanations of the dream,' I began.

Quick as a flash Adelaide gave a sniff of disbelief.

'Just as I told you, Bertha. Soothsayers are always devious.

They're deliberately vague so you can read into their prophecies whatever you want to believe.'

'Hear him out, Addy,' Bertha said, springing to my defence. 'Give him a chance to explain.'

I gave Bertha a grateful glance and went on.

'According to Artimedorus, a person who dreams of travelling through a foreign country while having only one eye means the journey will be hindered and full of difficulties.'

Adelaide looked doubtful.

'I've not heard that the king intends a foreign trip.'

'The interpretation of the dream does not allow one to say when it will come true,' I cautioned.

'More weasel words from the soothsayer,' Adelaide promptly accused.

Her open scepticism prodded me into saying what I had not intended.

'There is another interpretation of the loss of an eye,' I said sharply.

'And what's that?' Adelaide scoffed.

'The loss of an eye means the loss of a member of the family,' I said quietly.

That caught their attention. The two sisters looked hard at me.

'What member of the family?' asked Bertha. Her voice was flinty, but there was a trace of fear.

I was committed now, and could not draw back.

'A parent or a child.'

'Well, both the king's mother and father are already deceased,' said Adelaide. Her eyes were alert with interest.

'And does your Greek offer any further details?' Bertha asked slowly.

'You will have to tell me which eye was missing in your father's dream.'

'The right one.'

I smothered a sigh of relief.

'According to Artimedorus, the loss of the right eye means that the dreamer will lose a son.'

No sooner had the words left my mouth than I regretted them. I pictured the royal family seated at their table at the banquet. There had been only one son – Pepin. He was the heir, yet he was illegitimate, the offspring of a concubine. Both sisters in front of me were daughters of legal marriage.

I tried to hide my thoughts, keeping my face blank. But I noticed that the two sisters exchanged a quick, meaningful glance.

Then Adelaide said brightly, 'We are forgetting our manners.' She went to a side table, removed the glass stopper from a flask of wine and poured me a drink. 'Here, Sigwulf, you need something to warm you up before you go out into the cold again.'

It was clear that my audience with the royal sisters was at an end.

*

My thoughts were in turmoil as I left the royal residence. I had a queasy feeling that I was teetering on the edge of palace politics, a very dangerous area. What I had said about the king losing a son had struck a chord with both sisters. Yet nothing I had heard about Pepin led me to believe he was near death. I had not laid eyes on him for some time and he had not been with the royal hunting party, but that was not surprising in light of his physical attributes.

I was so engrossed in my thoughts that I did not look where I was putting my feet. All of a sudden I skidded, flailing wildly to keep my balance.

'Look where you're going!'

A building foreman, wrapped up in a heavy sheepskin coat, was waving at me to get out of the way. Behind him a squad of labourers were advancing in a line, tipping buckets of water on to the frozen ground. As the water spread it was freezing into a sheet of ice.

'Keep off if you don't want to break your neck!' bellowed the foreman.

His men were creating a smooth, slick pathway from the unfinished great hall. Behind them was another gang of men. They were hauling on ropes attached to a crude sledge. On it stood the great metal horse and rider which had shocked me on my first day. They were sliding their load along the ice.

I went across to the foreman.

'Where will the statue eventually be placed?' I enquired.

'Search me,' was his gruff reply. 'Right now the master mason wants it out of his way. Says it interferes with his brick hoists where it is.'

The foreman wiped a drip hanging from the end of his nose and turned round to yell more instructions to his men.

I continued on to the chancery where Osric was still engrossed in the Oneirokritikon. I asked him whether Artimedorus had written anything about seeing bronze statues in a dream.

He searched the pages of the book.

'According to him, a large bronze statute is a good sign as it symbolizes wealth. On the other hand, if the dream statue is truly enormous that portends extraordinary dangers.'

'What about a statue of a horse and rider?'

'I haven't come across anything like that. Artimedorus does say that a man who dreams of riding a well-schooled and obedient horse will have friends and family to support him throughout his life.'

'I'm sure he also provides a more bleak interpretation,' I said.

Osric gave a thin smile.

'If a poor woman dreams that she is riding a horse through a city street, he says it means she will become a prostitute.'

I sat down at my desk and took up my pen, but before I

started on Osric's dictation I told him what had been said during my visit to Bertha and Adelaide.

'As far as I know, Pepin's in good health. Yet one interpretation of the dream is that the king will lose his son,' I concluded.

Osric glanced towards the door to make sure that we would not be overheard.

'Master, as I mentioned earlier, slaves and servants gossip. Pepin has not been formally declared as the heir to the king. There are important men around him who fear that if the king has another son, Pepin will be passed over.'

'Because the king never married his mother?' I said.

'Precisely. These so-called friends of Pepin are encouraging him to seize the throne before it is too late.'

A chill ran through me. Should Pepin be plotting to seize the throne, and his scheme was discovered, he was almost certain to be put to death. Before that, there would be uproar within the royal family, accusations and counter-accusations as to who knew about the plot, and who was involved. Any outsider who might provide information would be questioned. If Bertha or her sister breathed a word of what I had said about their brother's doubtful future, I would be under suspicion of knowing about Pepin's plan and not warning the authorities. They would want details from me, extracted on the rack if necessary. I had already experienced the lengths to which a ruler would go to protect his position against rivals. My blunder with Bertha and her sister meant that King Offa was far from the only threat to my survival.

I found myself wishing that I had never told Bertha about the Book of Dreams.

*

Gerard mended very slowly. For his convalescence he was moved to a house within the town, the property of a rich contractor. I went there to tell him about the poison mushroom Osric had identified, and found the old man sitting up in bed, a marten fur cloak wrapped around his shoulders. His face looked strained and pale under the thick felt hat that hid his white hair. But Gerard was hardier than his frail appearance suggested. His eyes were bright with intelligence.

'So that's what nearly did for the two of us,' he said after I had explained.

'Osric came across it growing in the forest.'

The old man snorted.

'The kitchen is staffed with fools.'

'I've been wondering if it was more than an accident,' I said cautiously.

He shot me a glance from under bushy eyebrows.

'You think it was put into the pottage deliberately?'

'The thought had occurred to me, but I don't know who might want to injure me.'

He smiled grimly.

'In other words you believe that I have enemies.'

'I meant no offence,' I apologized. 'But if you do, it is best if you and I were aware of them.'

A thin, blotched hand emerged from under the cloak to scratch his chin.

'Everyone acquires enemies sooner or later.'

It was my turn to draw an inference.

'I don't believe I've been here long enough to merit them.'

'What about enemies you left behind. They could have a long reach.'

I thought about King Offa and my turncoat uncle.

'I'm much too insignificant,' I concluded.

'Less and less so,' he replied. 'I gather you made quite a stir at the hunt and that a certain princess thinks highly of you.'

I avoided the old man's sly gaze. It seemed that servants were not the only ones to gossip.

'Hroudland thinks I was poisoned as a means of getting at him.'

Gerard considered my suggestion.

'That's possible. Everyone has noticed that you and Hroudland are very close. He is the king's nephew and could be the target for ambitious rivals.' Abruptly he changed the subject. 'Did your servant Osric manage to translate any of that book I gave you?' he asked.

'He's about halfway through. It's not a leech book. It's about how to understand the meaning of dreams,' I answered.

'Does it contain any truth?'

I decided to take Gerard into my confidence. The old man was wise in the ways of palace politics. Maybe he could suggest how I could deal with the consequences should Bertha and her sister speak to others about my interpretation of their father's dream.

'I've put it to the test, but it's too early for any result.' I told him how I had used the book to interpret the king's dream of losing the sight of one eye.

Gerard sat very still, his face grave.

'If your interpretation is accurate, that book is more powerful than any sword.'

'Double-edged, then. Every dream has more than one explanation, and I'll need to learn how to choose the right one.'

When the old man next spoke, he was deadly serious.

'Patch, if the dream book is genuine, others will want to get their hands on it. The more you learn how to use it, the more danger you will be in.'

Chapter Eleven

PROOF OF THE DREAM BOOK'S accuracy came in mid-January when Bertha asked me to explain another of her father's dreams. The winter, though intensely cold, had brought very little snow to interrupt the king's favourite sport. Day after day he was away at hunting camp, returning to Aachen briefly to attend to affairs of state. In his absences I had spent several more nights with Bertha for I was far too besotted with her to pay any heed to the sly comments of Oton and the others. But on this occasion I was summoned in mid-morning and arrived to find her sister with her in the same reception room as before. Both women were dressed against the cold in long gowns of heavy velvet, the bands of embroidery at the neckline almost hidden beneath short fur capes.

'Last night the king dreamed of a strange horse,' Bertha informed me.

I had a momentary qualm, recalling my own vision of the bronze horse, its rider weeping blood. Her next words reassured me.

'It was a beautiful animal, a glossy, dark chestnut with white blaze on its nose. It had neither saddle nor bridle. Yet it was not wild, for its coat and mane were brushed and well cared for.'

'And what happened?'

'The horse came walking quietly towards where he was standing, and turned in through the gate of a paddock. My father was intrigued. He did not recognize the horse and he had no idea who owned such a magnificent creature.' She looked at me expectantly. 'What does your dream book have to say about that?'

I relaxed. The appearance of a riderless horse was one of the visions that the author of the Oneirokritikon had dealt with.

'Your father's dream means that he will receive a visitor, a person of importance. The more splendid the horse, the more powerful the visitor.'

Adelaide was as sceptical as before. She gave a sigh of exasperation.

'Bertha, I don't know why you pay any attention to this nonsense. Of course the king will have an important visitor. He receives important visitors all the time, whether from Byzantium or Rome or a hundred other places.'

I had to defend myself.

'But this visitor will arrive when he is not expected and the outcome could be far-reaching.'

Adelaide did not bother to conceal her disbelief.

'And when will this mysterious visitor grace our presence?' she asked. Her voice dripped with sarcasm.

'When did your father have this dream?'

'Last night, as Bertha just told you.'

I ignored her rudeness.

'That is not what I meant. Did the king have this dream last night soon after he retired, or in the middle of the night? The timing is all-important.'

'In the morning, shortly before he woke. He told us about it at breakfast,' snapped Adelaide.

'Then the visitor will arrive very soon, in the next day or two,' I said firmly.

'Why couldn't you say when the earlier dream would be fulfilled?' Adelaide asked caustically. 'The dream of my father losing an eye?'

'Because I had not yet come across the passage in the book that deals with the timing of dreams and their fulfilment,' I said.

'And now what can you add?' Adelaide demanded.

'The earlier in the night one has a dream, the longer it will take to come true,' I said.

Adelaide turned to her sister, and again I detected that air of conspiracy between the two sisters.

'Did the king mention at what time he had the dream?' I asked.

Bertha thought for a moment.

'I think it was soon after he retired to bed.'

Adelaide swung back to face me.

'How much longer could it be before the king loses a son?'

I did not like the ambitious look in her eyes.

'According to the book, the longest time between a dream and its fulfilment is twenty years.'

Her lip curled in disbelief.

'So no one would be around to see it come true.'

I held my ground.

'If you remember, Joseph dreamed of seven years of plenty in Egypt, followed by seven years of famine. So it was fully fourteen years between the dream and when the final year of near-starvation came about.'

She glared at me angrily, and then strode out of the room.

'Let's hope your interpretation of my father's latest dream is correct,' said Bertha. She was looking nervous, fearful of her older sister. 'Otherwise Adelaide may no longer keep our secret.'

*

The very next morning the stone masons and bricklayers on the scaffolding of the great hall stood gaping down at a foreign-looking cavalcade of strangers riding into the royal precinct. It was a Saracen embassy from Hispania. The newcomers had thrown open their heavy sheepskin riding coats to reveal long flowing gowns and broad silver-studded belts. Their heads were wrapped in great white turbans that contrasted with their dark skins and thick, immaculately barbered black beards. Two musicians preceded them blowing wind instruments of wood that looked like reed pipes and made an unearthly wailing sound.

The king had not received notice of their approach. He was away in the forest, hunting.

'Look at their horses. No wonder they made such good time,' muttered Berenger as he stood beside me in the small crowd, observing the spectacle. The embassy's horses were small and neat, with high arched necks and well-muscled hindquarters. They moved with a high-stepping grace, almost dancing, and their well-brushed manes had been allowed to grow like curtains until they reached almost to the ground. With bright red bridles and saddle cloths edged with gold braid, they made a splendid sight in the wintry sunshine.

The flamboyant procession made its way past the admiring spectators as far as the portico of the great hall. There the visitors dismounted in a swirl of expensive silks to be greeted by the count of the palace and led inside.

'Their leader is the governor of Barcelona, name of Suleyman al Arabi.' said Engeler. He had spoken with one of the officials making hasty preparations to accommodate the embassy. 'He's brought with him two other walis, as they call their governors, from Zaragoza and from Huesca.'

'What could possibly bring them all the way here in midwinter?' asked Berenger.

'Whatever it is, this is more than a courtesy visit,' said Gerin.

A royal messenger was hurrying across to intercept us. He headed straight for me and said in a loud voice.

'Your presence is requested by the Princess Bertha.'

Otto sniggered.

I gave him a nasty look and followed the messenger to the side entrance of the royal apartments. Bertha was waiting for me in the private audience chamber. She was jubilant, eyes sparkling with triumph. Adelaide was nowhere to be seen.

'The king is not yet back, but I'm sure he will want to meet you as soon as he hears how you interpreted his dream,' she said.

I recalled Gerard's warning about the dangers of being recognized as an expert in dream prediction.

'There's more than one way to interpret a dream,' I protested.

'That's why you must talk with the king,' she insisted. 'He will want to hear from you the different meanings.'

She laid a hand on my sleeve.

'Don't worry, Sigwulf. It will be for the king to decide which outcome to believe.'

*

The summons from the king came a week later. Whatever had been discussed with the Saracen embassy was kept confidential to the king and his advisors, so I had no idea what to expect when I entered the royal chambers. It was the same room where I had first met the king more than half a year before, and little had changed. The clay model of the palace was still on the central table, and Carolus, standing by the window, was again dressed in the belted tunic and leggings of an ordinary citizen. I noted that he had less of a paunch, doubtless the result of so much energetic hunting in the forests. As I bowed, I realized that his view from the window overlooked the private entrance that I used for my visits to Bertha. I felt suddenly uncomfortable.

To my surprise, Gerard was in attendance. The old man was seated in a chair, a heavy woollen shawl wrapped around his thin shoulders. I had not thought him well enough to leave his sick bed.

'Count Gerard has been sharing his knowledge of the Saracens with me,' began the king briskly. 'My daughter tells me that you foretold the arrival of their embassy.'

'You foretold their coming yourself, Your Majesty,' I said diplomatically. 'I merely interpreted your dream with the help of a book.'

The king looked unimpressed.

'You also claim that their visit will have important results.'

'That is what your dream would indicate, sire. But there is no clue as to what those results will be.'

The king turned to Gerard.

'What do you make of them?' he asked, referring to the three Saracen ambassadors.

'I do not know them personally, my lord,' Gerard said. 'I understand that they are seeking your help against their overlord.'

'And I have to decide whether to give it to them,' the king grunted. He began to pace up and down the room with long, heavy strides. Occasionally a floorboard creaked beneath his weight. 'The Saracen Lord of Barcelona takes the lead. He asks me to bring an army in Hispania to aid him against his rival, the Emir of Cordoba.'

'There is always much rivalry among the Saracens,' Gerard agreed. 'They form factions and fight among themselves. It was what saved Septimania in my father's day. The leaders of the Saracen invasion quarrelled among themselves.'

'So you don't think this embassy is here to draw us into a trap?'

'Treachery is possible, but unlikely,' said Gerard.

The king stopped his pacing and studied me, his grey eyes shrewd and probing.

'If I had more dreams to tell you, young man, perhaps they would reveal what answer I should give these Saracens.' He treated me to a sour smile. 'Or should I try taking one of those potions which produce strange and peculiar visions.'

'Only a dream that comes naturally to the sleeper can possess meaning. The author of the dream book is clear on that,' I replied meekly.

'But is it not also true that a person often dreams of people and places known from real life?'

'That is the case,' I agreed.

'You yourself dream.' It was more a statement than a question.

'I do, my lord.'

The king gave a short, mirthless laugh.

'So, if I cannot force myself to have a dream that will reveal the true intentions of these Saracens, I can do the next best thing.'

My heart sank as I realized what he was about to say.

'I can place a dreamer among them, someone to get to know them so well that they appear in his dreams, and he will learn what they intend.' He chuckled softly. 'You might say that I will have an insight into their minds as well as into the future.' The king shouted for an attendant, and a man appeared instantly at the door. 'Escort this young man to the chancery. I am attaching him to the mission that returns with the Saracens. They leave in two days' time.' Carolus looked down at me from his great height, his face a mask of royal authority. 'Speak with Alcuin. Tell him why you are going to Hispania. He will give more detailed instructions.'

I bowed and began to walk towards the door.

'And be sure to take your crippled servant with you,' the king added. 'He may overhear some useful information. I'll tell Bertha you may be absent for some time.'

I left the chamber, stunned. The king must have spies and

informants everywhere. It was reasonable to suppose that Gerard had told him that Osric was a Saracen by origin, but I wondered how often the king had stood at the window looking down at my comings and goings to his daughter's chamber.

*

Alcuin greeted me without enthusiasm when I tracked him down in the chancery. He was deep in conversation with two clerks from the office of records. They were discussing the correct wording for a charter document, and I had to wait until they had finished and moved away before I told him what the king intended for me.

'So that's why you asked about the meaning of Oneirokritikon,' the priest said. 'If I'd known, I'd not have told you.'

'I thought it would be a leech book, not a book of dreams,' I said.

'The Church does not approve of such writings.'

'I'm sure that the Oneirokritikon is harmless.'

Alcuin arched his brows in disbelief.

'Dreams are the raw material of necromancy and superstition. Often the Devil works through them.'

'Yet an angel of the Lord used a dream to tell Joseph the husband of Mary that her unborn child was conceived by the Holy Spirit,' I objected.

He drew a sharp breath of displeasure and stepped past me.

'If you will follow me, I will do my best to carry out the king's instructions.'

He led me to where the great map of tiles was still laid out on the trestle table. Instinctively I looked towards the range of mountains where I had pricked my finger. Today there was no glint of light.

Alcuin's sandals clacked softly as he made his way round to reach over the map and point to a spot on the coast of Hispania.

'The leader of the embassy, Suleyman al Arabi, governs this region centred on the two cities of Barcelona and Girona. He is accompanied by the governors of Zaragoza and Huesca. All three are at war with their overlord, the Emir of Cordoba. His name is Abdurahman.' Alcuin hitched back the sleeve of his gown. 'They are asking Carolus to bring an army into Hispania to aid them. In return they promise to place their lands under his protection. Note how their lands lie just beyond this mountain range which presently forms our border with Hispania.'

He brushed his hand across the tiles and I half expected him to flinch and draw back, his finger bleeding. But nothing happened.

'The allegiance of these Saracens would be immensely valuable,' Alcuin continued. 'It would provide Frankia with a broad march, a protective frontier zone, on the far side of the mountain range.' He stepped back from the map, allowed his sleeve to fall, and thrust both hands into the sleeves. There were cold draughts in the chancery. 'Equally, this might be a trap. The Saracens may be seeking to lure our army across the mountains so that they can fall on our troops and slaughter them. They consider us to be infidels, enemies ripe for destruction.'

He gazed for a moment at the map, shoulders sagging slightly as if imagining the dreadful consequences. I recalled how I had once pointed out the danger of over-extending the kingdom.

With a slight shake of his head, Alcuin brought his attention back to the present.

'If the king thinks he can discover the intentions of the Saracens through your dreams, so be it. But I believe he is badly mistaken.' Suddenly he was briskly efficient. 'If we are to send an army across those mountains and into Hispania, we require intelligence on the conditions of the road, where to obtain water and pitch camp, the danger points where we might be ambushed, and so forth. All this you can observe as you travel with the Saracens.'

'The king has already made a spy of me,' I said gloomily.

'So when you are not dreaming, keep your eyes open.'

'And what do I do with this information when I have it?' I asked.

'You write it down and include it with the official reports that our two ambassadors will be sending back to us here in the chancery whenever possible.'

'And if I am discovered or my despatch is intercepted?' There was no need for me to add that such a discovery would discredit the embassy in the eyes of their hosts and probably lead to my arrest. I had no idea how the Saracens dealt with spies they caught, but it was unlikely to be a pleasant experience.

A hint of a smile appeared on Alcuin's face.

'Let me give you something.' He led me to a small side room which had the appearance of being his personal office. One wall was lined with shelves holding neatly folded vestments, writing supplies of pumice, paper, quills and an ink horn. He took a small box down from an upper shelf.

'You can use this,' he said. From the box he took out a flat wooden disc about six inches in diameter.

'Caesar's Wheel,' he said. The disc had an inner and outer ring. Both were marked with letters of the alphabet. Alcuin rotated the outer ring so that the letters were displaced against one another.

I grasped the principle.

'I use the wheel to code my report. If I want to write an A, for example, and the A lies opposite the letter F, that is what I write.'

He gave a nod of approval.

'Correct. It won't fool an intelligent observer, but someone who scarcely knows how to read would be puzzled, especially if they are more accustomed to the Saracen way of writing.'

It occurred to me that anyone who could read both Saracen and Western script would be no fool, but I said nothing.

Alcuin returned the device to its box.

'To make matters a little more challenging for anyone who tries to decipher your code, we will vary the offset. Taking the letter A on the outer ring as your reference, I suggest you offset it differently at the start of each sentence you write, according to a sequence based on a single word.'

'What is this key word?' I asked.

'Something you can easily remember.' There was a hint of a twinkle in his eye. 'Why not Oneirokritikon? That should keep them guessing.'

He was about to hand me the box when I asked, 'Have the ambassadors been told that I will be acting as a spy?'

He shook his head.

'They will know only that they must give your despatches to their courier who in turn will hand it on to me. The courier, of course, will be bringing only a verbal report to His Majesty. Neither of his envoys is comfortable with pen and paper.'

'Who are these two envoys?'

Alcuin's reply shook me to the core.

'The king has selected Ganelon and Gerin.'

Chapter Twelve

'GANELON! THAT DEVIOUS REPTILE!' Hroudland let out a string of oaths. 'The king must be out of his mind sending him with the Saracens. There'll be double-dealing and lies. The only person who will come out of it unscathed will be Ganelon, that slimy bastard.'

My friend was falling-down drunk when I finally located him and told him my news. It was late afternoon and he was lolling with Berenger on a bench in the changing room of the thermae. The water in the pool was pleasantly warm even in mid-winter, and the count sometimes went there to swim and then carouse with his close companions. The baths, being some distance from the main palace, were a place to go for heavy drinking sessions as the king was known to discourage drunkenness.

Hroudland waved his cup, slopping the contents.

'Patch, you couldn't have a worse travelling companion,' he announced, slurring his words.

'He can't be that bad,' I protested.

Even intoxicated, Hroudland still had the look and manner of the handsome aristocrat despite the flushed face and owlish expression.

'Don't you believe it. Ganelon will always try to save his own skin. He tried to get the king to send me with the Saracens. Serve him right that he's been given the job instead.'

'I don't understand.' The sight of Hroudland helpless and groggy made me uncomfortable.

'The journey to Barcelona could prove to be a suicide mission. The Saracens turn against you, and you're done for.' Hroudland drew his finger across his throat and made a gurgling sound. He swayed on the bench and would have slipped off it if Berenger had not caught him and held him upright.

Hroudland belched and rose to his feet. He staggered forward and threw an arm around my shoulders and hugged me to him. Judging by the smell of his breath he was drinking hot red wine flavoured with blackthorn berries.

'Poor Patch, this may be the last time I see you. You will come to visit me in Brittany, won't you?'

Embarrassed, I pushed him away.

'I don't know what you're talking about.'

Berenger, who was more sober, explained: 'The king has appointed Hroudland to be the new Margrave of the Breton March. He leaves next week to take up his post.'

'So, Patch, you ride off to the sunshine, and I'll be heading for the rain and drizzle of the west,' said Hroudland.

My friend's melancholy was contagious. All of a sudden I felt depressed. I knew I would miss Hroudland. I valued him as a confidant and comrade.

'I'll have Gerin for company. He's being sent to Hispania as well,' I said.

Hroudland swayed back and hiccupped.

'Pity the king didn't think to send him to Brittany with me. Gerin gave Offa a hand with sorting out his neighbours.'

It was the first time that I had heard any reference to link Gerin to Offa since Osric had told me that one of Gerin's servants was curious whether I had ever been at Offa's court. But I had no chance to ask any questions because Hroudland had begun taking off his clothes.

'Come on, Berenger! Time for another swim,' he said with another drunken hiccup. 'We won't have thermae in Brittany. Let's make the most of it.'

I turned away dejectedly. I had not got over my dread of the murky green waters of the pool, and I had to go and find Osric and tell him to be ready to leave early next morning.

That night was my last in Aachen for many months and it was filled with foreboding. I had great difficulty in falling asleep, and when I did so I dreamed that I was on the side of a strange and barren mountain. It was in near-darkness and Hroudland was with me. Together we scrambled down the steep slope, descending at breakneck speed, careering off rough boulders, bruising hands and knees as we slipped and fell, then getting back to our feet and hurtling onward. Dragons with armoured scales flew around our heads and from clefts in the rocks sprang loathsome creatures that snarled and showed their fangs. I awoke drenched in sweat and wondering if the Book of Dreams could explain such grotesque fantasies.

One thing was certain: I would take the Oneirokritikon with me to Hispania so that Osric and I could finish the translation. I needed Artimedorus's writings to help me to spy into the minds of the Saracens as King Carolus had instructed.

A raw wind was lifting little spirals of powdered snow, sending them spinning across the frozen ground in front of the great hall as I joined the other members of Carolus's delegation to Hispania assembling on horseback. The icy blast was making my eyes stream and, although I was wearing heavy gauntlets, I had already lost all feeling in my fingers. It was only an hour after sunrise and Osric had brought my bay gelding from the stable and was riding a rangy-looking chestnut mare. He held a laden pack animal on a lead rope, and I noted a long package which I guessed contained my bow and sword. I had packed the Book of Dreams in my saddlebags, together with pages of the translation I had made so far. All around me the other riders were bundled up in thick clothes. I recognized Ganelon by the glimpse of a black beard poking out from the hood of his heavy jacket, and Gerin by the red shield slung across his back. The Saracens had not yet mounted but were holding their horses by the reins; there seemed to be some sort of problem.

An official emerged from the portico of the great hall and hurried across to Ganelon and said something to him. I saw Ganelon jerk the reins in an angry gesture, then wheel his horse round and come trotting across to shout to Gerin.

'The Saracens are refusing to leave until we have more horses,' he called.

'What's the matter with them?' asked Gerin. He sounded grumpy.

'They say we need to bring spare mounts, or we'll slow them down. They've already refused a cavalry escort for the same reason.'

I looked across at the Saracens. They wore heavy riding cloaks and soft boots, and carried short whips. Their small horses were no longer decked out in the finery of their arrival. Manes and tails were neatly plaited and tied up. Bridles and saddles were workmanlike, and when one of the Saracens picked up his horse's hoof to check, I saw a half hoop of metal armed with short spikes. I had never seen a horseshoe before. A Saracen was talking with a palace official and pointing with his whip towards the king's residence. The official set off at a run.

'What's going on?' demanded Ganelon. His horse was skittish. It stamped and snorted, edging sideways.

'They are insisting you bring couriers' horses as remounts,' the official called out, heading towards the outbuilding that housed the horses kept ready for the king's messengers.

'Impudence,' growled Gerin. He leaned forward and patted the neck of his tall stallion. With its shaggy winter coat, the animal looked even more powerful than when he rode it during our fighting practice.

Ganelon shifted in his saddle to make himself more comfortable. Apart from one slight nod, he had ignored me entirely.

'No point in making a fuss,' he said quietly to Gerin. 'We'll be in one another's company for a long time.'

After a short delay, a gang of palace ostlers appeared, leading a string of horses from the couriers' stables. They distributed the animals among us, handing out the lead ropes, and at last we were ready to set out.

We formed up in a ragged column, two royal heralds in the lead. Immediately behind them were the Saracens. Discreetly I took up my place towards the rear, just ahead of the grooms and servants. Osric was at my side and glancing at him I could see the resemblance to the Saracens in the embassy. His face had the same sharply defined features and dark complexion.

'Did you ever hear anything more about Gerin's time at King Offa's court?' I asked.

Osric's eyes flicked to where Gerin rode ahead of us.

'No, but his servant is travelling with us. I'll see what I can find out,' he replied.

'I had a strange dream last night. When we have a chance I want us to see if there is some meaning to it.'

Osric turned his brown eyes towards me.

'So you are beginning to have faith in the book?'

'I am, but it would be better if we kept quiet about it, at least for now.'

There was a shouted command from the front of the column.

One of the heralds blew a short blast on a horn, and we began to move. I twisted in my saddle and looked back towards the king's residence, wondering if Bertha was watching us leave. I doubted it. There had been no opportunity to say farewell to her, and my goodbye to Hroudland had been less than satisfactory. The newly appointed Margrave of the Breton March had been stretched out on his bed with his head under a pillow, suffering a bad hangover. He had groaned and with a muffled voice told me to go to the Devil.

*

The brisk pace of the Saracen riders came as an unwelcome surprise. Their horses moved with short, rapid steps, covering the ground with a smooth, measured beat while their riders sat at ease in their deep, comfortable saddles. To keep up with them the rest of us had to either trot or canter, and this tested our heavier mounts. Soon the muscles in my legs and back were aching and I felt my bay gelding beginning to flag. The groans and muttered curses from other riders told me that they too were suffering. From time to time someone would break the torment by pulling out of line and going up ahead at a gallop. But then his horse would tire and slow to a walk, and not long afterwards the Saracen cavalcade came stepping by at the same brisk rate, apparently unflagging. By the time we stopped for a brief midday break, most of our riders had already changed horses, glad that remounts were available. When we finally halted for the night and slid painfully down from our saddles, we had covered the same distance Arnulf's eel cart would have travelled in a week.

So it continued, relentlessly, day after day. We rose in the dark, set out on the road in half-light of dawn and often did not reach our day's destination until well after sunset. Many of our horses broke down or went lame. If they were not immediately

replaced, their riders were left behind. Our group steadily dwindled until we numbered less than a score of riders in addition to
the Saracens. Not one of them fell by the way. We had no need
of guides because our path was along the old Roman roadways.
Sometimes the original paving remained, the stone slabs cracked
and scored with grooves left by cartwheels over the centuries.
Elsewhere the surface had deteriorated into a rutted gravel track
that followed the lines of ancient causeways over marsh and
bogland, bringing us to sturdy Roman bridges whose solid stone
arches still crossed the rivers. During the first week of our journey
many of the smaller streams were frozen solid so that we could
ride across on the ice. The Saracen horses went ahead on their
spiked shoes, while the rest of us dismounted and cautiously crept
across, leading our nervous mounts.

The scenery changed very slowly. Our route avoided high
ground, as everywhere was in the grip of winter. The trees in the
vast forest tracts were leafless and stark, as were the orchards
outside the villages. The ploughed fields were bleak expanses of
bare soil. Nothing moved. The country people were keeping
indoors close to their fires and if no smoke rose from the chim-
neys we knew they shared their hovels with their cattle, huddling
together for warmth. We passed quickly through the towns,
having no need to buy supplies or seek lodgings. The king owned
royal farms all along our route, some so vast that they rivalled my
father's little kingdom in acreage. Every steward on them was
obliged to feed us from his stores and give us shelter. If no royal
demesne was convenient, the dukes and counts, who held their
lands from the king, provided all we needed. Our progress was so
swift and unhampered that I was able to measure it by the way
the weather changed. We left Aachen under skies so dull and
overcast that it was impossible to tell the direction of the sunrise,
and in the evening the daylight ebbed seamlessly into night.

Three weeks later we were riding in sunshine so bright that it hurt the eyes, and the night sky was so clear that the stars glittered in the bitter cold with an intensity that I had never seen before. By then we were already within sight of the jagged crests of the snow-covered mountains marking the limit of the king's realm.

Here, taking us unawares, the Saracens abruptly announced one morning that they would be going their different ways. Suleyman al Arabi, the Wali of Barcelona, was to continue straight ahead, taking the coast road direct to his own country. The governor of Heusca would accompany him. Husayn, the Wali of Zaragoza, intended to turn aside and use a different route home through a mountain pass further west.

We had spent the night in the hamlet that had sprung up at the fork in the road. It was a poverty-stricken place of small houses built of loose unmortared stone, their wooden roof tiles held down with heavy rocks. Ganelon, Gerin and I hurriedly met in a disused building on the central square to discuss the change of plan. Judging by the smell and the droppings underfoot, the place was used as a sheep shed.

'We have to decide whether to stay together or divide,' Ganelon announced.

'We should stay with Suleyman. He's their leader,' said Gerin. Throughout the journey he had been his usual taciturn self and had barely exchanged a dozen gruff sentences with me.

Ganelon turned to me.

'What do you think?' he asked.

I was surprised to be consulted. Ganelon had treated me as some sort of unwanted addition to the embassy ever since we had set off from Aachen. I recalled my instructions from Alcuin that I was to gather information on the possible routes for an army to enter Hispania.

'What do we know about the different roads the Saracens will take?'

'The coast road to Barcelona is well travelled. I have not heard anything about the road through the mountains which Husayn proposes,' Ganelon told me.

'Then I will go with Husayn,' I said promptly. Ganelon studied me for a long moment, his eyes watchful, and I wondered if he knew or had guessed the reason for my choice.

'I'm for Barcelona,' Gerin confirmed.

There was a sudden burst of some foreign language from outside. The words sounded angry. One of the Saracens was shouting, probably chasing away a villager who had got too close to their panniers and saddlebags. The Saracens were likely to set out at any moment.

Ganelon came to a quick decision.

'If Sigwulf is prepared to accompany Husayn to Zaragoza, he can rejoin us in Barcelona in, say, three weeks' time. I'll check with the Saracens that they agree to this arrangement.'

As we hurried out into the village square, Osric was standing beside the stone water trough in the centre of the village, talking with Gerin's servant.

'Ganelon and Gerin are accompanying Governor Suleyman to Barcelona, and we'll be taking the road through the mountains with Husayn, direct to Zaragoza,' I told him.

Osric waited until Gerin's servant was safely out of earshot before replying.

'I'm glad to hear it,' he said softly.

I gave him a sharp look. There had been no hint of trouble on the journey. No one had attempted to harm me. I was beginning to think that the mushroom poisoning and the attack in the forest were unrelated accidents, or that whoever wished to hurt me had been left far behind.

'What makes you say that?'

'I've learned a little more about Gerin.'

'He has no reason to do away with me,' I said.

'He sells his sword to whoever pays him. King Offa hired him during a border quarrel with the Welsh. Gerin served as leader of a war band.'

I recalled Gerin's expertise with lance and javelin.

'How long ago was that?'

'Maybe five or six years ago.'

'Poison is not his style; an arrow in the back, maybe.'

'Gerin was present at the hunt and also at the banquet,' Osric reminded me.

Out of the corner of my eye I saw Ganelon walking across the square to where the Saracens were clustered. They were tightening their saddle girths, getting ready to depart.

'There's something more. Ganelon has already had a private meeting with Husayn,' he said.

That startled me.

'Do you know what was discussed?'

'No, Gerin's servant was up early, tending to a horse with saddle sores. He saw Ganelon go and return. The meeting lasted less than an hour.'

There was a flurry of activity on the far side of the square. The Saracens were mounting up. A gaggle of villagers surrounded them, some begging, others holding up lumps of hard cheese and strips of dried mutton, hoping for a sale. Now we were in the borderlands, we were having to purchase our own supplies.

'Everything's arranged,' Ganelon shouted at me. 'I'll see you in Barcelona in three weeks' time! Go with God!' He hurried to where Gerin and the rest of our group were already mounted and circling their animals, preparing to head off. Osric and I had to grab the reins of our own horses and hold them back to prevent them joining the others. After three weeks on the road our animals had become used to travelling together.

I watched my comrades clatter out of the village at a trot. Gerin still rode like a cavalryman on campaign. He sat square and upright in the saddle, his plain red shield bouncing against his horse's flank, with his long heavy sword slung across his back. The handle projected above his left shoulder like a cross.

Deep in thought, I turned my attention to the Saracens who had stayed behind. Four of them were sitting quietly on their horses on the far side of the square, the hoods of their riding cloaks pulled up against the chill air. They were waiting for Osric and me to join them.

'Greetings, fellow travellers,' said the nearest Saracen in good Latin as we approached. He was a little older than me, perhaps in his early twenties, plump and expensively dressed. From his air of confidence I presumed that I was being addressed by Husayn, Wali of Zaragoza. This was the first time I had seen him close up and face to face. He had a clear olive skin and large dark eyes made even darker by the application of black dye around them. He had also painted his small, delicate mouth. His lips were a striking shade of pink. If I had not known that he had just ridden across Frankia in less than three weeks, I would have mistaken him as being effeminate.

'Ambassador Ganelon tells me that you wish to accompany me to Zaragoza. I look forward to your company, so let us be friends,' he said.

'Your Excellency is to be congratulated on his excellent command of my language,' I answered diplomatically. I was thinking that Husayn's Latin was so fluent that Ganelon would not have required an interpreter at their private discussion.

The wali smiled delicately, showing small, even white teeth.

'Then we shall be able to converse as we ride.'

'Does Your Excellency know how long the journey will take?'
I asked.

'A week at the most. We are fortunate there is so little snow
this year.'

Husayn, his curiosity evident, turned his gaze on Osric.

'Your Excellency. This is Osric, my servant. He has been with
me for many years,' I explained.

Abruptly the wali switched into what must have been the
Saracen tongue and asked Osric a direct question.

There was an awkward pause as Osric looked across at me. I
nodded.

When Osric had finished his reply, the wali treated me to
another of his engaging smiles.

'Now it is you who must be congratulated. Your servant tells
me that you are a good master, and he is happy to serve you.
Come, let us get started!'

*

Thankfully, riding in company with Husayn was less gruelling
than what had gone before. The young wali rode at a steady walk
so that I could match the pace of my gelding to his mount and
he encouraged me to ride by his side. He asked many questions
about my life and later, when I ran out of answers, we continued
together in companionable silence, the white-capped mountains
gradually coming closer and the land wilder and less inhabited.
Recalling Hroudland's comment that the Saracens could turn
nasty and cut my throat, it occurred to me that no one would be
any the wiser if it happened in these remote borderlands. Yet I
sensed no threat from the Wali of Zaragoza. Husayn was courteous
and friendly and, as it turned out, also very devout. Whenever we
stopped for him and his people to say their prayers, they took a
long time. This gave me a chance to dismount and wander away

from our little group under the pretence that I needed to stretch my legs. Then, privately, I wrote down my observations for Alcuin.

Our route continued westward for two days before turning south and beginning to climb steadily through the foothills. The landscape was a dreary succession of barren hills slashed by steep-sided ravines. Watering sources were few, forage non-existent and, in many places, the road narrowed to a single track difficult for carts. The inhabitants were a sturdy, taciturn people living in small, scattered settlements located on spurs of high ground. They provided food and shelter for us and our animals in return for generous payments in silver coins from a heavy purse carried by one of Husayn's attendants, but they showed no interest in who we were or where we were going.

On the fourth day of our journey, we passed above the snow line. Now the mountain slopes were speckled with boulders poking up through the snow crust. But the track itself was almost clear. It was another cold, crisp day of bright sunshine, and we had not seen a living soul since setting out that morning. I judged that we were approaching the crest of the pass itself and I could see that Husayn was pleased with our progress.

'Normally I would be worried that snow would block the road. But tomorrow we will be over the worst and our path will begin to slope downhill,' he said cheerfully. For the past mile he had been glancing up at the sun to determine when to halt and recite the Saracen prayers that are said just after noonday. I waited patiently. I had slipped behind in writing up my notes and this was the most crucial stage of the road through the mountains.

At length we came to a narrow defile, warmed by the sun but sheltered from the wind.

'This is a good place to halt,' Husayn announced. 'After prayers, we can take some food and rest the horses.'

I dismounted stiffly and handed the reins of the bay gelding to Osric.

'I think I'll go for a stroll,' I said.

'Stay close,' warned Husayn. 'There are bears in these mountains, and wolves. They have been known to attack travellers.'

I laughed.

'I haven't seen a bear or a wolf since we began our journey.'

'Then at least take a weapon with you, just in case,' Husayn insisted.

Dutifully, I unstrapped my bow case from the packhorse and took out the weapon and a couple of arrows. I noticed the look of mild interest on Husayn's face when he saw the type of bow I was using.

Leaving the others, I walked off, picking my way carefully over the loose rocks. Behind me I could hear the sounds of the Saracens unsaddling their horses. From past experience I expected we would halt for at least an hour.

The bare hillside was open and exposed, and I was obliged to walk a little distance to find somewhere to sit privately and write my notes. I angled up the slope until I could no longer be seen from the defile. There, I found myself a patch of ground free of snow in the lee of a large boulder. I laid down my bow and arrows, sat down and took the flat box containing my writing materials from the inner pocket of my coat.

I had just slipped off my gloves and taken up the stylus when a movement caught my eye. A bird, the size and colour of a crow, was flying in low swooping arcs across the hillside. Occasionally it stopped and landed on a boulder. It was the only living creature in the immense, frozen landscape, and I wondered what it found to feed on. I watched the bird come closer until it settled on a rocky outcrop below me. I turned my attention back to the work in hand and began to scratch out a diagram of our route for the past three days. The wax tablet had hardened in the cold and the metal point of the stylus skidded on the brittle glazed surface. I pressed harder, the wax chipping and flaking. I engraved the main line of the route then started to mark the location of the mountain villages I had seen and the distance between them. The air was so still and the silence of the mountains so absolute that I clearly heard the sound of claws scrabbling on rock as the bird settled on the crest of a boulder, not six feet from me. It cawed loudly. Its voice came back as an echo from the far mountainside.

I ignored the bird and worked on, head down. I was anxious to finish my work before the Saracens thought I was overdue and came looking for me. After a short while I heard the soft flap of wings as the bird flew away. Then came a tiny clink, the sharp sound of a pebble falling on rock. I vaguely thought that the sun melting the snow must have released a stone lying on the crust.

I was concentrating so fiercely on my work that I was shocked by the loud crack as something smashed into the boulder close to my head. I jerked back and felt a sharp sting on my cheek. A round pebble, the size of a hen's egg, fell to the ground beside me.

I dropped my writing materials and sprang to my feet. Fifty yards away and slightly up the slope a shaggily dressed man was standing and whirling a strap around his head. I recognized a slinger and threw myself to the ground just as he released his second missile. I heard it whirr overhead. If it had struck me in the head the blow would have split my skull.

Seeing that he had missed, my attacker turned and began to run, dodging from rock to rock up the hillside.

A cold rage seized me. This attack was too similar to the murderous assault in the forest to be a coincidence. This time I would not let my assailant get away. I picked up my bow, nocked an arrow to the string, and then turned to judge the distance to my target. The slinger had not gone far. He had chosen to run directly uphill, thinking no doubt that he could outdistance any pursuit, and his decision had slowed him down. Evidently he had not noticed my bow lying on the ground beside me. He was running straight, not bothering to weave from side to side. He was an easy target.

Taking a deep, slow breath, I took up the tension on the bow and waited. It was like one of the archery exercises that Osric had made me repeat so often in the royal park of Aachen. My target was a dark, shapeless figure, bundled in heavy fur clothing, moving steadily and predictably up the slope away from me. In another few yards he would cross an undisturbed patch of snow. I waited until he was halfway across the white background and clearly outlined. Then, in a single controlled movement that concentrated all my rage, I drew the bow to full extent, aimed and released, watching the arrow fly up the hill.

The arrow struck the slinger squarely in the back. He pitched face forward into the slope. There was a moment's pause as though he was embracing the mountain, then his body slithered back down a few feet in the snow and came to rest.

I put the bow down. My hands shook for the first time as I collected up the writing tablet and stylus, put them away in their wooden box, and then hid them safely out of sight inside my coat. I retrieved the bow and the second of the two arrows, though I knew it would not be needed. Then I began climbing towards the man I had struck down.

There was a shout from the hillside below me. One of the Saracens was calling my name. I did not answer but kept heading upwards, taking deep deliberate breaths, each step breaking through the crust of snow.

I reached my victim. He was still lying face down, the

feathered shaft of my arrow protruding a hand's span from the grimy fabric of his heavy wolfskin jacket. I had struck him square between his shoulder blades. Callously I put the toe of my boot beneath him and turned him so he lay on his side. He was a man of middle age, his face gaunt with hunger and burned dark by the sun. A few strands of dirty grey hair straggled out from under a tight-fitting cap, also of wolfskin. A long scar, perhaps the result of a sword cut, ran from his left ear to the side of his mouth. He was breathing but only just. I had never seen him before.

I kicked him hard in the ribs.

'Who sent you?' I snarled.

His eyes opened, revealing dark brown irises, and he mumbled something in a strange, spiky-sounding language.

I kicked him again, more viciously.

'Who sent you?' I demanded.

He had not long to live. My arrow, large and heavy enough to have brought down a bear, had transfixed the man. The bloody head, three fingers' width of sharp iron, emerged from the front of his coat which he had wrapped tight around his chest, using his sling as a belt.

I felt a hand on my elbow and turned to see Husayn. He looked shocked, staring down at the dying man for several moments before turning to face me.

'Are you hurt?' he asked. I put up my hand to my cheek. It came away streaked with blood. The first slingstone must have knocked a chip off the rock where I was sitting, and the flying shard had cut my face.

'Who is this wretch?' I asked angrily.

The wali bent down and asked the man a question, speaking in the Saracen tongue.

He got a faint reply, again in that strange-sounding language. Then there was a choking sound. A grimace of pain passed across the battered face, the eyes were now shut in agony.

'What did he say?' I demanded.

Husayn straightened up.

'He's a Vascon. I recognize the language but he is too far gone for me to make out the words.'

'Search the bastard,' I growled. 'Maybe we will find a clue about who sent him.'

By now Osric had reached us. He knelt down and began to rummage through the man's garments. He found only a pouch containing half a dozen sling stones, a lump of hard cheese in one pocket, and a knife with a short stubby blade in a wooden sheath. By the time he had finished, the man had stopped breathing, choking on his own blood.

'A brigand, surely,' said Husayn.

'Then he was a foolish one. He was on his own,' I pointed out.

Osric looked to me for instructions.

'What do you want done with the body?'

'Leave it for his friends, the bears and wolves,' I said sourly and began making my way down the slope back towards our horses. I did not want to stay a moment longer in that grim place and I needed to puzzle out who could have arranged the attack. Ganelon and Gerin were many miles away. My immediate suspect was Husayn, though the wali seemed genuinely shocked by what had occurred.

*

Husayn said little for the rest of that day's ride. The incident had delayed us and we were obliged to push our horses hard to reach our destination that night, a smoky shepherd's hut that doubled as a way-station for travellers. Fortunately the shepherd was there, and he lit a fire and prepared a pot of mutton broth for his visitors. With hot food inside me, I asked Husayn to tell the shepherd that we had left a dead man in the pass. I hoped that it might lead to some information.

Husayn relayed the information and the shepherd gave me a sideways look, furtive and mistrustful. Then his face closed and, without a word, he got up and left the hut and did not return.

'Is he a Vascon, too?' I asked Husayn.

'He belongs to one of their mountain clans.'

'And you speak their language, as well as Latin? I'm impressed.'

Husayn shrugged.

'I have to. My lands border with the Vascon territory. Sometimes they see me as their protector.'

'So they're not all a bunch of cut-throat robbers.'

Husayn looked mildly unhappy at my bluntness.

'They are an ancient people. They were here even before the Romans came.'

'It's a pity that the shepherd did not see you as his protector.'

The wali grimaced.

'His clan has no need for protection. If attacked, they can retreat into their citadel. It's set on a mountain peak and impregnable. From there they laugh at their opponents until they lose interest and go away.' Husayn made a sweeping gesture, encompassing the mountains. 'For generations the mountain Vascons have hovered around these passes, extracting treasure from travellers, by force or by guile. This clan's citadel is said to contain a great hoard of raw bullion, as well as plates and cups of solid gold, bowls studded with gems, loose jewels and precious fabrics.' He gave a bleak smile, adding, 'Naturally no outsider has ever seen such marvels with their own eyes.'

'So no excuse for murdering a lone traveller for his money,' I said bitterly.

The wali stared straight at me. His large intense eyes under their dark painted lids glittered in the firelight.

'You might have been attacked for something equally valuable.'

I looked back at him coolly.

'What do you mean?'

'Words on a page.'

I felt a cold lurch in my guts. Husayn knew that I was a spy for Alcuin. Either he had seen me making notes during the journey or perhaps Ganelon had told him.

Husayn's next words came as a surprise.

'I understand that you interpret dreams. With the aid of a book?'

Shakily, I recovered my poise.

'That is something I prefer to keep to myself. Some people regard it as devil's work.'

Husayn nodded gravely.

'They are wrong. The messenger of God – may the peace and blessings of God be upon him – was also an interpreter of dreams. God spoke to him through them.'

I let out a slow breath.

'So you know about the Oneirokritikon.'

'It is famous. My people know how it was lost, left behind in the hands of the infidels.'

'And someone told you that I have the Book of Dreams?' With a sudden surge of anger, I guessed Ganelon had passed on the information.

Once again, Husayn surprised me with his answer.

'I knew that Count Gerard's family had possession of the book. When I was in Aachen, I offered to buy it from him for a great price. But he told me that it was no longer in his keeping.'

'Did he say he had given it to me?'

'No. But one of your king's daughters was heard to boast that you had foretold the coming of our embassy to Aachen. So I guessed that the Book of Dreams had passed into your hands.'

'I may have left it behind in Aachen,' I pointed out.

The wali treated me to a veiled look.

'I don't think so. No one would leave behind such a precious object, least of all someone who travels with a servant who can help him read it.' Husayn leaned forward and laid a hand gently on my arm. 'I respect your ownership of the dream book. I would not take it from you by force. But should you ever wish to sell it, I would pay a great price.'

Chapter Thirteen

WE REACHED ZARAGOZA three days later. It was mid-morning and the air crisp and invigorating, the cloudless winter sky a pale washed-out blue. The city had been alerted to the governor's approach and an escort of Saracen cavalry came jingling out to meet us among the plum and apple orchards that ringed the city. The troopers made a cheerful show in their close-fitting mail jackets and burnished metal helmets, and they had tied banners of dark crimson silk around their spear heads. They swung in behind us as we passed through the main gate in the centuries-old city wall. Built of brownish-yellow blocks of stone, the wall was immensely thick and topped with dozens of semi-circular defensive towers, all of them in good repair. The gates themselves were plated with heavy iron sheets. I made a mental note to report to Alcuin that Zaragoza would not easily be taken by storm.

Within the wall, the city was a mixture of the familiar and the exotic. Some passers-by, fair-skinned and fair-haired, would have been unremarkable in Frankia. They dressed in tunics and leggings under warm outer garments, for winter in Zaragoza was cool without having the biting edge of more northern climates. Other citizens were more exotic. They wore bulky turbans in bright colours and stripes. A few preferred a close-fitting lace skull cap or a tall, stylish bonnet in black felt. When I asked Husayn about these differences, he told me that the bonnet-wearers were more traditional in their tastes and wished to emphasize that they came from the Saracen lands further east.

'I govern a city of many peoples and faiths,' he said ruefully and indicated a side street where it disappeared into a warren of narrow alleyways and lanes. 'Down there is the Jewish quarter. Next to it is the area where the Vascons live. It's no easy task controlling such a mix of citizens.'

He pointed out an officious-looking person fingering a bolt of cloth on a market barrow. The stallholder was looking on nervously, occasionally darting forward with obsequious gestures to help unroll the cloth.

'See that man there, with an assistant holding a set of weighing scales. He's one of my market inspectors. He's checking the quality of the goods for sale. If he finds a cheat, he will punish him with a fine or confiscation of all his goods, regardless of race or creed.'

My eye was caught by the sight of a black man, the first I had ever seen. Standing at the edge of the street, he was displaying a basket of what looked like fist-sized pine cones, greyish green in colour.

'What's that he's selling?' I asked.

'Alcachofa, we call it. It's a vegetable. You'll taste some this evening,' said the wali. He raised his whip to acknowledge a greeting from a distinguished-looking grey-beard wearing a long dark-brown woollen cloak edged in fur. 'The plant is said to be an effective cure for someone who has eaten poison.'

I gave him a sharp glance, but he seemed oblivious to the effect of his remark.

We continued down the main thoroughfare, which was lined with two- and three-storey houses. Most were in good repair, though some were losing their plaster, and a few were boarded up. Halfway along it we were obliged to pull aside our horses to squeeze past an immense load of firewood piled on a donkey, its head and tail scarcely visible. The donkey's owner was shouting abuse at the driver of a mule cart blocking the roadway. I commented that several words in his stream of insults had a familiar ring to them and was told that the citizens of Zaragoza had even more languages than religions.

Eventually we arrived in the central square. It was dominated by the gleaming newly built dome and spire of what the wali proudly told me was the place of worship his father had paid for. Directly across the square was a long, white-washed wall. Twice the height of a man, it was blank except for a single archway shaped like an upside-down horseshoe. This was closed with a pair of double doors of dark, oiled wood, which had been intricately carved and embellished with patterns of heavy, brass studs. In front, two armed men stood guard.

'Welcome to my home,' said the wali as we came to a halt in front of the doors. In the same moment they were pulled open from the inside to reveal an elderly man with a thin wispy beard waiting at the head of a band of at least a dozen servants. All of them were dressed identically in white gowns and turbans. Their waistbands were the same dark crimson as our cavalry escort.

We dismounted and grooms ran forward to take our horses and lead them away. Husayn spoke with the old man, the steward of the household, and then turned to me.

'You and your servant Osric are my guests. Your quarters are being prepared,' he declared.

Together we walked through the entrance and into a small, intimate courtyard paved with fine, pink gravel. A double line of carefully tended ornamental shrubs led towards the slim white pillars of the portico to the main building. Husayn accompanied me up a short flight of marble steps and into the antechamber. His house was built as an open square and through an archway ahead of me I observed another courtyard, even larger than the first. Flowerbeds bordered a long, rectangular pool. In the centre of the pool rose a jet of water which fell back, making a pleasant splashing sound. Like the phenomenon of a black man, it was the first time I had ever seen a fountain.

'You will forgive me if I leave you in the care of my steward,' said the wali. 'After such a long absence I have much to discuss with my councillors. God willing, we will dine together after evening prayers.'

He moved away to join two grave-looking men, both wearing high Saracen bonnets who had been hovering in the background. The elderly steward escorted Osric and me along the colonnaded gallery that surrounded the central courtyard. At the far end he turned to his left and, opening a door, showed us into a set of rooms. Our panniers and saddlebags had already been placed inside. The steward bowed formally and withdrew, closing the door behind him. I heard a click.

I gazed about me, overawed by the level of comfort. High glazed windows let in daylight and made the room bright and cheerful. The walls were covered with tiles painted with patterns of flowers, blue on white. The plaster ceiling was intricately moulded into geometric shapes that had been subtly picked out in muted shades of red and green. Rich carpets were spread on the floor and draped over low couches. A lantern crafted from perforated copper hung by a chain from the ceiling. On a low table a tray with a bowl of fruit, a jug and porcelain cups had been placed. By comparison, Carolus's private apartments in Aachen were a cowshed.

Osric had paused, as if reluctant to step further into the room.

'I once lived in a house like this,' he said quietly, his voice full of a wistful sadness, 'though not so large or opulent. My father was a well-known doctor.'

I turned to him in surprise. It was the first time he had ever mentioned his own family.

'I studied to follow in his profession. But he died of a fever he caught from one of his patients and, in my sorrow and anger at life's whims, I decided I wanted nothing more to do with medicine. I chose to go to sea as a merchant and, as you know, was wrecked on my very first voyage.'

There was such aching distress in his face that an impulse made me say, 'Would you like to return to that life when this is over?'

He thought for a moment, considering his reply, and then shook his head sadly.

'It would be all but impossible. These are not my people, and there is no place for me among them. You should realize that Saracens can be as different from one another as Greeks are from Franks, or Saxons from Romans.'

I went across to the door and tried to open it. As I suspected, it was locked.

Osric dropped his voice almost to a whisper.

'Politics here are dangerous. Today Husayn is an ally of the governor of Barcelona. Tomorrow he may switch his allegiance to Barcelona's most bitter enemy.'

I recalled what old Gerard had told me of the in-fighting among the Saracens and why the king had sent me to Hispania.

'Osric, I'm going to need your help more than ever before,' I said, speaking softly in case anyone was listening outside the door. 'I need to learn whether the wali is genuine in seeking the king's help against his enemies.'

'I'll keep my ears open,' murmured Osric. He seemed to have regained his usual careful poise and began unpacking our luggage. I explored our new quarters. Beyond the living area was a sleeping room and then a small marble-lined wash room. There towels had been laid out. A wall alcove held a display of jars containing various creams and on a wooden stand was a large metal basin. I dipped my finger into it. The water it contained was hot.

'If this is to be our prison, it's a comfortable one,' I said, returning to the main room where Osric had opened an inlaid chest and found a store of clean clothes in the Saracen style. I held up one of the garments for inspection. It was a long gown of fine wool with an embroidered edging. I sniffed. It had a pleasant slightly musty smell.

'What's that?' I asked.

'Kafur, a perfume to keep the garment sweet and the insects away. It's also used as flavouring in cooking.' Osric allowed himself a grim smile. 'Too much kafur in your food is fatal, and there is no known cure.'

'I doubt the wali is planning to do away with me just yet,' I said. 'We'll get on with translating the Oneirokritikon until I'm called for the evening meal. I have a feeling that the wali will want to talk to me about it.'

*

Washed and changed into a gown, I sat down cross-legged on a cushion to use the low desk the wali provided for his guests. There was a metal stylus in place of a quill, and though the inkpot was familiar there was neither parchment nor vellum, only leaves of what looked like pale stiff fabric.

'What's this?' I asked, holding one up to the light to examine it more closely. I could see what looked like matted fibres in the material.

'Old rags soaked in quick lime, then washed and pounded together and dried into a sheet you can write on,' explained Osric.

'It doesn't feel very durable,' I said dubiously and wrote out a trial sentence. The tip of the stylus scratched and skipped on the rough surface but the result was legible.

Osric resumed his place in the Book of Dreams where we had left off our translation, and we settled down to work. We had reached the last few pages of the book by the time the light began to fade, and not long afterwards we heard the call to evening prayer and then a knock on the door. The chief steward was outside, waiting to escort me to dine with the wali. To my surprise, I saw that the meal was to be in the central courtyard, in the open air despite the winter chill. Carpets had been spread under the arches of the colonnaded gallery, lamps and cushions for two people arranged, and a row of lanterns lit and placed along the marble rim of the pool. The reflections shimmered in the ripples radiating from the fountain which was still sending up its jet of water. Above, the dark immensity of a cloudless sky was full of stars.

Husayn was waiting to greet me. He had changed into a pale-grey robe edged with gold brocade and when he stepped forward into the light of the lamps I saw he had refreshed the black eye-lining and his lip colour. He looked relaxed and self-assured, very much the master in his own home.

'It is such a fine night I thought we should dine in traditional style,' he said.

I took my seat on to the carpet. To my surprise it felt warm. I laid my hand on its surface to make sure. Husayn noted my interest.

'We have to thank Zaragoza's early rulers for installing a system of sending hot air beneath the floor tiles as well as leaving us with strong city walls and a never-failing water supply,' he murmured, a subtle reminder of his city's strength to resist attack.

The wali was a gracious and attentive host. A relay of servants brought out the trays of food, and he explained in careful detail how each dish had been prepared: lamb baked within a coating of olive oil, salt and turmeric; rice flavoured with saffron and then a handful of dried and chopped jujube mixed in; sherbet prepared from the juices of crushed pomegranate and orange. So many of the names and tastes were new to me that I almost failed to notice the alcachofa roasted in oil that the wali had remembered to order from his kitchen.

'Nearly everything you have eaten this evening was produced within a day's journey of Zaragoza,' he said contentedly as we finished the meal. He gestured for the servants to clear away the remains of our feast. A plate of dried figs was set down between us, along with a silver ewer of water and a bowl so that we could wash our hands. Then the attendants collected up the nearest lamps and withdrew, leaving only the lanterns around the pool and, close to us, a single lighted wick floating in a small earthenware bowl of scented oil. The wali waited until we were alone, then he turned towards me. His face was in shadow making his expression inscrutable. I sensed that he was about to broach the main topic of the evening.

'How can I convince you to part with the Book of Dreams?' he asked gently.

'Your Excellency, Count Gerard is still the owner of the Oneirokritikon. The book is only on loan while I translate the text.'

'And will you return it to him when you have completed the work?'

'I will.'

The wali was silent for several moments, then in the same soft, even tone he asked, 'But you will keep your copy of the translation?'

'Yes, I suppose so.' The answer seemed obvious.

'Then you accept that you have the right to allow a copy to be made.'

Too late, I saw the trap that I had fallen into.

Husayn's voice took on a more urgent edge.

'That book belonged to my people for generations. It is written in our language and in our script. Wise men studied it. Rulers consulted it.'

I thought quickly. Rather than offend the wali by stubbornly denying him the book, I should use it to my advantage.

'Your Excellency, I am willing to allow a copy to be made, but on two conditions.'

Husayn leaned forward into the lantern light and there was a hint of a smile on his pink lips. 'Name your price.'

'I intend to give my servant his freedom. I want you to appoint him to a position in your court. If Osric later chooses to return to his own country, you will assist him in doing so.'

The wali reached forward and selected a dried fig from the bowl.

'Easily done, and what is your second condition?'

I took a deep breath.

'You must tell me what Count Ganelon discussed with you privately on the day that we left the others and took the direct route to Zaragoza.'

Slowly and deliberately Husayn sank his teeth into the fig, closing his eyes as he savoured the flavour. He swallowed and then asked, 'Why is that so important to you?'

'It may help me understand who my enemies are,' I replied.

Husayn finished eating the fig, picked up the silver ewer and began to trickle water over his fingers.

'Ganelon offered to advance my interests on his return to Karlo's court,' he said calmly, using the Saracen name for the Frankish king.

I was not entirely shocked. Hroudland had often spoken of Ganelon's double-dealing.

'What reward does he expect?' I asked.

'Money, of course. Naturally I accepted his proposal, though I told him that the amount would depend on results.'

'How did he react?'

'He asked for a down payment of five hundred dinars when I got back to my treasury in Zaragoza. He needed a note – he even had a document ready for me to sign – in which I promised to pay over the money.' Husayn dried his hands on a towel and there was a low popping sound in the dark. The wali was cracking his knuckles. He spoke casually, as if talk of treason was an everyday occurrence. 'Ganelon said that the down payment would help him to dispose of a rival at court and increase his influence as a royal councillor and that would therefore also be to my benefit.'

I already knew the answer, but I asked anyway.

'Did he say who this rival was?'

'Karlo's nephew. Ganelon intends to lay evidence before the king that his nephew offered to betray the Frankish army in return for my silver.'

'But that is absurd!' I burst out. 'The king's nephew, Count Hroudland, is too far away. He's been appointed the Margrave of the Breton March. How can he have made such an offer to you?'

Somewhere in the city a dog barked, and was answered by another. There was a furious storm of barking as other dogs joined in. When silence returned, the wali spoke quietly.

'The note I signed for Ganelon says that *you* would collect the five hundred dinars. It does not mention on whose behalf. I did think it odd, but I presumed Ganelon wanted to keep his role secret.'

Now I was truly stunned. I believed what the wali had just told me. Hroudland would know nothing of the deceit until the moment he was summoned before the king and asked to defend himself against a charge of treason. Then it would be his word against Ganelon's, and Ganelon would produce the note from the Wali of Zaragoza as evidence. No wonder Ganelon had been keen for me to go with the wali; Gerin would confirm that I had chosen to leave the other Saracens and ride off directly to Zaragoza. I was known as Hroudland's close friend and confidant, and the king would accept that I had acted as a go-between. I tried to think clearly.

'You seem dismayed,' Husayn said. There was a note of genuine concern in his voice.

'The person whom Ganelon seeks to destroy is a decent and honourable man. He does not deserve such treachery,' I said.

'A close friend of yours?'

'Yes, that too,' I said. I was heartsick to think that I had been selected as the instrument of Hroudland's downfall.

'Had I known, I would not have signed that document,' the wali murmured. He watched a small, white moth circle the flame in the bowl of scented oil. When it had fluttered away, he continued in a comforting tone. 'Surely Karlo will not condemn his nephew out of hand. He will cross-examine all those concerned and that will be your chance to speak up for your friend and establish the truth.' There was a brief pause, and then he added meaningfully, 'If you are still alive.'

The image of the dead slinger rose before me. It would have made sense for Ganelon to have me killed once Gerin had seen me ride off with the wali. If the king thought to ask what had happened to me, it would be presumed that I had stolen the five hundred dinars and run away. As long as I remained alive, I was the single flaw in Ganelon's scheme.

At that moment I knew I had to avoid Ganelon and reach Hroudland and warn him of his danger.

Husayn seemed to have read my thoughts.

'I can arrange for you to join your friend. It will mean a sea journey, possibly a difficult one as this is a stormy season.'

There was another upsurge of barking as the city dogs again challenged one another. I shivered despite the warmth of the carpet underneath me as I thought of another sea voyage.

'I accept your offer,' I said. There seemed nothing else I could do.

There was a gleam of gold in the darkness, the light from a lantern reflecting on the brocade of his gown as the wali shifted position. His manner became businesslike and brisk.

'Good. It will take a few days to make the necessary arrangements for your trip. In the meantime my scribes will make a copy of the Book of Dreams so you can take the original with you and return it to Count Gerard.'

'You are very gracious, Your Excellency,' I said. 'Men like Ganelon are dangerous. My friend Count Hroudland describes him as a reptile.'

The wali gave a low, grim chuckle.

'I'll know how to deal with him. Country people say that Zaragoza is so well favoured that a bunch of grapes suspended from the ceiling remains sweet for six years, and no article of dress whether it is wool, silk or cotton is ever eaten by moths.' His gown rustled as he rose to his feet. I also stood up and he came forward and took hold of me by both elbows. Looking into my eyes, he said, 'The country people also claim that in Zaragoza scorpions lose their sting, and snakes and other reptiles are deprived of their venom.'

He released his grip and stepped back as a body servant silently appeared behind him and settled a cloak across his shoulders. Then he turned and strode away, passing in front of the line of lanterns, the cloak swirling out behind him, as he went back inside the house. His grey-haired steward materialized out of the darkness and led me back to my own rooms. This time he did not lock the door behind me.

*

That night, perhaps not surprisingly, I dreamed of a snake. It was my first real dream since leaving Aachen. In my dream I was seated on a rock on a barren mountainside and dressed only in my loose Saracen gown. I was icy cold but dared not stand up. A poisonous brown snake, as thick as my wrist, lay curled in my lap. I felt its weight through the gown. The slightest movement would rouse it. Some distance away Hroudland stood talking with Husayn and Governor Suleyman of Barcelona. I wanted to call out to them, seek their help, but then the snake would strike. I sat, fearing the slightest movement.

It was at that point in my dream that I became half awake. I was stretched out on a couch where I had lain down to rest after returning from my meal with the wali. Something was indeed lying across my thighs. I thought I felt it stir, and the hair on the back of my neck rose in terror. I lay still, struggling to control my panic. After what seemed like an age, I took a shallow breath and gathered my strength. I tensed and then, in one terrified move, I sprang to my feet, flinging aside whatever was lying across me.

I was fully awake now, standing upright and shivering with fright. The room was in total darkness and I had no idea of the time. I stood stock still, listening for the sound of something slithering on the floor. I heard nothing. Gradually I calmed down and told myself that it had been a nightmare. After some moments I stooped and gingerly felt around the floor, still fearful. My fingers closed on a roll of cotton sheet. It had wrapped around me as I tossed and turned.

It took me a long time to get back to sleep, and it was well past dawn when I awoke. Daylight was flooding in through the high windows. Snatches of birdsong came from the direction of the central courtyard. I rose and went into the marbled washroom to splash water on my face. Osric was waiting for me in the adjacent room and I saw that breakfast had been delivered – a flat loaf of bread, some fruit and a jug of sherbet. I mumbled a greeting and went straight to the low desk where I had left my translation of the Oneirokritikon. I sat down on the floor cushion and began to skim through the text until I found the section on animals and their significance in dreams. It was a strange assortment of creatures. Mice, tapeworms, crickets, moles, owls, bats – as far as I could make out, they were listed in no particular order. Eventually I came to the page that dealt with snakes. The book left me in no doubt.

To dream of a snake was a sure portent of impending treachery.

With a sick feeling in the pit of my stomach, I looked up. Osric was standing beside the uneaten food, waiting for me to speak, his dark eyes troubled.

'Ganelon plans to destroy Hroudland,' I began, and told him what I had learned the previous evening and my nightmare.

He heard me out in silence.

'Do you remember what time of night you dreamed?' he asked, once I'd finished.

'No. It was pitch dark,' I said.

'Then the treachery will not occur for some time yet. What happened to the snake?'

It was such an odd question that I was taken aback.

'I don't remember.'

'The Book of Dreams tells us that the snake's behaviour is important.'

In my anxiety about the meaning of the dream, I had forgotten that, according to the Oneirokritikon, if the snake wrapped itself around the dreamer's leg, then he would be the victim of treachery. If the snake moved away, it meant that someone else would be betrayed.

'In my dream the snake was lying on me, curled up. Nothing more,' I said.

'Then you are not to be the victim. And it might not be Count Hroudland either,' Osric said.

'I'm going to warn Hroudland anyway. The wali is making arrangements for me to travel to join him. He says I can go by sea.'

'Let's hope that this time we don't sail with a crew of pirates.'

'Osric, you don't have to go with me,' I said slowly.

He looked at me as if he had not heard me properly. Choosing my words carefully, I told him what I had arranged with the wali and that there was a place for him in Zaragoza.

'You can decide whether to stay or not. It is up to you,' I said. 'Whatever happens, you will not be a slave. If you travel with me, it will be as a free man.'

An expression that wavered between reluctance and elation passed across Osric's face.

'I had not expected this,' he said huskily.

'You saved my life, if you remember.'

'Yesterday you said you would need my help more than ever before.' Osric put up a hand to massage the side of his damaged neck. It was a habit of his to knead the muscles there while he was thinking. I had forgotten how accustomed I was to his small gestures.

'Will you manage on your own?' he asked.

'Osric, three days ago I killed a man. I put an arrow right through him. Afterwards I would have preferred he lived a little longer, but only so I could beat some information out of him. I'm tougher now than when I left home, more cynical and suspicious. I will be on my guard.'

His eyes searched my face as he considered his reply.

'Very well. I will stay here in Zaragoza,' he said finally.

I reached across the floor to pull my saddlebags to me and rummaged inside them until I had found what I needed.

'Osric, can you write in Frankish script?' I asked.

'My father made me learn it. I expect I could just about manage, though I'd be very slow,' he said.

'Speed won't matter,' I told him. 'If you find out anything more about Ganelon's plot, you must write and let me know. You will need this.' I held up the little box containing the Caesar's Wheel.

He limped across and took it from me.

'I had wondered what this contained,' he said, lifting the lid and glancing inside.

'It's a device for writing in code. I'll show you how it works. If I'm going back to Frankia, I don't need the wheel any more. I can report in person,' I told him.

He raised his eyebrows questioningly.

'I've been gathering information for Alcuin,' I confessed.

He closed the lid and slipped the box inside his sleeve without comment. I felt guilty that I had not confided in him earlier that I was a spy. Worse, I realized that I had not given Osric the complete liberty I had intended. I still took it for granted that he would help me if he could.

Chapter Fourteen

I SPENT THE SEA JOURNEY to the Breton March lying on a pile of nets in the dank, foul-smelling hold of a Vascon fishing boat. The vessel pitched and rolled, and every time a wave crashed on deck above me the water dripped down through the deck planks. In the whirling darkness I dry-retched until I wished I would die.

The wali had warned that the voyage would be uncomfortable but he had understated the case.

'The mountain Vascons are tough,' he'd said, 'but for sheer hardiness they are exceeded by the sea Vascons. They'll set out from port in any weather if there's profit in the trip.' He should have added that he had paid the crew handsomely because the Bay of the Vascons, which we had to cross, is notorious for sudden storms and raging seas.

Husayn also arranged my travel across the Vascon lands which bordered Zaragoza. The guide who brought me to the ship took me through Pamplona, the region's capital. The place showed all the scars of a fought-over frontier town with a battered city wall, stumps of broken towers like damaged teeth, and gates that had been repaired time and again. Conscientiously I made notes of these facts because I still regarded myself as a spy for Alcuin.

At voyage's end, the Vascon fishermen set me ashore, wrapped in a sodden cloak, in a small, unnamed and deserted inlet on the Breton shore. They explained with gestures that I was to walk along the beach and around a headland to my left. It was a damp, drizzly morning, less than an hour after daybreak. Curtains of heavy mist drifted in from the sea, coating everything on land with a glistening wet sheen. Despite the dreary surroundings, I was very thankful to be finally off the ship, which hoisted sail and disappeared into the mist. I waited until the ground stopped tilting and swaying beneath me and then I set out in the direction they had indicated, slipping and sliding on the shingle, clutching the satchel, which contained the original Book of Dreams, my translation, and the purse of silver dinars the wali had pressed on me. All my other possessions, including my bow and sword, I had left behind with Osric and I had made him a present of the bay gelding.

I trudged round the headland, and there, immediately ahead of me, was a line of small boats hauled up on the shore and left upside down on wooden rollers to keep the rain out. Beyond them stood a row of fisherman's shacks.

'*Piv oc'h?*' said a voice suspiciously.

A man dressed in a shapeless knee-length smock and a broad brim hat stepped out from behind one of the boats. He was short and broad shouldered. On his feet he wore thick wooden clogs. '*Piv oc'h?*' he repeated, staring at me. He had eyes the same dull colour as the pebbles on the beach, and his face showed a week's stubble. Drops of rain hung on his hat brim and ran in trickles off his smock. I realized that all his garments had been soaked in fish oil.

'I am trying to get to the headquarters of Margrave Hroudland,' I said in Latin.

The man regarded me warily, suspicion mingling with distaste showing on his face. I was not understood.

'*Penaos oc'h deuet?*' he said.

'A Vascon vessel set me ashore, around that headland,' I explained uselessly, pointing back toward the cliff.

The man jerked his head for me to follow him and led me towards the largest of the huts. He pushed open the rain-streaked plank door, and I found myself inside a single, cramped room, dark and smelling of wood smoke, dirt and fish. A woman, her tangled hair streaked with grey and wearing a grimy shawl, was seated on a stool before the hearth and stirring the contents of an iron pot. Three young children – all boys – looked at me curiously, their eyes teary and red-rimmed from smoke. They were barefoot and their clothes were little more than rags, though they looked sturdy and well-nourished.

The man spoke briefly in his own language to the woman. I presumed she was his wife. She rose to her feet and wiped her hands on her heavy skirt. I noticed a small wooden cross threaded on a leather lace around her neck.

'My husband asks who are you and where are you from?' she asked in Frankish, speaking slowly and with a heavy accent.

I chose to distort the truth.

'I serve Alcuin of Aachen. He sent me to obtain a most holy book from the Saracens. I am bringing it to him for the new royal chapel.' I unlaced my satchel and pulled out the Book of Dreams, handling it with great reverence.

The woman eyed the volume respectfully and crossed herself, though I noticed that her husband was more interested in trying to see what else was in the satchel.

'I would be grateful for a guide and horses to take me as far as the headquarters of Margrave Hroudland. I can pay.'

A glint of avarice competed with the veneration.

'How much?' the woman asked.

I groped in the satchel, keeping the flap half-closed, until my fingers found the wali's purse. I extracted three silver dinars and held them out on the palm of my hand. Like the stab of a heron's beak, the woman's hand darted out and scooped up the coins. She looked at them closely and for a moment I feared that the sight of the Arab script on them would make her suspicious. However, she dropped them into a pocket in her skirt.

'My man will show you the way on foot. His name is Gallmau. We have no horses,' she said flatly. She gave her husband his instructions, and then turned back to stirring the pot, ignoring everything else except to snap at her oldest boy when he made as if to accompany us.

I followed Gallmau out of the hut and into the fine, penetrating rain that had replaced the earlier drizzle. The breeze had also picked up. Small, white-capped waves were now rolling in and breaking along the beach where the boats were drawn up. I guessed that Gallmau would not be losing any fishing that day. He picked up a stout wooden staff that had been propped against his hut, and called to two small shaggy brown dogs crouched in the lee of a pile of driftwood. They jumped up and bounded over, their ears flopping. Gallmau started up the muddy path that led inland along the rocky course of a small stream that flowed down from the high ground behind the village. Ahead, the two dogs scampered enthusiastically, splattering mud, as indifferent as their master to the wet weather.

I followed, pulling up the hood of my cloak. The rain had soaked through the cloth and was dripping down my neck and under my collar. Fortunately I had acquired stout new boots of greased leather while in Zaragoza and, while not watertight, they kept out most of the water as we tramped our way through the puddles.

We walked steadily uphill for at least an hour, following the line of a narrow glen until the track brought us out onto level moorland. Huddled inside my hood, I paid little attention to our surroundings. When I did raise my eyes, it was to note that we had climbed to where the mist had turned to low cloud and was even thicker. I could see no more than thirty paces in any direction, a bleak vista of rock, heather and low scrub. Everything was dripping wet. I presumed that there was only one track leading inland, and wondered just how far we would have to go before we reached the next settlement. It was useless to ask Gallmau. He spoke only his own language and showed no interest in trying to communicate with me. Also, I was growing increasingly uneasy about being on the moor alone with him. He could easily knock me down with his heavy staff, steal my money and disappear into the mist.

I was plodding along, head down and looking where I was putting my feet when all of a sudden the two dogs rushed away from the footpath. They were barking excitedly, doubtless chasing a rabbit or a hare. Gallmau roared at them so fiercely to come to heel that I glanced up to see the reason for his anger. The sight that greeted me made my skin prickle. Our way lay between two rows of huge grey stones. They were set at intervals, some fifteen paces apart, and a little way back from the track. Each stone was its natural shape, a massive boulder longer than it was broad and weighing many tons. It must have taken unimaginable labour to drag each one of them into its right place. Then, by some feat of ingenuity, they had been tilted and set on end so that they resembled gigantic tombstones. In the half-light of the overcast day they were eerie and mysterious, as if not of this world.

Gallmau treated them with great respect. After the two dogs had returned obediently to their master, he used the tip of his staff to mark some sort of shape in the turf, before bowing his head and dropping down to one knee as though to pay homage to the great stones.

The mist grew even denser as we proceeded, until I could barely make out the looming shape of the nearest stone on either side. As we moved through this silent, opaque world I became aware that we were not alone. Someone had joined us. It was just a fleeting impression at first, a shadowy figure a short distance ahead of Gallmau, someone walking along the path in the same direction as us. The figure was indistinct, appearing and then disappearing as the thickness of the mist varied. Gallmau was striding along ahead of me and the track was too narrow for me to overtake him to investigate. Besides, I had no wish to intercept the stranger. Only after several minutes did I realize there was something familiar about our new companion. He was dressed like me, in a long cloak. He had the hood pulled up so I could see only his general shape. It was the manner of his walking and the way he held his shoulders that was familiar. Finally I realized who it was: my twin brother. His fetch was travelling with us, leading the way. I wondered if Gallmau could also see him, but the fisherman gave no sign of it. Only the two dogs reacted. They ran forward along the path and I watched them investigate the distant wraith, sniffing at its heels, wagging their tails, and then padding back to their master. The confidence of the dogs reassured me. I knew I could not attract my brother's attention. The otherworld pays no heed to mortals, and if he wished to speak to me, he would do so. Yet I half-hoped that he would stop and turn to greet me. But he kept walking forward through the mist, and I tramped along behind him, strangely comforted by his presence. I was certain that as long as my twin brother was with me on my journey, no harm would come to me.

After some hours the path finally began to descend. We left the high moorland and emerged from the worst of the mist. About that time my brother's fetch vanished. He disappeared in much the same manner as he had first arrived, showing himself indistinctly for a few moments, then vanishing, only to reappear for another brief glimpse. When he did not show himself for several long minutes, I knew that I would not see him again that day.

We had reached a fold in the land, which sheltered a hamlet of a dozen small cottages. The two dogs ran ahead of us, straight to one of the buildings, and scratched at the door. A voice called out and when Gallmau answered, the door was opened by a bald, very overweight man of middle age. He had a round head, a neck that spilled over his collar in folds of fat, and his small sharp eyes looked as if they had been set in a pudding. His gaze travelled slowly over me, and then to Gallmau before he gestured at us to enter. We stepped into a room starkly furnished with a wooden table, a bench and three stools. There was a door to an inner room, a fire burning in the hearth and several farm tools propped in a corner. Gallmau's two dogs promptly ran to the hearth and lay down on the earth floor as if they owned the place. Soon the room filled with the smell of drying dog.

Gallmau spoke briefly to the fat man, who then turned to me.

'You travel to the king's palace at Aachen?' he enquired. He spoke far better Frankish than Gallmau's wife.

'I carry a sacred book for the library of the new chapel,' I said. I was uneasy. Something about the fat man made me distrust him.

He waved a chubby hand towards the bench by the table.

'Take a seat. It's a long walk from the coast, and you must be tired. I'll get something for you and Gallmau to eat and drink.'

He waddled out of the room and I went across to the bench, removed my cloak and sat down heavily. It was true. I was exhausted. I was also aware of Gallmau's interest in my satchel so I placed it on the bench beside me, trying not to make it obvious that I was keeping it very close.

Gallmau removed his dripping hat and took his seat on a stool opposite me.

We sat in strained silence, waiting for our host to return. Surreptitiously I scanned the room hoping to see some sign of another person living in the house – a wife, children. There was nothing. The fat man lived by himself, and I began to wonder if I should get up and leave while I still could. I was alone, a stranger in an unknown house and an easy target for a robbery, if not worse. Yet I had not seen anyone else in the hamlet as we arrived, and I knew that country people were clannish. There was no certainty that I would find a better reception elsewhere.

The fat man came back into the room. He was carrying three scuffed, leather tankards in one hand, and in the other a large earthenware jug. He put them down on the scarred table top and, wheezing slightly, pulled up a stool and sat down. His flabby bulk overflowed the stool. He tipped a stream of some pale straw-coloured liquid from the jug into each of our tankards. I sniffed it suspiciously. It smelled of apples, pears and honey. A quick taste confirmed that it was mead mixed with fermented apple and pear juice, something that had been my father's favourite. I took a long draught. It had been months since I had tasted strong drink. The tiny bubbles tickled the back of my throat as I swallowed. The sweet heady liquid was delicious.

The fat man was eyeing me speculatively. He reminded me of a large boar inspecting its next meal. He put down his tankard and licked his lips, about to speak. I forestalled him.

'Those big boulders up on the moor, what are they?' I began.

He blinked.

'Menhirs, the long stones.' He sounded as if he did not want to talk about them.

'Who put them there?'

'No one knows. They've always been there.'

'And do they have a purpose?' I asked.

He shrugged fleshy, round shoulders.

'Some believe that they are grave markers of giants.'

'Not only giants,' I said in a solemn voice. He looked at me curiously. I took another drink from my tankard and set it down carefully on the table. I had not eaten all day and could sense the strong drink taking effect. My tongue felt slightly thick and I knew I was already getting tipsy.

'I saw my twin brother at the menhirs this afternoon,' I said.

His piggy eyes opened wide in surprise.

'Your brother?' he asked.

'He walked with us for a while. The dogs saw him.' I nodded towards the two animals now asleep in front of the fire.

The fat man muttered something to Gallmau who shook his head, then looked flustered and ill at ease.

'Are you sure it was your brother?' asked the fat man.

'Of course. I haven't seen him for more than a week. He doesn't visit me that often,' I said, trying to sound casual.

The fat man's eyes flicked towards the satchel.

'Are you not a Christian?' he asked.

I belched softly. Judging by the aftertaste, the mead had been brewed with clover honey.

'My being a Christian has nothing to do with it. My brother visits me as often as he wishes,' I said. 'He drowned when we were youngsters.'

The fat man's eyes darted nervously around the room. A bead of sweat broke out on his scalp.

'Will he call on us tonight?' he asked.

I shrugged.

'Who knows.'

My host got up from his stool.

'Then we must not be found wanting,' he muttered, and shuffled his way out of the room.

In a short while he came back with four wooden plates, a loaf of stale-looking bread and some cheese, and an extra tankard. He set four places on the table, and we began to eat. Each time there was a sound outside, both my companions started. We hurried through our meal, and when I had finished, I drained my third tankard of the cider-mead and reached up and removed my eye patch. Then I turned to face my companions, staring straight at them for a long moment, unblinking so they could not help but notice the mismatched colours of my eyes.

'Leave my brother's place at the table as it is,' I said, 'in case he joins us later.'

Without asking, I stretched myself out on the bench, with my satchel as a pillow and allowed myself to drift off to sleep, confident that neither of them would dare harm someone who bore the Devil's mark and was the twin brother of a fetch.

*

A low growling awoke me, followed by a thud as a heavy boot kicked the front door, making it rattle in its frame.

'Wake up you tub of lard,' shouted a voice.

I sat up. I was still on the bench and had spent a quiet night. My brother's wooden plate and tankard sat on the table untouched.

The boot thumped into the door again. Gallmau was climbing to his feet from where he had been sleeping on the floor. The two dogs were barking furiously and dancing round the door, which shook to another heavy blow. The fat man was nowhere to be seen.

I put on my eye patch and went across to the door and pulled it open. Outside stood a thick-set, scowling man with a short, neatly trimmed beard and the weather-beaten skin of someone who spent his days in the open air. Behind him I saw two men-at-arms with spears. Further down the street, the faces of villagers were peering out from their front doors.

'Who are you?' demanded the bearded man aggressively. He spoke in good Frankish.

'Sigwulf, a royal servant,' I answered.

The man narrowed his eyes.

'Royal? Don't waste my time!' he growled.

I knew that I made an unimpressive spectacle, with a patch on one eye, travel-stained and unwashed.

'I am on my way to see Margrave Hroudland,' I said.

'And is the margrave expecting you?' jeered my interrogator.

I was feeling grouchy and hungover, and lost my temper.

'No, he is not,' I snapped, 'but he will be very pleased to see me, and I shall make it my business to report on your conduct.'

My sharp manner penetrated the man's disbelief. He gave me a calculating look.

'What do you want to see the margrave about?' he asked, a little less derisively.

'I'm bringing him a book.' Once again I slid the Book of Dreams out of the satchel.

The display had its effect. The man might have never seen a book before, but he knew that they were rare and valuable.

'Very well, you come with me and tell your story to the head steward,' he said.

He looked past me at Gallmau who had both hands full, holding back the two dogs that were eager to attack the stranger.

'Where's Maonirn?' he asked.

Gullmau stared back stonily without replying.

'He doesn't speak Frankish,' I said. 'He's a fisherman from the coast.'

'Smuggler, too, if he keeps company with Maonirn. I expect

that grease bucket slipped off to the moors when he heard us coming. No chance to find him now.'

He turned on his heel and I followed him out of the cottage and past the waiting men at arms.

*

I had encountered a bailiff, as it turned out. He had planned to arrest Maonirn, a known rogue, for the theft of some cattle. Instead he brought me before the head steward of the local landowner. He, in turn, was persuaded as to my honest character and provided me with a pony and directions to the town Hroudland had chosen for his headquarters as Margrave of the Breton March.

It was not much of a place.

A few hundred modest houses clustered on the floor of a shallow valley where the river made a loop around a low hill. The dwellings were a depressing sight under a dull winter sky, with their drab walls of mud and wattle, and roof thatch of grey reeds. There was a watermill on the river bank, a scattering of leafless orchards and vegetable patches, and a log palisade to enclose the hilltop. Just visible above this palisade was the roof of a great hall. The miserable weather was keeping the townsfolk indoors, and the only activity was in what looked like a soldiers' camp on the water meadows. Tents had been set up in orderly lines, smoke was rising from cooking fires, and numbers of armed men were moving about.

It had taken me two full days to ride there and I guided my tired pony through the town's muddy, deserted streets and headed straight for the gate in the palisade. It stood open and I rode in without being challenged. There I halted, overcome by a reminder of the past.

Hroudland's great hall recalled my memories of my father's

house, the home I had grown up in, except that it was much, much larger and intended to impress the visitor. The ridge of its enormous roof stood two-storeys high. The roof itself was covered with thousands upon thousands of wooden shakes and sloped down to side walls of heavy planks set upright and closely fitted. Every vertical surface had been brightly painted. Red and white squares alternated with diamond shapes in green and blue. There were stripes and whorls. Flowers, animal shapes, and human grotesques had been carved into the projecting ends of the beams and cross timbers and the door surrounds. These carvings, too, were picked out in vivid colours: orange, purple and yellow. Flags flew from poles at each corner of the building, and a long banner with a picture of a bull's head hung down above the double entrance doors. It was a spectacle of unrestrained and gaudy ostentation.

There was much bustle around the building. An impatient-looking foreman was supervising a team of workmen as they unloaded trestle tables and benches from a cart, and then carried them indoors. Servants were wheeling out barrows heaped with cinders and soiled rushes; others were taking in bundles of fresh reeds. A man on a ladder was topping up the oil in the metal cressets attached to the huge doorposts.

'Where's Count Hroudland?' I asked a porter. He was shouldering a yoke from which hung two water buckets and was on his way towards what looked like the kitchen building attached to the side of the great hall. Smoke was rising from its double chimney.

'You'll not find him here. He's down by the army camp.'

I turned my pony and rode back down the slope towards the water meadows. I was scarcely halfway there when I heard a sound that made my heart lift: a full-throated whoop of triumph. It was the yell that my friend let loose every time he scored a direct hit with javelin or lance, and it came from my right, just beyond the soldiers' tents. I kicked my pony into a faster walk and a moment later emerged onto a familiar scene. A couple of dozen cavalry men were fighting a mock battle. Watched by a ring of spectators, the opposing sides were a milling mob of armoured men on horseback chopping and thrusting with wooden swords and blunt lances, deflecting blows with their shields. I spotted Hroudland at once. He was riding his roan stallion with the distinctive white patches and he had a cluster of black feathers fastened to his helmet. A closer look showed that several of the other riders were wearing black feathers while their opponents sported sprigs of green leaves. Above the hoarse shouts, the thud of blows and the general grunting tussle of horses and riders, I again heard Hroudland's triumphant cry. He had barged forward with the roan, knocked his opponent's horse off balance, and then delivered a downward blow to the man's head. As I watched, he thrust his shield into his opponent's face so that he toppled backwards out of his saddle and crashed to the ground.

Hroudland straightened up and looked around, seeking his next victim. His eye fell on me where I sat on my pony looking over the heads of the spectators. His face lit up with a broad smile. Ignoring the chaos around him he spurred his stallion through the fighting and came towards me at a lumbering trot. The crowd in front of me scattered, dodging the great hooves as the horse came to a halt.

'Patch! Welcome home!' the count shouted. He was out of breath, the sweat pouring down his face. He tossed aside his wooden sword, slung his shield on to his back, dropped the reins and swung himself out of the saddle. I dismounted from my pony. Hroudland came forward, threw his arms around me and swept me up in a powerful bear hug. I was crushed uncomfortably against his chain-mail shirt, and had to duck to avoid the rim of his helmet.

'It's good to see you!' he said.

I became aware that another horse and rider had joined us. Looking up, I saw Berenger's cheerful face grinning down at me. He had taken off his helmet and his curly hair was plastered with sweat.

'Patch, where did you spring from?' he called down.

I disentangled myself from the count's embrace.

'From Hispania by way of the Bay of the Vascons,' I said. 'I've important news.'

Hroudland's unattended stallion was edging sideways, tossing its head and irritably stamping the soft ground. The nearest onlookers were scrambling back out of the way.

'Patch, I'll see you up at the great hall later,' said the count, hurriedly stepping back to gather up the reins. 'You could not have come at a better time. There's to be a banquet. My seneschal will look after you.' He vaulted easily up into the saddle. Someone handed back his wooden sword and he waved it above his head in salute, and then plunged back into the fray, Berenger riding at his side.

*

Hroudland's seneschal made no attempt to conceal his irritation at being distracted from the preparations for the banquet. He bawled at a groom to take my pony to the stables, then beckoned to a lad loitering nearby and told him gruffly to show me to the margrave's personal quarters. There he was to hand me over to the margrave's manservant. I followed the youngster into the great hall. The interior was as resplendent as the outside of the building. Painted in stripes of white and red, Hroudland's household colours, a double line of wooden pillars, each thicker than a man's waist, soared upward as piers for the great roof. Bolted to each pillar were brackets for dozens of torches. Although it was scarcely noon, many of these lamps were already lit, and their flames made the shadows dance and flicker in the rafters high above us. The trestle tables and benches I had seen earlier were already erected in the spaces between the pillars, and there were enough to accommodate more than a hundred guests. A team of servants was setting out wooden trenchers and glass beakers. The kindling in the fire pit was well alight, and the blaze had spread into the stack of fresh logs. I smelled pine smoke and somewhere in the background was the sound of a musician tuning up a stringed instrument. My guide took me the length of the great hall and past the high table, still bare except for a fine, linen table cloth. I presumed that the more valuable tableware would be brought out later. At the far end of the hall I was shown through a heavy door into what amounted to a large arms store. The walls of mortared stone had narrow slits for windows. Cressets added to the weak light, which shone on racks of spears and javelins, war axes and iron bound chests. Along one wall was a display of shields. All of them were painted with the margrave's red and white.

My young guide led me on and up a wooden staircase that brought us into an upper room furnished for comfortable living. There were rugs on the floor, and wall hangings embroidered with scenes from the chase and the classical tales. To my surprise I noticed that one of the wall hangings depicted the siege of Troy. I recognized the figures of Troilus and Achilles, whose story I had told in the presence of Carolus at the banquet where I was poisoned. Ironwork braziers kept out the chill and damp, and there was a large and comfortable-looking bed with a mattress, as well as the usual stools and chairs. Here the windows were glazed and larger than on the ground floor, allowing in extra daylight.

Nevertheless racks of expensive wax candles, some of them scented, were already burning. I found myself wondering how Hroudland could afford such luxury.

A manservant took me in charge and, after a condescending appraisal of what I was wearing, drew back a curtain to an alcove. Expensive clothes hung on pegs. There were fine shirts of silk and linen, jackets and leggings, fur-trimmed cloaks, tunics with silver and gold thread woven into the fabric, a selection of fashionable hats and bonnets. Lower down, shelves displayed an array of footwear; boots, slippers and shoes of all colours and styles. I was told that I could select whatever clothes I wanted, and that hot water would be brought up from the kitchens so I could wash and change.

*

The count himself arrived two hours later. I heard his footsteps thudding on the wooden stair and a moment later he came bounding into the room, his face flecked with mud and his eyes alive with energy.

'Patch, Patch! It's been far too long!' he exclaimed, and I received another exuberant bear hug. Then he held me at arm's length and gazed into my face. 'You're tanned and look well. Hispania must have suited you.'

'Being Warden of the March has suited you. Your great hall is magnificent,' I complimented him.

He pulled a face.

'It's to make up for this miserable climate and its equally miserable people. You have no idea what it is like to live among such sullen, dour blockheads. They don't know the meaning of what it is to enjoy oneself. We have to create our own amusements.' He brightened. 'But tonight there'll be good food and conversation and my steward will provide some decent wine. Also, I've arranged a special entertainment for you.'

His words tumbled out at such a pace and with so much fervour that I examined my friend more closely. I noticed the slight bags under his eyes and the broken veins on his face. He seemed overwrought and anxious. It was not how I remembered him. I wondered if Hroudland had been living a little too lavishly.

'I abandoned my mission to Hispania because I have to warn you of a plot against you,' I began.

But the count had already turned away, almost as though he was unable to keep still. He strode across to the bed and pulled off his shirt. His body was still as slim and athletic as before, the muscles sculpted under the pale skin. If my friend had been indulging in too much fine living, it had not affected his physique. The manservant reappeared with a basin of water, which he placed on a stand, and Hroudland began to wash his face and arms.

'Ganelon is plotting against you,' I said loudly, trying to get his full attention.

'That's nothing new,' answered the count dismissively. He did not bother to raise his face from the bowl.

'This time he may succeed,' I insisted. 'He wants to have you disgraced as a traitor.' I failed to suppress the note of irritation in my voice but I was frustrated that my friend should be taking my warning so casually after I had made so great an effort to reach him.

'Tell me about it,' said the count, straightening up. He began towelling his head and shoulders.

Point by point, I explained how Ganelon had obtained Husayn's signed promise to pay me five hundred dinars so he could use it as false proof of Hroudland's treachery.

When I had finished, the count threw back his head and laughed scornfully.

'Is that the best that Ganelon can do? It won't get him very far,' he scoffed.

I thought I detected a note of hysteria in my friend's response and I pressed on.

'You must contact the king. Tell him what is happening. Warn him against Ganelon.'

Hroudland came across to me and punched me lightly on the arm.

'Patch, my friend, I'll do better than that. I'll fight so well in Hispania that Carolus will have no doubt of my loyalty.'

'What do you mean? Is there to be a war in Hispania?'

Again Hroudland laughed.

'Of course!'

'But I was sent with Ganelon and Gerin to investigate whether or not the Saracens' request for military help was genuine.'

The count gave me a wicked smile.

'Carolus decided on war in Hispania long ago, well before the Saracens showed up to ask for his help. Despatching you and the other two to make a report was just a ruse, a way of concealing his intentions.'

From somewhere outside came the sound of a horn. The margrave's guests were being summoned to their places in the great hall. I heard someone else coming up the wooden stairs and Berenger appeared in the room with the words, 'Time to get ready.'

'Patch, any more trouble with people trying to kill you?' Hroudland asked.

I would have preferred if his enquiry had sounded less casual.

'There was an attempt when I was travelling through the mountains,' I said and told him about the Vascon slinger.

'Sounds like Ganelon at work,' said Hroudland. 'Berenger, what do you think?'

'Just like him,' replied Berenger, who was helping the count get his arms into a fresh shirt.

'Well, Patch,' said my friend, as he selected a belt studded with semi-precious stones from his wardrobe in the alcove, 'at least you don't have to worry about being poisoned at today's banquet. The cook and every scullion are on my staff.' He buckled on the belt, picked up a short cloak of white silk with a crimson lining and threw it over his shoulder. It was time to descend into the great hall and begin the banquet.

*

I was seated in the place of honour on Hroudland's right, while Berenger was on his left. The rest of the high table was occupied by senior members of Hroudland's entourage. Some of them I recognized from the mock battle earlier. There were no women. All of us sat facing down the hall so that the guests could look up and see us and their overlord. The table setting was as ostentatious as I now knew to expect from the margrave; plates and ewers of silver, drinking vessels of horn banded with gold and silver or made of coloured glass, candle holders with gold inlay or decorations of semi-precious stones. The food, by contrast, was disappointing. Pottage, lumpy and bland, was served with root vegetables. The bread was coarse and gritty. Hroudland grumbled to me that the local farmers were unable to grow good wheat due to the climate and poor soil. He was drinking heavily, right from the start of the meal, and Berenger and the others at the table kept pace with him. As more and more wine and beer was consumed, their raised voices and shouted conversations drowned out the efforts of a small group of musicians who were trying to keep us entertained. From the packed hall in front of us rose the steady babble of conversation as the margrave's less exalted guests ate their way stolidly through the meal. More than once I found myself having to stifle a yawn.

All of a sudden, Hroudland banged the handle of his knife down on the table, hard enough to make the nearest plates jump. Immediately everyone fell silent, looking to him. By now my friend was well and truly drunk.

'I want you all to meet my good and excellent friend, Patch,' he announced in a slightly slurred voice.

There was a tipsy nodding of heads around the high table. One or two of the more sober guests caught my eye and smiled at me tentatively.

'Some of you will have heard how he corrected the royal bard in Aachen when he was telling a story during a banquet in front of the king.' The count raised his voice so he could be heard the length of the great hall. 'Tonight I have arranged for one of the greatest bards of the Bretons to entertain us so Patch will know that we have storytellers the equal of any in the kingdom.'

There was a scatter of applause, and from behind one of the great pillars stepped a stooped, bony man of middle age. He was dressed in a plain, brown robe and a close-fitting skull cap. In one hand he held a small harp. The other hand rested on the shoulder of a lad no more than ten years old. They walked slowly into the open space in front of the high table, and the boy put down a small three-legged stool he was carrying. The bard took his seat and placed the harp on his lap, ready to begin.

'Tell us what tale you are going to sing,' called Hroudland.

The boy leaned forward and spoke quietly to the older man. Not only was the skald blind, but also he did not speak Frankish.

The boy looked up and in his high voice he said, 'With your permission, my lord, my father will tell a local story; the tale of Yvain.'

My neighbour on my right, a stocky red-faced Frankish

stalwart whose sour breath stank of ale, leaned closer and whispered in my ear, 'Let's hope this doesn't go on for too long.'

Hroudland was beckoning to the lad.

'Come up here,' he ordered. 'I want you to translate for my guest.'

Unembarrassed, the boy stepped up on to the dais, came round the end of the table, and stood behind Hroudland and myself.

Without any preamble the blind storyteller plucked a single note on his harp and launched into his tale, speaking in a language that I presumed was the local Breton tongue. He had a fine, strong voice and it carried clearly. On the high table most of the count's entourage looked bored, but the audience in the hall stayed silent, either out of courtesy or for fear of Hroudland's displeasure.

The lad was a competent interpreter. The bard would pause between each verse and the boy swiftly summarized the lines in Frankish, speaking quietly in my ear.

The tale itself was a strange one: Yvain, a nobleman, leaves the court of his king to go in search of a magical fountain, deep within a forest. Beside the fountain stands a boulder studded with gems, and a golden cup hangs from the branch of a nearby tree. Directed to the spot by a hideous giant, the nobleman pours water from the cup on the boulder. Immediately a great storm arises, tearing the leaves from the trees. When the storm ceases, flocks of birds descend from the sky, singing and settling on the branches. At that moment an armoured man mounted on a horse appears and proclaims himself the guardian of the fountain. He and Yvain fight until the mysterious stranger is wounded, turning his horse and fleeing, with Yvain in pursuit.

'Surely Yvain took with him the golden cup? It was his prize,' Hroudland called out rudely. I had not realized quite how drunk he was.

The skald broke off his recital, offended by the interruption. Hroudland turned to me, his face flushed.

'That's what would have happened at the siege of Troy, wouldn't it, Patch? To the victor the spoils.'

'It's a legend, a fantasy,' I said, trying to humour him and calm him down.

'No, my lord, it is how it happened,' the lad behind us spoke up.

Surprised by his boldness, I turned round to get a good look at him. He was standing with his hands clenched at his side, looking pale and upset.

'Nonsense,' snapped Hroudland. He was ready to pick an argument, even with a youngster. 'The entire yarn is a fabrication.'

'The fountain is there. You can see for yourself. At Barenton in the forest of Broceliande,' insisted the lad.

I feared that Hroudland was drunk enough to hit the boy so I waved the youngster away. He turned on his heel and stalked back to his father, his back stiff with anger.

Hroudland's mood had plummeted. He was aggressive and angry. He picked up his goblet unsteadily and took a long fumbling drink. A trickle of wine ran down his chin. Then he slammed the goblet down and slurred truculently, 'Patch, tomorrow you and I will search out that fountain and prove there is no magic to it.'

Out of the corner of my eye I noticed that the bard had risen from his stool, and he and his son were leaving the hall. The song had not been a success.

*

Next morning I hoped that Hroudland would have forgotten the episode. But a servant came to the guest chamber where I spent the night and woke me just after dawn to say that the margrave was waiting for me at the stables. Leaving aside my borrowed finery, I pulled on my travelling clothes and joined Hroudland. He seemed little affected by the evening's carousing and I wondered if he had grown so accustomed to regular drinking bouts that he no longer suffered from hangovers.

'Patch, I'm told that the magic fountain is no more than a three-hour ride from here,' my friend said brightly. 'We can get there and back in daylight.'

A stable-hand led forward two sturdy riding horses, and we rode out of the palisade gate, followed by an escort of four mounted troopers. The morning was dank and misty and beads of condensation glistened on my horse's mane as we made our way down the hill and through the streets of the little town, deserted except for an occasional thin cur scavenging for scraps.

'You have no idea how glad I am that soon we will be off to war in Hispania,' Hroudland confided to me as we rode side by side.

'In search of glory?' I asked mockingly.

He turned a serious face towards me.

'I need money badly. You'd be shocked to know how costly it is to maintain a great hall and its entire staff.'

I could have pointed out that he could save money by not being so lavish, but instead said, 'I thought the local taxes provided funds for your office as Warden of the March.'

'Nothing like enough.'

'Then you should ask the king to relieve you of your post. Go back to court.'

Hroudland shook his head.

'That would be to admit failure. In any case, being Warden of the March has given me a taste of what it is like to make my own decisions.'

'So it's plunder rather than renown that you want from Hispania.'

'I hope to win both,' he answered bluntly.

We made good progress along a rutted highway, which took us across low round hills covered with scrubby woodland. The only travellers we saw were on foot, walking between the small hamlets. Often they would deliberately leave the road, vanishing into the bushes, avoiding us. Eventually we overtook a family of father and mother and three small children trudging slowly along. One of our escorts spoke enough Breton to glean from them that the fountain at Barenton lay some distance off to our right.

The low cloud was thinning and a watery sun had begun to show itself as we left the main road and turned into an area of true forest. The ancient oaks intermingled with beech reminded me of the place the mysterious archer had tried to kill me while out hunting with the king. But here the trees were less majestic; they were gnarled and stunted, and the space between their thick, mossy trunks was choked with undergrowth. Little by little, the track narrowed until it became no more than a footpath, and the branches above the height of a man's head reached out and scratched our faces as we pushed our horses forward.

'Can't be much further now,' said Hroudland, finally dismounting when progress on horseback became too difficult. He handed the reins to our escort and told them to wait. Stiffly I got down from my horse and followed the count as he strode briskly onward. The forest smelled of earth and wet leaves, and – oddly – there was no sound of wildlife, no birdsong, not even the faint rustling of a breeze in the stagnant, still air. It was eerie, and I grew uneasy.

Hroudland did not appear to notice the silence. He drew his sword and, when the path became very overgrown, slashed back the undergrowth.

'If the legend was true, this is where we should encounter an ugly giant,' he joked to me over his shoulder. 'Someone to show us on our way.'

But we saw no one, though I thought I detected the occasional faint trace of a footprint on the muddy track we were following.

Eventually, just as I was about to suggest that we turn back, we emerged into a clearing. It was no more than twenty paces across and open to the sky. It had the serene, tranquil air of an ancient place. In the centre stood a great upright stone. The boulder was similar to the menhirs I had seen on the moors in the mist, but here it stood alone, its rough grey sides speckled with pale circular patches of lichen growth. Close to the foot of the boulder was a shallow pool, little more than a large puddle. In the stillness of the glade the only movement was a faint ripple disturbing the water's surface. A spring was bubbling out of the ground. My spine prickled.

'This must be the place,' said Hroudland confidently. He sheathed his sword and looked around at the bushes. 'But I don't see a golden cup hanging from a branch.'

He crossed to the stone and examined it more closely. 'Nor is it studded with gems,' he added with a derisive snort. 'Another fable.'

I walked across to join him. A small trickle of water overflowed from the pool and drained out of the glade to where it was soon lost under some bushes. Something caught my eye, a small shadow under the surface of the rill, a dark patch that came and went as the water washed over it. I leaned in closer. Lying on its side, submerged in the water, was a metal beaker. Reaching in, I picked it up tentatively. I knew instinctively that it was extremely old. It was the size and shape of a small tankard or a large cup without a handle. I shook off the drops of water and turned it this way and that, searching for distinguishing marks in the dull surface.

The cup was made seamlessly from a single sheet of metal, without joints or rivets; there were only patterns of dots, pecked into the surface with a pointed instrument. They swirled around it in mysterious whorls.

'What have you got there?' demanded Hroudland. He strode across, taking the cup from my grasp. 'Probably a drinking cup dropped here by a woodsman.'

'My guess is that it's bronze,' I said.

My friend pulled out a dagger from his belt and scratched the surface of the cup with the tip of the blade. It left no mark.

'It's not Yvain's cup of gold, that's for sure. Far too hard.'

He grinned at me mischievously.

'Let's see if it will work its magic as it did for Yvain.'

Hroudland knelt down by the little pool and filled the cup with water. Walking across to the great boulder, he tossed the contents over the grey rock, stood back, and looked up at a sky still covered with its thin veil of cloud through which the disc of the sun could just be seen.

Nothing happened. The forest around us remained completely still and silent, the air pressed down on us, heavy and clammy.

'There you are, Patch,' Hroudland declared. 'It can't even summon up a storm.'

The words were scarcely out of his mouth when, without any warning, there came a hard pattering noise all around us. It was the sound of a myriad of fat, heavy rain drops striking the branches and bushes, splattering on the soggy carpet of dead leaves. There was not a breath of wind so the rain fell straight, as if tipped directly from the sky. The freakish shower lasted only a few minutes, five at most. Then, as abruptly as it had begun, the downpour stopped. The eerie silence returned.

Hroudland looked down at the bronze cup in his hand and gave a nervous laugh.

'Coincidence, Patch. What about the gale? The story of Yvain says that when he poured the water on the stone, a great gale arose and ripped the leaves from the trees.'

'There are no leaves. It's winter,' I pointed out.

We looked at one another, both silent for a moment.

And into that silence came another sound, a hollow rushing noise. It filled the air, coming closer and louder though it happened so quickly and without warning that there was no time to say from which direction the sound was coming. Then my skin crawled as a shadow passed across me, momentarily darkening the sky above the glade.

I looked up. A great flock of birds, thousands of them, was swirling over the clearing. We were hearing the beating of their wings, a noise that rose and fell as the flock circled twice and then came spiralling around our heads to land on the boughs and twigs of the trees and bushes around us. There were so many birds that it was impossible to count their number. They settled on every possible perch until the thinner branches began to sway and sag under their weight. I had never before seen birds like them. They were the size of thrushes, brownish-black and with short yellow beaks. They clung on their perches, seeking to keep their balance, occasionally shifting to get a firmer grip with their feet or to allow yet another bird to land beside them, but never settling on the ground. Then a faint, subdued chatter arose, and the entire circle of the glade seethed with birdlife.

Hroudland and I stood motionless for the few moments it took for the vast flock to rest. Then, just as abruptly as they had arrived, the birds took wing. They leapt from the branches and twigs in a great rustling and flutter of feathers, and a moment later they were climbing up into the air and streaming away over the tree tops like a thick plume of dark smoke.

Hroudland gave a short, staccato laugh.

'They knew about the pool. They probably came wanting to drink, but our presence frightened them away,' he said.

'There were far too many to drink at that tiny pool. And there must be other pools and lakes all over the forest.'

Hroudland looked down at the cup still in his hand.

'Can you imagine anything more pointless? Even if this thing does summon rain and storms, it would be far more valuable to this soggy country if it caused the clouds to roll away and the sun to shine.'

He tossed the cup into the air, and caught it as it spun back down to his hand.

'I think I'll keep this, and wave it under the nose of the next fool who tries to tell me that there is truth in the childish tales of these Bretons.'

'Perhaps we should leave the cup where we found it,' I said, trying hard not to sound craven. 'It may be nothing more than superstition, but the cup was there for a purpose.'

But Hroudland ignored my feeble protest. He turned on his heel and headed back down the way we had come. I started to follow him, but before I left the glade I turned for one last look, and stopped with a jolt.

My brother's fetch was standing by the stone, watching me silently.

A chill came over me. Hroudland had made a terrible error. The cup should remain where we had found it. For a long moment my brother just stood there and I could find neither anger nor reproach in his face, only regret. Then I heard Hroudland call my name, shouting that we should hurry if we were to get back to the great hall before dark. I had no wish to be left alone in that ominous, supernatural place, so I dropped my gaze and stumbled away, fearful that what I had allowed to happen would have calamitous results, yet knowing that nothing I could say would deflect Hroudland from his chosen course. What had happened at the fountain of Barenton was another step along the path that Fate had chosen for him.

*

It was only when our little group was back on the main road that I had the chance to ask Hroudland the question that had been troubling me.

'Why did we go to the trouble of visiting the fountain?' I asked. 'What's so important about disproving an ancient folk tale?'

We were riding at a brisk trot. Hroudland pulled on the reins to slow his horse to a walk so that he did not have to shout. He threw a glance over his shoulder to make sure our escort was out of earshot.

'As Warden of the Breton March it is my duty to defend the frontier and maintain the king's authority,' he said.

'What has that got to do with a tale told by a blind bard?'

My friend's face clouded for a moment.

'The Bretons expect the Franks to be driven from this land.'

I laughed out loud.

'By whom? They can only dream.'

'That is precisely my problem – their dreams.'

I looked at him in surprise. I had never told him about the Oneirokritikon or my own dreams. But he had something else in mind.

'Patch, the Bretons await the return of a war leader who will restore their independence. As long as they think like that, the March is not secure.'

'What's the name of this saviour warrior?' I enquired with more than a hint of disbelief.

'They know him as Artorius.'

Something stirred in my memory, something that I had heard as a child. My teacher had spoken of an Artorius, a king who had led the resistance against my own people when they first came to settle in Britain.

'If it's the same person I'm thinking of, you don't need to worry,' I said. 'Artorius has been dead for a couple of hundred years.'

Hroudland threw me a sharp glance.

'What do you know about him?'

'He fought my Saxon ancestors and was mortally wounded in battle. His followers set his corpse adrift in a boat.'

Hroudland's mouth was set in a grim line.

'Exactly the same story is told here. Bretons and Britons share a common history. They claim that the boat drifted on to our coast and Artorius was buried with a great boulder as his tomb-stone, a stone like the one we saw by the fountain. They say he will rise and lead them to victory.'

I had to chuckle.

'That can't please their Christian priests. It's too much like their own story about their risen saviour.'

Hroudland frowned at me. He was impatient that I would not take him seriously.

'You're wrong. The priests are adding fuel to the fire. They've begun using this Artorius as an example of a good Christian ruler. They say he did good deeds and encouraged his very best men to track down the holiest relics from the time of Christ himself.'

'And did they find any?'

The count reached into his saddlebag, drew out the cup he had stolen from the fountain and held it up.

'If they did, maybe they looked something like this.'

At last I understood.

'So you went to the fountain intending to discredit the stories about Artorius. You knew that there would be neither a gem-studded stone nor a golden cup. They were as fanciful as the legend of Yvain himself, and as he was supposed to be one of Artorius's men, then he and his lord were both make-believe.'

Hroudland casually tossed the cup into the air and caught it again. 'You hoped to show that the gem-studded stone and golden cup did not exist. Yvain was one of his men.'

'And I found that the famous gold cup is nothing but a small, bronze beaker. I think I'll put it on display in the great hall or I might even drink from it at my next banquet. That will make both the priests and the pagan stone-worshippers think again about the truth in the wonderful adventure of Yvain.'

'What about the strange shower of rain, and the flock of birds?'

He shrugged.

'There are natural explanations for both of them, but neither you nor I need mention them.'

I was silent for several moments as I thought over his reply.

'And if the story had been true? If we had found a cup of gold and a stone studded with gems?'

He showed his teeth in a wolfish grin.

'That would have been even better. I would have prised out the gems with my knife and brought them and the gold cup back with me as plunder. As I said, I need the money badly.'

He spurred his horse into a canter, cramming the bronze cup back into his saddlebag.

Chapter Fifteen

NEXT MORNING, HAVING RISEN EARLY and feeling in need of fresh air, I climbed the wooden ladder to the lookout platform on the palisade surrounding the great hall. The day had dawned cold and clear, and a shallow bank of fog pooled in the valley floor below me, obscuring the soldiers' camp. Judging by the noise, the camp had grown in size in the short time that Hroudland and I were away investigating the fountain. From the fog rose a medley of sounds: shouted commands, ribald laughter, axes chopping into wood, the distinctive ring of a blacksmith's hammer on an anvil, the neighing of many horses. Shivering in the chill, I descended the ladder and fetched myself a breakfast of hot milk and bread from the kitchen beside the great hall. Then, loaf in hand, I strolled down the slope to get a closer view of the preparations for the expedition to Hispania.

Where the ground levelled out, I found myself walking between dimly seen rows of army tents. They stood empty, their door flaps fastened open and I could see the baggage of the occupants whom I supposed were now out and about on their duties. Occasionally the ghostly figure of a man appeared on foot leading a saddleless horse on halter, only to disappear into the mist without a word of greeting. When the smell of manure grew overpowering I knew I had reached the horse lines. The picket ropes to which the animals were tethered hung slack, but somewhere in the mist, a handful of horses was still being groomed.

I heard the impatient stamping of hooves, the occasional vibrating fart of a horse breaking wind and the soothing sounds made by unseen ostlers, whistling between their teeth or murmuring soft nonsense as they attended to their animals. Finally I came to the river bank where the ground was churned to deep mud by the animals brought there to drink.

Here I turned to my left, intending to walk upriver. Before I had gone a couple of hundred paces a breeze sprang up and began to clear away the fog in slow-moving tendrils. I discovered that I had ventured on to a broad open expanse of turf and mud – the cavalry training ground. Men on foot were gathered in groups of about twenty, holding their horses' reins while they listened to instructors. Compared to the escort of smart troopers that had greeted Wali Husayn when we had reached Zaragoza, the men were very scruffy. They wore an assortment of helmets and mailcoats, no two of them alike, and their mounts were shaggy in their winter coats.

The nearest instructor, a lean, grizzled fellow with a horseman's bow legs, had his sword slung across his back. The handle protruding over his shoulder reminded me of the last time I had seen Gerin as he rode away with Ganelon in the company of the Wali of Barcelona. The instructor was standing with the reins of his horse looped over his arm and holding up a small iron hoop, about the size of his palm. One side of it was flattened.

'Any of you know what this is?' he was demanding of his listeners.

One or two members of his audience looked down at the ground and shifted awkwardly. No one made any reply. I guessed that many of them knew the answer but did not want to risk being singled out later.

'It's a stirrup,' announced the instructor. 'Now some of you think that stirrups are womanly, that a good rider doesn't need them.' He jabbed a stubby finger at a tall, rangy recruit in the front row who had removed his helmet to reveal a shock of red hair. 'Carrot Top, you're a big lad. Mount up and let me show why every one of you will have stirrups attached to his saddle by tomorrow morning.'

The red-headed recruit put on his helmet and vaulted on to his horse. He was an accomplished rider and sat easily in his saddle though I noticed that his legs hung down each side of the animal, without the benefit of stirrups.

By now the instructor was also on horseback. He drew his sword and nudged his mount forward until the two riders were facing one another, knee to knee.

'Strike at me, lad!' he commanded.

The redhead pulled out his own blade and aimed a half-hearted blow that the instructor easily blocked with his shield. Then the instructor rose in his stirrups until he was half a head taller than his opponent. Reversing his sword, he thumped the pommel down hard on his opponent's helmet. Dazed, the redhead reeled in the saddle.

A hand clapped me on the shoulder, making me jump. Hroudland had walked up behind me.

'Skulking on the sidelines, Patch, instead of training?' he queried cheerfully.

'Where are those men from?' I asked.

'They're locals. I've stripped the March of men and animals. The king's marshals want cavalry, not foot soldiers, for the expedition to Hispania.' He turned to look at the recruits who were now lining up under their instructor's eye, ready to tilt at a line of straw dummies. 'Let's hope this latest batch of levies are quick learners. We don't have enough fodder to keep so many animals for more than a few weeks.'

'If you want me to join them, I'll need to borrow some armour from you, as well as a sword,' I said.

'What happened to the sword I selected for you from the royal armoury in Aachen?' he demanded, his face suddenly serious.

'I left it in Zaragoza with my servant Osric. He's a free man now. I also gave him my horse.'

For a moment the count was lost for words. Then he snapped angrily, 'You blockhead. That sword was something special. Have you forgotten that it is forbidden to export such weapons from Frankia?'

His outburst was so unexpected that it took me a moment to respond.

'I'll ask Osric for it back when we get to Zaragoza,' I said.

The count scowled.

'If Osric is still there, or hasn't sold it.'

'I'm sure he would keep it until I return,' I said.

Hroudland drew a sharp breath, clearly annoyed.

'I'd rather shatter the blade of my own Durendal than let it fall into the wrong hands.' He swung round to face me and, in a sudden change of mood, treated me to an apologetic smile. 'I'm sorry, Patch, I didn't mean to be boorish. Of course, it was impractical for you to bring that sword back with you. The Vascon sailors would have cut your throat for it.' He waved his hand towards the great hall on the crest of the hill. 'Pick yourself a shield and helmet from my armoury and find yourself a mail coat that fits.'

*

With the prospect of real fighting in Hispania ahead of me, I did as Hroudland suggested: I devoted all my energy to becoming a skilful mounted warrior. There was no time to think of anything else. I pushed aside any thoughts of making contact with Bertha, for I was still wary of palace politics in Aachen. Besides, I suspected that she had long ago found other lovers. I was now the margrave's man and I owed him my duty, and that meant following him unquestioningly wherever he might lead. After six weeks' practice with lance and borrowed sword I was fit to accompany the margrave's cavalry when they set out to join the main invasion force. We struck camp two weeks after the equinox and made an impressive spectacle, the mounted column splashing across the ford at the edge of the training ground in the pale spring sunshine. Hroudland himself took the lead, a stylish figure in a scarlet riding cloak trimmed with marten fur, bareheaded, with his long blonde hair falling to his shoulders. Immediately behind him came his standard bearer holding the staff with the bull's head banner. Then followed the rest of his entourage – household servants in red and white livery, a groom leading the roan war horse, his councillors and his confidants, of which I was one.

Our supply carts had gone ahead and we followed them southward in easy stages. We were travelling across pleasant wooded countryside, the trees were bursting into leaf and the underbrush was full of small, flitting, rustling creatures and birdsong. The air had a rich, loamy smell of new growth and, except for the occasional heavy rain shower during the first week, the weather was kind to us. Day after day, the sun shone from a clear, pale-blue sky, disappearing only briefly behind the legions of puffy, white clouds that sailed overhead on a westerly wind, their shadows racing across our path and then over the open landscape to our left.

Frequently Hroudland invited me to ride beside him, in full view of the rest of the company, cementing my reputation as his close friend.

'I'm not sorry to be leaving the Breton land,' he confided to me on the fourth day of our journey. The road was taking us through a birch forest on the edge of a heathland. The greyish-white bark on the trees reminded me of my stay in Zaragoza. The bark was the same colour as the sheets of unknown writing material I had found in wali Husayn's guest chamber.

'Does the winter weather depress you?' I asked.

'That and the people. They keep their feelings so shuttered. I'd like to have their loyalty, not just have their sullen obedience. You never know what they are thinking.' He nodded towards the forest around us. 'Those birch trees, for example. To me, as a Frank, they are trees full of bright life, hope for the future. But, to the Breton, the birch is a tree that grows in the land of the dead.'

'My father once told me that the birch is a symbol of a new beginning, a cleansing of the past. Perhaps that is what you need,' I said.

Hroudland suddenly became very serious.

'Patch, if I have anything to do with it, this new campaign will indeed provide me with a fresh start.'

I stole a quick sideways glance. His face was clouded.

'What do you mean?' I asked.

'Remember our excursion to the forest of Broceliande to investigate the story of Yvain and the fountain and how it ended?'

'The cup of gold turned out to be made of bronze. I saw it recently with the other tableware in your great hall.'

'What if we had found a real gold cup?'

'As I recall, you proposed to have it melted down and added to your treasury.'

'But supposing the cup had been something of such extraordinary value that no one would ever think of destroying it.'

'Now you are talking in riddles,' I said to him.

'Those Breton bards are always singing about something called a Graal, some sort of a bowl or a platter. It was the most precious object known to their mystical king Artorius.'

'And what happened to it?' I asked.

He did not answer my question directly but said, 'Many of Artorius's best men went looking for this Graal. Yet only a couple of them ever laid eyes on this mysterious object.'

'I don't see what this has got to do with our expedition to Hispania,' I said to him. I was beginning to believe that Hroudland had spent far too many evenings swilling wine with his friends and boasting of exploits past and future.

He turned to face me and I saw that he was in complete earnest.

'The Breton bards say this mysterious Graal is kept in a heavily guarded castle, a place difficult to reach because it is surrounded on all sides by mountains. They make it sound as if the castle is somewhere in the south.'

I had to scoff.

'If you're thinking that the Graal is to be found among the mountains on the way to Hispania, let me tell you there are few forests in that region. It's a bleak and barren place where someone nearly knocked out my brains with a sling stone.'

Hroudland was not to be deflected.

'A little danger won't deter me from looking for the Graal there, no more than it stopped me from riding into the forest of Broceliande.'

I sighed with exasperation.

'And what will you do, if you lay hands on this Graal? It could turn out to be like the little bronze cup, something you could buy for a penny in a market.'

The look Hroudland gave me was almost triumphant.

'Don't you see, Patch? It doesn't matter whether this Graal is made of gold or brass or even wood. Imagine how the Bretons would respect the man who returned this treasure to them!'

I had to stop myself from shaking my head despairingly. Once Hroudland fastened on an idea, he was impossible to reason with.

'And if there is no Graal and the whole thing is a myth?'

Sensing my misgivings, Hroudland laughed.

'In that case this expedition is still my chance for a new beginning. As I've said before, I will serve with such distinction that when we have conquered our Saracen opponents, my uncle Carolus will make me Margrave of the new Spanish March.' He leaned across from his horse and cuffed me affectionately across the head. 'And then, Patch, you will come with me as my close advisor, and enjoy the sunshine instead of the Breton drizzle.'

He clapped his heels to the side of his horse and broke into a canter, clods of earth flying up from his horse's hooves.

*

A week later we found ourselves looking down into a ruined valley. It was as if a great wind of destruction had swept across the land. Hedges and thickets were smashed into tatters. The young crops in the fields trampled and ruined. The ground was all torn up and wrecked. Not a tree or sapling was left standing in the coppices, and their stumps showed fresh axe marks. It was a truly dismal spectacle and I was astonished when Berenger gave a whoop of delight.

He began humming to himself as we rode side by side down the slope and into the scene of devastation.

'What happened here?' I asked.

'An army,' he retorted with a grin. 'The ground will soon recover. Look at all that manure.'

Indeed there were piles of dung dotted here and there, as well as an ugly spew of rubbish – discarded sacking, traces of cooking fires, chicken feathers, gnawed bones, a broken earthenware pot, a split shoe that someone had tossed away. I pulled my horse aside before he stepped into what was obviously a pile of human excrement. It took me another moment to realize that all this squalor lay in a broad swathe leading along the bottom of the valley.

Hroudland was riding a little distance ahead of us. He swivelled in his saddle and called back, 'Come on! They must be just over that hill crest!' He put his horse into a fast trot and began to ascend the far slope.

Berenger and I followed, and as we crested the rise I pulled my mount to a halt and looked on in amazement. I knew now why my comrades always seemed so confident of the success of the Frankish army.

Along the bottom of the next valley crawled a huge serpent. It was formed of ox-drawn vehicles, creeping forward in a long line. There must have been four or five hundred of them. Most were substantial two-wheeled carts, though a few of the larger ones had four wheels similar to Arnulf's eel wagon. All were tented and drawn by two animals, their drovers walking beside them or riding on bench seats in front of the canopies. Even from a distance I could hear the squealing and groaning of the huge solid wheels turning on wooden axles, and hear the occasional crack of a whip. Out on the flanks of the column were parties of foragers stripping the countryside of any vegetation that might provide food for the draught animals. Closer to us a great herd of cattle meandered along, eating every blade of grass or green leaf in its path.

'Everything the army needs is down there,' Berenger called out to me proudly. He waved his arm towards the wagons. 'Tents, spare weapons, grain, cooking pots, trenching tools. That cattle herd is a moving larder of fresh meat.'

'Where's the king himself?' I asked.

He pointed. At the head of the column, in the far distance, was a dark swarm of horsemen, the main body of the army. I could just make out some flapping banners and the occasional glint of sunlight reflected from a shield or spear point.

'Sloppy of them not to have posted a rearguard,' observed Hroudland tartly, interrupting us. He spurred his horse down the slope to join the army, and Berenger and I cantered along behind him.

We overtook the column and rode along beside it. Now I could hear the deep grunting breaths of the draught animals, saliva dripping from their mouths as they plodded forward. We came level with a company of infantry, tramping along stolidly, one of many such companies dotted along the column. This group were husky, well-built men, who shouldered short-handled axes. Their sergeant, a craggy figure with cropped hair and a great beak of a broken nose shouted out a question at us in a strange hoarse voice, in a language none of us could understand.

'They'll be some of Anseis's Burgundians,' Berenger explained. 'Carolus has summoned troops from all over the kingdom. Each man is obliged to serve under arms for up to sixty days a year.'

'Do they fight only with those axes?'

'Their shields and spears will be somewhere in the wagons along with the rest of their gear. There's no point in carrying an extra burden on the march.'

Ahead of us one of the ox carts pulled out of line. The right hand wheel was wobbling and it looked as if an axle pin had come loose.

Someone, a wheelwright probably, jumped off an ox wagon. Tools in hand, he was already on his way to repair the stranded cart. It appeared that the column was self-repairing.

'What happens when the column needs to cross a river?' I asked.

'If there's no bridge strong or big enough to take so many vehicles, the scouts find a ford. Provided the oxen can keep their footing, the army moves forward. Nothing should get wet. The carts and wagons are built like boats, to keep out river water as well as rain.'

I noticed that the wooden sides of the nearest cart were sealed with pitch, and the cover was made of greased leather. Nevertheless, something was missing. It was only after Berenger and I had ridden the entire length of the column and were approaching the mass of cavalry up ahead that I identified the flaw. Among all the hundreds of supply wagons and carts, mobile smithies and workshops of the army on the move, there was not a single large siege engine. If Carolus met with resistance from the walled cities of Hispania, he risked failure.

I thought of voicing my concern to Hroudland, but he had gone ahead to catch up with the leaders, and by the time I had a chance to speak to him privately, too much had happened to make me think that my opinion would be taken seriously.

In mid-afternoon the army halted on open ground. Nearby was a lake where the horses and oxen were led to be watered. The ox carts and wagons were parked in orderly lines, the infantry and cavalry set up their tents, camp fires were lit, and cattle selected from the accompanying herd were slaughtered and butchered. Soon so much smoke rose into the air from the cooking fires that a stranger would have thought he had stumbled on a small town.

Hroudland went to report to the official in charge of the practical arrangements for the campaign, a man named Eggihard who held the title of seneschal to the king. Meanwhile Berenger and I set off in search of the other paladins. We found them drinking wine and lounging around a camp fire close to an enormous square pavilion, striped in red, gold and blue with the royal standard flying from the centre pole. Several paladins I remembered from the winter in Aachen were there — Anseis of Burgundy, handsome and swaggering Engeler, and Gerer, Gerin's friend. Old Gerard was missing and I was saddened to be told that he had never fully recovered from the poison he had eaten at the banquet. His agonizing stomach cramps had returned and his new doctor had advised him to chew laurel leaves, swallow the juice and then lay the wet leaves on his stomach. This treatment had been no more help than the prayers of the attendant priests, and a winter chill took him off while he was still in a weakened state.

Guiltily I wondered if I had been selfish to have taken Osric with me on the mission to Zaragoza. If Osric had stayed behind, perhaps his medical skill would have saved the old man. Now, even if I had wished to return the Book of Dreams, it was impossible.

'Patch, Berenger! I want you to hear our orders from the king.' Hroudland was standing at the entrance to the royal pavilion and summoning us. All thoughts of Gerard vanished from my mind. Inside the tent I might come face to face with Ganelon and he was a man best avoided. I had not seen him since he had gone off to Barcelona with Gerin. Even if Ganelon was not responsible for the attack by the Vascon slinger in the mountains and the earlier attempts on my life, he would see me as a threat to his plan to discredit Hroudland as a traitor in the pay of the Wali of Zaragoza.

So I stepped cautiously into the royal pavilion. The interior was more spacious than most houses. I caught a whiff of some sort of incense, and I guessed that the royal chaplain had recently been conducting a service inside. The evening light filtering through the canvas was strong enough to show a heavy curtain of purple velvet partitioned off the far end. Beyond it, I presumed, were the king's private quarters. The rest of the pavilion was arranged as a council room. Wooden boards had been laid to make a temporary floor. In one corner two clerks sat at a portable desk with parchment and pens. A travelling throne of gilded, carved wood stood on a low plinth, and the centre of the room was entirely taken up by a familiar object – the great tile map that I had last seen in the Aachen chancery. It had been reassembled on trestle tables.

A dozen senior officers and court officials were already standing around the map, talking quietly among themselves. My heart was in my mouth as I scanned their faces, looking for Ganelon. But he was not there, nor among the outer circle of lesser attendants and advisors. I quietly joined them just as the velvet curtain was abruptly pulled aside and the king strode into the room. Carolus was bare-headed and dressed in his usual workday clothing, brown woollen tunic and hose with cross garters of plain leather, and he wore no badges of rank. Outside the tent one might have mistaken him for a common soldier; tall but unremarkable.

His glance swept round the assembled company and I could have sworn that it lingered for a moment on my face as he recalled who I was. Ignoring the wooden throne, he walked straight to the map table, and was straight down to business.

'I have summoned this meeting so that you are all familiar with our plan for the campaign in Hispania,' he announced in his strangely high, thin voice, so much in contrast with his air of authority. He gestured toward the map on the table beside him. 'I want you to take careful note of our dispositions because tomorrow I propose to divide the army.'

All around me was a collective intake of breath. Men shifted uncomfortably, clearly disturbed by the royal decision.

Carolus was aware of the disquiet he had caused.

'I know it is considered foolhardy to divide one's forces, but now that my nephew Count Hroudland has arrived with his Breton cavalry we have sufficient numbers to do so.' Again he indicated the map. 'A wall of mountains lies between us and the Saracens in Hispania who seek our help, here at Barcelona, Huesca and Zaragoza.'

I was standing too far away to be sure, but I had the impression that he was pointing out the three cities on the map without reading their names on the tiles because he could not do so.

Carolus paused briefly while he looked at his senior officers. He had their full attention.

'I myself will lead that part of the army – the larger part – that will go around the eastern end of the mountains. We head directly for Barcelona to meet with the wali there.'

There was complete silence in the room. No doubt many of his audience were silently wondering which units would be detached from the main force.

The king turned to face Eggihard.

'You as seneschal will lead the western division that will go around the mountains and head for Zaragoza where the wali is expecting us. The margrave will be your second in command.'

I felt a glow of satisfaction. It meant that I was likely to see Osric again..

Carolus once again addressed his wider audience.

'Our spies tell us that our entry into Hispania may encounter opposition. By entering Hispania from two directions we will crush our opponents between us like a nutcracker. That is why I divide the army.'

His audience relaxed. There were murmurs of approval.

The king held up a warning hand and the assembly immediately fell silent.

'The success of my plan depends on both halves of the army acting in concert.'

'Your Majesty, what about the supply train?' asked Eggihard.

'Allocate the vehicles by their size. The smaller, lighter carts will go with the western division as it has further to travel and must move more quickly. Those details I leave to you and my other captains to arrange.'

Amid the general shuffling and conversation which followed, I heard someone ask his neighbour, 'Anyone know who we're likely to be fighting?'

The questioner was a pear-shaped, rather worried-looking man with a strong accent. I guessed he was the commander of one of the contingents from the further reaches of the kingdom, possibly Lombardy.

I missed the answer because Carolus had disappeared behind the velvet curtain and Hroudland was beckoning to me and Berenger. We pushed our way through the press of people and caught up with the count as he was leaving the pavilion and heading in the direction of the tents allocated to the Breton cavalry. The count was in a foul mood and scowling.

'Eggihard knows how to put pottage into soldier's bellies and boots on their feet, but if it comes to a fight, he'll be useless.'

It was obvious that Hroudland resented Eggihard's appointment over him. I also wondered if the count would have preferred staying with the main army where he would have been more directly under his uncle's eye to impress the king with his military prowess.

'Maybe there won't be any fighting,' I suggested. 'We are entering Hispania at the invitation of the Saracens.'

Hroudland gave a snort of disbelief.

'The Falcon of Cordoba won't stand by idly.'

'Who's he?' I asked.

'The most dangerous man in Hispania. He claims that he is rightful overlord of those three rebellious Saracen walis who have invited us to help them. The last time there was an uprising against him, he lined up a hundred of their leaders, kneeling on the ground, and had their heads chopped off.'

'Then all the more renown for us when we defeat him,' boasted Berenger.

This was dangerous vainglory, but I held my tongue. Besides, something was nagging at the back of my mind. We were walking past the horse lines and a tall, big-boned stallion had caught my attention. It had its head in a feed bag while a groom brushed its coat. I had seen that same horse on the day I had gone to hunt deer near Aachen; it was the horse that the king had ridden. The memory brought a shiver to my spine. The next animal in the line was another stallion, not as tall as its neighbour, but broader and more heavily muscled, a true war horse. There was something eerily familiar about it, too. I stared long and hard at the creature, wondering where I had seen it before. With a sudden lurch of recognition, I knew. It was the same animal I had seen in my nightmare many months ago, looming over me, one hoof raised. I had looked up in terror and seen blood seeping from the eyes of the rider. It was also the bronze horse of the statue Carolus had brought from Ravenna, the statue I had seen dragged across the sheet ice.

I came to an abrupt halt, unable to take another step. A strange prickling sensation had come over me, paralysing me from head to toe. Unaware of what was happening, Berenger and Hroudland walked away, leaving me behind. I remained rooted to the spot, unable to take my eyes off the war horse until a hand touched me on the elbow and I turned to see a messenger, dressed in royal livery. He was looking at me strangely, and I heard his words through a haze. He repeated them.

'Follow me, please. The king wants to speak with you.'

*

I was so numb with shock that until my boots were echoing on the wooden flooring I did not realize that I had been led back inside the royal pavilion. A small group of courtiers was in the outer chamber and they eyed me curiously as I was taken straight past them and handed over to an attendant. He peeked in through the velvet curtain, and then held it aside just far enough for me to slip into Carolus's private quarters. As I entered I caught a whiff of roast flesh.

The king was eating a late meal. Seated at a plain wooden table, he was gnawing the stringy flesh from the leg of a partially dismembered goose carcass. A manservant was hovering nearby with a jug of water and a napkin over his arm, ready to wash the grease off the royal fingers. The inevitable clerk lurked in a corner, wax tablet in hand, ready to take down notes. Otherwise the king was alone.

He gnawed a strip of meat from the bone. His teeth were big and strong, a match for his great size. When he raised his face towards me, I again saw the grey, watchful eyes. A morsel of food was trapped in his moustache.

'Have you anything to report?' he asked, not unkindly but with a simple directness.

My mind was in a whirl. The face of the king and the image of the man on the horse crying blood were overlapping as if in a waking nightmare. I blinked hard, feeling confused and nauseous.

'Well, what have you to say?' The tone was harder now. Carolus did not like to waste time.

'Your Majesty, I returned from Hispania some two months ago, by sea. I have been with Count Hroudland,' I stammered.

'I know that,' Carolus snapped. 'Did you learn anything among the Saracens? Did you dream among them?'

Desperately I thought back to all that happened when I was

with Husayn. All I could remember was the horrible dream of the snake lying across my lap.

'Just once, Your Majesty. I dreamed of treachery.'

The king pointed the half-chewed goose bone at me as though it was a sceptre.

'Tell me.'

I described my dream and how I had consulted the Book of Dreams to interpret its meaning.

Carolus listened in silence.

'This happened when you were staying with Wali Husayn in Zaragoza?' he asked when I finished.

I nodded.

'Thank you. I shall be on my guard.'

I began to edge away towards the curtain. I was still deeply disturbed by my vision of the king on horseback, crying blood. I knew I should not speak about it, at least not until I knew what it might mean.

'One moment!' he commanded suddenly.

I froze, wondering if he was about to cross-examine me.

'My nephew is headstrong. If there's to be any fighting in Hispania, he'll be in the thick of it.' It was a flat statement of fact.

'I am sure he will acquit himself nobly, Your Majesty,' I answered diplomatically.

'And you? Do you know how to wield a sword as well as you can manage a bow?'

It seemed that Carolus had not forgotten the day I killed two royal stags. I thought it wiser to say nothing and waited for his next remark.

'I am very fond of my nephew. I hope that you and your companions among my paladins will see to it that his enthusiasm does not lead him astray.'

I bowed my head obediently. The king had already reached out and was twisting the second leg off the goose carcass. It was clear that my interview was over, and I slipped gratefully out of the room.

*

Hroudland's poor opinion of Eggihard's military leadership was to bring near-disaster on the western army and on me in particular. When we entered the foothills of the mountains marking the border with Hispania, the count persuaded Eggihard that a detachment of picked cavalry should scout in front of the main column. Naturally Hroudland put himself at the head of this detachment. He took Berenger, Anseis, Gerin and me with him, in effect creating his own roving command. His motive became clear within days. Simply put, our advance unit had first choice of any plunder that lay in the army's path. We ranged across the countryside and helped ourselves to any valuables in the towns and villages. We met little or no resistance from our victims, and each evening gathered at our chosen campsite and piled up the booty we had found that day. Though the booty was meagre it reminded me of the scene when King Offa's troops had sacked my father's great hall. So, whenever possible, I waived my share of any loot. My comrades thought I was behaving strangely. To them the chance for plunder was a powerful reason to go to war, and Hroudland had an impatient, hungry look as he presided over the division of the spoils. He always kept a tenth for himself declaring that his expenses as Margrave of the Breton March had left him in debt.

Understandably the villagers and townsfolk were glad to see the back of us when we moved on. Quite how unpopular we made ourselves was made evident to me one bright day in mid-May.

By then we were advancing around the end of the mountains, with their foothills to our left. That morning, as our unit prepared to fan out across the countryside, Hroudland asked me to take a couple of troopers and investigate a low range of hills in the distance. He believed there might be a rich village hidden somewhere in that direction.

I rode off as instructed, the two cavalrymen trotting behind me. We were so accustomed to lack of resistance that all three of us left behind our cumbersome lances and shields. Our only weapons were our cavalry swords and daggers. Very quickly we left the cultivated land and came into an area where the soil was too poor to sustain anything but thin, scrubby grass and clumps of small thorny trees. We came across an occasional cattle byre built of dry branches but saw neither cattle nor people, and resigned ourselves to a long ride as the hills were some distance away. Gradually the land sloped upward and, riding along reins slack, we allowed our horses to go at their own pace. By midday it was uncomfortably hot in the sunshine and when we stopped to water the horses at a small pool of tepid water I removed my brunia, the leather jacket covered with metal scales worn by every cavalryman, and tied it to my saddle. I had already taken off my metal helmet. The two troopers did the same.

We remounted and jogged along, following the faint trace of a path through the bushes. We reached the hills themselves and the land closed in around us as the path led higher. Here the ground was bare of vegetation, and the track grew more and more stony, twisting and turning around the spurs of the hills. After some time, one of the troopers called out to me that his horse had gone lame. The animal had stepped on a sharp stone; the sole of the hoof was bleeding. We were deep in the hills and I told the trooper to turn round and begin walking his horse back to where we had watered before. His companion and I would continue ahead for another hour and if we found nothing, as seemed likely, we would turn back and rejoin him.

We rode on. Soon the road dwindled to little more than a footpath, obliging us to walk our horses cautiously in single file. To our left the hillside rose very steeply, a bare slope of loose scree and shale. It climbed at least a hundred feet to a ridge whose jagged outline reminded me of a cock's comb. On our right the ground fell away equally steeply, dropping into a dried-up river bed. Here, the slope was dotted with boulders of every size and shape. They had broken away from the crest and rolled down the hill. Some had come to rest part of the way down, but most had tumbled all the way into the ravine below.

My companion was the more accomplished horseman, and as the path grew even narrower, he offered to take the lead. My own horse, a chestnut mare, had a nervous disposition and was reluctant to proceed.

After some twenty minutes of slow progress she lost her nerve entirely. She came to a halt, shivering and sweating, and would go no further. I kicked her hard in the ribs and shouted at her. She put back her ears, stiffened her legs and refused to budge. I kicked again and shouted even louder. My shout came back to me as an echo from the steep slopes all around. As the sound faded I heard a gentle clatter. Looking up and to my left, I saw that a small section of hillside close to the path had come loose and was sliding downhill in a thin trickle of gravel. The flow halted, there was a final rattle of the last few pebbles, and a brief silence. Then a sharp, much louder crack sounded. I shifted my gaze higher up to the cock's comb of the ridge above me just in time to see a moderate-sized boulder break free and slip downward a fraction. It was about the size a man could encircle with his arms. It hung motionless and time seemed to stand still. In a heartbeat it began to roll, tumbling end over end. It gathered speed, first making small leaps, and then as it struck a rocky ledge it was thrown outward, bounced, and flew with even greater force, hurtling downward in a series of destructive arcs.

I shouted a warning to my companion, less than ten paces ahead. He had already seen the danger and put heels to his horse's flanks. The animal jumped forward, and this action saved them. The boulder went spinning past them and crashed on down the hill.

'Are you all right?' I called out. I was struggling to control my mare. The animal had been terrified into action and was scrabbling with its hooves, lunging from side to side. I feared we would slip off the loose surface of the path and plunge to our destruction.

'A near miss,' came back the call, and the trooper gave a confident wave to reassure me. 'We'll be on safer ground soon.'

Underneath me the mare was still shaking with fright so I nearly missed the same ominous warning, a sharp crack and then the first thud as another rock, slightly smaller than the first, broke away from the ridge line and began its lethal descent towards us.

'Look out!' I yelled.

Again the boulder was careering a deadly path down the slope.

By then I knew it was no accident. Someone on the crest was trying to kill us.

For a second time the boulder missed. It leaped through the gap between us, bounding down the slope with a great crashing. Shards of rock flew up whenever it struck another boulder.

I bellowed at the trooper to come back. He flung himself sideways from his saddle, landing on the slope above him. He had the reins in hand, hauling on them, trying by brute force to make his horse turn on the narrow path. The animal gave a whinny of protest and spun on its haunches, turning so that its front hooves were clawing on the loose gravel of the upper slope as it tried to find a purchase. At that moment the trooper himself lost his footing and, arms flailing, slid down under the belly of the horse.

The tangle proved fatal. A third rock came tumbling down. It was larger than the others, and halfway towards us it struck an outcrop of rock and split into two. The smaller part, no larger than a blacksmith's anvil, bounced higher and higher until it struck the trooper squarely and with tremendous force. I felt the thud of the impact, and then the scream of the horse as in the same instant the collision smashed the beast over the edge of the path. The trooper, his hand still twisted in the reins, was dragged away with his mount. Beast and man went slithering down the slope in a sickening whirl of hooves, arms and legs, bouncing off the rocks as they followed the fatal boulder that had outstripped its victims. Finally they came to a rest in the bottom of the ravine. Neither could have survived that terrible fall.

Now the hidden enemy turned his attention on me. I was the only target remaining. I kicked my feet out of the stirrups and swung myself down from the saddle, stumbling as I landed on the broken ground. I made no attempt to make the mare turn but pushed past her flank, leaving her where she was as I ran for my life back the way we had come. The loose ground crunched and shifted beneath my boots, though thankfully not loudly enough to drown out the warning thud and clatter of the next boulder as it was launched down the slope. I looked up and judged its path. Then I dived to one side, flattening myself against the hillside, feeling the ground shudder beneath me as the rock careered off the rocks. It missed me by a yard or more, and then I was up and running, away down the path and around the next corner in terror.

I had gone perhaps twenty paces when, to my horror, I heard someone chasing down the track behind me. I dared not look over my shoulder and expected a lance point in my back at any moment. Then, to my relief, my panic-struck mare came slamming and barging past me, almost knocking me off the trail. The creature had managed to turn herself around unaided, and was bolting. I reached out, grabbed a stirrup with both hands as she pushed past me and clung on. I was bounced and dragged beside her down the path, and I feared she would run off the track and fall, taking us both down to our deaths. But somehow she managed to carry me, half running, half dragged, for more than a mile before she slowed enough for me to heave myself back into the saddle and gather up the reins.

By then we were well away from the ridge, and I rode on shakily until I caught up with the trooper walking his lame horse. By a stroke of luck we came across Hroudland very soon afterwards. He was out with a score of cavalrymen, checking on his patrols.

As soon as the count heard what had happened, he went galloping off at full tilt, hoping to catch the hidden attackers before they left the scene.

But it was too late. He returned some hours later, riding up to our camp at the head of his men, faces covered in dust, their horses lathered and weary. His first words were, 'Patch, you were lucky. We found marks up on the ridge where a lever was used to dislodge the rocks. But the enemy was gone.'

'What about the trooper who was knocked off the track?' I asked.

'A mangled corpse. One of my men clambered down to take a look. All blood and broken bones.' He swung himself down from the saddle and walked over to the campfire, his face serious. 'Tomorrow I'll call the men together and warn them to be more on their guard.'

'Any sign of a village where the attackers could have come

from?' asked Berenger, who had been scouting out on our left flank.

The count shook his head.

'If there had been, I'd have got the truth out of them.'

Then I noticed something odd. One of Hroudland's riders had come back with an extra brunia tied to his saddle which, I presumed, he had salvaged from the corpse of the dead man. A brunia was a costly piece of equipment and most of the mailed jackets worn by the men were on loan from the royal armoury; it seemed strange that the mysterious assailants had not stayed long enough to plunder their victim.

Chapter Sixteen

THE AMBUSH AND THE TROOPER'S death cast a shadow over our advance. We were still in Vascon land, yet to enter Saracen territory. So we should have had a peaceful journey because the Vascons were Christians like ourselves. Instead with every mile we travelled, we were met with increasing hostility. The Vascons hid their stores of food, blocked or polluted wells, and if we asked directions, they sent us in the wrong direction. Hroudland had begun drinking heavily again and, in keeping with the prickly mood of our troops, he became erratically aggressive and surly. When we reached the Vascon capital at Pamplona, he proposed to Eggihard that the army should storm and ransack the city to repay the Vascons for all the trouble they had caused us. The city walls were still as derelict as when I had seen them on my way to Brittany; they would not have withstood a determined assault. Eggihard bluntly told the count that the army had come to Hispania to assist the rebel Saracens, not plunder the Vascons, and there was a blazing row between them. Hroudland stormed out of the meeting and rode away with his vanguard, leaving the main army to fend for itself.

With Hroudland in such an ugly mood I made a habit of keeping out of his way as we pushed on to Zaragoza. I was thinking about Osric and wondering what had happened to him. It was three months since I had given him his freedom and left him with Wali Husayn. Part of me hoped that he had been able to leave Zaragoza and return to the place where he had grown up, but another part of me was looking forward to meeting him again. I had come to appreciate that nothing had replaced his companionship since the days when King Offa had sent me into exile. I suppose that I was falling victim to long-delayed feelings of loneliness. No longer having Osric by my side had made me realize just how much I had relied on him as a mentor and a confidant, and so I eagerly anticipated our meeting and the renewal of trust that it would bring.

With this in mind I rode ahead of everyone else during the final few miles of our approach to Zaragoza, through the orchards that surrounded the city. After several days of uncomfortably hot sunshine, the sky had partially clouded over and a slight breeze made the morning pleasantly cool. I had decided to put on full armour, helmet and brunia, and was carrying my battle shield and sword, hoping to impress any herald that Husayn would send out to welcome us, for the wali would surely know of the approach of Hroudland's vanguard, even if Eggihard and the main force lagged several days behind.

Riding through the lines of plum and orange trees, I was reminded of the day I had first come there with Wali Husayn after our journey through the mountains. We had used the very same track for I recognized a small wooden bridge that crossed one of the many irrigation channels. Now, of course, the trees were in full leaf, their fruit nearly ripe, and there was just enough breeze to gently sway the laden branches. I was happy and relaxed as I rode, turning over in my mind what I might discuss with Wali Husayn. I hoped there would be the chance to share another pleasant evening meal beside the reflecting pool in his palace. All around me the orchards were very quiet except for the croaking of several ravens that circled over me. I saw no one. The hoof beats of my horse, the same nervous mare that had saved my life, were muffled by the soft earth between the fruit trees. I savoured the calm and stillness, glad to be clear of Hroudland and his snappish temper. He and his escort of riders would be at least a mile behind me. I felt an unexpected surge of pride at the idea that after two months' march from Brittany, I would be the first person in the army to sight Zaragoza.

A movement some distance ahead caught my attention. A small troop of horsemen was moving at a walk across my path. They appeared and disappeared among the lines of tree trunks. It was difficult to tell their exact number but I recognized them immediately as Saracens; their mounts were their typical small, high stepping horses. They wore flowing mantles and I identified them as cavalrymen, for they wore helmets and carried lances. I congratulated myself that Wali Husayn had sent out an escort to greet Hroudland and bring him into the city, showing the count the same honour that the wali received from his own followers. For days I had been telling the count that Husayn was a civilized and cultured nobleman and I was hopeful that such a courtesy would help dispel Hroudland's sour temper.

The riders were crossing my path about a hundred paces ahead and had not seen me. Perhaps they were not expecting a lone rider. So I called out a greeting. I saw the little group stop and turn in my direction. I reined in my horse and sat quietly as they trotted towards me. In my mind I was already rehearsing the formal phrases of welcome in the Saracen tongue which Osric had taught me.

The Saracen cavalrymen must have been fifty paces from me when I noted the colour of the scarves around their helmets and the banners tied around their lances. It was a plain green. With a sudden lurch in my stomach I recalled that every one of Husayn's servants and soldiers had worn crimson.

Something was very wrong.

The riders were still coming towards me at a purposeful trot. My alarm sharpened my senses. Even at that distance I could detect that they were deliberately keeping their horses in check. It was not the disciplined riding of well-trained cavalry. Belatedly it dawned on me that they were hoping to get very close before I realized who they were – the enemy.

I snatched on the reins and wrenched my horse's head around and kicked hard. The mare threw up her head in outrage and broke into a gallop. I leaned forward in the saddle and shouted in her ear, urging her on as we flew between the trees. Behind me I heard a triumphant cry and then whoops of excitement as the troopers took up the chase.

For them it must have been as easy as running down a wounded deer. My mare was not a creature to win races. She was very ordinary, more suited to a thirty-mile march than a mad, short sprint. Her timidity gave her extra speed at the outset, but she could never outpace the Saracen horses now in pursuit.

I stayed low, ducking under the branches of the fruit trees, occasionally feeling the lash of twigs and foliage whipping across my helmet. I felt the mare leap an irrigation ditch, and urged her on. The whoops and yells grew louder and nearer, and in what seemed only a few minutes I could feel the mare tiring beneath me. Her head began to droop and her breath was coming in gasps. I knew that very soon she would stumble and go down. We came to a clearing in the orchard, no more than thirty paces across, and rather than take a spear in the back, I pulled up the exhausted beast, and turned.

If I was to die, I thought to myself, I preferred to be facing the enemy. In a sudden flashback to my childhood, I knew my martial father would have wanted it to be that way.

My pursuers had strung out in a line. The leader was a lancer mounted on a small chestnut horse. He gave a shout of confident anticipation as he saw that I had turned and was at bay. Scarcely breaking stride he lowered his lance and rode straight at me. The point with its fluttering scrap of green cloth was aimed squarely at my chest.

Whether it was luck or the hours of practice I had spent on the training ground below Hroudland's great hall, I responded as the instructors had taught me. I gripped my horse with my knees and thankfully the mare steadied for a moment, too tired to fidget. I concentrated fiercely on the lance tip. The green cloth tied around it made it so much easier. As it came darting towards me, I swung up my shield and slapped aside the point so that it missed entirely. My enemy was riding at a full gallop and went racing past me on my left hand side, lying forward in the saddle so that the small round shield slung between his shoulder blades protected his back. He was a youngster, scarcely into his teens, and his lighter weight had brought him to the front of the pursuit. He was probably in his first hand to hand combat, for when I looked into his brown eyes for an instant I saw they were bright with the excitement of battle.

Then, without deliberate thought, I was rising in my stirrups as I had seen my instructors demonstrate time and again. My borrowed sword was in my right hand, and as my attacker drew level, I chopped down the blade almost vertically. It caught the lad in the back of the neck, below the rim of his helmet. I felt the shock as the blade hit something solid, and then it was nearly ripped from my hand as the lad slumped forward on his horse's neck. A moment later he tumbled to the ground, his mantle tangling around his corpse.

My hand and wrist was tingling from the shock of the blow, and I was gasping for breath as I turned to face my next attacker. Beneath me the mare was weaving unhappily from side to side, wanting to turn and flee. I knew she would be overtaken in a few strides so I struggled to keep her head toward the remaining Saracens. There were four or five of them – it was all happening too quickly for me to be sure exactly how many – and they had reached the far edge of the clearing. After witnessing the fate of their comrade, they were getting ready for their next attack. One man turned and handed his lance to a comrade, then drew a short, wide-bladed sword. For an unsettling moment, I had a vision of my family's final battle. The shape of the Saracen's weapon recalled the seaxes that my father's followers had held when they faced King Offa's warriors. I saw dark, bearded faces beneath their helmets, faces set in grim calculation. The trooper with the drawn sword rode forward a pace or two, and was joined by a companion who had kept his lance. Now I saw what they intended to do. One would ride at me on my left hand side with his lance, and while I fended off his attack with my shield, his companion would cut me down on my exposed side.

The two troopers took their time. I heard them exchange a few words and then they edged their horses sideways to increase the gap between them and make it harder for me to defend myself against their double-pronged assault. Now they settled in the saddle, adjusted reins, and prepared to charge. I saw the horses gather their hind legs under them, ready to spring forward. I knew I was finished.

At that moment, another Saracen rode out from the tree line. He was dressed like the others in flowing gown and metal helmet, but he carried a short staff instead of a spear. I guessed he was some sort of officer for he barked an order, and, to my relief, the two who had been preparing to charge me pulled back their mounts, and resumed their places in the line. I sensed that they were disappointed at being denied their victim.

My relief was short lived. The officer gave a second order, and one of the other troopers reached behind his saddle and produced an object I recognized. It was a curved bow, the twin of the one that I had learned to use in Aachen. Still mounted the archer strung the bow, then reached into a quiver hanging from his saddle and drew out an arrow. I sat there helplessly, thinking back to what Osric had told me in Aachen and I had scarcely believed: at seventy paces distance a mounted Saracen was expected to hit a target of less than three spans across.

The bowman facing me was no more than half that distance away. The Saracen officer saw no point in risking further loss to his men. He preferred that I was despatched like a mad dog.

For a brief moment I wondered about turning my horse and trying to flee. But it was hopeless – I could not outrun the arrow.

So I sat on the mare without moving. I stared at my executioner, wondering what was going through his mind as he drew back the bowstring and took aim.

I saw the arrow fly. It was no more than a very brief, dark blur and then, appallingly, I felt it thump into the target. It was not my chest. Beneath me the mare quivered as if she had been struck with a hammer, and her forelegs buckled as she collapsed on the ground. As I flew over her head I realized that the Saracens did not want to kill me. They wanted to take me alive.

I landed on soft ground, sprawling awkwardly. My sword flew from my hand, and I felt a sharp pain in my elbow as the shield straps held firm, twisting my arm sideways.

Dazed, I struggled up on all fours and managed to haul myself upright, my pride forcing me to remain facing my enemies. The mare was on the ground next to me, her legs kicking feebly. I saw the ribs heave one last time and heard a hollow grunting sigh emerge from her throat. Then she lay still. The mounted officer gave his reins a gentle flick and his mount, a particularly fine

stallion, stepped delicately towards me. His expression framed by
the rim of the iron helmet and its two metal cheek guards was of
cold, bleak certainty.

He had no need to tell me what to do. I pulled my left arm
free of the shield straps and let the shield fall to the ground. Then
I reached up and began to unfasten my helmet, which had
somehow remained in place.

I was fiddling with the lacing knot when something flew over
my head from behind me. It smashed into the chest of the officer
and the impact threw him backward over his horse's haunch. He
flung up his arms and, as he fell, I had a momentary glimpse of
the butt end of a heavy spear buried in his chest. The next instant
I heard a full-throated whoop of triumph that I had heard on my
first full day at Aachen, and many times on the training ground
below Hroudland's great hall. It was the yell of victorious pleasure
that the count released whenever he scored a direct hit on his
target.

An instant later Hroudland himself burst out of the trees
directly behind me. He was riding at a full gallop, hallooing and
yelling, and charging straight at the Saracens.

He deliberately rode over his victim. I heard the sickening
crunch of bones as the powerful war horse trod on the officer's
body. Then the animal crashed headlong into the next Saracen
trooper in line and sent his lighter horse staggering backward.
Hroudland already had his sword in his hand and before his
opponent could recover his balance, the count had delivered a
downward cut at the Saracen's shoulder. The man must have been
wearing shoulder armour under his mantle; otherwise he would
have lost his arm. He swayed in the saddle, his arm now hanging
useless, blood gushing from the wound. His horse saved his life;
before Hroudland could deliver a second sword blow, the animal
leaped sideways and carried its rider out of range.

Now Berenger and the rest of the count's escort came pouring out of the tree line. Suddenly there was the thunder of hooves, yelling and shouting, and all the headlong chaos of a cavalry charge.

The Saracens knew at once that they were outnumbered. Without hesitation they pulled around their horses. It was astonishing how nimbly their mounts turned. They pivoted on their hindquarters and, like cats, sprang forward. Moments later they were in full flight, racing away from the pursuit. They had been driven off but they were not in disarray. The group split up, each man taking his own line through the orange and plum trees, weaving and twisting, and making the chase difficult. I doubted if Hroudland, Berenger and the others would catch them.

I stood in the clearing, shaken and exhausted. My legs were trembling with fatigue, and I could feel my left elbow stiffening where the shield straps had wrenched my arm. All of a sudden everything seemed very quiet. The skirmish had been very brief, yet had taken a bloody toll. My chestnut mare lay dead just a few feet away, and beyond her was the body of the young Saracen I had killed. Further off, right in the centre of the glade, was the corpse of the officer with Hroudland's lance sticking out of his chest.

The very same qualities that often irritated me about Hroudland – his lack of forethought, his belligerence, his vain confidence in his own prowess – had saved me. His impetuous, raging attack had been typical of the man. If he had not been riding out ahead of his escort, he would have arrived too late. If he had not been so prone to acting on the spur of the moment, he would never have intercepted the Saracen officer in time. If he was not such a good fighting man, he would never have hit his target with his thrown lance.

Without question I owed him my liberty and very likely my life as well.

The count and the others rode back into the clearing some time later, their horses flecked with lather. There were no Saracen prisoners.

'They got away,' Berenger called, frustrated.

The group gathered round me and dismounted. Their presence was comforting. Never before had I felt so close to my Frankish colleagues.

'Who were they?' I asked through dry cracked lips. My throat felt raw and I was parched with a sudden, fierce thirst.

'A patrol of the Emir of Cordoba's cavalry, probably.' Berenger lifted off his helmet and removed the felt cap he wore under it. He ran his hand through his crop of curls.

'How did they come to be here?' I wondered.

'The Falcon didn't get his nickname for nothing. He strikes fast. They must have been probing the defences of Zaragoza.'

One of the men sauntered over to the corpse of the young Saracen I had killed. Doubtless he was checking what there might be worth plundering from the body. With his foot he rolled the body over on its back. Now I saw the face clearly. It was indeed that of a young man, not old enough to have grown a full beard. He had smooth skin and fine, regular features. As I watched, the head lolled loosely to one side. My downward stroke had nearly decapitated the trooper. A great red gash opened, and I saw the white gleam of bone.

My stomach heaved. I doubled over and threw up its thin, slick contents at the feet of my rescuers.

*

'Here, take a drink.' Hroudland was holding out a waterskin to me. I straightened up and took it from him. The water had a rancid taste and was lukewarm. I drank it gratefully.

'No point in hanging around,' Hroudland said. 'We ride ahead to the city and let them know we are here. They'll be grateful to know we've driven off the Falcon.'

Instinctively I looked around for my horse, forgetting for a moment that the creature lay dead. Hroudland noted my error.

'We caught one of the Saracen cavalry mounts running loose. You can ride that.'

One of his escorts led forward the animal. It was the thorough-bred that the Saracen officer had been riding. Someone helped me up into the saddle, another man handed up my helmet and shield, then the sword. The blade was chipped where it must have struck the neck bone. I hung it from a loop on the Saracen saddle, settled the helmet on my head, and rode after Hroudland who was already moving away at a brisk trot.

Half a mile further on we emerged from the orchard and there ahead of us was the city wall of Zaragoza just as I remembered – huge blocks of yellow stone carefully fitted to form a sheer rampart forty feet high with circular watch towers at regular intervals. Husayn's crimson banner flew above the arch of the main gate. The great double doors with their iron sheets were firmly shut.

We sat on our horses, taking in the spectacle. Unlike Pamplona with its semi-derelict defences, the walls of Zaragoza were in perfect condition. There was no sign of dilapidation or weakness. The ground around the city wall had been cleared for the distance of a long arrow flight, and an occasional glint of sunlight on a metal helmet or spear point marked where Husayn had posted his soldiers along the ramparts. Doubtless they were watching us.

'Even the Falcon would have trouble storming a city like that,' commented Hroudland with grudging admiration. He turned to me. 'Patch, ride up to the main gate. They might know who you are. Announce our arrival and say that we have come to relieve the city.'

The words were scarcely out of his mouth when one half of

259

the main gate swung open, and a man on horseback came out and began to make his way towards us at a sedate trot.

Even from that distance I knew at once that it was Osric. His misshapen leg stuck out awkwardly to one side, and he held himself slightly aslant to allow for his crooked neck. His ungainly posture was in stark contrast to the perfect proportions and elegant gait of his horse, a pure white Saracen stallion that must have come from the wali's personal stable.

When Osric was some fifty paces away, I heard an angry intake of breath and realized Hroudland had just recognized who it was.

'What's this insult, sending a slave to greet me?' he growled.

I stole a quick sideways look at him. Hroudland had removed his helmet so that his yellow hair hung around his shoulders. Mounted on his war horse and still in full armour, he cut an imposing figure, but the effect was ruined by his expression: his face was red with anger and pouring with sweat.

'Osric is no longer a slave,' I reminded him quietly. 'He deserved his freedom and I gave it to him.'

Hroudland responded with a low grunt of disdain and spat deliberately on the ground.

Osric came to a halt a few feet from us. He was wearing the full livery of the wali, crimson turban and sash, soft leather boots patterned with matching red silk stitching. The rest of his garments, the baggy trousers and loose shirt, were made of fine white cotton and his short over-jacket was embroidered with silver thread. He looked more like a rich Saracen nobleman than the former house slave of a Saxon kinglet.

After acknowledging Hroudland's presence with a slight bow, he addressed me.

'I bring a message from His Excellency, the Wali Husayn of Zaragoza,' he said in Frankish.

Hroudland broke in rudely.

'Go back and tell your wali that we have come two months' journey to meet him and to confirm our alliance with him and his fellow governors in Barcelona and Huesca. We look forward to being received by him,' he rasped. I knew that Hroudland was annoyed that Osric had chosen to speak to me and not to him.

Osric ignored the outburst.

'My master, His Excellency the wali trusts that your journey was not too uncomfortable.'

Hroudland shifted impatiently in his saddle.

'You can also tell the wali that we encountered a patrol from Cordoba and have put them to flight,' he snapped.

Again Osric was imperturbable though I noticed his eyes flick towards the Saracen horse I was riding.

'His Excellency the wali is aware that the emir's troops are in the vicinity. That is one reason why he ordered the city gates to be closed. He anticipates that they will soon be discouraged and go away.'

I knew from Hroudland's tone of voice that he was close to losing his temper. Before the storm broke, I intervened.

'Please inform the wali that we would be grateful for food and lodging in the city for our men, and for the army which follows,' I said.

There was a long, meaningful pause before Osric said quietly.

'His Excellency the wali regrets that will not be possible.'

I could hardly believe my ears. I asked Osric to repeat what he had just said.

'Husayn, Wali of Zaragoza, has told me to inform you that your army may not enter Zaragoza. The city is closed to all Franks.'

Hroudland exploded.

'What nonsense is this!' he roared.

'On my master's orders,' Osric said firmly, 'the gates will remain closed. Anyone coming within range of the archers on the city wall will be regarded as hostile.'

'Osric, can you explain this?' I asked, using his name for the first time.

'It is repayment for treachery,' he replied simply.

I goggled at him.

'Treachery?'

There was a trace of sympathy in his dark eyes as he looked straight at me.

'Then you have not heard?' he asked.

I shook my head.

'King Karlo has betrayed Wali Suleyman of Barcelona. The wali has been seized by force and is now a prisoner of the Franks.'

I gaped at him.

Beside me Hroudland guffawed in utter disbelief.

'Nonsense! We come as friends and allies.'

Osric raised an eyebrow.

'That is what my lord the wali truly wished to believe. Unfortunately your king acted otherwise. He has broken faith. His army has done great harm to Barcelona and now he holds the wali captive.'

'I don't believe a word of this,' snarled Hroudland, swinging round to glare at me. 'Slaves are natural liars.'

Osric did not flinch.

'You do not have to believe me. At this very moment your King Karlo is marching here with his army. When he arrives, you will see for yourself that Wali Suleyman is his prisoner. Perhaps you now understand why my lord will not open the gates of his city to your people.'

Osric turned his attention back to me. He seemed reproachful.

'It was written,' he said simply.

For a moment I thought he was talking about the Saracens' holy book, their divine scripture revealed by a desert prophet. Then with a jolt I realized he meant the Book of Dreams. In Zaragoza I had dreamed of the snake, the sign of impending treachery. Stupidly I had presumed it meant that the Saracens would betray Carolus. But it was the Franks who had behaved treacherously. I had ignored Artimedorus's statement that when a snake slithers away from the dreamer, it signifies that the treachery will be found elsewhere.

I must have been silent for quite some time because it was Hroudland who spoke next, his voice thick with anger.

'You insult my family. My uncle would never commit such a base act.'

Osric shrugged.

'Then he was badly advised.'

'By whom?' The count's voice dripped disbelief.

'I understand it was by one of his chief counsellors. A man named Ganelon.'

Hroudland looked as if he had been struck across the face. There was a long pause, and then he spoke again, slowly.

'Now perhaps I might believe you.'

'As you wish,' said Osric drily. He touched his reins to his stallion's neck and as the horse obediently turned aside, he added, 'Make no mistake, the gates of Zaragoza stay closed.'

For a long moment we all sat on our horses watching him ride back to the city. I had no idea what Hroudland was thinking, but my own thoughts were in turmoil. I had been looking forward so much to meeting Osric again, renewing our friendship, and learning about his life at the wali's court. Now it seemed that Frankish double-dealing meant we were on opposing sides. I regretted that I had ever tried to use the Oneirokritikon to help me understand my visions. I had allowed myself to be led disastrously astray with my interpretation of the snake dream. Was I also wrong about other dreams where I had found explanations? I had jumped to the conclusion that my own adventure in the hunting forest explained the king's vision of the huntsman attacked by wolves and desperately blowing his horn to summon help. Lost in the forest I had sounded the horn dropped by my unknown attacker, hoping to hear an answering call. But I had seen no wolves in the forest. Perhaps the huntsman in the royal dream was someone else entirely.

A clammy chill spread into the pit of my stomach as I recalled those other troubling visions that still haunted me – the rider on the great horse crying blood, and the ghoulish incident when Hroudland and I were on a mountainside and attacked by monsters and flying demons. I had no idea what either dream meant, though I knew now that they were of great significance. But I did not know whether I wanted to understand what they might foretell, or if I should throw the Oneirokritikon into the fire and give up the interpretation of dreams entirely.

Chapter Seventeen

CAROLUS ARRIVED A WEEK LATER at our camp outside Zaragoza's walls, leading an army that was weary and much reduced in size. Many of his levies had returned to Frankia, having completed their days of service. Others had deserted. The great baggage train had dwindled to less than a hundred ox carts and the accompanying herd of cattle no longer existed. The troops had eaten every last animal and were now living off the land like locusts.

The king lost no time in summoning a council of war. It was held in the same royal pavilion, its bright colours now faded by sun and rain, and once again Hroudland required Berenger and me to attend him.

This time, as I entered the great tent, I saw Ganelon. He was dressed in exactly the same clothes he had been wearing at the first banquet in Aachen. Apart from a deep tan on his bearded face he appeared to have changed not at all since he rode off with Gerin to negotiate with – or rather betray – the Wali of Barcelona. I quietly took my usual place in the outer circle of attendants and stood watching him, waiting for his reaction when he noticed me. Halfway through a conversation with his neighbour, he happened to look up and saw me. His eyes widened and for a fraction of a moment he froze. Then he recovered himself and glanced briefly towards Hroudland. If he was busy calculating whether or not the count knew of the plot to discredit him, it did not show on his face. Without the slightest change of expression he turned back to continue his conversation with his companion. At that moment Carolus appeared from behind the velvet curtain.

In just a few months, the king looked as though he had aged by ten years. He no longer walked with quite the same confident stride, and his face was more deeply lined than I remembered. His long moustache, once straw-yellow, held flecks of grey and he looked tired. As usual he was dressed in the ordinary cross-gartered leggings, tunic and trousers of a well-to-do Frankish noble, though, as a concession to the heat of Hispanian summer, the cloth was now of light linen rather than heavy wool. In his right hand he carried a mace of dark wood, gnarled and polished and banded with gold. I imagined it was some sort of sceptre.

He walked across to his portable gilded throne and took his seat. His attendants had already set up the trestle table with the map of tiles, and Carolus looked across it at the assembled company. His gaze was the same as ever, the grey eyes shrewd and penetrating, knowing each and every one of the people before him. Despite myself I held my breath and stood straighter as I waited for his pronouncement.

'I have summoned you to council,' he began, 'to hear your advice on how we should proceed with the campaign. As you are aware, our allies are in disarray. The Emir of Cordoba has defeated the Wali of Huesca in battle. The Wali of Barcelona was unable to offer us the help he promised. Our original plan for Hispania must now be modified.'

The king's words made me realize how little I knew of the overall progress of the campaign. Evidently the Falcon of Cordoba had moved decisively against the rebellious Saracen governors before the Franks had arrived.

'We now find ourselves in front of Zaragoza, whose governor is the third of our so-called allies,' Carolus continued. 'He has closed its gates to us. I await your suggestions as to what we should do next.'

There was a long awkward silence. I sensed the Frankish nobles trying to gauge the king's frame of mind. None of them wanted to speak up and risk the king's wrath by making an unwelcome proposal. It was the ever-cautious and practical Eggihard who spoke first.

'Your Majesty, we are running low on supplies. The army cannot keep in the field for more than a few weeks.'

Carolus toyed with his wooden sceptre, stroking the polished surface.

'So how do we put those few weeks to good use?'

'We teach the Saracens a lesson they will remember so they never cross into Frankia again,' called out a swarthy, heavily built nobleman I did not recognize.

'How?' grunted the king.

'We've already dealt with the Wali of Barcelona as he deserved. Now we should do the same to the Wali of Zaragoza. Take his city, and hold him to account.'

The man looked around for the support of his fellows. Most of them avoided his gaze and stared instead at the map table. The mood of the meeting was decidedly pessimistic, even sombre.

To my surprise, it was the normally aggressive Hroudland who urged caution.

'I have seen the walls of Zaragoza,' he said. 'Believe me, without large siege engines we cannot take the city in less than six months.'

'Then our engineers must build siege engines,' insisted the swarthy nobleman. He scowled angrily at Hroudland. The man was evidently another of the margrave's rivals at court.

'It will take far too long to construct heavy siege engines,' argued Eggihard. 'By the time they are ready, our supplies will be finished.'

There was another long interval as no one else spoke. The king stirred restlessly on the wooden throne. Close to me someone coughed nervously. I was aware of the faint, musty smell of mildew; the canvas of the great royal tent had begun to rot. It occurred to me that this decay symbolized the threadbare, worn-out state of the Frankish army.

Finally Hroudland again spoke. He raised his voice so everyone could hear him clearly, and his words were delivered with a confident flourish.

'I suggest, Your Majesty, that instead of laying siege to Zaragoza, we extract its wealth like honey from the hive, and leave the city so impoverished that it will be unable to trouble us in the future.'

'And how do we keep the bees at bay?' demanded his uncle. I could see a glint of interest, even affection, in the gaze he turned on Hroudland.

'We have the Wali of Barcelona as our prisoner. He is both the brother-in-law and the close ally of the Wali of Zaragoza,' the count answered. 'I'm told that there is a strong bond between the two men. I propose that we demand a very great ransom for the release of the Wali of Barcelona plus an additional sum to recompense the expenses for bringing the army into Hispania.'

Like a shaft of sunlight suddenly lighting up gloomy countryside, his words lifted the atmosphere in the pavilion. Noblemen exchanged knowing glances. Most of them had come to Hispania for loot, not to stay and settle. There was a mutter of excitement; they could carry back the spoils without having to fight for them.

'Is there enough wealth in Zaragoza to meet such a heavy demand?' the king asked Hroudland mildly.

'Your Majesty, Zaragoza is one of the richest cities in Hispania. The wali has enormous personal wealth,' Hroudland assured him.

A low rumble of approval greeted his announcement.

By now I knew this was the way of the Frankish world. The naked greed of the Franks was unpleasant to observe but, however distasteful I found it, I had to accept that I had committed myself to helping satisfy their craving for riches when I rode into Hispania as a loyal member of Hroudland's entourage.

'And how do we persuade the wali Husayn to part with his wealth?' asked the king.

With a sinking heart I anticipated what Hroudland would say next.

'I have just the man to act as a go-between. He will know how best to present our demand,' answered the count. He looked in my direction.

The king followed his glance and there was a flicker of recognition as his shrewd, grey eyes came to rest on me.

Unexpectedly Ganelon spoke up. His voice was measured and serious, with no hint that he was raising an objection. He was too clever for that.

'Your Majesty, the noble margrave's plan is admirable, but it may come to nothing unless we can provide the wali with some sort of surety of our good faith.'

It was a fair comment but Ganelon rarely did anything without a hidden reason.

Hroudland blundered into the trap set for him.

'Your Majesty, I am willing to offer myself as that surety. I will go into Zaragoza as hostage for the honest fulfilment of our bargain. Only when the Wali of Barcelona is set free and rides in through the gates of the city will I bring back the wealth of Zaragoza.'

I detected a hint of a smile under Ganelon's black beard. He was evidently relishing the success of his intervention. If something went badly wrong with the payment of the ransom, Hroudland might well have forfeited not only his freedom, but also his life.

The king looked around the assembly.

'Does anyone else wish to make a suggestion?'

When there was no reply, he announced that Hroudland's plan was to be put into immediate effect and declared the meeting closed.

As soon as the king had left, a cheerful group of Hroudland's supporters clustered around him, congratulating him for his proposal and applauding him for his personal courage. I held back. I recalled describing Husayn's splendid palace and its luxury to the count as we rode side by side on our journey to Hispania. I should have known that my description of such wealth would attract Hroudland's craving for riches. I had also let slip that Wali Husayn was married to the sister of the governor of Barcelona. That pleasant conversation intended to pass the time would now lead to the ruin of the wali and Zaragoza. Crassly I had betrayed Husayn's hospitality and kindness. Perhaps the snake in my dream of treachery should have coiled itself around my leg. Sick at heart, I felt soiled and dirty.

*

The next morning the army engineers constructed a small ballista capable of throwing a heavy arrow three hundred paces. They dragged it to the edge of the cleared ground around the city, and Hroudland had me write a note to Wali Husayn outlining the ransom plan. I suggested that it would be easier for a messenger to deliver the message under a white flag, but was told that the ballista would serve as a reminder to the Saracens that the Frankish army was capable of preparing siege engines.

The arrow carrying the message was shot over the city wall.

The wali's reply came within an hour, delivered by a messenger who rode out of the city and dropped it disdainfully on the ground. Husayn had agreed to our terms. He would pay four thousand pounds weight of silver coin for the governor of Barcelona to be handed over, in good health. Additional treasure including silks, gold and jewels to the value of another five thousand pounds of silver would reimburse Carolus for the expense of bringing his army into Hispania. Husayn made only one condition: he required four days to assemble such a colossal sum.

On the appointed day, Hroudland and I crossed the open ground towards the city gate. The count had chosen to ride his great roan war horse and he towered above me on the small, sturdy cob that had been provided for me. Neither of us carried weapons, though we wore full armour, intending to put on a brave show. The sun was already well above the horizon so the heavy war gear was hot and uncomfortable. Behind us was the wreckage of the orchards. The troops had set up camp, hacking down the carefully tended trees to make shelters and for firewood. The irrigation ditches were crumbling under the constant trampling of horses and men, the water in them was muddy and foul. Swarms of fat flies buzzed over mounds of human filth, and the air reeked with the smell of horses, men and dung.

'Let's get this over as quickly as possible,' Hroudland muttered to me as we approached Zaragoza's main gate. The note of resignation in his voice made me take a quick glance at him. His face had a fixed expression, downcast yet determined. I guessed he was thinking how he had once hoped to become the Margrave of the new Hispanic March. Now he knew that it would never happen. When the campaign was over, he would be returning to the rain and mists of Brittany.

'Wali Husayn will keep his word,' I said, trying to reassure him.

The city gate swung open as we came closer and there waiting on his white horse was Osric, again dressed in the wali's livery. Beside him was a single mounted cavalryman, also wearing Husayn's colours.

I sensed Hroudland's surprise. He must have expected that we would be met by at least a troop of horsemen to escort us through the city. Instead it seemed that we were being treated as little more than a passing nuisance.

Osric did not speak a single word in greeting. I felt a pang of acute disappointment at his frigid reception. I had expected at least some small gesture of recognition for the years we had shared. But he had merely nodded to the both of us and now, stony-faced, he led us in silence.

This impression strengthened as we rode through Zaragoza on Osric's heels. Life was continuing as normal. It was as if there was no foreign army camped outside the walls. The streets were crowded with people going about their business, shopping, gossiping, and haggling in the market. The air was full of the rich odour of street food being cooked over open braziers. I even recognized the same pavement seller with his tray of fruit whom I had noticed when I rode into the city for the first time with Husayn. The vendor's display of fruit was piled high, and the butchers and vegetable sellers had no shortage of goods. It was a stark contrast to the camp we had just left where disgruntled soldiers were ravenous for provisions and sweltered in the heat while mounted patrols scoured the countryside seeking supplies.

The passers-by were as dismissive as Osric. Whenever I caught someone's eye in the crowded streets, that person would simply turn his back on me. It was very unpleasant to be treated as being beneath contempt.

Eventually we arrived in the main central square. It was almost deserted of people. I had expected that we would be brought to the arched doorway that was the entry to Wali Husayn's own palace. Instead, we crossed towards the mosque that Husayn had told me his father built. Beautifully proportioned, a central dome was tiled in green and blue, spiral patterns in the same colours twisting up the columns of the four thin spires that surrounded it. To the left was a low, squat building, its thick white-washed walls pierced with a few windows barely large enough to be pigeon roosts. A horse was tethered in front of it. Hroudland recognized the animal before I did.

'Patch, that's the gelding I picked out for you in Aachen,' he exclaimed.

The horse wore the same saddle I had used on the ride across Frankia. Dangling from it was my curved bow and the sword that Hroudland had selected for me in the royal stores of Aachen the previous year. I had an uncomfortable feeling that I knew why they were there.

Our little group halted before the building and dismounted. The Saracen trooper took the reins of our horses and led them away while Osric limped ahead of us to the massive iron door and knocked. It was pulled open from inside and Hroudland and I followed Osric in.

Immediately I was reminded of the strongroom at Hroudland's great hall. The interior of the building was a single chamber, some fifteen paces squared. The small windows seen from the outside had been deceptive. The chamber was lit by a dozen shafts of sunlight shining down through a pierced dome in the ceiling. Specks of dust floated in the sunlight, and the thick walls kept out the noonday heat so that the air inside the room felt slightly chilly. It also had a faint smell that I could not identify. The floor was made of massive stone slabs and there was no furniture apart from a tall metal-and-wood contraption whose function escaped me until I recognized a set of over-size weighing scales. Waiting for us were two men, dressed in the wali's livery. One of them was the grey-bearded steward who had looked after me when I had been Husayn's guest. Ashamed at my role in this sordid ransom, I could not look him in the eye and could feel the distaste oozing from him as he stepped around me and firmly closed the heavy door to the outside. We were standing inside Zaragoza's treasure house.

Arranged on the floor was a neat row of stout leather panniers. They were the size normally carried by mules, and it was the rancid smell of leather saturated with mule sweat that had perplexed me. The flap of each pannier had been unlaced and thrown back so that their contents glittered dully. Each pannier was full to the brim with silver coins.

At last Osric broke his silence.

'Each bag contains one hundred pounds weight in silver coin,' he said. There was no emotion in his voice.

I quickly counted the number of panniers. There were forty of them.

Hroudland bent over the nearest one and plunged both hands into the contents. He held up a double handful of coins and let them trickle through his fingers. They made a rippling, metallic clatter as they landed.

He looked at me.

'What do you think, Patch?'

I walked across and picked up one of the coins. Clean and shiny, it looked as if it had been minted very recently. Both sides were stamped with lines of Saracen script across the centre and in a circle around the rim. I looked questioningly at Osric.

'A silver dirhem issued last year by the Emir Abd al Rahman. The coins in the bags were struck by many rulers and come from many places, but all are genuine.' His voice was still flat and expressionless.

Hroudland moved along the row of panniers, peering into each of them, stirring their contents with his fingers like a grain merchant dabbling in sacks of barley. He beckoned me to stand close to him. Bending close he whispered in my ear, 'Maybe there is dross deep down beneath the surface.'

Osric could not have overheard but he knew well enough what was said.

'We can arrange to have the coins weighed out in front of you, bag by bag, if you wish,' he announced, disdainfully.

'That will not be necessary,' I said firmly. Before Hroudland could raise an objection, I muttered to him, 'It will take far too long to weigh this amount.'

The count turned to face Osric.

'What about the rest of the payment?' he demanded.

The wali's elderly steward walked to the far side of the chamber where a low shapeless mound was covered by a dark cloth. He took hold of the cloth and, with a sudden swish of silk, drew it to one side, revealing what it had concealed.

Despite his attempt to remain aloof, Hroudland sucked in his breath with amazement.

'By our calculation, this should suffice to cover Karlo's costs,' observed Osric icily.

Laid out on the stone floor was a sensational array of valuables. Most were made of silver. There were cups and goblets, plates, ewers, censers, bowls and trays engraved with interlocking geometric patterns. There were belts studded with silver discs, silver scabbards for knives, silver bangles and necklaces, medallions and hanging lamps of silver filigree. A separate much smaller pile was made of similar objects in gold. Several of these were set with coloured stones. These items had been artfully placed so that the beams of sunlight sparkled off polished surfaces or struck a glow of colour in their depths. Without examining them more closely it was impossible to tell which were true jewels and which semi-precious. I supposed the dark reds were rubies and garnet, and here and there was a spark of blue from a stone unknown to me.

Two special items had been arranged on their own, laid out on a square of dark green velvet. Seeing them, I knew instantly that Osric had advised Husayn what would most arouse the greed of any Frankish envoy.

The first item was a glittering crystal salver. Around the rim ran a band of gold as thick as a man's thumb and inlaid with intricate enamelwork that captured all the colours of the rainbow. I had seen its exact twin on display on Carolus's high table at a banquet in Aachen. How this second crystal salver had found its way into Zaragoza's treasury was a mystery. Possibly it had been plundered in the days when the Saracens raided deep into Frankia. What was certain was that Carolus would be delighted to match this crystal salver with the one he already owned.

The other object lying on the velvet cloth was proof that Osric also knew how to appeal to Hroudland's aristocratic love of lavish display. It was a superb hunting horn, its surface embellished with delicate carvings. Its colour was a lustrous pale yellow, almost white, and I supposed that it was made of ivory. Yet I had never seen ivory of such great size. If I had held it against my arm, the horn would have measured from my elbow to my finger-tip. Ivory, as far as I was aware, came from the long teeth in the whiskery mouths of large seal-like creatures far in the north. The size of the monster which had sprouted such a monstrous tooth was difficult to imagine.

Overcome with curiosity I picked up the hunting horn to look at it more closely. The horn was lighter than its size suggested. The carver had hollowed out the interior so that the instrument sounded the note he wanted. The ivory was delightful to the touch, cool and smooth yet not slippery. The mouthpiece and the band around the open end of the horn were both of silver. Wonderingly I turned the horn over in my hand to examine the carvings. They ran almost the full length with an area left clear for the huntsman's grip. There were hunting scenes, which formed a continuous story along its length. Near the silver mouthpiece a trio of mounted huntsmen were riding among trees. Further along the horn they were attacked by a shaggy cat-like beast. I suspected it to be a lion, though I had never seen one. The creature had leaped on the hindquarters of a hunter's horse and sunk its claws and teeth in the animal's hindquarters. In the next scene a hunter had put his arrow into the beast's chest. The great cat was reared up and arching with pain.

I kept turning the horn in my hand following the story of the hunt until I reached the end of the tale close to the silver rim. I froze in shock.

The final scene showed a lone huntsman. He was no longer mounted. His dead horse lay nearby. He stood with one foot on a rock, his head thrown back, and a hunting horn to his lips. But I knew for certain he was not sounding the note to announce the successful end of the chase. He was blowing on the horn, calling desperately for help. He was the huntsman Carolus had seen in his dream, the nightmare his daughters had described to me.

I stood there, dumbstruck, until someone took the hunting horn from my grasp and in a delighted tone said, 'The tooth of an oliphant!'

It was Hroudland. A moment later he put the horn to his lips and was trying to blow a practice note. He failed. The horn made a low sad sound, half moan, half growl. It was the noise of air rushing out, expelled uselessly.

The hair rose on the back of my neck. I had heard that sound once before. It was on the day that Hroudland had rescued me from the Saracen troopers after they had dropped my horse with an arrow. It was the last sound my horse had uttered as she lay on the ground, her final groan.

*

I spent the next few hours like a man stunned. I never saw Wali Husayn. He did come to see us at his treasury and must have relied on Osric's clever guidance on how to deal with the unwanted visitors to his city. Hroudland, by contrast, was childishly eager to complete the ransom arrangements. He lusted after the magnificent hunting horn for himself and he knew that his uncle the king would be delighted to receive the priceless crystal salver. The immense amount of silver coin was enough to be shared out with the army and keep the other nobles happy.

So in late afternoon, the ransom accepted, we rode back to the main gate of Zaragoza accompanied by a score of Vascon muleteers leading their pack animals loaded with the ransom of silver coin. As I had anticipated, my gelding, bow and sword had been returned to me. Husayn wanted no reminder of my former presence, and I had found the animal tied to the tail of one of the horse-drawn wagons that carried the remainder of the ransom. The great iron-plated gates were dragged open and we waited there, under the archway. Out from the distant line of orchards, Berenger appeared on horseback. He was holding the lead rein of the horse on which sat Suleyman, the Wali of Barcelona. As the two men approached us, Suleyman was staring straight ahead. He looked a broken man, tired and withdrawn. He passed me close enough for me to reach out to touch him, and as he did so he deliberately lowered his eyes and gazed down at his horse's mane. I wondered if he knew of my role in arranging his ransom, and wished that I could tell him that I felt ashamed. Carolus's grand adventure of Hispania had been reduced to a grubby exercise in banditry.

At a nod from Hroudland, Berenger released the lead rein. The humiliated Wali of Barcelona rode on into the city, and our heavily laden little procession began to make its way slowly towards the Frankish camp. It would soon be dusk and I looked back over my shoulder, thinking that Osric or even Husayn had come to greet the ransomed wali. But there was no one to be seen beneath the archway except the soldiers hauling shut the two heavy gates. They closed with a solid thud, and there was the sound of a heavy crossbar dropping into place. The gates would open when our Vascon muleteers returned with their unloaded pack animals, but against me Zaragoza was sealed tight.

I had one more thing to do. As soon as we got back to the Frankish camp, I went directly to the tent that I shared with Gerin and the other paladins. There, I took out my copy of the Book of Dreams. I leafed through the pages, searching for a passage that I remembered from happier times when Osric and I had sat in Wali Husayn's guest rooms working together on the translation.

It did not take me long to find what I was looking for. The author of the Book of Dreams had an explanation for a dream about trumpets. They were symbols for man himself because air had to pass through them just as a man requires air to pass through his lungs if he is to live. And when the air is totally expelled, a trumpet falls silent, just as a man expires with his final breath.

I put down the Book of Dreams and stared unseeingly at the walls of tent. A trumpet and a hunting horn were alike. Was I now able to glimpse the future in day-to day events as well as in my dreams? If so, when Hroudland took the oliphant hunting horn from my hand and blew that false dying note, he had announced his own impending death.

Chapter Eighteen

I HAD NO TIME TO BROOD. Someone was shouting my name.
I peered out of the tent flap, expecting I was being called to
supervise the unloading of the ransom from the mule train and its
transfer into the army's ox carts, but the royal messenger who had
been sent to fetch me announced that I was to attend the count.
The matter was urgent.

'The bad news came while you were away,' the messenger told
me as he waited for me to put away the Oneirokritikon safely.
'The Saxons have assembled a huge raiding force in the northern
forests and are threatening to invade across the Rhine. The king
has called a meeting of the army council.'

As we hurried through the gathering dark I wondered why
I should be needed at such a high level conference. I entered the
royal pavilion to find it lit by clusters of candles on tall, metal
stands. The air in the tent was stifling, and there was a tense
atmosphere among the dozen or so people gathered around the
map table. One of them was Carolus, and beside him was
Hroudland. To my relief there was no sign of Ganelon.

Hroudland saw me enter and beckoned to me to approach.

'The king wants to know about the route you took through
the mountains when you first came to Zaragoza,' Hroudland told
me.

I felt the colour rising in my face.

'Alcuin asked me to make notes,' I stammered, 'but I never

got round to sending them to him. I don't have them with me now.'

The king ignored my embarrassment.

'Tell me what you can remember.'

I swallowed nervously.

'The road is very narrow in places but an army would be able to use it.'

'Show me exactly where the route goes.' Carolus was briskly efficient.

I reached out to touch the map, and then checked myself. The rough tiles had once pricked my finger and drawn blood.

'From this side the road climbs through the foothills in easy stages. There's a narrow pass just here.' My finger was quivering slightly as I pointed out the exact route. 'Once you're over the pass, the descent on the far slope is awkward but should present little difficulty.'

'Is the track passable for ox carts?' Eggihard the seneschal asked. I recalled that he was in charge of supplies and stores.

'In single file, and taken slowly,' I said.

'Water? Pasture? Food supplies?' Carolus demanded more detail.

'There are only rocks and bare slopes in the higher sections, Your Majesty. But there are several springs and wells along the route, though not in the throat of the pass itself. Beyond that, the nearest water would be a day's travel on the far side.'

Carolus grunted. He was deep in thought. I had been forgotten. After some moments he turned to Hroudland.

'We must get the army north urgently. That route will save us three or four days.'

The count leaned forward, and the shadow of his arm fell across the map as he pointed to a spot close to where he stood.

'Our flank will be dangerously exposed if we don't deal with this place,' he said.

I looked to see what he meant. He was indicating the Vascon city of Pamplona. I was puzzled. Pamplona was too far away to be a serious threat, and though the Vascons were hostile, they were unlikely to launch a full scale attack on a large army. They would keep out of the way, glad to see the Franks retreat over the mountains. Then I remembered the count's intense dislike of the Vascons and the ambush that had killed one of his troopers. I stole a quick glance at Eggihard. He had restrained Hroudland from attacking Pamplona during our advance into Hispania. The result had been a bitter falling-out between the two men. But now Eggihard, even if he guessed what Hroudland had in mind, said nothing. I supposed it was because he knew the count was high in the king's favour after his stratagem to extract a ransom for the Wali of Barcelona.

Carolus accepted his warning without any questions.

'Go with your cavalry and deal with Pamplona. Then catch up with the army. Eggihard can take command of the rearguard and cover the withdrawal through the mountains.'

I saw Hroudland's mouth set in a grim line as he nodded, acknowledging his uncle's instructions. There was something chilling in his reaction. My presence was no longer needed and I stepped back from the map table. Already I was trying to think of how I could avoid riding against Pamplona with the count. I had no quarrel with the people in the city. They had treated me fairly when I passed through on my way to Brittany. After what had just happened in Zaragoza, I feared that if I was again swept up in Hroudland's plans I would only add to my sense of guilt.

*

Hroudland raised no objection when I told him that I preferred to remain with the main army as a guide. He rode off for his raid on Pamplona taking Berenger, Gerin and five hundred picked troopers with him. I did not see him again for two weeks. By then I was high in the mountains and our leading units had already crossed the pass and begun to descend the other side. Behind them straggled a disjointed, weary line of foot soldiers, transport drivers and camp followers. Saracen mounted archers were harassing our rear. Whether they were the Falcon's men or soldiers from Zaragoza, it was impossible to tell. They would appear at first light and skulk around, sending arrows at long range. Eggihard organized sorties to ride out to drive them off. But the Saracens would simply melt away and return the following morning.

On the afternoon Hroudland got back, I was camped beside a shepherd's hut close to the pass where the road ran between high cliffs in a narrow defile. It was the same hut where Wali Husayn and I had discussed the slinger who had attacked me in the mountains. I had gone there with Eggihard to investigate an accident with the baggage train. An ox cart had smashed a wheel at a narrow section of the track and was blocking the roadway. Fortunately the damaged cart was one of the last transports in the column, and there were only three more carts behind it. Alarmingly we discovered that the stranded vehicles carried the ransom money from Zaragoza though they should have been in the well-protected centre of the column. The group of four carts was becoming increasingly isolated, and Eggihard decided that we should stay with them until the wheel was repaired, and the order of march could be rearranged.

So we greeted Hroudland's arrival with relief. He came clattering up the rock-strewn trail at the head of his troops and immediately agreed to detach fifty men to stand guard over the stranded vehicles. The remainder would ride on and rejoin the main force. Their horses were lathered and exhausted and their riders seemed reluctant to talk about the raid on Pamplona.

Hroudland's unkempt appearance was shocking. His eyes were

raw and red-rimmed, staring from a face where every line was engrained with soot. His yellow hair, normally clean and lustrous, was streaked with ash. When he passed a hand across his face to rub away the dirt, I saw that the nails were jagged and grimy. In his sweat-stained and crumpled clothes he looked nothing like the handsome nobleman who had ridden out so jauntily to win his wardenship of the Spanish March. The only fine thing about him was the splendid hunting horn of carved ivory. He wore it like a badge of conquest, slung from a silk cord across his chest.

His companions were even worse for wear. A rough bandage on Gerin's left arm partially covered a painful looking burn that extended from his elbow to his wrist. Berenger had lost most of his eyebrows. They had been scorched away and only the stubble remained. Their clothes reeked of smoke and there were holes where sparks or hot cinders had landed.

The sun had dropped behind the mountain ridge and the air was turning so chilly that Eggihard suggested we discuss the next day's plans in front of the hearth in the shepherd's hut.

'We wondered why the Saracen skirmishers disappeared this morning,' said Eggihard, as we took our places on the rickety benches. He was eyeing the oliphant horn with more than a touch of envy. 'They must have known you were coming up behind them.'

Hroudland had found himself a wineskin. He held it up to his face and squirted out a long draught into his mouth before wiping his lips with the back of his hand.

'If they return,' he growled, 'we'll soon see them off.'

Eggihard bridled at Hroudland's bluntness.

'I take it, then, that you've also disposed of the Vascon threat?' The simmering antagonism between the two men was close to boiling over.

The count gave a bitter laugh.

'Pamplona will no longer bother us.'

There was an awkward pause, and then Berenger broke the silence.

'Pamplona has been taught its lesson.'

Eggihard turned towards him, eyebrows raised.

'Or have you only succeeded in rousing the citizens against us?' His voice was waspish.

'There's not much left to rouse,' Berenger answered. 'Their fault for neglecting the walls. We were charging down the streets before they could put together a defence.'

'And then?'

'Some idiot set the place on fire. The blaze spread too fast.'

'Too fast for what?'

'For us to sack the place properly.'

Eggihard smirked. I wondered if he was pleased that his earlier caution about attacking Pamplona had been proved right.

'Poorly handled, then. A pity.'

Hroudland flared.

'Better handled than this botched withdrawal. If we hadn't got here today, you might have lost the Zaragoza ransom, taken back by the Saracens.'

The two men bristled at one another, and then out-faced by Hroudland and his comrades, Eggihard got to his feet and stalked out of the hut.

Hroudland shot me a resentful glance.

'Can't see how you put up with that incompetent fool,' he said.

I kept silent. I was reminded of my father's bad temper, quarrelsome and tetchy, when he came back from an unsuccessful day out hunting.

Hroudland squeezed another drink from the wineskin, and then spat into the flames of the fire.

'The loot we took from Pamplona wouldn't pay a month's expenses.'

'Thankfully you can look forward to your share of Wali Husayn's ransom money,' I ventured.

He raised his chin and glared at me.

'When we charged into Pamplona, the place had already been emptied out. Most of the treasure had been carried away to safety.'

'Are you sure?'

'Of course I'm sure,' he snapped. 'We got into the cathedral before it burned. Nothing there. All the church plate gone. The same story with the merchant houses. We found just a few baubles.'

He turned his bloodshot eyes towards me.

'And now there's a far greater prize.'

I looked at him baffled.

'What prize?'

The count leaned forward and tugged a length of firewood clear of the hearth. The end was smouldering. The count blew on it until the first flames began to flicker.

'Patch, think back to your earlier trip through these mountains. We spoke about it when we were riding south. You told me then that the people of these mountains are an ancient race who have lived in their mountain strongholds for centuries.'

'It was how Wali Husayn described them to me,' I said.

'And didn't he say that they demanded tolls from the people who used the passes, or robbed them if they did not pay?'

I was growing uneasy with the line of questioning.

When Hroudland next spoke, it was in a dreamy tone as if he was far away. He was staring at the flames on the firebrand in a half-trance.

'A priest in Pamplona gloated to me, even as his cathedral burned around his ears. He crowed that their greatest treasure was worthless to us.' With a sudden fierce gesture, the count jabbed the end of the piece of wood back into the fire, and left it there deep among the glowing embers. 'The priest should have kept his mouth shut. But he was too intent on having his paltry victory – the church's spiritual value outweighs any wordly price was how he put it. I asked him what he meant, and he said that their greatest treasure was a chalice fashioned from stone. It came from the Holy Land.'

I felt the hairs on my neck prickle for now I knew why Hroudland had ridden up into the mountains with such haste.

The count turned to face me. It was as though he was seeing me for the first time.

'I asked the priest why the chalice was so special. He informed me that Christ had used this very same chalice at the Last Supper.'

'I suppose he even told you where to find it?' I forced as much disbelief as possible into my voice, but Hroudland ignored my scepticism.

'It took a little persuasion. The chalice doesn't belong to the cathedral but is brought there for special feast days. For the rest of the year it is kept in a mountain refuge.' He reached out and caught me by the sleeve. 'Don't you see, Patch. Everything fits. The castle in the mountain, the ancient guardians, the chalice from the Holy Land. This has to be the Graal. Somehow the Vascons got hold of it from a group of travellers who were on their way through the pass. If I bring it back to the Bretons, I will become more than just a margrave.'

I made another attempt to deflect him.

'Everyone knows that Vascon mountain refuges are impregnable.'

'How about robbery by stealth?' he said, suddenly sly. 'Less than five miles from here a stronghold matches the description we extracted from the Pamplona priest. It's worth a look.' He gave my sleeve a slight shake to emphasize his words. 'Patch, tomorrow I'm going to see what I can find there. I want you to come with me.' He called across to Berenger. 'Fetch in that prisoner.'

Berenger left the hut and came back moments later, pushing ahead of him a short, wiry man with a weather-beaten look. The side of his face was cut and bruised. Someone had beaten him up badly. A faint memory stirred. He was the Vascon shepherd in whose hut we were sitting.

'We caught this fellow spying on us from the side of the track as we came up the road,' said Berenger. He kicked the shepherd's feet from under him so that the man fell heavily to the ground.

'This hut is where the man lives,' I said defensively.

'Then he must know the mountains as well as anyone. He'll tell us where we want to go,' said Hroudland. There was a more ruthless edge to his voice than I had ever heard before.

I should have refused at that moment, or at very least I should have made another effort to convince Hroudland that the Graal was a fantasy. Yet there was something so intense about his conviction that I knew my words would have no effect. It was the same stubborn, self-obsessed Hroudland that I had seen before. Once he had decided on a course of action, he was adamant. This time he had persuaded himself that the Graal was hidden nearby, and he was determined to take it. I could either stand aside and refuse to be involved in such a madcap venture or I could accompany him and assist in whatever way I could. A quick, stealthy raid might achieve surprise but I doubted it. The mountaineers would be keeping a good lookout, knowing the Frankish army was moving through the pass. If there was fighting, the count's reckless bravery might win a skirmish. But his rashness could equally draw him far into danger.

Conscious that I already owed my life and liberty to Hroudland's impetuous actions, I decided that I would go with him. If I was the cool head by his side, there might come a moment when I could repay the debt.

*

Just three of us set out in mid-morning – Hroudland, Berenger and myself. Hroudland had decided to keep our group as small as possible to attract the least attention. Eggihard raised no objection to our departure. Indeed he was so keen to see us go that I suspected he was hoping that Hroudland would get himself killed. Our plan was that we would be back by the time the broken cartwheel was repaired so we could catch up with the main army. Gerin was to stay behind, partly to help stand guard over the disabled treasure carts, but also to make sure that Eggihard kept his word and waited for our return. At Hroudland's request I carried my bow, and he and Berenger were armed with swords and daggers. None of us wore our armoured jackets for we intended to travel fast and light, and we left behind our horses for the trail we followed was a thread of a footpath that branched from the main track.

The path looped its way around the flank of the hillside and by the time we had gone less than a mile, we were out of sight of the main track behind us. The surface was crumbly and treacherous, and we had to walk cautiously. To our right, the land was a series of steep slopes scarred with dry gullies and an occasional deep ravine. In places a few scrubby plants had managed to take root, but in this season they were parched and shrivelled. To our left the mountainside rose so abruptly that the path was often broken in places where land slips had carried away the trail. It was a bleak, rocky wilderness where the only signs of life were a large bird of prey hanging in the air far above us, and, very far in the distance, a small group of animals on an upper slope that I guessed were wild goats. They took fright and went bounding off across a ridge as soon as they detected our presence.

The weather was in our favour. The day was sunny and bright, and there was enough of a breeze to make the air feel pleasantly cool. I began to hope that Hroudland's notion of locating the Graal was misplaced, and our venture would prove to be no more than a pleasant stroll. It took us another hour of steady walking before we turned a corner around a spur and Hroudland, who was in the lead, came to a sudden halt. He dropped to one knee and gestured to us to wait where we were. After a few moments he beckoned me forward and pointed. I could just make out some sort of building in the distance. It was perched on a rocky crag that jutted out from the mountainside like the prow of a ship. The building was made of exactly the same grey stone as the surrounding landscape so it was difficult to make out any details. It was much smaller than I had expected, little more than a substantial hut surrounded by what looked like a wall built of boulders. The line of our footpath continued on, doubling back and forth, climbing across the face of the mountain in that direction.

'That has to be the place,' Hroudland muttered.

We retreated to a small patch of level ground.

'Berenger,' instructed the count, 'you stay here and keep a look out.'

Berenger started to object but Hroudland cut him short.

'This is our only way back. I trust you to make sure it stays open. Use force if necessary. If that's impossible, sound a warning.'

He unslung the oliphant horn from around his neck and handed it to Berenger who accepted it reluctantly.

'I would prefer to go with you,' Berenger told the count sulkily.

Hroudland shook his head.

'I need Patch to accompany me. His bow could make the difference.' Then he turned to me. 'You and I will climb up the mountainside immediately behind us. We'll be out of sight from anyone in that building. After we've gained enough height, we begin to work our way sideways.'

I glanced up the rugged slope and must have looked doubtful because he added, 'There's no hurry. We must wait until late afternoon before we cross into view of anyone in that building. They'll have the sun in their eyes, and we'll be able to take advantage of the longer shadows as we get closer.'

The boulder-strewn mountainside looming over me brought back a memory of the rock slide that had almost killed me. My attention wavered for a moment as I wondered who had been behind it. Since Zaragoza there had been no attempt on my life, and I had almost forgotten the series of mysterious attacks.

Hroudland was speaking again.

'In our final approach to the building, Patch, I want you to be higher up the slope from me, looking down so you have a clear shot if necessary.'

I had removed the bow from its cover to check that everything was in order.

'You'll need both hands while we're climbing. So keep your bow slung across your back. When it's time to take up your position I'll pause and give you a signal.'

I selected an arrow and ran my thumb along the barb. It was murderously sharp. I had a vague recollection that I had used the identical arrow to despatch the Vascon slinger who had ambushed me in that same area.

'How many arrows should I carry?' I asked.

'Four or five. That building looks as if it contains no more than one or two men. If I can get close enough, I should be able to rush the place before anyone knows what is happening.'

We waited until the sun was dropping towards the horizon before we began our climb. We had to grope our way up the steep face of the mountain, handhold by handhold, and made such slow progress that I feared the count had left it too late. He was in the lead and I tried to avoid being directly behind him because he occasionally dislodged large stones which bounced down around me dangerously. Once or twice I nearly came to grief through my own fault when a stone that I was holding worked loose. There was a very bad moment when my foot slipped and I slid backwards for several yards towards the lip of a small precipice. I came to a stop just short of the edge, my heart pounding. Ahead of me Hroudland paused only to look back down at me, glare, and gesture to me to hurry. Soon the muscles of my arms and shoulders were aching with the strain, and I began to worry that even if we reached our objective before dark, my hands would be shaking so much that I would be useless as an archer.

Eventually Hroudland halted his upward climb and waited for me to come level with him. Then he began to angle sideways across the face of the mountain. I followed close behind him, hampered by my bow slung across my back. The going was easier now and we made better progress, stretching from one handhold to the next, spread-eagled in our effort to cover the most ground. When we crossed the ridge line and into view of the building we chanced on to the faint vestige of a trail made by sheep or, more likely, by wild goats. It meant we could move more quickly. Otherwise we would have found ourselves scrambling about the mountainside in the gathering dark.

After we had crept within a long bowshot of our target, Hroudland waited until I was close behind him, and then said quietly, 'I don't see any sign of life. Maybe they haven't posted a lookout.'

I looked past him. We were high enough to see over the surrounding wall and gain a better idea of the unknown building. It was on the far side of the walled-in enclosure, overlooking the cliff face beyond. Constructed of cut stone blocks, it had an unusual barrel-shaped roof of weathered tiles. It was definitely not a shepherd's hut. There was no chimney or soot marks from a smoke hole, and, from where I was positioned, I could see only a low wooden door and no window. Nor was there any sign of fortification and it was much too small to hold a garrison.

'More like a tiny chapel than a mountain stronghold,' I said to Hroudland.

He turned his face towards me and I saw the gleam of excitement in his eyes.

'Just the place for the Graal!' he said. 'Another fifty paces, then I want you to find a spot from where you can put an arrow into anyone who might put his head up over that wall. I'll go on alone.'

A slight ruffle of breeze made me glance up at the sky. The weather was changing. The leading edge of a heavy veil of cloud was advancing over the mountain crest to the north. Once it moved over us, we would quickly lose the evening light and then it would be a black and starless night.

'Better hurry. But be careful,' I told him.

For a moment he was his old, blithe self as he treated me to a confident, light-hearted smile. Then he scurried off, stooping as he picked his way from boulder to boulder and made towards the building.

I found my place, half-hidden behind a great slab of tumbled rock, took my bow from my back, and tied on an arm guard of stiff leather. It might help steady my aim. My muscles were still shaking from the exertion of the climb. Below me Hroudland was sprinting in short, quick bursts from one hiding place to the next. There was still no movement from what I now thought of as the mountain chapel. Everything was eerily quiet.

When Hroudland was not more than twenty paces from the surrounding wall, he stopped, unsheathed his sword, then turned and waved to me. I stepped out into the open, nocked an arrow to my bow, and took aim at a spot just above the flimsy-looking wooden gate. It would be an easy shot. Hroudland ran the last few yards and I saw him give the gate a heavy kick. It flew open and he dashed inside. Afterwards there was an occasional glimpse of his head and shoulders above the wall as he searched the enclosure.

In a short while he reappeared at the gate and called up to me, 'There's no one here. The place is empty.'

The tension drained from me. I let my bow go slack, and then began to descend the slope to where Hroudland stood waiting.

'All that climbing and hiding for nothing,' he smiled ruefully. 'We could have walked directly here along the path.'

We went in through the broken gate and I looked round. The enclosure did duty as a sheep pen. The dusty ground was strewn with animal droppings. A length of canvas had been draped over branches propped against the outer wall to make a lean-to shelter. Someone had kindled a fire on the ground in front of it. The charred fragments looked fairly recent.

'Whoever stays here didn't want to occupy the building itself,' said Hroudland. He was checking the door. It was locked.

'I would have expected there to be some sort of caretaker or a guard?' I said. The emptiness of the place struck me as unnatural.

'He could have gone off to Pamplona,' said Hroudland. He was probing the door jamb with his sword point to see if he could find a weakness. 'His friends needed help to empty the city of valuables and carry them up into the mountains.'

'No point in damaging Durendal,' he commented, slipping his sword back into its sheath. He walked over to a boundary wall made of rocks. They were neatly stacked one on top of the other without any mortar. He picked out a large stone and brought it back.

'Stand aside!' he warned, and then slammed the rock against the timber. The door was sturdy and it took a dozen hefty blows before the lock gave and it finally burst open.

Hroudland peered inside.

'It's too dark to see much.'

The lintel was so low that he had to duck his head as he stepped over the threshold. I followed him cautiously.

There was a faint aroma of burned herbs. The interior was more like a cave than a room. If I stretched my arms out sideways I would nearly have touched the opposite walls, and I could barely stand upright. The only window was a fist-sized hole left open in the far wall and close to the ceiling. The light from it scarcely penetrated the deep gloom. Both of us had to stop for a moment to allow our eyes to adjust to the darkness.

I heard Hroudland give a low grunt, part astonishment, part satisfaction.

'There, straight ahead.'

I moved aside to allow more light to enter through the smashed doorway behind me. A thick stone slab set in the far wall made a broad shelf running almost the width of the building. On each end of the shelf stood a small wooden block. They were holders for rush lights, though both were empty. On the shelf between them lay two commonplace items that might have been found in the kitchen of a modest home. One was a small goblet. Five or six inches high, it looked dull and very plain. Beside it was a plate that was even more ordinary, the sort of serving dish for a small joint of meat or a fish. Otherwise the little room was bare.

Hroudland stepped forward.

'Could this be the Graal?' he asked tentatively. He sounded more than a little disappointed. He picked up the goblet from the shelf and carried it back to the doorway to look at it in better light.

The sun had now sunk far below the horizon and the chapel, if it was that, was deep in shadow. Nevertheless as he held up the goblet up, I saw a very faint glow, tawny brown within the bowl.

'It's made of some sort of stone,' the count said. On the middle finger of his left hand he wore a gold ring set with a large piece of amber. He tapped the goblet with it and it rang with a hard, flat sound.

He handed me the goblet.

'What do you make of it, Patch?' he asked.

If I had seen the goblet displayed on an altar I might perhaps have described it as a small chalice. The upper part, the bowl, appeared to have been hollowed from a single piece of a dark coloured stone, which had a brownish tint in its depths. This bowl had been fixed on to a base made from a dense dark wood that contained black streaks. The effect was rather clumsy and heavy, and the goblet with its thick rim looked neither valuable nor very elegant. I turned it over in my hand, half-expecting to find some pattern or decoration like that I had seen on the bronze cup from the fountain of Broceliande. There was nothing.

'Maybe this is not the Graal, if such a thing even exists,' I said carefully.

'Then why hide it away up here in the mountains?' demanded Hroudland, taking it back from me and returning inside the chamber.

He replaced the cup on the shelf and picked up the dish that had been lying next to it, and brought that into the light. Again I saw the tawny brown glow. The plate was made from the same material as the goblet. I could only compare it to a fine marble. The dish had swirls of other colours – grey and pale white – within the stone. I had never seen anything like it before.

Hroudland examined both sides of the dish. Again there were no marks. The plate had been carved from the unknown stone and then polished.

'Those tales you heard from the Breton bards, do they say what the Graal looked like?' I asked.

He shook his head.

'The stories were more about the journeys of those who went searching for the Graal, the strange places and the mysterious people they met . . .' His voice tailed off as he saw the expression on my face.

I had been looking past him, over his shoulder at the mountainside. The fading light had lengthened the shadows, changing the appearance of the rocky slope behind him. There were patterns and shapes among the boulders that had not been there previously. I knew exactly where I was. I was in the landscape of my dream, the nightmare of the monstrous beasts and winged creatures that attacked Hroudland and me.

'What's the matter?' the count asked sharply. 'You looked as if you've seen a ghost.'

I forced my gaze back to the plate he had in his hand.

'We have to get out of here, immediately,' I said shakily.

Hroudland did not hesitate.

'We'll take both the cup and the platter. Later we can decide which is the true Graal.'

He turned and disappeared inside, the plate in his hand, to fetch the cup. At that instant a series of high-pitched whistles sounded from the side of the mountain above me. There were several different notes, one after another. My skin crawled. I swung round on my heel, scanning the slope. But it was impossible to locate where the sound came from. The mountain was shrouded in the gathering darkness. There was a short silence; then came a series of whistles from a different spot. Another succession of notes, rising and falling almost as if they were words. I jerked around, again seeking the source of the sound. But it was futile. I was still peering into the gloom when the original caller responded. Now there was no doubt. The whistlers were communicating with one another in some sort of secret language.

I was about to duck into the building to summon Hroudland outside when there was a fierce scrabbling sound. A dark shape came hurtling out of the shadows straight at me with shocking speed. There was a terrifying snarl, and I was knocked off my feet by the impact of a heavy body. I heard a deep-throated murderous growl and had a glimpse of white fangs beneath drawn-back lips. My nostrils filled with a powerful scent of dog.

I flung up my arm to ward off the gaping jaws. The beast was appallingly strong and determined. It was thrusting and snarling, trying to snatch my throat. I rolled from side to side, attempting to throw it off. I was faintly aware of two more animals. They streaked past me and bounded into the dark entrance to the chapel. From within came the sounds of a vicious tussle.

My archer's arm guard saved me. The dog had locked its jaws on my forearm, and the leather prevented the teeth from penetrating. I managed to struggle up on my knees, and then regain my feet. The brute was thrashing its head violently from side to side, trying to drag me down again. I reached forward with my free hand, intending to pull it off by the scruff of the neck. There was an agonizing stab of pain as my hands closed on the sharp metal spikes of a thick collar designed to deter wolves.

I backed away slowly, step by step, holding off the dog with my left arm while it continued to growl savagely, shaking and tugging frenziedly. I retreated, just managing to stay on my feet, until I could feel the wall of the chapel behind me. That is where I had left my bow leaning against the stonework. I searched behind me with my right hand and fumbled in the arrow bag until my fingers closed on an arrow. Gripping the shaft firmly I pulled it out. With a great heave I swung the brute to one side and, when its flank was exposed, I rammed the razor-sharp metal head into the dog's belly with all my strength. There was a yelp of pain and it released the grip of its jaws.

But the brute did not abandon the attack. It stood a yard away, stiff-legged, teeth bared and growling murderously, watching for an opening when it could fling itself on me once again.

I shouted for Hroudland, and he backed slowly out from the chapel in a half-crouch, facing towards the frenzy of brutish snarls that sounded within the gloomy interior. He had set down the dish because he had his sword, Durendal, in one hand and in the other a short dagger. Both blades were pointed towards the doorway. He had scarcely got clear when the other two dogs emerged. They were even larger than the one that had knocked me down. One had a gash in its shoulder, the blood dripping down on the dust. Both animals had their eyes fixed on the count, and they were stalking slowly towards him, ready to spring.

Again I heard that unearthly whistling from the mountainside behind me. This time it seemed closer.

'They're somewhere on the mountain,' I gasped. 'I don't know who they are or how many.'

'If they send in more dogs, we're in trouble,' said the count. 'I can deal with three or four. But a pack of them would pull us down.'

We were out in the open now, standing back to back, facing the growling dogs. They were massive brutes, each as big as a small calf, with bear-like shaggy pelts and heavy square heads. All of them wore spiked collars, and it was clear that they were trained for fighting.

Even at that late stage, Hroudland might have successfully completed his raid. He could have risked going back inside the chapel, snatched up the goblet and the plate, and the two of us could have fought our way back down the track. But then there was a sudden movement in the air above us. It was so unexpected that neither of us had time to prepare ourselves. Out of the gloom swooped down a half-seen shape, a darker form against the already dark sky. It came at an unnatural speed, at head height. I felt the rush of air on my face. A whisper of something flashed overhead. Hroudland let out an oath and doubled over as if he had been struck. Durendal clattered to the ground as he let go his sword and clapped his hand to his face. For a moment he stayed bent over, hunched in pain. When he stood upright and removed his hand, blood was streaming from a gash just beside his right eye.

I had barely time to take in what had happened when again I felt that sinister rush of air. This time there was a sharp blow and searing pain across my scalp as something sharp raked across my head. I caught the quick flap of broad wings and the large bird that had attacked me was rising up and away. It was circling, ready to attack again.

In the distance we heard the oliphant horn. Berenger was signalling that there was danger along the path where he stood guard. Our escape route was threatened.

So we ran. We blundered out of the broken gate and down the dimly seen track. The huge dogs harried us every step. They lunged at our heels, snarling and barking, driving us off like the sheep stealers. I had abandoned my bow but Hroudland had managed to snatch up Durendal from the ground. Occasionally he stopped and stabbed and slashed at our tormentors, making them keep their distance. There was nothing we could do about the birds. They swooped out of the darkness and tried to rip out our eyes. Like the huge dogs, they must have been trained to guard the Vascon flocks from wolves and thieves.

Only when we were well clear of the chapel did the onslaught finally cease.

The night sky then clouded over completely. Without light from moon or stars to show us where to put our feet, our progress was like groping through a black pit. We tripped and fell, got up and stumbled forward a dozen or more times. We dared not stop, fearing that our enemies would have time to set an ambush on the track ahead of us. We lost all sense of time or how far we had got, and it must have been well past midnight when someone called out a challenge from directly in front of us. It was Berenger. He heard the noise we made coming down the track.

'Thank God you're back,' he said. The relief in his voice was very evident. 'The place is swarming with Vascons, hundreds of them on the move.'

'Which way are they headed?' asked Hroudland sharply. Even exhausted, he kept his wits about him.

'Towards the road. They passed me a couple of hours ago. I stayed out of sight until it was safe to sound the alarm.'

'We press on at once,' Hroudland announced. It was an order, and he was once again a war leader. 'I must be back in command of the rearguard before the Vascons fall on us.'

Chapter Nineteen

THERE WAS NO REARGUARD, as it turned out. The three of us limped out on to the main road just as the first glow of sunrise seeped into the sky. In the cold light we found the treasure carts gone. The area around the shepherd's hut where we had previously camped was strewn with the usual rubbish left behind by retreating soldiers. The place was abandoned.

Wearily I sat down on a roadside boulder. My knees were sore and bruised and the palms of my hands skinned raw from the number of times I had fallen.

'Back on your feet!' Hroudland hissed at me. The gash on the side of his face where the eagle had clawed him was crusted with dried blood. 'Gerin and the others can't have gone far and the Saracen skirmishers will be here soon.'

I rose slowly. Every part of my body ached.

'Over here!' Berenger shouted. He had gone across to the shepherd's hut in search of something to eat.

The count and I joined him. Lying in the dust behind the hut was the Vascon shepherd. His throat had been cut. The front of his wolfskin jacket lay open. Someone had searched the corpse for anything worth stealing. Our dispirited soldiers had been reduced to corpse robbers.

We heard the clatter of horses' hooves. Someone was riding at speed down the road from the direction of the pass. Berenger and Hroudland drew their swords and ran to take up positions where they could defend themselves. With only a dagger in my belt, I considered whether to take refuge inside the hut but thought better of it. I did not want to be accused of cowardice.

The rider came in view. He had a plain red shield on his arm and Hroudland's roan war stallion on a leading rein. It was Gerin.

'I thought you might come back,' he called out. 'We don't have much time.'

He tossed the stallion's reins to Hroudland and leaned down, extending an arm towards me so that I could scramble up behind him.

'How far ahead are the others?' Hroudland demanded, settling himself into the saddle of the roan, and then hoisting Berenger up on to the crupper.

'Five or six miles. Eggihard ordered the carts to move on as soon as the broken wheel was fixed.'

We set off at a canter, the sound of the hooves echoing off steep rocky slopes. Hroudland had to raise his voice to make himself heard.

'I told you to make him wait for our return.'

Gerin snorted.

'Carolus sent Count Anselm back to find out what the delay was all about. The king is worried about the gap between the main army and the last of the carts. Anselm accepted Eggihard's suggestion that the carters should travel through the night.'

Hroudland cursed both Eggihard and Anselm. The latter was count of the palace and could act with the king's authority.

'Where's Carolus now?' he called to Gerin.

'Already through the main pass. He's taken the main cavalry with him and intends to push on to face the Saxons.'

The road was rising steadily, one bend after the other. I was glad I was no longer on foot. I doubted I had enough strength left to have made the climb. I twisted around, looking back over my shoulder, trying to recall what I had seen when coming in the opposite direction with Wali Husayn. The rocks and slopes all looked alike, featureless and forbidding.

Only when we reached the treasure carts did I know where we were. Up to my left I recognized the rocky slope on which I had killed the Vascon slinger who had ambushed me.

The four treasure carts were halted at the place where Husayn and his men had stopped to say their noonday prayers. Here the road widened out, and there was enough space for the drivers and their oxen to pause and rest. Their escort of some thirty heavily armed cavalrymen was standing around, looking bored and impatient, waiting for the journey to continue. I wondered which one of them had murdered the Vascon shepherd.

Hroudland sprang down from his horse and strode off to confront Eggihard and a tubby, balding man in an expensive-looking war coat of chain mail that extended right down to cover his ample thighs. I guessed he was Count Anselm.

Hroudland was furious, and his voice carried clearly.

'Where are the rest of my men? I left fifty of them as guards. I can see barely a score of them now,' he snarled.

Eggihard shrugged. He seemed to accept that Hroudland had a right to take charge again.

'Count Anselm brought more soldiers with him. I relieved the others, and they've gone ahead.' He treated Hroudland to a look full of malice. 'While you were away on your private escapade, we outstripped any Saracen pursuit by travelling through the night. In a few more miles we'll be through the pass and back on Frankish soil.'

Hroudland glowered.

I had to get away from the incessant bickering. I slid down from the back of Gerin's mount and picked my way up the slope and sat down on the exact same spot where I had written up my notes for Alcuin. The rock was already warm from the sun. It was going to be a hot day.

I sat quietly, gazing toward the plains in Hispania just visible in the distant haze. Somewhere out there was Osric. I wondered whether he would spend the rest of his life in Zaragoza as an official of the wali's court or whether he would eventually find his way back to the city of his birth. It was strange that fate allowed him a choice, while I could not return to my own homeland as long as King Offa ruled. Thinking about Offa reminded me that Gerin had once served the King of Mercia. Looking down towards the road I could see Gerin with his red shield slung on his back. He was chatting to one of the troopers. Previously I had suspected him of being behind the attempts to have me killed. Now that seemed unlikely. He had been just as quick to get me out of danger as to extricate Hroudland and Berenger.

My gaze drifted back to the mountain opposite me, on the far side of the road. The slope was a jumble of boulders and broken rock with an occasional ledge and overhang. There were no trees or shrubs to add a touch of green. Everything was grey, from the darkest shade of slate to the colour of cinders left in a cold hearth. I slid my eyepatch up on my forehead. A speck of grit had worked its way under it and was lodged in the corner of my eye. It pricked painfully and made my eye water. I rubbed the eye to clear it, and before putting the patch back in place I blinked several times to clear my vision. Perhaps because I was using both eyes I saw the far hillside much more clearly. A dark shape that I had thought was a boulder was nothing of the sort. It was a man. He was sitting motionless, his clothing the exact colour of the rocks around him; even his head was swathed in grey material. He was watching the ox carts on the road below him. After I had spotted the first man, it was much easier to see the others. They were spread out across the slope, waiting and watching, not moving. There must have been a dozen or more. My heart thumped wildly, and I replaced my eye patch. Slowly I got to my feet and began to descend the slope, careful not to hurry.

'There are men lying in wait on the slopes above us,' I said under my breath to Hroudland, forcing myself to act as though everything was normal.

He did not even glance upward.

'They'll be the Vascons that Berenger saw earlier. Any idea how many?'

'At least a dozen, maybe twice that number.'

'There'll be many more waiting at whatever place they've selected for an ambush,' he said calmly. He beckoned to Gerin to come to join us.

'Patch tells me that there are Vascon watchers on the slopes above us,' he told Gerin. 'Is there someone who might know where their attack is likely to take place?'

Gerin signalled to one of the guards to join us. The man's battered face with its broken nose seemed familiar. I recalled him as the Burgundian sergeant I had seen marching at the head of his troop on the way to Hispania. He had his short-handled axe slung from his belt. I wondered why he was now a mounted soldier and what had happened to the rest of his unit.

'What's your name?' Hroudland asked him.

'Godomar, my Lord.'

'You came with Count Anselm?'

'I did, my lord.' The man spoke with an unnaturally husky voice and there was the scar of an old wound on his throat.

'So you've travelled this road a couple of times,' said Hroudland. 'If you were to set an ambush, where would it be?'

'About half a mile ahead, my lord,' the Burgundian replied without hesitation. 'The road runs through a small ravine, low cliffs on either side. Ideal spot.'

'Any way we can avoid it?'

Godomar shook his head.

'Gerin, I'm putting you in charge of the vanguard,' said Hroudland briskly, 'with Godomar as your second in command. You'll have ten men.' He sounded purposeful, almost eager. 'Expect an attack. It's likely to come from both sides – arrows and slingstones followed by a charge.'

The Burgundian's eyes flicked to where Anselm stood with Eggihard. He was worried about taking orders directly from Hroudland.

The count noted his hesitation.

'Godomar, the king appointed me to command the rearguard,' he said firmly.

The veteran raised his hand in a salute and was about to leave when Hroudland warned, 'The Vascons will try to block the road with boulders. Tell your men that they will have to clear away any obstacle. The treasure carts must get through, at whatever cost.'

As the Burgundian went off to carry out Hroudland's instruction, Gerin's mouth twisted in a sardonic smile.

'Cavalry men won't like getting off their horses in order to roll boulders around.'

'By the time the Vascons have finished with us, we'll be lucky if there are enough horses left for anyone to ride,' retorted Hroudland grimly. He was in his element, issuing orders. 'Berenger, I'm putting you and Patch on either side of the carts. I'll assign five troopers to each of you. The enemy will try to cripple the draught animals. Your job is to protect the oxen.'

'Where will you be?' I asked him. My horse, the bay gelding, was tethered at the tail of a cart. I had left my sword for safe-keeping with the carter.

'At the rear with the rest of the troopers. That's where the Vascons will concentrate their attack.'

The halt was over. The drovers were fussing around their oxen, getting ready to move off. Godomar was talking quietly to several of the troopers and they were mounting up and taking their position ahead of the carts.

Eggihard and Anselm sauntered across, making it obvious from their casual manner that they did not care much for Hroudland or his leadership.

Hroudland allowed his irritation to show.

'It's time you were mounted up. I'm assigning you to the rearguard,' he snapped at them. He deliberately turned his back and put a foot into the stirrup of his roan, ready to climb into the saddle.

Eggihard paused for a moment. Then he observed in a voice loud enough for the nearest soldiers to hear him, 'I would have despatched a messenger to the king by now.'

Hroudland's back went rigid. He removed his foot from the stirrup and swung round to glower at Eggihard.

'A messenger to say what?' he demanded icily.

'To ask the army to turn back and assist.'

Two red spots of anger appeared on Hroudland's cheeks.

'I have not the slightest intention of running to the king asking for help,' he snapped.

Eggihard raised an eyebrow insolently.

'And if we are outnumbered, what then?'

'We fight our way through. That's what the king expects of us.' Hroudland pointedly allowed his gaze to settle on Anselm's bulging waistline. 'Unless you and your companion no longer have the stomach for it.'

Anselm looked as though he would explode with anger.

'I'll hold my own against any man who cares to go against me,' he spluttered.

'Then I suggest you reserve your fighting prowess for the coming battle,' snarled Hroudland. Without bothering to put a foot into the stirrup, he vaulted into the saddle. A moment later he was trotting off, shouting encouragement at the ox drovers, encouraging them to pick up the pace.

*

Riding beside the treasure carts brought back memories of the days when Osric and I had tramped along behind Arnulf's eel wagon. There was the familiar farmyard smell from the oxen, and the four heavily laden carts rumbled along at the same sedate walking pace. The road surface was very rough, and their solid wheels juddered and shook as they rolled over small rocks or dropped into pot holes. Arnulf had handled his well-trained oxen by himself, but here in the mountains each cart needed two men, one walking beside the animals, the other seated on the cart and armed with a whip to urge the animals on. The axles worn down by months of travel produced a continuous, high-pitched squealing that announced our presence to anyone within half a mile and set one's teeth on edge.

It was unnerving to know that the Vascon sentinels were watching our every step. I found myself wondering how often they had tracked the progress of other travellers labouring along the same narrow road. Perhaps this was how the stone platter and the little chalice had come into their possession, looted from victims of an ambush sometime in the distant past. I had no doubt that the Vascons knew about the ransom that Wali Husayn had paid. The bags of silver would be sufficient enticement for an attack, and Hroudland's brutal sack of Pamplona had given the Vascons a powerful reason to wreak bloody revenge.

So, despite the blazing sunshine, I wore an iron helmet over a felt skull cap. The metal plates of a brunia protected my body. Thick, padded gauntlets covered my hands and forearms. Only my legs felt vulnerable. I sweltered in the searing heat and the perspiration ran down my body until my saddle was slippery with sweat. Like the troopers riding with me, I knew there would be no time to don our war gear when the Vascons chose to launch their assault.

It was the trooper just behind me who first spotted the danger. He gave a sharp cry of alarm and pointed up to our right. I swivelled in the saddle and looked up the steep slope of the mountain. The Vascons had struck early, well before we reached the gorge. The mountainside was sprouting men, a hundred or more. They had been lying in wait, concealed among the rocks. Now they rose from the ground and began to descend, leaping and slithering. As they advanced they raised a war cry, the most chilling sound I had heard. It was a terrible wolfish howl, mournful and without pity.

There was momentary panic along our line. The drovers struck out with their long whips. Troopers cursed as they swung their shields off their backs and slid their arms through the straps. Everyone grabbed for their weapons. Hroudland was bellowing at us to close ranks and keep moving and face the danger.

The Vascons had another surprise for us. We had expected their first attack to come as a hail of sling stones and arrows. But we had misjudged their ferocity. There was a clatter of slingstones, though only a few. At the same time a couple of dozen arrows fell among us without doing much harm, though a wounded horse screamed. It was the reckless savagery of the Vascon charge that was dismaying. They came seething down the hill in a surge of raw hatred and hostility. They were determined to engage us hand to hand. At that moment I knew for certain that it was not the wali's ransom that drew them on but the burning desire to exact retribution for the destruction we had inflicted on their city.

Their leading warriors had concealed themselves within a few yards of the track. They sprang up from the ground and lunged at our horses' bellies with daggers and short swords. Few succeeded in reaching their targets. Our troopers spitted them on their lances. Their iron sword blades cut down through muscle and bone, severing outstretched hands and limbs. The Vascons wore no armour. They were dressed in jackets of wolfskin and leggings of coarse cloth, and they took fearful losses. The man who had selected my gelding as his victim scuttled out of the roadside ambush and came straight at me like a scorpion, dagger raised. I swung my sword at him and the well-balanced Ingelrii blade made an effortless arc. The razor edge lopped off the man's dagger hand as easily as a woodsman prunes a small branch. The Vascon reeled away, leaving a smear of blood behind him.

There was a confusion of shouting and the clash of steel from where Gerin was in charge of the vanguard. Near me the trooper who had first seen the Vascon ambush was swearing steadily as he tried to wield his sword and at the same time bring his mount under control. The howls of the Vascons and the smell of blood had panicked the animal. It was skittering from side to side, trying to bolt, hooves scrabbling on the rocky surface of the road. The trooper was roaring angrily and, unbalanced, he failed to connect as he cut at a Vascon lunging at him with a spear. The point of the weapon gouged a deep gash in the horse's hind-quarters before the trooper recovered himself enough to make a backhanded sword swing and hack the man to the ground. Out of the corner of my eye I saw a lad dart past me. He could not have been more than ten years old. He headed for the nearest ox cart and had a small knife in his hand. Before I realized what he was doing, he stabbed the blade into a full water bladder that hung from the side of the cart. Quick as a weasel, he dived under the cart and escaped. Behind him a jet of fresh water sprang from the punctured water bag and splashed to the ground.

All the while the oxen plodded on. Heads held low, they ignored the chaos of battle. Their huge dark eyes were intent on the road immediately ahead of their hooves. Long, glistening strings of drool hung from their muzzles. They toiled forward against the slope, goaded by their frightened drovers.

Gerin was managing to keep the road clear ahead of us. Whenever numbers of Vascons blocked the path, his Frankish lancers formed up and charged. They swept aside the men on foot, killing or wounding those who were too slow to run back up the hillside. Then the troopers reined in, turned and trotted back to resume their station in the vanguard. Each charge left a handful of Vascon corpses on the ground.

'They're out of their minds!' Berenger yelled across to me. He was on the far side of the cart, riding escort. He had seen little action yet because the Vascons had launched their ambush from our right.

'Hroudland ought to send a messenger to summon help from the main army,' I shouted back. 'This is just the first attack.'

Berenger laughed aloud and I heard a note of battle frenzy in his response.

'Not a chance! The count is much too proud. We can fight our way past this rabble.'

I glanced over my shoulder. The Vascons were concentrating their attack on the rear of our little column. Hroudland and the rear guard were engaged against a grey-clad mob of the enemy.

Eggihard and Anselm were mounted on tall, powerful horses so they were very visible. They had been reluctant to take orders from Hroudland, but in battle they were proving fearsome. Both men were using their long swords with deadly effect, slashing and thrusting, forcing back the attackers. A few yards away, Hroudland sat on his roan, roaring encouragement to his troopers as they drove off the Vascons.

It was impossible to tell how long the fury of the initial assault lasted. Eventually the Vascons saw how effectively we resisted and they began to withdraw, though only for a few yards up the mountainside where they were safe from our cavalry. There they kept pace with us, moving across the slope as our column crept forward.

To my surprise Hroudland took advantage of the lull in the fighting to ride up and congratulate me. His face under the rim of his helmet was running with sweat, and his eyes were bright.

'Well done, Patch!' he exclaimed. 'You and your men held our flank.'

'The enemy are only biding their time,' I answered.

'Then we'll drive them off again and again until they learn that they can't defeat well-trained cavalry,' he assured me.

'We're not yet at the place Godomar thought suited for an ambush,' I reminded him.

Hroudland was not to be put off.

'Then that's their mistake. They've thrown away the advantage of surprise.'

'Maybe the Vascons are planning to delay us or to wear us down,' I objected.

Hroudland drew his eyebrows together in a scowl. He did not like his judgement to be questioned.

'What makes you such an expert soldier, Patch?' he demanded, his congratulatory tone suddenly gone.

'One of their lads slipped through our defence earlier. He put a hole in that waterskin over there,' I said and nodded to where the punctured waterskin hung limp from the side of the cart.

Hroudland shrugged.

'So we'll be thirsty for a while,' he said, though I noted that his eyes flicked towards the other carts. Several of their waterskins were also dangling empty.

I lowered my voice so that no one else could hear.

'The next water source is the far side of the summit ridge.'

Hroudland recovered his poise.

'Then all the more incentive to fight our way there,' he retorted.

While we had been speaking the column had advanced perhaps a hundred paces. I wondered how many more hours it would be until we were out of danger.

*

The Vascons attacked us twice more before the sun was directly overhead. Each time we succeeded in driving them off though we lost a dozen horses, lamed or disembowelled. Their riders now walked or, if they had been wounded, they rode on the carts. We had not suffered a single death and I began to think that Hroudland was right; we would manage to force our way along the road until we were safely over the pass.

Two miles later everything changed.

Gerin rode back past me, his face grim. He was on his way to report to Hroudland. I was close enough to overhear him say to the count, 'We're in sight of the ravine now. It looks very narrow. A dangerous place.' There was a short pause, and then Gerin added, almost apologetically, 'We could always leave the carts behind. We still have enough horses to carry everyone to safety if they double up. I'm confident we could slip through.'

Hroudland's answer was delivered in a harsh whisper.

'I thought I made it clear: I have no intention of abandoning the treasure we have won. Have the enemy blocked the roadway?'

'Apparently not, though there's a bend in the road and I can't see the full length of the ravine,' said Gerin.

'Then the passage lies ahead, and we take it,' Hroudland confirmed.

'I will do my best, my lord. But I fear that is what the enemy want us to do,' Gerin said. He spoke in a flat, resigned tone in contrast to his usual air of steely competence.

He returned past me, looking distracted and chewing his lip. I had a queasy feeling that he was right. We were doing what the Vascons had planned for us. Only Hroudland's absolute self-confidence kept driving us forward.

The enemy left us alone for the time it took us to reach the point where the road narrowed to no more than four or five paces width, just before entering the ravine itself. To the right was a low cliff, not more than fifteen feet high. To the left a steep broken slope covered with rocks and small loose stones extended all the way up to the mountain ridge. I noticed the troopers casting worried glances from side to side. We were roasting in the summer heat and my mouth was dry. I summoned up some saliva and swallowed in an attempt to moisten my throat.

Two of Gerin's troopers accompanied by Godomar broke away from the vanguard and went forward at a trot, presumably to scout the passage. They were gone for several minutes. When they returned and delivered their report, Gerin rose in his stirrups, turned and called back to the drovers behind him, 'Close up! Keep moving! The road is partially blocked by a barrier of boulders at the far end. My men will clear the way for you.'

We continued forward, our little column more compact now as we reduced the distance between each cart. The narrowness of the roadway obliged the flanking cavalrymen to close in. My knee was almost touching the wooden wheel of the nearest cart.

'Maybe we've reached the boundary of their territory,' Berenger called across to me. He nodded toward the Vascons on the hillside who had been keeping pace with us. They had halted, and were standing and watching us leave.

'Or they know that there's a relief force on its way back from the main army,' I said hopefully, though I did not believe it. There was something unnerving about the way the Vascons were holding themselves in check.

As Gerin and the vanguard entered the ravine, I paid close attention to the top of the low cliff to our right. I was expecting to see Vascon slingers or archers appear there at any moment.

I was looking in the wrong direction.

After the first of our carts entered the ravine, I heard a gasp. It came from a wounded trooper riding on the cart next to me. He was looking up the long, steep slope to our left. I followed his gaze. It was as if the mountainside was sloughing off its grey skin. The entire slope was alive and moving. Grey-clad men, hundreds of them, covered its surface and they were swarming down towards us. They were not hurrying, but picking their way purposefully among the boulders, converging on the roadway. They held spears and swords, and they moved with deadly earnest.

My guts turned to water as, behind us, the massed wolf-like howl we heard when the Vascons first attacked rose again. I swung round. The men who had been tracking us had now descended into the roadway. They were blocking any attempt at retreat.

'Face left! Keep moving!' Hroudland was bellowing. Most of us were still gaping at the sheer number of fighting men the Vascons had assembled.

Berenger was dumbfounded.

'Some of them must be the men I saw yesterday. But where did all the others spring from?'

He had drawn his sword and now he looked down at the weapon in wonder as if he knew that it would be useless in the face of such overwhelming odds. Behind me I heard Eggihard's voice, railing at Hroudland, shouting that he should have sent to Carolus earlier and asked for reinforcements from the main army. Even the oxen sensed that something had changed. The squealing of the wheels fell silent as they came to a gradual halt and stood meekly. We were halfway into the entrance to the ravine.

Hroudland changed his instructions.

'Stand! Form a defensive line. Shift the carts to make a barricade!' he roared.

But it was impossible. The road was too narrow. The drovers did not have enough space to turn and manoeuvre their beasts. The carts remained where they were, one behind the other. The Vascons had pushed us into the ravine like forcing a cork into the neck of a bottle.

Gerin squeezed his way past me.

'It'll take more than an hour to clear away enough boulders from their barrier,' he reported to Hroudland.

Anselm, the count of the palace, was within earshot. He was sweating heavily, his fleshy face scarlet under his helmet and his fine chainmail covered in dust.

'Is there enough of a gap for a rider to get through?' he demanded savagely. His stallion, trained to battle, was tossing its head and pawing the ground nervously.

When Gerin hesitated with his reply, Anselm bawled to one of the troopers nearby.

'You there! Change horses with me and get through to the main army. Tell them to send help!'

He slid down from his own horse, handed over the reins, and a moment later the man was galloping into the ravine on his fresh mount.

Hroudland had no time to react to this challenge to his authority. Our men were milling about in confusion. The close-packed carts were making it difficult to form up in a defensive line. He rode in among the troopers, pushing and shoving them into some sort of order. I glanced across at Berenger. He was sitting still, his eyes fixed on Hroudland, waiting to carry out his commands. I realized that Berenger would follow the count whatever happened, his faith unshakeable.

The swarm of Vascons on the mountainside merged into a single dense mass as they reached more level ground. Now they flowed towards us like a rising tide. They filled the roadway and lapped up the sides of the track until they came to a stop, some twenty paces away. There was neither semblance of discipline nor any plan of attack that I could see. Among their weapons were ugly-looking cudgels as well as their swords and short spears. A few held woodsmen's axes. For an unhappy moment I was reminded of the homespun levies my father had assembled when our family fought and lost its last battle against King Offa and his Mercian men-at-arms. But the resemblance was false. These Vascons were hardy mountain men, not peaceful farmers, and they out-numbered us so vastly that it was clear to everyone that we had not the slightest chance of victory.

For a long, tense moment the two sides stood and faced one another. The Vascons brandished their weapons and shouted insults and threats in their outlandish language. We stood silent except for the occasional stamping of a restless horse. The wounded trooper on the cart next to me was mumbling some sort of prayer over and over again as some sort of lucky charm that would save him. The sun beat down and the heat reflected off the rocks. My head ached and I was parched with thirst. I licked my cracked lips and tasted the gritty road dust.

Vaguely I became aware of someone getting down from his horse. Then he was pushing through our front line and walking towards the enemy. It was Godomar, the veteran from Burgundy. He had taken off his brunia and his helmet and was wearing only a pair of loose trousers and a light jerkin which left his arms and shoulders bare. A strip of cloth held back his long, thick hair which was the colour of forest honey. In his right hand he held the short handled axe that usually hung from his broad leather belt. All of us, Vascons and Franks, looked on as Godomar strode out on to the open ground between us. Then, in a deep husky voice from his wounded throat, he began to recite what must have been a battle ode in some ancient tribal dialect. With each line he tossed his axe in the air so that it spun in a circle, and caught it with the opposite hand. Finally, as he declaimed the last words, his voice rose to a shout and he threw the axe, not to the other hand, but high in the air, towards the enemy. It spun round and round, and by the time it fell back, Godomar had run forward and was ready to catch its handle. He was no more than an arm's length from the Vascon line. In a sudden blur of axe strokes he cut down three or four Vascons. Then they closed in around him, and he was gone.

His death broke the spell that had held us in our places. With a bellow of shock and anger the Vascons charged. They crashed into us, and there was pandemonium. Lances were useless at such close quarters. Troopers used their swords to hack and thrust at the men on foot surging around them. The Vascons ducked and feinted. They stooped to get in under the riders' guard, and if close enough, they hacked and stabbed with their weapons. The bravest grabbed for the riders' legs and tried to drag them out of the saddle.

Amid the curses and grunts, the clash of metal, the cries of anger and pain, the Vascons were badly mauled. Dozens of them died, their bodies overridden by the horses or trampled underfoot by their comrades. Yet they kept pressing forward, ignoring their losses. Charge after charge, they were like waves pounding on a rocky beach. With each attack they reduced our numbers. Our troopers went down one after another, hauled from the saddle or their horses were killed beneath them. Few survived for more than a moment if they were unhorsed. The Vascons swarmed over them and killed them. With their third headlong charge our line broke, and the Vascons were among the drovers and their oxen. With the expertise of butchers, they slit the windpipes of the cattle and brought the beasts to their knees. The drovers were massacred.

The press of the mob was so powerful that my mount was thrust back and pinned against the wheel of the nearest cart. I flailed with my sword, uselessly. Strong hands grabbed my leg and I was hauled to the ground. Without a rider, the horse kicked out and a hoof struck the forehead of the man who held me. I heard the crack of hoof on bone. He let go and I rolled away between the wheels of the cart. My attackers were obliged to stand back as the terrified animal reared up, then bolted through the mob. It gave me enough time to scuttle away on all fours to the far side of the cart and rise to my feet. I had lost my sword and I could think of nothing else to do but hoist myself up on the cart itself. From there I looked around and saw the carnage that had taken place. Only one man was still on horseback – Hroudland. His powerful roan was rearing and plunging, faced by a half circle of Vascons. They were being kept at bay by the lashing hooves and by Hroudland's menacing sword blade. Every other Frank was on foot. They were drawn up in a compact mass behind Hroudland, their backs towards the carts. I estimated there were no more than a dozen of them. Berenger had lost his helmet and I recognized his head of tight curls. There was no sign of either Eggihard or Anselm. Their bodies would be lying among the ugly jumble of corpses in front of the Frankish position. Dead and injured Vascons were scattered everywhere, the ground streaked and splashed with blood.

Hundreds of Vascons still filled the roadway, and many more were poised on the slopes on each side of the road. With their next assault they would swamp us.

First, however, they dealt with Hroudland. A single Vascon stepped out from their ranks. He was a squat man of middle age, wearing a wolfskin cap and very broad across the shoulders and chest. He held a loaded sling which he began to whirl rhythmically around his head. He watched Hroudland, judging his moment. As the roan stallion turned towards him, the Vascon released a slingstone as large as a man's fist. The stone travelled less than five paces and struck the roan between the eyes. I heard the thud from where I stood. At that short range the impact was spectacularly effective. The front legs of the horse buckled and the stunned animal tipped forward on to its knees and Hroudland just had time to leap clear. He landed on his feet and, sword in hand, ran back across the blood-soaked ground to join the other Franks. I noticed he was limping. Behind him, the dazed stallion stayed down for several moments, then groggily heaved itself back upright and wandered off.

The Vascons held back a little longer, waiting to see what we would do next.

I jumped down from the tail of the cart and picked up an abandoned sword from the ground. Berenger glanced at me over his shoulder. His red-rimmed eyes looked out from a mask of dust. His hair was sweat-soaked, and there was a rent in his brunia where several plates had been torn off. 'This is where the fight gets interesting, Patch,' he said to me with a tight smile, then turned back to ask Hroudland, 'What are your orders?'

The count was so calm and self-possessed that I wondered if he appreciated the hopelessness of our situation.

'We leave behind the carts. Looting them will delay the Vascons. It will give us time to make an orderly retreat.'

Even now a flicker of regret passed across his face. The idea of losing all the treasure still grated on him.

'We take with us only what we value the most,' he continued. He turned to me. 'Patch, can you find the oliphant for me? It should not fall into the hands of the Vascons. Also the crystal salver from Wali Suleyman's ransom. I still intend to give it to the king.'

I climbed back on the cart and searched. I came across the oliphant wrapped in a soft leather covering but the crystal salver must have been locked away in a treasure chest and I had no time to locate the key. Instead I picked up my most prized possession – the packet of loose pages of the translation of the Book of Dreams. Unlacing the side of my brunia, I slid them inside my armoured jacket.

By the time I rejoined the others, Hroudland had marshalled our few survivors into two ranks. There was only one direction for our retreat – deeper into the ravine. One rank was to stand firm while the other ran back a few yards, then turned to face the enemy and allow the first group to filter back among them before they again took up position. I remembered practising the same manoeuvre when I had first arrived in Aachen and joined the paladins in their war games. I had never expected to rely on it in real combat.

The Vascons harassed us every step of the way. Inside the ravine they could only attack us on a narrow front but they were recklessly brave and showed no mercy. Any Frank who slipped and fell, or dropped his guard for a moment, was despatched on the spot. As the afternoon wore on and the light began to fade, we fought and retreated, turned and fought again. Our numbers dwindled as we grew more and more weary. I allowed my shield to droop and felt an agonizing pain in my left shoulder. A Vascon, screaming with anger, had run his spear point over its rim. Beside me Berenger was clumsy in countering a thrust from a Vascon dagger. He was stabbed, low down on his right side. Only Hroudland continued to wield his sword as if he would never tire, but with every pace he left a bloody foot print on the ground. I could not see where he had been injured, but he was losing blood rapidly.

The Vascons drove us along the ravine like obstinate sheep until our backs came up against the barrier of boulders that they had created earlier. By then it was almost dark and only four of us were still standing – Hroudland, Berenger, myself, and an unknown trooper with a hideous stomach wound. As if to gloat, the Vascons drew back so we would know that they had us at their mercy. Occasionally one of them let out the dreadful wolf's howl in victory. During the retreat I had seen such hatred in their faces that I knew that they would not let us live.

'We managed to hold them off,' said Hroudland proudly. He was leaning on his sword, his chest heaving as he sucked in great breaths of air. Beside me, Berenger slumped on a boulder, a wet bloodstain seeping down his leg. I too found a place to sit as I was dizzy from the pain of my wounded shoulder.

I looked at Hroudland. There was just enough light to see how he was deathly pale. He was smiling and his eyes held a faraway look that convinced me that he had lost touch with reality. I wondered if he still clung to the idea that he could never be defeated in battle by a horde of uncouth mountain men.

With an effort he turned his back on me and began to climb

up on to the rock barrier behind us. The oliphant hung on a cord around his neck. When he reached the highest boulder, he stood up on it, raised the great horn to his lips and blew a long, quavering blast, which echoed and re-echoed down the ravine.

'What in God's name is he doing?' I demanded of Berenger. He was gazing up at Hroudland, awestruck.

Berenger turned to face me, his eyes shining.

'Listen!' he exclaimed.

Hroudland sounded the horn again, and I recognized the notes. It was the call when a huntsman announces the death of a great stag. In the deepening gloom there were only shades of black and grey. There, up above me, I could only make out the outline figure of the Margrave of Brittany. A cold lump gathered in my guts as I remembered that the same scene was carved on the oliphant itself, and that long ago in Aachen the king himself had dreamed of a huntsman standing on a rock surrounded by wolves and blowing a horn calling for help. But Hroudland was not summoning help. He was announcing his own passing.

'Do you remember when I first laid eyes on you,' Berenger suddenly asked. The question was completely unexpected and his voice sounded strained, almost as if he was ashamed to speak. 'It was evening. You walked into our living quarters, unannounced. None of us had any idea who you were.'

'You, Gerin, Anseis and the others were playing a game. Asking one another riddles,' I said.

Berenger's voice sank almost to a whisper as he began to recite:

'Four strange creatures travel together, their tracks were very swart.
Each mark very black. The bird's support moves swiftly, through
the air, underwater.
The diligent warrior works without stopping, directing the four over
the beaten gold.'

I knew the words.

'That was the riddle I set. Hroudland was the only one who knew the answer,' I said.

'That was the moment I began to fear you,' he murmured.

I was so astonished that I could only blurt, 'Why?'

I heard him shift uncomfortably. Another shaft of pain must have struck him.

'I was terrified that you would take Hroudland away from me.'

'I don't know what you're talking about,' I said, baffled.

'Jealousy feeds easily. Hroudland paid you every attention from the moment you arrived.'

'He saw that I was a stranger and in an alien land. He only wanted to help me,' I said.

'I know that now,' Berenger answered, 'but not then. The very next day I walked in on you at the bath. He was half-naked, holding you by the arm.'

I was appalled.

'He was trying to drag me into the water, that's all. I didn't want to go. I have a fear of water.'

In the darkness Berenger laughed mirthlessly.

'As time passed I persuaded myself that you were luring him on. I decided I had to get rid of you and waited for a suitable opportunity.'

The memory of the banquet when I had nearly died came back clearly. Berenger had been seated next to me.

'So you were the one who put poison in my food. I never thought of you as a murderer,' I told him.

'Neither did I. I had the poison hidden in my sleeve and even at the very last moment I hesitated. Then I had to listen to you brazenly telling the story of Troilus and Achilles to everyone at the banquet. That was too much for me.'

I remembered seeing a tapestry depicting the same story

hanging in Hroudland's room in his great hall. Achilles's lust for the beautiful youth Troilus lay at the core of the Greek tale. Berenger, already jealous, must have been driven to distraction.

'And when poison didn't work, did you also try to have me killed while hunting in the forest?' I said.

'Yes.'

From above us came the sounds of the oliphant. Hroudland was blowing the same hunting call again and again, each time less vigorously. He was tiring.

'First I thought it was Gerin who wanted to do away with me on King Offa's orders,' I said, 'More recently I believed it was Ganelon who was trying to have me murdered. And all along it was you. You even tried to have me killed here in these mountains by that Vascon slinger.'

'There you are wrong,' Berenger said. 'I had no hand in that. It must have been a genuine attack, though I did roll some rocks down on you when we were on our way here into Hispania.'

Hroudland had come to the end of his strength. Halfway through the next hunting call, the notes died away in an ugly rasp. From the darkness where the Vascons waited came a derisive spine-chilling howl of wolves.

Ignoring the pain in my shoulder, I twisted around so I could look up towards Hroudland. The moon had risen above the lip of the ravine and its cold light showed Hroudland facing towards the enemy. He was swaying on his feet. With an effort he raised his sword Durendal in defiance, and then smashed it down on the rock, trying to break the blade. He failed. Twice more he tried to destroy his sword, and then he gave up the attempt. He knelt down and laid the sword on the boulders before him. Then with the oliphant still hanging against his chest, he lay face down, the sword beneath his body. With an awful sick sensation I knew that he would never rise again.

'Patch, you are a hard man to kill,' hissed Berenger.

He managed to struggle to his feet. His injured leg was too weak for him to remain standing so he put his back against the rock barrier. He had his sword in hand, and I thought he was about to attack me. Instead he croaked, 'I die here with Hroudland. You have no right to be here at his side. Go! I will make sure you are not followed.'

I dragged myself over the rocks, away from the Vascons. I had no idea how far I had the strength to go, and there was no reason that the Vascons would let me escape. But the urge for survival was powerful. I gritted my teeth against the pain and stumbled forward. Twice I tripped and fell on to my knees and, weirdly, an image of Hroudland's roan stallion came to my mind. I saw the animal, stunned by the slingstone, getting back on its feet. I forced myself to do the same. In the darkness all around me I imagined the shapes and blurred outlines of people and grotesque creatures. One of them was my brother's fetch. He was seated on a rock ahead of me and I longed for him to come forward and help me. But all he did was watch me in brooding silence as if to chide me for ignoring his warning that I should trust my enemies and beware my friends. Then my legs gave way one last time, and I sank to the ground in a dead faint.

Chapter Twenty

MY SHOULDER WAS ON FIRE. A hand pulled away my eye patch and something wet pressed on my forehead. I opened both eyes and struggled to concentrate on the crooked figure stooping over me. In the thin light of dawn, Osric was using his moistened head cloth to dab my face. I wondered if I was wandering in my wits.

'Here, Sigwulf, drink,' he urged. He held a leather water flask against my lips. I sipped and my choking cough produced an agonizing spasm of pain in my shoulder. I was back in the real world. We were still on the mountain roadway, but alone.

'Where are the others? Where's Hroudland . . . and Berenger?' I asked, struggling to connect Osric dressed in Saracen robes with what I remembered from the previous evening.

'Nothing can bring them back,' he said. 'Wali Husayn sent me.' Osric squatted down on his heels so he could look me directly in the face. 'The wali asked the Vascons not to harm you. He still values your friendship.'

I winced as yet another stab of pain clawed my shoulder. Osric gently pulled open the rent in my brunia and checked where the Vascon spearhead had pierced my flesh.

'In the heat of battle it was difficult for every Vascon to remember the wali's instructions,' he observed.

'So the Vascons were fighting on behalf of the wali?' I mumbled. Every bone and muscle in my body ached.

Osric shook his head.

'They fought for themselves. After Pamplona, they wanted revenge.'

I remembered the skirmishing Saracens who had tracked the army's withdrawal from Zaragoza. They would have been providing the Vascons with daily reports of the army's progress.

'Try to get to your feet,' said Osric.

Looking past him, I saw two horses standing patiently. The Vascons must have told him that I had been seen abandoning my comrades, and Osric had brought a spare mount with him.

He put his arm around me and eased me to my feet.

'I have a message from Wali Husayn to deliver in person to Carolus. On the way I'll deal with that injury,' he said. Carefully he hoisted me up on to one horse, mounted the other and began to lead me along the track, heading over the pass.

We crossed the watershed and were descending the far side when we met the first of the Frankish outriders coming towards us along the track. They raised a halloo of triumph seeing a lone Saracen and spurred into a gallop. But when they saw that Osric was leading a wounded man wearing a brunia, they reined in.

'I'm bringing this man for medical help,' Osric called out.

'And who might you be?' enquired the patrol leader. He was bull-necked and beefy, with an accent from somewhere on the Rhine. He was eyeing Osric with suspicion. In his fine, white cotton gown, it was difficult to recognize Osric as a former slave. He had the manner and bearing of a Saracen of rank.

'I come as an envoy, with a message to your king from the Wali of Zaragoza,' said Osric smoothly.

'And you?' asked the Frank, examining me. His slight hesitation when he met my gaze reminded me that I had lost my eye patch.

'Sigwulf, companion to Count Hroudland.'

The cavalryman frowned.

'A rider came through to us in the middle of the night, sent by Count Anselm. Said the rearguard had been attacked and needed help.'

'Any help will be too late,' I answered wearily. 'Count Hroudland, Count Anselm and all their men are dead.'

The Frank looked shocked. I guessed that the fate of the treasure chests was going through his mind. They held the bulk of the army's loot.

'Very well,' he said after a moment's pause. 'You two may go forward. I'll have one of my men keep an eye on you. The king turned back when Count Anselm's request for help arrived. He's anxious for news of his nephew.'

He rode on with his patrol and we continued on our way. It was going to be another blisteringly hot day, and the trooper who accompanied us kept glancing sideways at us. He was eager to know what had happened but I was too tired and hurting too much to satisfy his curiosity. I had decided that Carolus should be the first to hear a full account of how his favourite nephew had died.

After a while we began to overtake the laggards of the army's main column. Groups of bedraggled men on foot mingled with camp followers plodding behind the slower supply carts. They looked to be in low spirits already, and I wondered how they would greet the news of the loss of the treasure carts. Osric enquired if any of the vehicles carried medical stores, and eventually a friendly storekeeper provided him with vinegar, needle and thread, and bandages. Osric sat me down on the roadside and unlaced my brunia.

'Hold still a moment, this will hurt,' he warned. I closed my eyes and there was a painful tug as he peeled something from my skin. I thought he was removing my undershirt but when I opened my eyes I saw he had in his hands the blood-soaked wreckage of the Book of Dreams.

Osric gave a grim smile.

'It caused you enough trouble so it's only fair that it probably saved your life. It deflected the Vascon spear away from your vital organs. Then staunched the worst of the bleeding.' He tossed the soggy pages aside and leaned forward to examine my shoulder closely. 'The gash is deep but not wide. I'll clean it, and then sew the lips of the wound together. It will hurt, but it's best done before it putrefies. You'll feel better afterwards.'

He was right. The stitching was agony and the thread he had been given was old and rotten. It broke several times. Eventually he plucked a hair from the tail of one of our horses and used that after soaking it in vinegar.

'Can't we save even a few pages?' I asked as I got back on my feet, stifling a gasp of pain.

He stooped down and picked up the gory mess that had been our translation of the Book of Dreams.

'Maybe we can salvage one or two pages, but I doubt it,' he said. 'We'll check later.' He wrapped the fragments in a cloth and placed them in his saddle bag. 'What happened to the original?'

'I left it on one of the treasure carts. It'll be with the loot taken by the Vascons.'

Osric shrugged.

'Then it's probably in Husayn's hands.'

I felt a sense of relief.

'I'm glad. Old Gerard obtained the Oneirokritikon from the Saracens as war loot in the first place.'

There was genuine affection in Osric's voice as he said, 'You and I are going to have to stick together if we want to try to remember what Artimedorus wrote.'

*

We rode on, the discomfort in my shoulder now an insistent, very painful throb beneath the bandages. The sun beat down, giving me a headache to add to my woes. The various units of the retreating army were moving slowly along the road, strung out in clumps, and we had to work our way past them with the help of our escorting trooper. He shouted at people to move aside, and was frequently cursed or ignored. Osric was treated to hostile glances and sometimes spat at. By mid-afternoon I was doubtful that I could continue much further. I was swaying in the saddle, dizzy and weak.

'I have to stop and rest,' I told Osric. We were passing a roadside halt where a long stone trough provided a watering place for travellers and their animals. Thankfully the soldiers had not wrecked the place. Water was too precious in such a baked and barren land.

'We can pause here until the sun drops. As soon as the air cools down, we should push on and try to reach the king wherever he is camped,' he said, turning aside his horse.

I dismounted with a groan and walked unsteadily to sit on a large flat stone near the water trough. I closed my eyes, trying to shut out the pain from my shoulder. In the distance there was the creak of cart wheels, the tramp of feet, the voices of groups of soldiers passing by. Much closer and more soothing was the sound of water trickling down the wooden pipe which brought the water from a distant mountain spring. It served as a balm for my senses, and I must have drifted off into a semi-stupor for the next thing I was aware of was the clatter of many horses' hooves.

To my annoyance I heard the riders turn in towards where I

sat. The noise came very close, and then ceased. Resolutely I continued to sit with my eyes closed, making it plain that I did not wish to be disturbed. One set of horse's hooves came right up to me. A shadow blocked the sunlight and I sensed the animal looming above me. I heard a loud, deep snuffle. Finally, very reluctantly, I opened my eyes.

I was looking directly into the gaping nostrils of a broad-chested war horse. It was standing over me, so close that if the creature had taken another step it would have trodden me under its vast hoof. Beyond the massive animal, I found myself locking eyes with Carolus himself. Dusty from the road and dressed in plain travelling clothes, the king was gazing down, his expression careworn and impatient. Behind him his retinue was drawn up in a circle.

Alarmed, I scrambled to my feet. But my legs failed me, and I sank to my knees, startling the great war horse. Trained to battle, it raised one hoof and would have struck me down if the king had not pulled on the reins and made the stallion step back a pace. I picked myself up and made an unsteady bow.

'The young man who interprets dreams,' Carolus said.

'Your Majesty,' I blurted.

'Shouldn't you be with my nephew? I hear that the rearguard is in trouble.' He spoke in that unmistakable high-pitched voice, and his words rattled around inside my skull.

I swallowed hard and managed to croak, 'Your Majesty, the news is bad.'

His eyes narrowed as he regarded me closely. For a long moment he sat on his great horse, taking in the extent of my exhausted condition, the bandaged wound, my state of near collapse. Abruptly he turned to his attendants.

'Clear the area! I need to speak with this man in private. And set up an awning so I am out of this cursed sun.'

There was a jingle of harness as the royal party wheeled about. A groom ran up and held the war horse's head while Carolus dismounted, then led the great animal away. A line of guards took up position along the roadside to prevent anyone intruding, and I saw them hustle Osric away. Within minutes a small open-sided tent had been erected from a bundle of canvas and poles carried on a pack pony, and stools, benches and a travelling chair appeared. Two servants held me up, one on each side, as I walked unsteadily to where the king had taken his place seated in the shade.

Carolus subjected me to a long, brooding stare. Then, seeing that I was swaying on my feet, he added, 'You may sit.'

Gratefully I sank down on a stool.

'Tell me what you know about my nephew,' he commanded as soon as the two servants were out of earshot.

'Count Hroudland is . . . dead, Your Majesty,' I said. 'He and Count Anselm and Eggihard died defending the rearguard of your army.'

'When and where did this happen?'

'Yesterday, just short of the mountain pass. The rearguard was ambushed and badly outnumbered.'

'By whom?' The question was delivered in a flat voice.

I told him about the Vascons, and all that had happened from the moment we had been ambushed. I omitted any details about the foray to find the rumoured Graal. I did not want to give the king any indication that Hroudland might have been irresponsible.

When I finished my description of the catastrophe, the king sat very still.

'Strange,' he said quietly. 'Last night, just as I was falling asleep, I thought I heard the sound of a horn. Not once, but several times, far in the distance.'

'The battle took place half a day's ride from here, Your Majesty. No sound could carry that far,' I said.

He gave me a strange look.

'Maybe I was already asleep and dreaming,' he said. 'You would understand that.'

I was too exhausted to make any reply.

'I should have paid more attention to the rearguard,' Carolus continued, as if speaking to himself. 'It was my mistake to let them lag so far behind.'

My moment had come.

'They were betrayed,' I said.

His head came up sharply and he stared at me.

'How do you mean "betrayed"?'

'The enemy knew when and where to ambush the rearguard, the size and number of its troops.'

He drew his eyebrows together in a scowl.

'Have you any proof?'

I pointed to Osric standing at a distance behind the cordon of soldiers.

'That man can tell you. He is an envoy from the Wali of Zaragoza.'

'A conniving Saracen,' muttered Carolus, but he beckoned to the soldiers. 'Bring that fellow over here.'

The guards searched Osric for hidden weapons, and then led him to the little tent. Once again the king's memory for people astonished me.

'Haven't I seen that limp before,' he demanded as Osric stood before him.

'He was my servant in Aachen,' I intervened. 'Now he is a free man and in the service of Wali Husayn of Zaragoza.'

'I'm told that my rearguard was betrayed.' There was an undertone of menace in the king's statement.

'That is what Wali Husayn has instructed me to inform you.' Osric managed to be respectful yet very sure of himself.

'Why would the wali want to do that?' growled the king.

'He wishes to re-establish good relations with Your Majesty.'

Carolus gazed at Osric thoughtfully.

'So this is some sort of peace offering?'

'That is correct,' said Osric.

'Is he prepared to identify the traitor?'

Osric nodded.

Carolus turned his shrewd grey eyes on me. There was no warmth in the look he gave me, only calculation.

'Do you know who betrayed my nephew?'

I shook my head.

'I only know that we stood no chance.'

Carolus's voice took on an edge that was chilling.

'Name this traitor,' he demanded of Osric.

'He is one of your inner council, a man called Ganelon,' Osric replied. 'He has been supplying information to my master for months.'

*

Osric and I had discussed this moment while he was stitching up my shoulder wound. It was then, to distract me from the needle's pain, he had told me why Wali Husayn had sent him as an envoy to Carolus.

'The wali intends to destroy Ganelon. He holds him responsible for what went wrong with the plan to invite Carolus into Hispania.'

I had sucked in my breath, stifling a yelp as the needle pierced my flesh.

'I remember when you met Hroudland and me outside the walls of Zaragoza,' I'd said, 'and refused us entry to the city. At that time you told Hroudland that it was Ganelon who persuaded the king to turn on his ally, the Wali of Barcelona, and make him a prisoner.'

'And later? Did you see the look on Wali Suleyman's face when he rode into Zaragoza after Husayn had paid his ransom?'

'He looked crushed. I felt very sorry for him.'

'He was deeply ashamed. When Wali Husayn greeted him, he drew back from his embrace. Since then Suleyman has scarcely emerged from his living quarters.' Osric had given a grunt of annoyance. The cotton thread had snapped again. I'd felt the loose end slither through my skin as he'd pulled it free of the stitch hole. 'Saracens value family honour. Wali Husayn and Wali Suleyman are brothers-in-law. To humiliate one is to humiliate the other.'

'So Husayn seeks to avenge his brother-in-law's dishonour?'

'Already he's recovered much of the ransom he paid. That was his agreement with the Vascons, and it makes things somewhat easier between himself and his brother-in-law.'

'Is that why Husayn agreed so easily to the payment of such a huge ransom?' I'd asked.

Osric hadn't answered, and instead re-threaded the needle, this time with the horse hair. Finally he'd said, 'He was already planning how to get the money back. His spies would have told him that the Franks would soon have retreated over the mountains. That meant passing through Vascon territory. When we stayed overnight with that Vascon shepherd, he told us himself that he was on good terms with the Vascons.'

'So now it remains for him to destroy Ganelon. Just how will he do that?'

'With your help we dispose of Ganelon using the same weapon he plotted to use against Hroudland.'

I had forgotten the note that Ganelon had asked Husayn to

sign, that had promised a payment of five hundred dinars, with me as the named person to collect the money but without an eventual recipient named. Ganelon had planned to accuse Hroudland of selling out to the Saracens and produce the note as evidence.

My friend's brown eyes had searched my face.

'Sigwulf, it will mean lying to Carolus.'

I had hesitated.

'I'm not sure I want to get mixed up in this. Hroudland and Ganelon hated one another. But now Hroudland is dead and I have no quarrel with Ganelon. There was a time when I believed he was trying to have me killed to get at Hroudland through me. But this wasn't true.'

'You have a different score to settle with Ganelon.'

I'd looked at my friend questioningly.

'Have you thought what would have happened to you if Ganelon's plot against Hroudland had succeeded?' he'd asked softly.

It had taken me a moment to grasp the subtlety of the Wali of Zaragoza. He had known he could count on me to help him once I'd realized that if Carolus believed that I had acted as a go-between for Hroudland collecting bribes I would also have been branded as a traitor and put to death.

'It should be easy for you to persuade Carolus that the rearguard was betrayed,' Osric had said. 'A little harder, perhaps, that Ganelon was responsible.'

*

Carolus sat without moving. It was a measure of the man that his face gave no hint of what he was thinking. Finally he said, 'Have you any proof?'

Osric did not falter.

'Ganelon insisted that my master sign a note promising him a first payment of five hundred dinars in return for his help.'

'And was the money ever paid?'

'Sigwulf here can answer that,' Osric murmured.

The king fixed me with a stare.

'Ganelon was a rival to my nephew, that is well known. But how do you come into all this?' he said.

I knew that I would have to lie convincingly in the face of those penetrating grey eyes.

'When I was sent to Zaragoza,' I lied, 'Ganelon asked me to collect five hundred dinars from the wali on his behalf. I was to bring the money to a Jewish moneylender in the town who would arrange for it to be sent on.'

Carolus leaned forward, peering into my face.

'You are prepared to swear to this?'

'Yes, Your Majesty.'

'You are both dismissed,' said the king. 'You will not speak to anyone about this.'

*

I did not see Ganelon's execution, though it was a public spectacle. It took place two days later and there was no trial. The damning note signed by Wali Husayn had been found among his possessions. He was taken to an open space where a stout rope was fastened to each limb. The ends of the ropes were then attached to the yokes of four ox teams whose drovers then urged their beasts to walk off in opposite directions. They tore Ganelon into pieces. This method of execution was normally done with horses, but Carolus decided that oxen would be more appropriate. The drovers had been carefully selected: each of them had lost a brother, cousin or nephew in the massacre at the pass.

I was in a delirium at the time. My shoulder wound began to fester alarmingly and I was placed on a pile of blankets in the back of a supply cart, soon to head north in the army's supply train. I raved and thrashed, shouting that flying monsters were attacking me or that a vixen was a mortal danger. At other times I lay still, the sweat beading on my brow, and mumbled of flocks of birds at a sacred spring.

Osric stayed with me, fending off the physician sent by the king who took a personal interest in my survival. The royal doctor wanted to stuff the putrid wound with a paste of cobwebs and honey, but Osric would not let him.

'I also had to stop him bleeding you,' Osric told me as I began to recover on the third day, 'you were weak enough already. The loss of any more blood would put you in your grave.'

His remark prompted a faint memory of a sentence he had translated from the Book of Dreams.

'Osric, do you remember anything in the Oneirokritikon about tears of blood?'

'Why do you ask?'

'When we first came to Frankia, I dreamed of a great horse and its rider crying tears of blood. Later, I saw the identical horse and rider as a statue at the palace in Aachen. On the march into Hispania I recognized the king's own war horse as the same animal.'

'Go on.'

'On the day I told the king about Hroudland's death,' I explained, 'I was seated by the water trough and he rode up on his horse, so close it nearly trod on me and I looked up. I knew exactly what was happening. It was all so real that I watched the king's face and waited for the tears of blood. Yet they never came.'

'Some people would say he had no reason to weep. He had yet to hear that his nephew had been killed.' Osric studied me, his expression serious. 'Yet, if we are to believe Artimedorus, there's another meaning for your dream.'

'What is it?' I asked. 'Can you remember something about horses?'

There was a long pause as Osric searched for the exact words as he remembered them. But the extract from the Oneirokritikon he quoted was not what I had expected.

'To see blood flowing is unlucky for a man who wishes to keep his actions secret.'

I sank back on my blankets, too exhausted to keep my head raised.

'So my dream was not about the horse and its rider. It was about me, the dreamer.'

Already I was wondering if one day Carolus would find out that I had lied to him about Ganelon and what I would find when I returned to Aachen. Did Bertha still expect me to continue with our affair? And how many of her intimate circle had she told that I had predicted the death of the king's only son? With Osric's help perhaps I could remember or reconstruct a few pages from the Book of Dreams and steer a safe path through the intrigues of the royal court. But Hroudland's death meant that I had lost my patron and protector, even as I had started to come to terms with being *winelas guma*, a 'friendless man', an outcast from my own country. Once again, my future was uncertain.

Historical Note

Sigwulf's story is based very loosely on the events surrounding Charlemagne's failed military expedition into Moorish Spain in August 778 AD. The rearguard of his army was cut off and massacred as it was withdrawing across the Pyrenees. Several high officials of Charlemagne's court were killed in the action, among them Anselm, the count of the palace, Count Eggihard the royal seneschal, and – notably – Count Hroudland or Roland, Prefect of the Breton March. Medieval poets and bards transmuted what had been a bloody defeat into a tale of valour and chivalry. Above all they celebrated the heroic last stand of Count Roland and his companions against an overwhelming foe whom they identified as Saracens but who were almost certainly Christian Vascons (Gascons/Basques). Their romanticized version of the battle became the best known of the *chansons de geste*, the 'songs of deeds', in the repertoire of tales known to jongleurs and minstrels as 'The Matter of France'. Another collection, 'The Matter of Britain', told of the exploits of King Arthur and his knights.

The exact location of the fateful battle when Roland was killed is not mentioned in the early versions of the story. Tradition places it in the pass at Roncesvalles in Navarre, Spain, 7 km from the French border. Roncesvalles became a popular stopover on one of the pilgrim routes to the shrine of St James at Compostela. 'The Song of Roland' as it became known was probably spread throughout Christian Europe by returning pilgrims. When Taillefer, one of William of Normandy's warriors, was granted the honour of striking the first blow at the battle of Hastings, it is said that he advanced against the enemy singing of Roland and Charlemagne.

Some of the leading characters in the *chansons de gestes* are authentic historical figures: King Offa of Mercia described himself as Rex Anglorum; the scholarly Alcuin moved from the cathedral church of York to teach at the royal palace school in Aachen; and three Saracen walis or provincial governors came to seek an alliance with Charlemagne against their overlord, the Emir of Cordoba.

*

The Oneirokritikon, or 'The Interpretation of Dreams', was compiled in the 2nd century AD by the Greek writer Artimedorus and translated into Arabic by the 8th century, probably via a Byzantine Greek source. It became a popular dreambook in various languages throughout the Middle Ages when the meaning of dreams was considered highly significant. The meanings of various dreams in Sigwulf's tale – seeing a snake, blood, an unknown riderless horse, etc. – are taken from the Oneirokritikon.

*

Charlemagne's unusual family arrangements have attracted scholarly comment. He kept his numerous daughters close to him. There were at least eight legitimate princesses, and an unknown number by other women. One of them had for her partner an unnamed courtier who wrote verse. Over the years the animals in Charlemagne's zoo included a lion, peacocks, bears and an elephant . . . of which more will be written in the next volume of Sigwulf's adventures.